Strange Tales from Liaozhai

Strange Tales from Liaozhai

Volume One

Pu Songling

Translated and Annotated by
Sidney L. Sondergard

Illustrations by Ben Grant, Matt Howarth,
Christopher Peterson, and Megan Williams

JAIN PUBLISHING COMPANY
Fremont, California

jainpub.com

Jain Publishing Company, Inc. is a diversified publisher of college textbooks and supplements, as well as professional and scholarly references, and books for the general reader. A complete, up-to-date listing of all the books, with cover images, descriptions, review excerpts, specifications and prices is always available on-line at **jainpub.com.** Our booksPLUS® division provides custom publishing and related services in print as well as electronic formats, and our learn24x7® division provides e-learning related products and services.

Cover art by Matt Howarth.

Table of Contents

Acknowledgments

For all the many reasons that he wrote these tales, from reflecting his love of the otherworldly to providing a natural extension of his work as a teacher, Pu Songling composed them most importantly to be enjoyed by a broad audience, not just by literary scholars. For over three hundred years this has indeed been their legacy in China, and I have tried while preparing this translation to remain respectful of that popular tradition. Many of these stories are unapologetically earthy, but never crude; they are occasionally quite violent or disturbing, but never gratuitously so; and they are frequently sad, but never morose or maudlin. What makes them so compelling is a barely-contained exuberance of tone that celebrates their excursions into the world of ghosts, demons, foxes, and immortals.

For this first complete translation of *Strange Tales from Liaozhai* into English, I have attempted to follow Pu Songling's syntax, punctuation, and phrasings faithfully, providing annotations for the reader when he makes allusions to personages or events unfamiliar to English readers, and I have profited enormously from the unabridged and newly-annotated edition of the *liaozhai zhi yi* edited by Zhu Qikai, published in Beijing (1995), my source text for the tales. In those cases where a long series of clauses has made it difficult or awkward for the reader to follow the flow of Pu's images, I have subdivided them into discrete sentences. I have resisted idiomatizing Pu's writing because I have found that translations which attempt to appeal to the slang and colloquialisms of the translator's immediate contemporaries tend, like topical humor, not to age well.

I wish to thank the Freeman Foundation for the generous grant support that allowed me to pursue research in 2005 on Pu Songling's life and work at Zibo and other sites in Shandong province. Every trip to China has been filled with serendipitous discoveries for me; I often share the astonishment there of Pu's characters, who, walking the mundane world one moment, in an instant find themselves in the presence of wonders.

My *laoshi* and colleague, Cai Hong/Anne Csete, has been keenly supportive of my efforts to translate Pu Songling's stories, and I wish to express my profound gratitude for her generosity of spirit and her scholarly devotion. I am particularly indebted to my meticulous Chinese Editors, Li Lin and Helen Zhang Peng, who have painstakingly reviewed my pinyin transliterations and have offered very helpful suggestions regarding the translations. The blame for any errors in the text, then, must fall solely to me. I wish as well to recognize my enthusiastic Editorial Assistants, Hu Shan, Hu Wensi, Liu Nan, Liu Ying, Shen Chaoer, Shen Wanghui, Wang Yifan, Wang Yingying, Yang Huidong, Yang Shanshan, Ying Lin, Zhou Jiayi, Zhou Lining, Zhou Nan, and Zhu Liang, for their careful proofreading. My gratitude also extends to Zhu Yimei for her support of the Editorial Assistants.

If you would like to receive copies of the transliterations of any of the particular stories in this volume, please feel free to e-mail me at sson@stlawu.edu, and I will gladly send electronic copies to you.

Since black and white illustrations are a traditional complement for Pu Songling's stories in popular Chinese editions, I solicited the artwork of Ben Grant, Matt Howarth, Christopher Peterson, and Megan Williams as unique individual responses to some of Pu's strange tales. I admire and treasure the results of their efforts.

For raising the kinds of questions that are always useful for me to ponder, for listening with genuine interest as I read each new translation aloud, I am indebted to Ran Rongming/Ramona Ralston, 我的妻和我的生。

Introduction

I. The Mystery of the Disappearing Artist: Pu Songling's Voice and Persona in the Stories

In 2004, I was visiting a small town in southwest Henan province called Xinye, because of its importance to the epic narrative of the *Three Kingdoms* (*sanguo yan yi*), when my two students and I were invited to the local office of the Ministry of Culture. There I was asked what Chinese literary works I had been teaching or researching, so I included a description of my project to translate all of Pu Songling's stories into English. One woman took me aside and confidentially told me, with no little pride, that her family had hidden their copy of *Strange Tales from Liaozhai* (*liaozhai zhi yi*) during the Cultural Revolution and refused to give it up when the call came around for subversive literature to be surrendered and destroyed. Since then, I've heard several similar testimonies. The Chinese people have a powerful affection for this collection of tales of the supernatural, the folkloric, and the simply odd, an affection due in part to the belief that Pu Songling (1640-1715) was acting as a moralist. As an early modern Aesop, Pu offered his readers entertainment, edification, and—perhaps most attractive of all—a heart-felt critique of the bureacratic structure of early Qing dynasty China. Although the imperial civil service retained its own idealistic mythology of maintaining a scholarly meritocracy and Confucian social philosophy through a system of advancement-by-examination, the reality was that it was deeply flawed by a tradition of corruption and abuses of power already centuries old by the time Pu composed his weird short fiction.

At the heart of this collection of 494 short stories is a mystery that in some ways is as fascinating as the magic performed by Daoist priests or shape-shifting foxes: the author's depiction of himself as a mere editor rather than as the stories' creator, or at very least as the craftsman who gives them their literary shape. In the idiosyncratically personal postscripts or addenda that accompany many of his tales, Pu refers to himself as *yi shi shi*, adapting the model of historiographer Sima Qian to identify himself as the archivist, or historian, of the strange tales. I've chosen to translate *shi* as "collector" to honor the traditions surrounding the manuscript's compilation. Pu pointedly notes in his preface to the collection that individuals from all over China "who share my enthusiasm for the unusual have sent me stories by post," and he modestly claims that "I have written down what I have heard, and this collection is the result." This assertion was reiterated by the author's grandson, Pu Lide (1683-1751), and later authors such as Zou Tao (fl. ca. 1884) have also perpetuated the story of Pu's solicitation of stories from travelers who would stop when offered some tea and relate their unusual stories and experiences to him (Hammond 206-7). At the Pu Songling theme park outside Zibo City (near Pu's home village of Zichuan) in Shandong province, visitors are shown the Liuquan (Willow Spring) Well, "the very well" from which Master Pu, then in his thirties, drew the water to make the tea that he served his story-telling visitors from a thatched shed nearby.

Pu's self-deprecation, his deemphasis of himself as author, is further exhibited in the nickname that he gave to his writing studio and incorporated into the title of his story collection: *Liaozhai*, the "studio of chit-chat" or "studio of leisure" (I've also seen this translated as "studio of idleness"). This is the place where he crafted the narratives for his story collection, where he constructed the descriptions of visitations, manifestations, and possessions that characterize the majority of his tales. But to credit the stories to his studio (although Liaozhai was also a nickname Pu took for himself) is another way for him to resist taking credit for their existence. There are two tensions, then, at the heart of the mystery of Pu's reluctant authorship: the first consists of a compulsion to retreat from making any claims for himself to fame or to literary talent, while simultaneously desiring to demonstrate his knowledge of literary tradition and his aptitude for narrative prose by presenting his collection as a literary work rather than as a compendium of interviews or field reports.[1] As you'll see, many of the stories open with assertions of the impressive reputations of their scholar protagonists or of their main characters' extraordinary talents.

The second tension involves his adopting a persona in the often moralistic addenda to his stories that is at times reminiscent of the philosophical commentaries by other great Shandong thinkers—like Kongzi (Confucius) and Mengzi (Mencius). Of the eighty-three stories included here, Pu writes formal postscripts in his own voice for twenty-six of them, though he often intrudes in first-person narrative voice, as when he speculates about whether the magician in "Stealing Peaches" (*tou tao*) was actually a practising descendant of the Song dynasty's mystic White Lotus Cult, or offers a stoic reflection on life and death at the end of "Forty Thousand" (*si shi qian*). At the same time that he takes the opportunity of telling the tales in order to offer explicit and implicit object lessons, Pu also embraces the irrationality of the magical world for its own sake, empathizing with troubled spirits and supporting the punishment of those who compromise principles of social justice for personal gain, arguing that encounters with the inexplicable may help to reorient or to guide an individual positively.

The preface to the collection, entitled "Liaozhai's Own Account" (*liaozhai zi zhi*), clearly reveals Pu Songling's ambivalence about his role as author. While he's a self-professed fan of strange tales (who sees himself as a literary inheritor of writers like Song dynasty poet Su Shi, enthusiastically asserting that "I, too, delight in hearing ghost stories"), he also feels so undervalued that he fears the "only ones who truly know me are those spirits of the green woods and of the dark places we cannot pass!" With typical self-effacement, he attributes the authorship of the tales to fellow aficionados who have sent them to him, "since things tend to gravitate to those who appreciate them," yet he also acknowledges that he's learned from experience that "the cultivation of my pen and ink yields me as little as a monk's begging bowl," which makes it all the more "lamentable that I have so many hopes riding on it." Nevertheless, his brief preface is sprinkled self-consciously with literary allusions to eight different writers, betraying a desire to display his knowledge of the tradition that he wishes his collection to extend, and implying that he wishes his anthology to be considered a literary work rather than a mere accumulation of others' words. Perhaps the authorial presence that he's surrendering here is simply replaced by a different investment of emotion in his seeming identification with the undervalued scholars of his stories, from Zhou, a man framed by enemies and removed from a list of successful civil service examinees ("Cheng the Immortal" [*cheng xian*]), to Xing Chou, a successful candidate in the highest level of the imperial civil service examination, who is rewarded for having once saved another person's life by being reborn as an official, thanks to the support of the Hell King ("A Certain Gentleman" [*mou gong*]).[2]

Though he fails to acknowledge his own artistry when doing so, Pu uses the composition of poetry by characters in the stories as a means of paying tribute to authorial integrity and veneration, to literature's power to confer immortality through memorial verse (as Fourth Lady Lin [*lin si niang*] does when she writes a poem for Chen, her beloved, just prior to being reincarnated), and even to poetry serving as a vehicle to instill humility by measuring the limits of one's talents (as "The Fox Duo" [*hu lian*] demonstrates when a pair of female foxes un-

successfully attempt to seduce a scholar by tricking him
into competing in a poetry contest that will end up with
them all in bed together—recognizing the impossibility
of beating them at their game, the scholar simply refuses
to participate). The hand behind the verse in the stories,
of course, is Pu's own, additional evidence of his craft as
an author; moreover, his specific commitment to poetry
was confirmed as early as 1660, when at the age of 20 he
helped friends organize the Yingzhou Poem Society.

The addenda which Pu appends to his tales place
him in the position of social critic, yet they also seem to
function for him as self-justification, self-authorization,
and even self-admonition, as he explicitly praises the
deeds of worthy characters and warns of the consequences
of misjudging others. The individuals whom Pu lauds
most effusively are generally underappreciated in some
manner, like the title character of such stories as "Yu
Jiang," who's praised for his exemplary bravery despite
his impoverished background. He also includes a number of stories that warn of the negative consequences
of judging by appearance, like "Yingning," where the
quasi-hebephrenic laughter of the female protagonist
is nearly allowed to obscure the fact of her compassion
and filial devotion, or like "Painted Skin" (*hua pi*), in
which superficial attraction to a woman's beauty is not
only deceiving—it almost kills scholar Wang.[3]

Joined with the respect his stories frequently show
for undervalued scholars, these emphases call to mind
the writer's own adventures and misadventures in his
attempts to secure preferment through the imperial civil
service examination system. At the age of eighteen, Pu
passed the county level examination (*xianshi*), and later
the two examinations at the prefectural level (*fushi* and
yuanshi), receiving his licentiate (*xiucai*) certification.
He failed his subsequent attempts at the provincial level
examination (*xiangshi*) which was offered every three
years (Hucker 233), and he seems to have made his
final official attempt at the age of fifty, in 1690. He was
disqualified in the 1687 examination under the pretext
that he had submitted inappropriate content—that is,

he skipped a page in his essay book. He didn't complete the 1690 examination; we don't know why he failed in 1660, 1663, 1666, 1672, and 1678. Frustration over his repeated attempts helps to suggest why some of his stories explicitly celebrate successful circumvention of the entire examination system: even the very first story, "Taking the Examination to Become Town God" (*kao chenghuang*) opens with the success story of the "grandfather of my elder sister's husband," Song Tao, whose talents qualify him to be directly summoned to a markedly "higher" level examination by immortals, superceding the conventional process before the civil examiner even arrives. The notion of reading personal resonance in Pu's stories is nothing new; one nineteenth-century commentator, for example, explicitly reads "Scholar Ye" (*ye sheng*) as Pu's "own covert autobiography" (Zeitlin 51), which hardly seems surprising, given that Pu laments that Scholar Ye is someone whose talents go unappreciated despite his being a resourceful person who is "serious and clear-minded all the time."

Candidates who succeeded in the provincial examinations were certified as *juren* and became eligible to take the metropolitan exam (*huishi*) in the capital. Even if one failed this latter exam, it remained possible to become an official; hence Pu's failure to pass the provincial exam, even after showing so much early promise, effectively denied him access to a government position. This must have proven exasperating for him, particularly as scholars like Pu Songling were prevented by personal morals and financial constraints (poverty, for example, kept Pu out of school when he was a child) from participating in the practice of purchasing the support of corrupt examiners through "ample funds or influential connections" (Barr 1986:99), the means by which many men far less talented than Pu received access to official appointments. Pu's stories often punish those who abuse authority or who obtain power under false pretenses,[4] from the *juren* Zhu in "The Frescoed Wall" (*hua bi*), who's sucked into a painting because his intentions towards a young woman in it are improper;

to the foolish scholar Wang in "The Daoist of Laoshan" (*laoshan daoshi*), who abuses the Daoist magic that enables him to pass through walls and as a result is punished by a wall that resists him; to the title character of "The Buddhist Monk's Sin" (*seng nie*), who is saved from hellish punishment for his misdeeds when his brother sees a vision of the torments awaiting him—and Pu delivers an explicit warning in the story's postscript that "punishment in the underworld comes as a result of wicked behavior in the mortal world."

Though the suprahuman and human realms were considered in Pu's era to be coterminous and "equally real," many storytellers engaged in the composition of *zhiguai*, or strange stories, were "more concerned with presenting the supernatural realm than with illustrating truths in the human world through their stories" (Chan 197). Pu's treatment of problem solvers in his stories often seems to acknowledge his authorial awareness of the appeal of heroic engagement with supernatural enemies by mortal intellectuals. Old Master Zhang (*zhang laoxiang gong*) resolves the horrible problem of a monster river turtle that demands animal sacrifices, and depletes the people's resources, by offering it a lump of hot iron: subsequently, the locals revere him as a water deity. Even when the perceived enemy isn't supernatural—as in "The Wu Official" (*wu ling*), where a city engaging in over-elaborate worship of its local patron god is corrected in a no-nonsense manner by the title official and is established in the people's heart as "a second city god"—the reward for agility of mind is proportionate to the efficacy and ingeniousness of the problem solver. This is perhaps another vicarious compensation for the undervalued Pu, who believes himself capable of precisely such intellectual acuity and unfairly denied the opportunity to demonstrate it in an official capacity.

Since Pu feels that anger and vindictiveness are ultimately self-destructive, his stories involving the humiliation and/or destruction of corrupt individuals may be functioning as harmless outlets for him to vent his frustrations at being denied what others less worthy had been granted. In "King of the Nine Mountains" (*jiu shan wang*), for example, the Li family is destroyed in retaliation for its patriarch having ruthlessly wiped out a fox clan. The author's use of the stories as an innocuous compensation for professional slights and the frustration of personal ambition likely also explains two patterns of tales involving *over*valued scholars in the collection: one involves scholars who are betrayed or destroyed when their lust entangles them with supernatural creatures (like the title character of "Scholar Dong" [*dong sheng*], who ignores his suspicions about a woman's fox nature and dies from his sexual relationship with her; or Wang Qihou in "The Temple Demon" [*miao gui*], who fails to discern that an apparent woman is really a demon and falls ill as consequence; or the scholar in "The Lord of the Sea" [*hai gongzi*], who recklessly makes love with a woman who turns out to be a serpent spirit). Other tales punish characters for not being more vigilant and seeing through the meanness of their own deeds or the trickery of others: in "The Man in the Ear" (*er zhong ren*), Tan Jinxuan goes mad after deluding himself about the efficacy of his Daoist meditative exercises; in "Ventriloquism" (*kouji*), a group of practicing spiritualists and diviners prove to be nothing more than scam artists; in "Scholar Huo" (*huo sheng*), the title character receives lip sores as rebuke for his practical joking: Pu calls the chancres "a kind of divine practical joke."

Like Ning in "Nie Xiaoqian," who suffers for years before passing the metropolitan level of the civil service examination to become a *jinshi*, a success that proves largely due to his compassion for others, Pu's empathy with unsuccessful examinees, or with individuals who are undervalued despite being intellectually adept, leads him to feature a number of stories that glorify individuals who demonstrate the wisdom and resourcefulness to solve problems others cannot or dare not address. Frequently the problems involve fox-spirits, who were very popular in the Qing-era folklore of northern China provinces like Shandong (Wang 241-5), and Pu demonstrates the need for a flexible intellect when encountering them—a response perhaps to the inflexibility of intellect he perceived in the examiners who repeatedly rejected his examination responses. Daoist priest Jiaoming (*jiaoming*) outwits a pesky, irrepressible fox, while the similarly "irrepressible scholar" Geng Qubing ("Qingfeng") exercises his bold cleverness to make Qingfeng the fox his secret love. The resourceful son of a merchant ("The Merchant's Son" [*gu er*]) manages to solve several fox problems despite seeming to be a pretty peculiar individual himself. In "Fourth Sister Hu" (*hu sijie*), Shang releases a fox sister who becomes trapped by the magics of a man from Shanxi; in gratitude, she rewards him by assisting him in becoming an immortal spirit after death. These situations, of course, offer considerable opportunity for their author to display his own cleverness in crafting them, and hence further beg the question of the fictionality of Pu's serving merely as their collector.

An important facet of Pu Songling's resonance as an artist is displayed in his passion for presenting the fantastic to the reader as something that should be accepted at face value: the soul can separate from the body and subsequently reunite with it (e.g., "The Changqing Monk" [*changqing seng*] and "Scholar Ye" [*ye sheng*]); animals may, by nature, act more compassionately towards each other than humans do (e.g., "The Snake Man" [*she ren*] and "The Faithful Mouse" [*yi shu*]); magic is real and only the abuse of it should be condemned (e.g., "Sorcery" [*yaoshu*] and "Old Man Zhu" [*zhu weng*]); demons and ghosts still manifest human qualities, meaning that they may be as prone to love and devotion as to evil and deception (e.g., "Lian Xiang" [*lian xiang*] and "The Weeping Ghosts" [*gui ku*]). Perhaps due to his own self-image as an outsider, he commiserates with spirits rather than simply treating them as "others" and suggests that encounters with what is strange or otherworldly may help to redirect or otherwise to influence the individual positively. Indeed, Pu reveals in "Official Lu" (*lu pan*) that he would be excited rather than frightened to serve the fierce underworld judge even in a menial capacity, knowing that in the end he would be equitably, justly assessed. Given his study of the Confucian canon in preparation for the civil service examinations, it seems quite possible that Pu's modesty as a writer/artist and his insistence upon justice as a commentator are informed by the same source text, the *Book of Rites* (*li ji*): "In dealing with important matters, [the scholar] is cautious and careful as though he were fearful; in dealing with trivial matters, he is also cautious and careful as though ashamed of his own incompetence" (Lao 373).

The weird landscape of these strange tales, then, becomes for Pu a place to exhibit and to condemn foibles, even when the author chooses not to intrude explicitly into his narration of them. The longstanding tradition of employing supernatural elements in Chinese folklore to function as signifiers in social allegories (see, e.g., von Glahn 78-97) helps to shape Pu's tales, as does a possible reaction against the prevailing attitude in the Confucian texts, where the absence of discussion of the world of foxes, ghosts, and demons, indicates an attitude "not of indifference but rather of studied avoidance," since they represent "a problem for the this-worldly" Confucian philosophy of civic harmony and reciprocity (Campany 127). Hence in celebrating the talent and resourcefulness of writers who encounter the strange in the *liaozhai* stories, Pu can reinforce his belief in the essential value of his own work, and in so doing he can surreptitiously protest the Confucian canon's resistance to consideration of a world beyond the mundane.

The most valued scholars in *liaozhai zhi yi* are those who acknowledge the reality and power of the strange (*yi*) without being frightened of it or intimidated by it. An official who is respectful but not overawed by the Hail God (*baoshen*) is named by the deity to become the overseer of burial mounds. Zhu, who performed meritorious deeds for others while alive and gained a reputation for forthright action, is named a magistrate to the four Dragon Lords after being destroyed by the poison of the *shuimang* plant (*shuimang cao*). Yin, in

"The Fox Marries Off His Daughter" (*hu jia nu*), proves himself bold enough while just a young man to sleep in a haunted house, and after living a life both brave and gracious is in time named a magistrate. Pu the author— who also serves as redactor and social commentator, using his addenda to personalize the narratives he crafts for his collection even when he "disappears" from his manuscript by identifying himself as a collector or editor rather than as a creative artist—identifies with the undervalued or unsuccessful scholar, an individual singled out for "strange" validation, in a metaphor for what he wishes his collection of stories, the anthology on which he admits to having "so many hopes riding," to demonstrate. Further personalizing the anthology, his authorial voice in the addenda, that of a chronicler/ historian/archivist, is as distinctive and intriguingly idiosyncratic as that of any of the other great figures from Shandong literary history.

While the magical world described by Pu's stories is rewarding in its own right, the modern English-language reader can also learn a great deal from the stories about the Confucian values inculcated within the Chinese family: from the filial duty of children to parents, to the importance of public rituals and festivals that unite the country, like Qingming, or Tomb-Sweeping Day, the time each year when families go to care for the burial sites of their relatives and to revere the memory of their ancestors. It's also intriguing to discover the rather different aesthetic focus of Pu's strange tales, which tend to be more episodic and centered upon the personal values of their protagonists than the weird fiction of westerners like Edgar Allan Poe or H.P. Lovecraft, where plotting is central to their stories' shape and flow. Pu's stories also include descriptions of purely natural phenomena (e.g., "The Alligator" [*zhupolong*], "The Whales Surface" [*hai da yu*], or "An Earthquake" [*dizhen*]), and treat the subject of sexuality with immediacy and frankness—suggesting that an assessment of "strangeness" must ultimately be measured against the routines of daily life. What occurs only in "other places," or in the imagination, qualifies as strange; commonplace emotions and desires are simply what make us human and fallible. But it's the juxtaposition of the two, the supernatural and the mundane, that makes them uniquely the creations of their modest author, Pu Songling.

Notes

[1] There are, however, some rare exceptions—like the purportedly verbatim report at the end of "Dragons" (*long*).

[2] For discussion of Pu's allusions to other figures from literature and history in order to connote unappreciated talent, see Barr (1986:89). Janet Zeitlin has noted that although it would appear that by comparing himself unfavorably in his preface with literary luminaries like Li He, Qu Yuan, Gan Bao, and Su Shi, Pu is rhetorically belittling himself, in effect he is actually "casting himself in exalted company" (46).

[3] On these stories as well as others in which Pu employs "alien women" as challenges to social norms or customary perceptions, see Barr (1989: 501-17).

[4] On the other hand, in a few cases Pu curiously intervenes through his addenda to pardon someone who likely seems unambiguously guilty to the reader. Pu offers a wry posthumous pardon, for example, to the bawdy title character of "The Adulterous Dog" (*quan jian*), blaming the dog's owner for training her pet to copulate with her in her husband's absence and hence concluding that the dog shouldn't have been tortured (as the wife was) before being executed. On the erotic themes in the *liaozhai zhi yi*, see Lanciotti (75-6).

II. Pu Songling's Exercise of the Fox Tradition: Moral Allegory and Social Critique

For over two millennia, Chinese writers have been recording accounts of strange phenomena: encounters of individuals with "denizens of the spirit-world" (Campany x), demonstrations of magic by spiritual masters, descriptions of exotic plants and animals, and accounts of meteorological or geological anomalies. All of these appear in Pu Songling's stories, along with familiar characters associated with China's spiritual traditions, from Yama, the gruff Hell King, to Guan Yin, the bodhisattva who functions as goddess of mercy, a figure whose empathy for individual sufferers parallels that of the Christian tradition's Virgin Mary. Pu's short stories are also part of a broad literary tradition of *zhiguai*, or strange tales, and while their ghosts and demons may be familiar to western readers of weird fiction, the most familiar context for the prominent presence of fox-spirits in them is perhaps the European folkloric tradition of Reynard the Fox, of the fox as a trickster figure.

In the work of Pu's literary successor, Ji Yun, whose own strange tales appeared in collections dated 1789 and 1791 (at a time when *zhiguai* were experiencing tremendous eighteenth-century popularity, as testified by the reissue of Pu's *liaozhai zhi yi* in 1766), fox-spirits are described as seeking the ultimate goal, shared by Daoist alchemy, of immortality, and those who cultivate their spiritual essence in pursuit of this goal are like scholars who seek advancement by dedicating themselves to the acquisition of knowledge. Those, however, who seduce men in order to drain them of their *jing*, or sexual essence, do so in an attempt to find a short-cut to becoming one of the celestial immortals—an attempt doomed to failure, according to Ji, for the harm that they bring to such men directly conflicts with the laws and mandates of the celestial realm. Thus the actions of fox-spirits are subjected to the verdicts of underworld judges, including the Hell King. In addition, foxes operate according to specific codes in terms of their interaction with humans: fox-spirits may "give birth to human babies but not vice versa"; "licentiousness among fox-spirits is excusable"; and fox-spirits "on a low level of spiritual cultivation live in the wilderness while others who have attained the Way mix freely with mankind" (Chan 121-22). The seductive, shape-shifting fox, then, can take on a predatory or a beneficent role, destroying or rewarding human mortals as a means to their ends.

The twenty-nine stories in this volume that feature fox escapades have a figurative function for Pu Songling that becomes apparent upon recognition of his two primary settings for fox activity: the lonely studies/studios of scholars, and the offices of government officials—those individuals who successfully used the imperial civil service examinations as a springboard for professional and social advancement. Although Pu was denied the opportunity to advance through governmental positions, he spent the majority of his life in the presence of young scholars and would-be officials, serving as a highly-regarded teacher for thirty years at the home of Bi Jiyou in Xipu village, Zichuan county, from 1680-1711. From his observations in that capacity, he derived a unique perspective on the life of the scholar and completed the majority of his tales in the early years of his teaching career. In addition to their function as descriptions of intersections between the mundane and the spirit worlds, his fox tales also function allegorically to express the author's own frustration at the problems of corruption and deprivation associated with single-minded pursuit of public advancement. Hence Pu's strange tales seem particularly pointed in their critique of officials who are unworthy of their government appointments (and who consequently prove susceptible to fox attacks, or who make inappropriate decisions involving foxes), and of the conditions that force young men to become isolated from the rest of the world as they devote all of their time and energy to preparing for the examinations that can offer them the only significant opportunities for social advancement within their culture.

In making his tales implicitly didactic, employing his fox characters to impart ethical lessons, Pu follows the principles established by the fourth-century B.C.E. philosopher, Mozi, in his defense of the existence of spirits. Mozi presents argument and proof that spirits can return to the mortal realm to punish individuals responsible for the deaths of innocents, priests who have been negligent in their duties, and individuals who have perjured themselves (Bonnefoy 255). The tenth-century monk, Yunming Yanshou, argued that the changeling powers of fox spirits could be employed for good or for evil, and that "only the accomplished adept can discern truth from falsehood. Thus most laypersons fall prey to the deceptions of demonic spirits" (von Glahn 184). Pu exposes the moral lapses associated with the political advancement of undeserving individuals, which result from a distorted sense of personal entitlement, by placing such individuals in situations that force them to interact with foxes. These scenarios offer the people in power opportunities to demonstrate diplomacy, beneficent leadership, and personal resourcefulness, and failures on their part to demonstrate these talents function collectively as an indictment of the very system that empowers them.

Li, a low-level imperial examination candidate from a wealthy family, eschews negotiation for genocide after "darkly entertaining thoughts of killing" a fox clan which offers him money to lease his unused garden in "King of the Nine Mountains" (*jiu shan wang*). The surviving member of the clan recognizes Li's overweening ambition and manipulates him to believe that he will achieve his destiny to become emperor through conquest, by becoming the leader of a powerful bandit enclave. Li is just successful enough to become a danger to the existing government—which then retaliates by showing his family no more mercy than he showed the foxes. Pu's postscript to the story defends the fox's revenge by asserting that he merely exploited the corruption already present in Li: "the man who killed the foxes was savage and that shows that his heart already possessed evil roots, so the fox encouraged those roots to sprout and then conducted his plan of revenge." A similar vendetta, also fox-initiated (though in response to criminal acts performed against humans rather than foxes), results in the murder of the brutal official Song in "Hongyu."

The lessons directed at corrupt officials by foxes are not always fatal—often they are simply punishment-in-kind or public humiliation. The attraction of malicious foxes to government buildings[1] is an ongoing motif in Pu's stories, identifying the public offices as natural magnets of corruption. "The Foxes in the Zunhua Office" (*zunhua shu hu*) may be maleficent characters, but Pu's commentary appended to the end of the story reveals what he sees the moral imperative here to be: "Foxes that plague people deserve to be severely punished. However, if they obey and abandon their wickedness, we should also treat them humanely." Official Qiu rejects an offer from one of the foxes to bring the others into line; instead of negotiating, he chooses to annihilate the nuisances and brings cannons to bear on the tower where the foxes are congregated. When Qiu is caught in a bribery scandal involving misappropriation of military funds later, he realizes it as retribution by the foxes. One of the characters in "The Wei County Fox" (*weishui hu*), a loutish magistrate who was an ass in a previous incarnation and who attempts to solicit a fox's magical patronage by ingratiating himself insincerely, is eventually denounced for passing judgment on civil offenders impersonally and for being "so greedy that even helping himself to somebody's rice soup makes him drunk with power." Pu's postscript advises the reader to emulate the fox, not the ass, in the story.

But in addition to feeling the acute frustration of having witnessed men undeservedly advanced into official positions, privileged men who subsequently proved unworthy of their authority, Pu's experience as scholar and teacher also led him to empathize with the lonely path of the individual who becomes fixated on achieving political advancement: namely, devoting years of one's life solely to the study of the Confucian classics and the works of other revered thinkers in hopes of being able to distill their wisdom into successful essays written for the imperial civil service examinations. While the fact is that marriage with influential families and emphatic recommendations from already-successful officials were the only guarantees a scholar might have of advancing from low-level government appointments, the poor scholar without such advantages had to accept that single-minded commitment to preparation for the civil service examinations would likely mean both limited social interactions with women and delayed marriage. Pu sees the vulnerability of such men to the seductions of foxes who disguise themselves as beautiful women—a traditional element in *zhiguai* for centuries before Pu was writing—as an opportunity to test their mettle, to propose what a truly virtuous individual can do when faced with unexpected opportunities and temptations.[2] This also becomes his tool for insinuating that moral integrity is perhaps the most important consideration when determining whether an individual is truly fit to become a public servant.

Kang Xiaofei has noted that the fox figure in Chinese folklore and *zhiguai* has served the function of allowing people "to draw boundaries between symbolic oppositions at multiple levels, be it personal, familial, social, or cultural" since the eighth and ninth centuries of the Tang dynasty, thereby using the fox tales "to order the world they lived in" (37). Human interaction with foxes in Pu's collection of stories provides precisely this kind of "ordering," as the author offers models of positive and negative behavior from foxes to serve as catalysts for human reactions. There are lessons—moral, philosophical, spiritual—implicit in the fox stories, then, even when Pu offers no explicit commentary on them.

The concept of *ren*, of empathetic benevolence towards others, for example, is central to the lessons in Confucius' *Analects* and is proposed as being essential to the behavior of an exemplary individual. In Pu's stories, the individual whose first impulse towards others (whether human or fox) is some kind of friendly gesture of *ren*, is someone worthy of trust and authority. Scholar Che comes from a poor family in "The Drinking Buddy" (*jiu you*), but when he discovers a drunken fox, he thinks of it as a kindred spirit rather than as a magical benefactor to be exploited—and the fox (who proves himself a kindred spirit indeed, by adopting the appearance of a Confucian scholar) subsequently rewards him for his joyful generosity, making him a rich man. Spontaneous, empathetic friendship is similarly rewarded in "The Magistrate of the Heavenly and Mortal Worlds" (*lingguan*), when a Daoist priest escapes danger thanks to the warning of an old man he'd befriended, in actuality a fox in disguise. A character who exhibits *ren* will ultimately be either resistant to, or rescued from, the seductions of malevolent, or potentially malevolent, fox spirits. Magistrate Zhu, for example, falls for "The Fenzhou Fox" (*fenzhou hu*) once his office is overrun by them, but the relationship is a benevolent one because Zhu treats the fox with the respect afforded a wife, inviting her to accompany him to his hometown to mourn his deceased mother.

Pu doesn't unilaterally condemn the scholars and other individuals in his tales who succumb to the seductions of foxes, for the real issue seems to be whether lust or loneliness is driving their desire; if the latter, there's hope that the character will recognize and value the beloved for herself, rather than simply for her sexual allure. Sang Xiao, in "Lian Xiang," becomes intimate with both Lian Xiang, who identifies herself as a prostitute, and Li, who claims to be the daughter of a good family, simply for sexual gratification, and consequently becomes life-threateningly ill. But his feelings turn to genuine love, and though his sickness proves to be the result of his beloveds being, respectively, a fox and a ghost, the female spirits curb their mutual jealousy in favor of sisterly harmony and make personal sacrifices in order to heal Sang. In "Yingning," on the other hand, when a neighbor's son arranges to climb over the dividing wall to *xiucai* Wang Zifu's house for an assignation with Wang's beloved, the giggly fox-girl Yingning, she tricks the lustful young man into thrusting himself into a log that he believes to be her—where a scorpion stings him and he dies.

Tales that initially seem to focus exclusively on the malicious nature of certain foxes present the reader with harmful acts that can range from simple vandalism, as in "Jiaoming," to causing physical illness, as in "The Merchant's Son" (*gu er*), to actual murder (as in "Scholar Dong" [*dong sheng*]). However, these negative portraits themselves often function as vehicles for cautionary lessons. In "The Swordswoman" (*xianu*), Gu, a poor but talented scholar, sells calligraphy and paintings to support his aged mother, and hence is unable to afford a wife; a young neighbor woman begins caring for the mother, but seems quite indifferent to Gu himself. He then becomes infatuated with a pretty young man, who in time proves to be a wicked fox; the neighbor proves to be a skilled swordswoman who dispatches the fox and bears Gu a son. That son eventually qualifies as a *jinshi* and outlives his father to care for his grandmother. The implication is that Gu's initial impulse to be a filial son and care for his mother was subverted by his lustful infatuation with the fox.[3]

Adding to the moral complexity of the stories is a parallel emotional complexity, for the stories can follow distinctly tragic or comic directions, celebrating or condemning the foxes and the responses they provoke in the humans who encounter them.[4] There is frequently a sad undertone to many of the successful relationships between foxes and mortals, concluding in the female fox having to leave her mortal beloved in order to move forward in the progression towards immortality. It is a commonplace of *zhiguai* generally, and of Pu's tales specifically, that a fox "can surpass all mortal women in virtue, but still she does not become quite human" (Huntington 1993:63). This creates an essentially tragic romantic dynamic: the fox wife or concubine works hard to prove herself "human," though her ultimate spiritual goal must be to become something considerably more than human. Because the title character of "Jiaona," a relative of scholar Kong Xueli's own fox wife, Song, had once allowed him the temporary use of the "red pellet" (immortality pill) she'd been cultivating for many years in order to cure a necrotic wound he'd suffered, Kong later sacrifices his life to save the lives of Jiaona and Song's fox family. Jiaona is so distraught by his death that she forfeits her immortality pill permanently in order to bring him back to life—and learns that her own mortal husband, Wu, and his household have been wiped out by the same "evil spirit, with sharp beak and long talons." While she is welcomed into Kong's household along with other members of the extended fox family, her loss is irrevocable and the reader is encouraged to empathize with her because of it. Her sacrifice is noble, but she isn't spared from suffering simply because of it. Nor, Pu suggests, are any of us.

Not all of the moral didacticism implicit in the stories is expressed seriously, however; Pu also employs humor and ridiculous situations to entertain the reader while his fox catalysts are being used to test human characters. In "Qiaoniang," Fu Lian, son of a government official and extremely bright, is denied promotion and any hope of future happiness associated with marriage simply because he was born with extremely small genitals. But because he unselfishly agrees to deliver a message, a crafty fox named Auntie Hua, who recognizes his positive attributes, applies a magical medicine that enlarges his modest endowment, with the result that he eventually marries both of her beautiful charges, the ghost, Qiaoniang, and the fox, Sanniang. Scholar Jiao wins a moral victory by resisting the seductions of "The

Fox Duo" (*hu lian*) beauties, but their bawdy poetry is so full of clever double entendre that it's also hard not to admire their bravado. Pu even enters into the narrative with his own comic voice at times, to defend foxes against anti-supernatural prejudice; not only does this kind of moralizing require no special exegesis, it also helps to explain why Pu Songling remains one of China's most beloved creators of natural and supernatural tales.

Notes

[1] Perhaps this is simply because they are more ostentatious, or physically larger, than other public buildings and the homes of the people, and hence offer more opportunities for the foxes to hide (Fatima Wu, for example, notes that foxes "like to hide in the rafters" [293]). But it seems equally as likely that Pu is implying that wicked and mischievous foxes are drawn to concentrations of corruption and corruptibility—like government offices or the studies of lonely scholars—where the chances are best that their seductions will succeed.

[2] Rania Huntington observes that one of Pu Songling's innovations with the fox tradition is to treat "the vixen as romantic heroine": "Although intimately related to vulpine sexuality (acquiring much of its interest from the containment and eventual exclusion of wantonness)"—particularly as regards the isolation of scholars who are tempted and/or tested by female foxes—the Qing tradition, particularly following Pu, is to emphasize "wantonness and virtue as two distinct paths foxes could choose to follow" (2000:79n3).

[3] Lest the modern reader misconstrue this as no more than a reflection of cultural homophobia on Pu's part, however, it's useful to note that in his postscript commentary on "The Swordswoman," he doesn't take the same sex relationship in that story as a matter of any serious concern.

[4] The fluid nature of the fox's signification in Chinese weird fiction is both facilitated and made meaningful by the fact that the stories are extrapolated from real-life dynamics and recognizable cultural values. The use by Pu, his predecessors, and his followers of the fox figure to impart moral or social principles reminds us that there are mundane corollaries even for the very folklore upon which they draw for inspiration. The superstitions surrounding the fox in Chinese culture,

for example, undoubtedly have some of their roots in simple observation of the animals: "An old tumble-down grave is easily transformed by a real fox into a convenient burrow, and this fact may have helped to increase the uncanny reputation of the beast" (Willoughby-Meade 123).

Preface

Liaozhai's Own Account

"A cape of cotton rose and a belt of usnea": Qu Yuan was inspired and so he created his "Sorrow"; "ox demons and snake gods": Li He was addicted to chanting their names even though they were imaginary creatures. These

---

Cotton rose . . . usnea: The Cotton Rose (*hibiscus mutabilis*), a Chinese shrub, has the "magical" quality of its white or pink flowers turning a deep red at night; it is cultivated in the United States as the Confederate Rose. Usnea, also known as Old Man's Beard, is a lichen that has been used in Traditional Chinese Medicine both externally as a dressing thanks to its antiseptic qualities and internally to stimulate the immune system.

Qu Yuan: Qu (c. 373-278 B.C.E.) was a courtier and poet who "initiated the paradigm of the virtuous man of genius, who, misprized during his lifetime, expresses his alienation in strange and intensely personal images" (Zeitlin 45), since he was slandered while holding a high position at court and was banished. Ensuing political chaos between the states of Qu and Qin led him to despair and he drowned himself. The "Sorrow" is his poem "Encountering Sorrow" or "The Sorrows of Departing" (*li sao*), a poetic milestone in Chinese literary tradition.

Li He: A major poet of the Tang Dynasty, the reference to Li (790-816) continues the motif of the undervalued scholar here. Having passed the first level civil service examination, he traveled to Chang'an (now Xi'an) to take the exam to qualify as a *jinshi*, but was denied the opportunity on a technicality. A Daoist, Li employs mystical imagery in his poetry, drawing on Daoist, shamanic, and mythological traditions for imagery, while his verses contain "many allusions to the restrictions suffered by the literati, whom the government often neglected in preference to those with a military or moneymaking" orientation (Perkins 276).

1

poets' works come from expressing what they truly felt, regardless of social approval. Qu Yuan and Li He both had their reasons for expressing themselves as they did. I am the failing light of an autumn firefly and evil spirits fight over my fading glow; I chased after vanity while drawing the derisive laughter of demons and monsters. Though my talent is nothing like Gan Bao's, I also love "searching for spirits"; and like Su Shi in Huangzhou, I, too, delight in hearing ghost stories.

I have written down what I have heard, and this collection is the result. For some time now, men from all four corners of China who share my enthusiasm for the unusual have sent me stories by post, and so, since things tend to gravitate to those who appreciate them, I've accumulated more and more of these stories. And here's the thing: for those of us who dwell in the mortal world, there may be stranger things among us than what occurs in "the land of those who chop off their hair"; if we just look around us, we may witness stranger sights than what people can see in "the land of the flying heads."

My enthusiasm quickly gets away from me and sometimes my comments are out of control—basically,

---

Gan Bao: Historian of the Jin dynasty and editor of the collection, *Searching for Spirits*.

Su Shi: Also known as Su Dongbo (1036-1101), a statesman, poet, and scholar. An outspoken critic of the popular courtier and poet Wang Anshi, who gained power by comparing emperor Ying Zong favorably with the wise monarchs of antiquity and was given unprecedented power in extending the duties of governmental administration, Su was dismissed in 1079 from his position as a Minister and "degraded" to the governorship of Huangzhou where he lived until he was restored to favor under a new emperor in 1086 (Mayers 204-5).

"The land of those who chop off their hair"; *"the land of the flying heads"*: Zeitlin notes that historian Sima Qian describes barbarian tribes with tattooed bodies and short-cropped hair, while Duan Chengshi records an account of "a legendary tribe of people whose heads could sprout wings and fly away at night," before returning and reintegrating with their bodies at dawn (44).

I just can't restrain these remarks; I always express my feelings, since I feel no need to hide them. Won't I simply provoke outbursts of laughter from circumspect individuals? However that may be, at the Crossroads of the Five Fathers I definitely heard some considerable exaggerations; and those stories carved on the Stone of Past Lives certainly make one realize some things. But just because a person speaks fervently is no reason to ignore him utterly.

When I was born, my late father dreamt of a sickly, frail Buddhist, his upper torso left bare by his robe, who entered the room with salve spread over a coin-shaped circle in the middle of his chest. By the time father awoke, I'd been born with a black mark like the Buddhist's in his dream. Furthermore: when I was young, I, too, was frail and constantly ill, and as I grew, I realized that my fate would be not unlike that monk's.

The dreary quiet of my front entrance and courtyard make them seem as desolate as a monk's cell; the cultivation of my pen and ink yields me as little as a monk's begging bowl. Often I've scratched my head and wondered: mustn't it be the case that the monk was my previous incarnation? Yet there must have been something inadequate about my karma, hence I couldn't attain to Buddha nature; and so I was tossed around by the wind, till I ended up a flower blown into a latrine. The Six Paths may seem boundless and inscrutable, but no one can say they're arbitrary!

All alone here at midnight, my dimming lamp flickers as I'm about to trim the wick; the wind whistles outside

---

Crossroads of the Five Fathers . . . Stone of Past Lives: References to the burial place of Confucius near Qufu in Shandong province, drawn from *The Book of Rites*. See Zhu (4n15).
Six Paths: These are the paths that can be taken by beings during transmigration in the cycle of existence, including, in ascending order, the realms of hell/hatred, animals/ignorance, hungry spirits/greediness, asuras/good intentions (but with failings that negatively affect others), human beings/desire, and heavenly beings/enlightenment.

my dreary study while the table inside is icy cold. Patching small pieces of story together into a large collection, I presumptuously create here my sequel to the *Records of the Underworld*; emptying my cup of wine and filling my brush with ink, I've almost finished this book with its cynicism about the ways of the world; how lamentable that I have so many hopes riding on it! What a shame!

Frightened by the frost, the shivering sparrow huddles close to a tree that has no warmth to offer; hanging in the moonlight, an autumn insect nestles against the railing to keep itself warm. The only ones who truly know me are those spirits of the green woods and of the dark spaces we cannot pass!

—Springtime 1679, in the reign of Kangxi.

Records of the Underworld: Title of a collection of strange narratives attributed to Liu Yiqing (403-44 C.E.).
Kangxi: Qing dynasty emperor (reigned 1662-1722).

The Tales

1. Taking the Examination to Become Town God

The grandfather of my elder sister's husband was named Song Tao, a scholarship student in his county. One day, while he was ill and lying in bed, an official leading a white-blazed horse brought him a formal document and told him, "You are requested to attend an examination."

Song replied, "The civil examiner hasn't arrived yet, so why has an examination been set so hastily?" The officer didn't answer him, but just urged him to go. Though weakened by his illness, Song rode out after him on his horse. The route was very unfamiliar.

Finally they reached a city which looked like a king's capital. After a while they entered a palatial building. Seated there were over ten officials, all unknown to him except for Guandi, patron god of war.

Town God: Each town has a "guardian deity who appoints local deities for each area," and many of these town deities are "former officials who ruled a city or area well" (Palmer 205).
Scholarship student: Song is a *linsheng*, a scholar who lived on government grants during the Ming and Qing dynasties.
Guandi, patron god of war: Guan Yu (d. 219 C.E.), one of the three peach garden oath brothers from the epic *Sanguo yanyi* (*Romance of the Three Kingdoms*), a valiant warlord for the Shu kingdom's attempts to restore the Han dynasty to power. Variously deified as the God of War (particularly to Daoists), Guandi (an imperial aspect associated with Cai Shen, God of Cash) and as the Qie Lan bodhisattva (Sangharama) to Buddhists.

Underneath the eaves of the house, two tables had been set up with a seat at each, and a *xiucai* had already been seated at the one on the right, so Song sat by him at the other. On each table was a pen and a writing tablet.

Suddenly the topic, on a piece of paper, fluttered down from above. Upon looking at it, they found eight words: "One man, two men; intentionally or unintentionally."

When the two men finished their compositions they submitted them to the examiner. Song's essay included the words, "He who does good deeds intentionally should not be rewarded for it; he who does evil, but without malicious intent, should not be punished." The deities passed it around, and gasped with praise for it.

They called Song forward and told him, "Henan is in need of a Town God, and you would suit the position."

The significance of this dawned just then on Song, and bowing his head, sobbing, he said, "It's a great honor to me, so I shouldn't have any excuses, should I? Yet my old mother is in her seventies and since there's no one else to wait upon her, please let me stay with her until she finishes her natural span of years. Then I will obey your bidding."

One of the deities, resembling an emperor, at once commanded that the mother's longevity record be examined. An official with a long beard held a volume and leafed through it, then stated, "She has nine years of life left in the mortal world."

When all of the deities hesitated about what should be done, Guandi replied, "Why not just let scholar Zhang take the seal and hold the position for nine years—then, later on, Song can take his place once he's ready."

Guandi told Song, "You ought to attend to your appointment at once; but for now, due to the benevo-

---

Xiucai: The lowest degree conferred on successful candidates under the old civil service examination system (see Hucker 248-9).
Henan: One of the provinces bordering on the western portion of Pu's home province of Shandong.

lence and filial piety in your heart, we'll grant you a leave of absence for nine years. When that period is through, we'll summon you again." He also gave some words of encouragement to Zhang.

The two scholars kowtowed and left together. *Xiucai* Zhang took hold of Song's hand, accompanied him to the outskirts of the city, and introduced himself as Zhang from Changshan. He offered a poem as a parting gift and though Song subsequently forgot most of the words, part of it went, "When there's wine and flowers, Spring is always here; / Even without candle or lantern, the night itself is bright." Song then rode away, leaving his fellow behind.

When he returned to his own neighborhood it was as if he'd just awakened from a dream. In reality, he'd been dead for three days. His mother heard a groan from inside his coffin, helped him out, and after half a day had elapsed he was finally able to speak. He inquired about Changshan and found that there really was a Zhang there—who'd died the very day he had.

After nine years, his mother did, indeed, die. Once her funeral service had been concluded, he washed himself, went into his room, and quietly died.

The family of his father-in-law, who lived in the city by the western gate, suddenly saw Song—among a multitude of carriages and horses with engraved belts and red trappings—enter their main hall, make an obeisance, and then leave. In their mutual surprise and bewilderment, they didn't realize that he had become a god. They hurried to his neighborhood for news about him and discovered that he had died.

Song had recorded a brief autobiography, but, regrettably, in the chaos that followed his death, it did not survive, and this is merely a summary of it.

In the chaos that followed his death: An allusion to the privations associated with the violent treachery of the Manchu overthrow of the Ming dynasty in 1644.

2. The Man in the Ear

Tan Jinxuan was a county scholar. He was a practicing enthusiast of Daoist breathing exercises, ceasing neither in cold or heat, and carried on like this for several months as though sure he would gain some special advantage through it.

One day he was just meditating cross-legged when he heard a tiny voice like a fly's, saying, "Okay, it can be revealed now."

As soon as he opened his eyes, he could no longer hear anything; closing them and calming his breathing, again he could hear the voice as before. He figured that he had achieved this by focusing his vital energy and was secretly overjoyed. From then on, every time he sat in meditation he would listen for it. He figured he'd just wait until the voice came back again and spoke, then he could open his eyes and have a look at it.

One day, it started to talk again. So Tan said in a tiny voice, "Okay, it can be revealed now."

Immediately he felt something flying around in his ear, and then it seemed to come out.

Looking sideways at him was a little man about three *cun* long, with a fierce and terrifying appearance like that of a yaksha, whirling around and around on the ground.

Cun: A measure equal to 1/3 decimeter.
Yaksha: Creatures sometimes appearing as demonic figures, sometimes as "pot-bellied dwarfs, guardians of treasures and secrets, who live in caves" (Bonnefoy 124).

Tan, surprised at it, fixed his attention on watching to see what it would turn into.

Unexpectedly a neighbor came to borrow something, knocking upon his door and shouting. The little man heard this, became alarmed, and circled the room like a mouse that's gotten lost from its hole.

Tan felt himself lose consciousness, and when he came to, he had no idea where the little man had gone. Thereupon he went mad, howling ceaselessly, and after taking medicine for half a year only then began to recover.

3. The Restless Corpse

An old man once resided in the village of Caidian, in Yangxin county. About five or six *li* from the village, the man and his son established a roadside inn to lodge traveling merchants. There were a number of cart drivers carrying goods, coming and going, who often stayed there.

One evening at dusk a group of four men came up to the door wanting to put up for the night, but the old man's lodge was already filled up with guests. The four men considered there were no other options and strongly requested to stay. The old man muttered to himself and thought of one place, but worried that it might not meet the approval of the guests.

"Provided there's a single space even in your halls or under your eaves," the visitors said, "we wouldn't ask for anything more."

At that time, the wife of the old man's son had just died. Her corpse lay in a room, his son having gone out to purchase a coffin and not yet having returned. Because the mourning area was quiet, the old man guided them there through a passageway.

In the room with the corpse, a dim lamp was set on a table; behind the table hung a curtain, and there was a paper bedspread covering the deceased. They looked

---

Yangxin county: Located in northern Shandong province.
Li: A measure of distance approximately equal to 1/3 mile.

over the place where they were to sleep on a big bed in the adjoining room. The four visitors were exhausted from their day's busy travels, so as soon as they laid down on their pillows, their breathing turned to snores. One of the men, however, was still only half asleep.

Suddenly he heard a swishing sound coming from the bed of the deceased. Anxiously opening his eyes, he found that the lamplight shining before the bier revealed everything clearly: the woman's corpse tore off the coverlet and sat up; soon she left the bier and crept over to where the men were lying. Her face was a slightly jaundiced color and she wore a strip of thin silk tied around her forehead. Lowering herself near the head of the bed, she exhaled three times on the three guests laying there.

The man was terrified; fearing she was about to reach him, he stealthily covered his head with the bedspread and held his breath to listen for what would happen. Soon the woman took her place and exhaled at him as she had done to the others.

Becoming aware that she had left their room, he then heard the sound of the paper coverlet again. He stuck his head out a bit to spy, and saw her stretched out stiff, as she had been originally. Horribly frightened, the guest dared not make a sound; he covertly prodded the other men with his leg, but they didn't move a bit. Though lacking a plan, he figured there was no alternative but to throw on his clothes and flee.

No sooner had he jumped up to pull on his clothes than he noticed that sound again. In terror, the visitor laid down and pulled his head back under the bedspread. He became aware of the woman returning, repeatedly exhaling at him several times, then leaving again.

After a while, he heard the noise from the bed, so he knew she was lying down again. Then he inched his hand out from under the bedspread to get his pants, hastily yanked them on, and ran outside barefooted. The corpse also rose up to chase him. By the time it started to move away from the curtain, the guest had unlatched the door and gone outside. The corpse sped after him in pursuit.

The man ran screaming through the village, but not a person was awakened. He wanted to pound on his host's door, but he was also fearful of being caught from staying too long in that place. Thereupon he ran as fast as he could go along the road leading away from the village.

Once he'd made it to the countryside east of town, he spied a monastery, and hearing the sound of a wooden fish, he was quick to rattle the gate. This surprised the monks as something totally unexpected, so they didn't admit him right away. The corpse, right on his heels, was soon within a *chi* of him. The man became even more frantic.

Outside the gate was a white poplar, its trunk four or five *chi* around, so he used the tree as defense; when she went to the left, he'd go to the right, and when she went right, he'd go left. The corpse grew more and more frustrated, but both were now feeling exhausted. The corpse paused while the guest, sweating and out of breath, hid behind the tree. Suddenly she pounced, stretching both arms around the tree to find and attack him. Terrified, he fell down. The corpse proved unable to seize him and stiffened up while hugging the tree.

The monks listened for a good long time, and upon hearing no further sound, ventured out to see the man lying on the ground. They saw he was near death, like a candle burning out, but his heart was still beating slightly. They carried him in and it wasn't until the night had passed that he revived. They got him to drink some broth and asked him about himself, giving the visitor time to compose his answers.

By that time the morning bell had finished ringing, and as the dawn's colors spread everywhere, the monks were able to sneak a peek at the tree outside—and as a result saw the stiffened corpse of the woman. Greatly

---

The sound of a wooden fish: Actually a rhythmic instrument used to accompany the chanting of scriptures.
Within a chi of him: A unit of measure approximately equal to one-third of a meter.

astonished, they reported it to the county magistrate.

The magistrate personally paid a visit to determine the facts. He sent his men to pry off the woman's arms, but they were so rigid they couldn't be moved. Examining the corpse carefully, he noticed that four fingers of each hand were curled like hooks and sunk up to the nails into the tree. They tried again with all their strength to pull them loose. Upon succeeding, they found finger holes that looked like they'd been dug in.

The magistrate dispatched some servants to the old man's household which was in an uproar since the corpse had disappeared and guests had been killed. The servants reported what had happened. The old man then followed them to retrieve his daughter-in-law's corpse.

The guest wept as he wondered aloud to the magistrate, "We four men went out together, and now only I return—what will the people in our home village believe about this?" The magistrate gave the man an official document and bestowed on him sufficient means to pay for his return home.

4. Squirting

When Mr. Song Wan, whose hometown was Laiyang, worked as a ministry official, the house he rented was very desolate and isolated. One evening, while two maids were looking after his mother as she went to sleep in the main hall, they heard a squirting sound in the courtyard, just like when a tailor sprays water from his mouth onto a cloth before ironing it.

The mother urged the maids to get up, and when they poked a hole in the window paper they saw an old woman, short and hunchbacked, with broom-bristlely, snow-white hair coiled up on top of her head, about two *chi* in length, walking around the courtyard in a circle, taking long, quick steps like a crane, spouting water endlessly as she walked. Stunned, the servant girls returned and described it all.

Song's mother was also startled and got up, the two maidservants helping her to the window where they watched together. The old woman suddenly rushed close to the window, spraying directly inside through the frame, splitting the window paper, and the three women fell down as though dead, though the family members knew nothing of this.

Song Wan: A famous poet (1614-1673) of the early Qing dynasty.
Laiyang: City in Shandong province.
Chi: a Chinese unit of measure approximately equal to a foot (about fourteen inches).

17

When the sun had already been up for awhile in the east, the family members gathered together and knocked at the door, but to their surprise they received no answer. Prying open the door to enter, they saw the mistress and the two maidservants, lying side-by-side in the room, apparently dead.

One of the servant girls was still warm under the breast. When they helped her up and got her to drink something, she came to her senses and began to give an account of what she had seen. After a while Song arrived, filled with sorrow and anger.

They checked carefully around the spot where the hag disappeared, while digging more than three *chi* deep, till some white hair was gradually revealed; they dug further till they found a woman's corpse that matched what the servant girl had seen, the face as fat and puffy as if she was alive. When they were ordered to strike it, the flesh and bones became all pulpy, as everything inside the skin turned to clear water.

5. The People in the Pupils Communicate

In the capital, Chang'an, there lived a scholar named Fang Dong with a reputation for being quite talented, although his behavior was inappropriately frivolous and discourteous. Every time he caught sight of a woman wandering the streets, he'd follow behind her, without regard to manners.

On the day before the Qingming festival, he was walking outside the city by chance when he spotted a small carriage with bright red curtains and an embroidered canopy; a number of servant girls followed at a fairly slow pace. Among them, one servant girl, riding a small horse, was radiantly beautiful.

Approaching slightly for a better look, Fang found the carriage curtains open, and inside sat a sixteen-year-old lady in stunning red attire, more exquisite than anyone he had ever seen. His eyes were dazzled, his heart ravished, and he was unable to look away from her—so sometimes from in front and sometimes from behind, he followed at a gallop for quite a number of *li*.

The capital, Chang'an: A city just south of Xi'an in Shanxi province, constructed during the Han dynasty, in the third century B.C.E. In older literature, it is used generically to signify "capital."

Qingming: The day of "pure brightness" on April 5th-6th is when one pays respect to dead relatives at the site of that individual's tomb or grave.

Li: A measure of distance equal to about 1/3 of a mile.

19

Suddenly he heard the lady ask a servant girl to come near the carriage, saying, "Let down the curtain for me. Where does this crazy young man who keeps peeping at me come from?"

So the servant girl drew down the curtain and looked at him angrily, saying, "This is the recent bride of the Seventh Lord of the Hibiscus, making a visit to her parents, not some female country bumpkin that a *xiucai* can outrageously stare at!" With these words, she grabbed some loose dirt from a wheel rut and threw it at him.

It got in his eyes, so he couldn't open them. Fang rubbed them in order to take another look, but found the carriage and horses nowhere to be seen. Surprised and bewildered, he returned home.

He became aware that his eyes weren't getting any better. He sent for someone who opened his eyelids, poking and examining them, and found a small, cloudy spot growing over each eyeball; through the night it became more severe, causing his eyes to water continually.

The spot gradually built up and in a few days had become as thick as a coin. A kind of spiral pattern developed on the right eyeball, and no medicine proved effective for it.

Annoyed and depressed, he wanted to put an end to himself until he began thinking about repenting his misdeeds. He'd heard that the "*guangming* sutra" would be able to resolve his distress. He got hold of a copy and asked a man to teach him to recite it.

Seventh Lord of the Hibiscus: As subsequent action will indicate, the Lord and his bride are *xian*, or immortals/fairies, and Hibiscus City is one of the fairylands in Chinese tales. In terms of consequences, Fang's sighting of the lady is analogous to Teiresias' sighting of the goddess, Athena, and his mother, Chariclo, bathing—for which he was blinded.

Xiucai: See "Taking the Examination to Become Town God."

Guangming: This "shining golden light" (*jin guangming*) sutra was translated into Chinese during the Sui dynasty (581-618 C.E.).

At first Fang had trouble because he was too impatient, but in time he became more calm. From dawn to dusk he did nothing but work at it, sitting cross-legged while fingering his beads. After having done this for a year, he achieved a state of absolute clarity.

Suddenly from his left eye, Fang heard words as tiny as a fly's: "It's so black here it's unbearable, enough to kill a person!"

From the right eye came the reply, "Let's get out and take a little stroll together since it's stifling in here." Soon he began to feel a wriggling on both sides of his nose that made it itch, as if something was coming out of his nostrils, and then went away.

After a long time had passed, he felt them come back, returning up his nostrils and entering his eye sockets.

Again a voice spoke: "It's been a long time since I had a peek at the garden—the Pearl Orchids are all dried up and dead!" Fang had been very fond of these particular orchids, having planted many of them in his garden and often watering them himself; following his sight loss, however, he hadn't even inquired about them.

Suddenly, upon hearing these words, he anxiously asked his wife, "How is it that my orchids have withered and died?"

The wife inquired how he knew this, and he proceeded to inform her about the incident. She hastened away to test this information and found the flowers withered indeed. This seemed very strange to her.

Quietly concealing herself in the room to wait, she saw tiny people, no bigger than beans, appear from inside the scholar's nose and zip right out the door. They moved further and further away, then vanished from sight. Instantly they linked arms and returned, flying up to his face like bees or ants whizzing into their nests.

This went on for two or three days. Once again Fang heard a voice from his left side: "It isn't very convenient coming and going in this winding tunnel, not as good as if we'd open a door."

The right side answered, "My wall's pretty thick, so

it's not going to be easy."

"I'll try to open up mine so we can both get through," said the left. Thereupon Fang felt something like a scratching and ripping in his left eye. Instantly upon opening his eyes to look, he was able to see a table and other things. Full of joy, he informed his wife.

She examined him and found a little hole torn in the thick cloudiness, through which the dark eye gleamed like a split peppercorn. By the next morning, the opaqueness had disappeared entirely. Upon careful inspection, the pupil could be seen again in one eye, while the old spiral remained over the right eye—so they knew that the people in the two pupils had made their home in the same eye.

Fang was blind in one eye now, but comparatively speaking, he could see more clearly than other people using both eyes. Because of this advantage, he became more reflective about his behavior and in his homeland was widely praised for his virtue.

The collector of these strange tales remarks, "In a rural area there was a scholar who, along with two friends, was out on the road when in the distance he saw a young woman riding a donkey in front of them, so he jokingly taunted, 'That's a beauty there!'

"He turned back and said to his two friends, 'Let's catch up with her!'

"They laughed with each other and rode on, soon catching up with the lady. When they did, the scholar saw that she was his own daughter-in-law. Feeling himself blushing and ashamed, he fell silent and had no more to say. The scholar's friends pretended not to know her and commented on the woman in very vulgar terms.

"The seemingly bashful scholar stammered as he spoke these words: 'She's my eldest son's wife.' Each of the other men concealed a snicker and dropped the matter.

"Being flippant usually turns into an act of self-insult that's really self-ridicule. In terms of the dirt that got into Fang's eyes and caused him to lose his sight, that's just the vindictiveness of ghosts and supernatural beings.

We don't know which god the Lord of the Hibiscus may be. Is it another physical appearance of a bodhisattva? Yet even if ghosts and supernatural beings are sometimes wicked, they still give people a chance to correct their errors and to make a fresh start."

6. The Frescoed Wall

Meng Longtan, from Jiangxi province, was visiting the capital with a *juren* named Zhu. By chance they found themselves at a Buddhist monastery, where neither the hall nor the meditation chambers were particularly spacious or grand, and which was occupied only by a single aged monk. Seeing the visitors, he made his robe look respectable and came out to greet them, then showed them around.

In the midst of the hall was a statue of Zhigong, a magic monk of the Han dynasty. On either side were murals painted in intricate detail, vividly depicting life-like human figures. The east mural was of the "Heavenly Maidens Scattering Flowers," in which a teenage girl picks a flower with a wistful smile, her cherry lips on the verge

---

Juren: A successful candidate in the provincial examination under the former civil service examination system (the text actually reads *xiaolian*, the term for *juren* used during the Ming and Qing dynasties).

Zhigong: Common name ("the Just Zhi") for the zen master, Baozhi (c. 417-514), founder of the Pilu line of Chan Buddhism.

"Heavenly Maidens Scattering Flowers": A common motif of offering in Buddhist art, the heavenly maidens, known as Devatas in India and as Tennyo or Tennin in Japan, are frequently pictured in illustrations of the sutras, strewing lotus flowers that become the seats for pious Buddhists. For more bawdy lotus symbolism, see Eberhard (169-70).

of opening and the waves in her eyes about to flow. Zhu stared at her for a long time, unaware of how his mind was wandering, until he fell into a trance.

His body suddenly began floating and fluttering as though sailing on a cloud, till he found himself entering the mural. There he saw countless halls and pavilions totally unlike those in the world of mortals. An aged Buddhist monk sitting on a dais preached the Dharma while a considerable crowd of monks, wearing robes that bared one shoulder, watched. Zhu mixed in and stood amongst them.

Soon, he seemed to feel someone covertly yanking at the front of his garment. He turned to find the mural's teenage girl. She smiled and walked away. Following her along a winding railing until she entered a small chamber, Zhu then held back, hesitantly, rather than venturing any further.

The girl turned her head, raising the flower in her hand in a beckoning motion, so he hurried to her.

Since there was no one else inside the quiet chamber, he hastily embraced her, and meeting very little resistance from her, they proceeded to make love. When they were finished, she locked the door and left, advising him not even to cough. Then she returned that evening. This went on for two days.

The girl's companions perceived that something was up and searched together until they found him, then made fun of the girl by teasing, "A little guy's already getting big inside your belly, yet you still wear your hair loose like a virgin?" They held out hairpins and earrings, urgently insisting that she put her hair up. The girl, feeling ashamed, did not speak.

One of the other girls said, "Sisters all, we mustn't hang around any longer—otherwise they'll be unhappy."

Insisting that she put her hair up: Children under fifteen wore their hair loose; when a girl was married, there was an elaborate ceremony for changing her hair style, often to a coil-like fashion.

Laughing, then, the group went away.

Zhu took a good look at the girl, her hair coiled up high while her phoenix earrings dangled low, and with the contrast he found her even more lovely than when she wore her hair down. Checking to be sure no one else was around, he began taking more indecent liberties with her; with her orchid and musky fragrance suffusing his senses, he indulged his pleasures without ceasing.

Suddenly they heard the heavy clomping of boots and something like the clanging of chains; soon there was the vague clamor of arguing. Alarmed, the girl got up and they secretly peered out. They saw an emissary in soldier's golden armor, his face black as lacquer, holding up chains in one hand and a hammer in the other, with the girls surrounding him.

He demanded of them, "Is that everyone yet?"

"That's everyone," they replied.

Then the emissary said, "If you're hiding someone from the world of mortals, you'd better make it known or you'll be sorry about the consequences."

Again their voices insisted, "We're not."

The emissary turned his mighty body around and scanned like a hawk hunting for something hidden. It seemed that he intended to conduct a search. The girl was terrified, her face pale as ashes, and in her fright she said to Zhu, "Hurry, you must hide under the bed." Then she opened a tiny door in the wall and abruptly escaped through it.

Zhu lay hidden, hardly daring to breathe. Presently he heard the sound of boots entering the room, then turning to walk back out. Not much later the noise receded into the distance and he began to feel more secure; however, there were still voices speaking as somebody came and went outside the door.

After Zhu had been trapped like this for quite a while, his ears began to feel like a cicada was chirping in them, while his eyes felt inflamed. Though the situation was in danger of becoming unendurable, he tried to calm himself while listening and waiting for the girl to return; besides, in addition, he could no longer recollect how he'd come to be there.

About that time, Meng Longtan, still standing in the hall, in the twinkling of an eye suddenly could no longer see Zhu, so he asked the old monk what was going on. The monk, smiling, said, "He's gone away to hear the Law explained."

"In what place?" inquired Meng.

The monk answered, "Not far away." Not long thereafter, the old man tapped the wall with his finger and called out, "Patron Zhu, after taking a stroll for such a long time, why not come back?"

Soon they witnessed an image of Zhu appear on the wall, inclining his ear towards them as he stood there, as if listening for more from them.

The monk again cried out, "Your associate has been waiting a long time for you." Thereupon Zhu floated down out of the mural and stood there like a block of wood, his eyes staring wide open and his legs turning weak.

Meng, though extremely shocked, slowly proceeded to question him. Zhu said that while he'd been hiding under the bed, he'd heard some knocks like thunderclaps, so he'd left the room to spy on the cause.

Together the men searched the mural for the girl holding the flower and they noticed that her hair was coiled up in a spiral, not long and loose like a child's. Zhu, astounded, bowed down before the old monk and asked him the reasons for this.

Smiling, the monk replied, "The individual creates his own illusions. How can I hope to explain them?"

Zhu was demoralized and downcast, while Meng was shaken to his very core and confused. They stood up, then walked down the steps and away from the monastery.

The collector of these strange tales remarks, "'The individual composes his own illusions': these sound like the words of one who profoundly understands the philosophy and wisdom of Buddhism. When one has indecent thoughts, one will experience an obscene illusion; when one has obscene thoughts, one will experience a horrific illusion. The bodhisattva enlightens the ignorant and uncultured through numerous transformative illusions. Everything comes from a person's own change of heart. The old monk spoke earnestly, but the young man heard no enlightenment in his words, nor did he give up his mundane life to seek the wisdom of Buddhism without pretension."

7. The Mountain Spirit

Sun Taibai has said that his paternal great-grandfather studied in Nanshan at the Willow Ravine Monastery. At harvest time he returned to his village, spent about ten days there, and then went back. As he opened the door to his study, he found that dust had collected upon his table and the window to the room was full of spider webs. He asked a servant to clean it up and by evening the room was clean enough for him to have a seat. He swept off the bed and shook out his old bedding, bolted the door, and went to bed as the moon rose and its light filled his window. He tossed about in bed for a little while until everything finally became still.

Suddenly he heard the rumbling of the wind and the creaking of one of the Buddhist monastery's doors. He figured it must be because one of the monks had failed to shut a gate. Engrossed in his thoughts, Sun's great-grandfather wandered toward the sound, which was coming nearer to his hut, till abruptly the outside door of his dwelling came open. He became quite suspicious.

Mountain Spirit: More precisely, a *xiao* is a trouble-making, single-footed spirit that lives in the mountains. Schafer finds "a trace of puckish humor" in accounts of these beings, variously described as "a kind of mountain troll," as shape-shifting birdmen, or even as "arsonists, prone to burning houses and huts" (112). Those from Lingnan were "compounded of ghosts, gibbons, and pile-dwelling pygmies" (113).
Cun: A measurement equal to 1/3 decimeter.

His thoughts were further unsettled as the noise drifted into his study; there was also a sound like that of boots tromping, gradually drawing near his doorstop. In his heart, he began to be afraid. Suddenly the inner door opened up. As he stared at it anxiously, a huge spirit bowed and squeezed in to enter. It leapt forward to stand before his bed, its head nearly touching the roof beam.

Its face was the color of an old gourd; its eyes flashing, it looked around the room and then opened up its gigantic, tub-like mouth to reveal sparse teeth over three *cun* long. Moving the tongue in its throat, it uttered a cry in a scolding, chattering voice, so the walls rang with the sound.

The great-grandfather's dread reached its limit; but he thought about the fact that the space in the room was so limited that there was no place to flee from its power, so he'd have to strike out at it instead. He drew out a knife that he'd hidden under his pillow, hastily raised it and cut right into its belly, making a sound like he was smashing a stone crock. The spirit was greatly enraged and extended its enormous talons, lashing out to seize Sun's great-grandfather. He managed to draw back just a bit. The spirit instead snatched at and grabbed his quilt, dragged it off the bed, then left angrily. The great-grandfather fell to the ground with the quilt and lay there, wailing in terror.

His family's servants arrived with torches and found his door closed as it had been originally, so they pushed through his window and entered—for upon seeing the ravaged state of the room, they'd been utterly terrified. They helped Sun's grandfather up onto the bed and he began to talk about what had happened.

Together they checked around, finding the end of the large quilt squeezed into the crevice where the door closed. Opening the door and holding some lights up to examine it, they found that the quilt had been pockmarked like a sieve, and wherever the spirits' five fingers had touched it, they'd slashed holes into it. After waiting until daybreak, they didn't dare delay any longer, but carried the great-grandfather's bookcase and left together.

Later on, they asked a monk about it and he said that they'd encountered no other strange things there.

8. Biting the Ghost

Shen Linsheng says his friend, a certain old man who was sleeping in the daytime during the summer months, in his drowsiness saw a woman lift the door curtain and enter, wearing a white cloth to cover her head and a mourning skirt of rough sackcloth, then head toward the inner rooms. He suspected that the woman was from the neighborhood and had come to visit his wife, but then he had second thoughts: for what urgent reason would someone hastily put on such ominous clothing and then walk into someone's household?

While he lay uneasy and puzzled, the woman stepped out from the inner rooms. He carefully examined her and found her age something beyond thirty, her face a swollen yellow, and her features wrinkled in an expression of fear. She hesitated and didn't leave, then gradually came near the bed where he was resting. He pretended to fall asleep in order to observe what she would do.

After a while, the woman lifted up her clothes, stepped up on the bed and pressed down on his stomach, making it feel like she weighed a ton. Though his mind was as clear as usual, when he attempted to raise his hand, it was as if it was tied up; when he tried to lift his leg, it was as if the leg was paralyzed. In his panic he tried to howl for rescue and bitterly discovered that he was

---

Weighed a ton: Literally, she weighs one hundred *jun*, an ancient weight equal to approximately thirty *jin*, itself equal to about ½ kilogram, for a total of about 1500 kilograms.

unable to utter a sound. The woman used her nose and mouth to sniff the old man's face, all over his cheekbones, nose, eyebrows, and forehead—he felt the mouth that was cold as ice, and her breath was so cold that it penetrated to the bone. In this urgent predicament, the old man worked out a suitable scheme: he'd wait until she sniffed up to his jaw or cheek, then at once he'd bite her.

Not a minute later, she arrived at his jaw as expected. He used all of his might to bite her cheek and his teeth sank into her flesh. In her suffering and pain the woman tried to pull away, both struggling to get free and weeping aloud. The old man increased the force of his bite. He felt her blood run down his cheek, soaking the side of his pillow.

They had hardly arrived at this deadlock when suddenly from an outside yard he heard his wife's voice, so he shouted at once that there was a ghost. In that moment, as he relaxed his mouth to speak, the woman seized the chance to float away.

His wife rushed over and came inside, didn't see anything there and laughed that it must have been just a nightmare. The old man related the strange details to her and in addition reported that there was blood, proving that it had all happened. She helped him inspect the premises and they discovered that something like water had leaked in from the roof, flowing down the pillow and soaking into the bed.

They bent over to sniff it and it had a bizarre, disgusting, fishy smell. The old man then began vomiting violently. After a few days, it was said that he still had the disgusting stink in his mouth.

9. Catching a Fox

Old man Sun was an uncle on my wife's side. It was widely known that Sun was a brave man. One day when he was taking a nap in the daytime, it seemed to him like something had climbed up on his bed, and he began to feel a sensation of his body rising as if it was sailing on a cloud.

Is this some fox spirit teasing me? he wondered.

He spied something as big as a cat, with yellow fur and a blue-green mouth, crawling towards him from near his feet. It crept slowly, being afraid of waking Sun. It wavered close to his body: one touch paralyzed his foot and leg, while the next made his thigh and hip go flaccid.

Just as it reached for his stomach, Sun suddenly rose up, put his hands on it and caught it, grasping it by the nape of the neck. The thing made nervous yelps since it was unable to escape. Sun urgently shouted for his wife to strap her belt around its waist.

Then as he held the belt by its two ends, Sun laughed, "I've heard about your skills at transformation. Now I'll keep my eyes on you to see how your changes work." Within seconds of his speaking, the fox suddenly drew in its stomach till it was as thin as a tube and almost managed to slip away.

Sun was greatly stunned and with anxious strength bound it tighter till the fox puffed up its stomach round as a bowl, so firm that the belt couldn't be tightened any further; as soon as Sun relaxed his force a bit, the fox drew in its stomach again. Sun, still worried about it escaping, quickly ordered his wife to kill it.

His wife panicked, looking high and low, not knowing where his knife was. Sun jerked his head to indicate its location. When he looked back, the belt in his hands was just an empty loop and the fox had disappeared.

10. Something Strange in the Buckwheat

In Changshan, there was an old man named An who enjoyed farm work very much. When the buckwheat ripened in autumn, he'd cut it down and heap it into mounds on the boundaries between fields.

At that time there were grain thieves in the neighboring village, so old An advised the tenant farmers to bring their buckwheat to the threshing ground in wheelbarrows by moonlight. Once they left, An stayed behind on guard duty. Resting his head on a spear, he lay down in an open area.

He had just closed his eyes a bit when suddenly he heard someone trampling the buckwheat, then making the sound of biting and gnawing, so he suspected it must be a thief. Swiftly he raised his head—and there was a huge ghost, well over three meters tall, with red hair and an ominous moustache and beard, already close to An. Terribly afraid and too mortified to think, he jumped up and poked the thing forcefully. The ghost made a sound like thunder and then vanished. Terrified that it might return, he took his spear and got away.

He met with the tenant farmers on his way home, telling them what he had seen and warning them that no one should go there again. The people, however, didn't really believe what he was telling them.

Changshan: Former prefecture now part of Zouping county, Shandong province.

The following day, while the wheat was drying in the sun at the threshing ground, they suddenly heard a sound from the sky. An, startled, cried, "The evil ghost is coming!" Then he ran away, and the other people also fled. More than two hours later, they turned back around and assembled, with old An commanding them to set up with bows or crossbows and then to wait for it.

The next day, the ghost came around once again. They fired many arrows simultaneously and the thing was scared away. Two or three days passed without it returning.

The buckwheat had already been stacked up in the storehouse, leaving behind copious amounts of wheat straw, so old An asked the others to collect the straw and pile it up neatly, then he would personally climb up and stamp it down, until the pile accumulated to a certain height.

Suddenly he looked off in the distance and shouted in fright, "The evil ghost is here!" While the people anxiously sought for their bows and arrows, the thing itself rushed at An. As he fell down, it gnawed at his forehead, then left.

The others went up together to look at him—and there was a section of bone the size of a hand missing from the unconscious old man's forehead. Carrying him on their backs, they took him back inside his home, where he died. No one ever saw the ghost again. Indeed, nobody knows what kind of ghost it was.

11. Goblins in the House

In Changshan lived a Master Li, the nephew of an important Ming dynasty Minister of Justice. His house there was full of weird goblins. One day he spotted a long, narrow wooden bench of a meaty red color that looked curiously decorated and smooth. Since Li knew that the thing hadn't been there before, he approached to touch and prod it, but immediately knew something was wrong, for it felt horribly like soft flesh. Shocked and repelled, he turned away from it.

As soon as he turned back to look at it, its four legs began moving and gradually it disappeared inside the wall. In addition, he saw a white stick standing up against the wall, an immaculate luster adorning it. Coming closer, as he leaned upon the stick wearily, it collapsed, then slowly began to penetrate the wall like a snake and disappeared into it.

In the seventeenth year of Kangxi's reign, a young man named Wang Junsheng lived and worked in a household as tutor for the family's children. Late one day, when the lamps had just been lit, Wang was still wearing his shoes as he lay down on his bed.

Kangxi: The seventeenth year of Kangxi's reign would have been 1678, for he succeeded his father Shunzhi in 1661. Born in 1654 as Xuan Ye, he became known for his studies, his wisdom, and his humanitarian policies within China.

Suddenly he saw a tiny person, maybe ten centimeters tall, enter from the outside, walk around a bit, then at once turn and leave.

In less than an instant, the tiny person carried in two small benches, looking like the kind made from plant stalks by children, and put in them in the middle of the room.

Again in just an instant, two tiny people entered, carrying a coffin perhaps four inches long, then stopped and set it upon the benches. They hadn't had time to get everything secured when a woman arrived, following some male and female servants, all as small as the first little fellow. The woman wore mourning clothes, with hemp threads around her waist and a cloth wrapped around her head; she used her sleeve to cover her mouth, wheezing and weeping, making a buzzing sound like a giant fly.

Wang watched her for a very long time, so frightened that his hair was standing on end and he felt as though he was frozen in place. He burst out with a loud cry and tried to run away, suddenly tripping over the bed, shaking and shuddering so much that he was unable to get up.

Hearing these sounds, his family members huddled together while the tiny people in the hall all disappeared.

12. Sixth Brother Wang

A man named Xu, whose family lived near the northern edge of Zichuan, was a fisherman by trade. Each night he went down to the river, carrying some wine, and drank while he was fishing. As he drank, he'd pour a libation on the ground and kindly say, "May the spirits of those who drowned in the river have this to drink." He did this so often that it became part of his routine. Other people who fished there came away without catching anything. Only Xu filled his baskets.

One evening, just as he was drinking by himself, a young man showed up, casually wandering near him on the bank. Xu offered him a drink and he gratefully accepted a share of the wine. Then for the rest of the night, Xu didn't catch a single fish, so he felt quite disappointed.

The young man got up and said, "I'll head down stream for you and drive them here." Thereupon he breezily drifted away. A little later he returned to report, "The fish are arriving." As a result, Xu heard sounds like a school of fish on a feeding frenzy. He raised his net and caught quite a few of them, each one of them over a foot long.

Overjoyed, he expressed his gratitude. Since he was about to return home, Xu offered the young man some of the fish as a present, but he wouldn't accept them, explaining, "Time and again I've enjoyed the favors of

---

Zichuan: Near modern Zibo, located in Shandong province.

your good wine, so this trifling thing isn't worth talking about. If you wouldn't reject such an offer, I'd like to do this for you more often."

Xu replied, "We've only shared drinks for a single night, so why do you say 'time and again'? If you're willing just to hang around with me that would be great; but I'm embarrassed that I have nothing to give you to show my feelings."

When Xu asked him his name, he answered, "My family name is Wang, but I don't have a courtesy name—so when you see me, you can just call me Sixth Brother Wang." Thereupon they went their separate ways.

The next day, Xu sold the fish and bought more wine. Later, when he returned to the river bank, the young man was already there, so he cheerfully gave him some of the wine. They drank several cups, then Wang drove the fish for Xu again.

It was like that for half a year. Then, suddenly, Wang announced to Xu, "It's been an honor to have known you, and my feelings for you surpass even those for a blood relative. However, the day has come when we must part from each other." His words were profoundly sad and sorrowful.

Alarmed, Xu asked him for a reason. Wang tried to speak but then faltered and kept on trying until finally he said, "Since we two are so fond of each other, perhaps I can explain without startling you. Now that we're about to part, there's no harm in telling you the truth: I'm really a ghost.

"I've always had a taste for the wine, and once several years ago, when I was really drunk, I drowned. You've been able to catch more fish than anyone else because

---

Courtesy name: Also known as a style name. In pre-modern China, after reaching the age of 20 and adulthood, one either selected or was given a courtesy name, composed from two characters, as an alternative to one's given first name; it was considered impolite for anyone but one's self and elders to use the given name, hence the "courtesy" name was employed in public exchanges and correspondences.

I've been driving them to you secretly in gratitude for the libations of wine you've made for the dead.

"Tomorrow my time will expire, and someone else will die so I can be reincarnated. We won't be able to meet together after this evening, and that's why I can't help feeling sentimental now."

At first, Xu was very shocked upon hearing this; but since they'd been close for such a long time, his fears went away. He sighed and sobbed, pouring them both some wine as he spoke these words: "Sixth Brother, drink this and don't be sad. To have met each other and to have to separate so soon is certainly cause for grief, but you've already completed your sufferings and now you can escape them, so it's appropriate that we should celebrate. Being melancholy just doesn't make sense." Thereupon the two began drinking freely.

"What person will take your place?" Xu asked.

Wang answered, "Elder Brother, if you watch from the riverbank tomorrow, at high noon a woman will try to cross the river but will drown—she's the one." Since they could hear the rooster in the village already crowing, they let their tears fall and parted.

The next day, Xu respectfully waited beside the river in order to witness the strange event. A woman did indeed arrive, holding a baby in her arms, and as she walked close to the river, she fell in. She managed to cast the baby up on the bank, where it flailed its arms and legs, bawling. Time and again she would sink and then resurface until suddenly she climbed out on the bank, dripping wet, and rested on the ground there briefly to catch her breath before gathering up her baby and leaving.

While he was witnessing the woman's drowning, Xu initially didn't have the heart to watch without hurrying to her rescue, but then realized that she was to be the substitute for Sixth Brother. He determined not to intervene—then the woman pulled herself out, leading him to wonder why Sixth Brother's words hadn't come true.

That night, Xu went to fish at their old spot. Sixth Brother, who was there once again, turned to him and said, "We're back together now, so for the time being there'll be no words of farewell." Xu asked him what was going on. He explained, "That woman had come to be my replacement; but when she fell in, I took pity on the babe in her arms. Though that one person might have been substituted for me, it wouldn't be right to ruin two lives for one. For that reason, I couldn't let it happen. There's no telling when another substitute may happen by the river. Perhaps it's because the two of us haven't come to the end of our friendship yet."

Xu was moved by this and declared in praise, "The compassion in your heart may touch even the Emperor of Heaven." From then on, they were able to continue meeting there as they had originally.

After several days, Sixth Brother came again to take his leave. Xu figured that another substitute must have turned up. "Not at all," Wang said. "My deed of compassion has been recognized by the Emperor of Heaven. Now he's appointed me to become the Earth God for Wuzhen, in Zhaoyuan county, and I leave in the morning to take up my position. If you don't wish to forget our friendship, you must come and visit me. Don't be afraid of any obstructions posed by the long distance."

Xu congratulated him: "Your forthright honesty has made you a god, which comforts my heart greatly. Nevertheless, the paths of men and gods are quite different. Even if there's no worry about the long distance, how could I find you?"

Wang urged him, "Just come, don't give it another thought." He reiterated this over and over and then left.

Xu returned home and began at once to prepare for a trip to the east. His wife, laughing, said, "That's a trip of

---

Earth God: An oracular figure, as depicted in the ancient Chinese almanac, the *tong su* (see Palmer 119-21). This City/Town God, given the charge of a particular region or district, is also called the *sheshen*.

Zhaoyuan: Located in the eastern portion of Shandong province.

several hundred *li*, and even if there was such a place, I'm
afraid you'd only find a dirt idol there that you couldn't
engage in much conversation."

Xu refused to listen and eventually reached Zhaoyuan County. He made inquiries of some of the locals
and found that there really was a place called Wuzhen.
After having arrived there, he stopped at an inn where he
could rest from his travels and asked about the location
of the town's temple. The host seemed rather shaken
by this and asked, "You wouldn't be a visitor named Xu,
would you?"

"That's correct," Xu replied. "How'd you know?"

The host asked again, "Your hometown isn't Zichuan,
is it?"

Xu answered, "That's right. But how'd you know?"

The owner hastily rushed out without answering.
Presently, husbands carrying children in their arms, along
with married and unmarried women, were peering inside,
with many more arriving, crammed together surrounding
the wall outside. Xu was even more surprised.

People in the crowd then explained to him, "Several
nights ago, a dream sent by the Earth God told us that
his friend, Xu, would be arriving soon from Zichuan and
that we should offer him assistance with expenses and
supplies. We've been looking forward to your arrival for
a long time." Xu found this strange as well.

Then he went to make an offering at the Earth God's
temple. Xu prayed, "Since we parted, brother, awake or
asleep I haven't been able to get you out of my mind, so I've
traveled a long way to honor the appointment we made.
The dream you made known to the townspeople about
treating me generously touches me deeply in my heart.
I'm ashamed I have no more handsome gift to offer than
this goblet of wine; if you don't find it too undignified,
please drink it as we used to do beside the river." Once

Li: A measure equal to about 1/3 mile, so Xu does indeed have a
long journey by foot ahead of him.
Burned some paper money: Also known as ghost money (or bank
of hell notes, or joss paper), burned at funerals and festivals.

he'd finished paying his respects, Xu burned some paper money. Immediately he saw the wind rise up behind the pedestal of the God's statue, whirl around for a long time, and then disperse.

That night he dreamt of Sixth Brother coming to see him, dressed neatly, a considerable change from the ordinary. In gratitude, Wang said, "You've journeyed from far away to visit me, and I'm so happy that I can't hold back my tears. But since I'm in this official position—insignificant though it is—I can no longer meet with you face-to-face, so even though we're so close to each other now, it feels like the distance between rivers and mountains. This saddens me to the very heart. The townspeople have some modest presents to offer you, to acknowledge our long-standing friendship. When it's time for you to return home, I'll come to see you off properly."

After staying for several days, Xu decided to take his leave. The crowd of residents courteously asked him to stay, presenting him with invitations in the morning and requests to entertain him in the evening, throughout the day bringing offers from an increasing number of potential hosts. Xu graciously declined, reiterating his need to be on his way. The crowd then brought armloads of offerings, all vying to present him with their farewell gifts. In less than a morning, the gifts filled an enormous sack. Old and young alike gathered together then to wish him a safe trip and to see him off as he left the village.

All of a sudden a cyclone of wind rose up, and followed for more than ten *li* as he went. Xu repeatedly bowed to it, saying, "Sixth Brother, take good care of yourself! Don't bother keeping up with me. Your benevolent and loving soul will certainly bring good fortune to your people, so you don't need your old friend to say anything more." The wind whirled around then for quite some time before moving on. Some of the townspeople who'd been traveling with him, marveling at all of this, also turned back. Xu returned home and became modestly wealthy, so he didn't have to fish any more.

Ever after, whenever he ran into someone from

Zhaoyuan, he asked about Sixth Brother Wang, and they reported that his spirit granted whatever his people requested. Others say that he's actually in Shikeng village, in Zhangqiu County. It's hard to know which it actually is.

The collector of these strange tales remarks: "To occupy the position of a high official but not to forget about old friends in humble and destitute circumstances—that's why Wang could become a god. Today a noble travels in a coach, but will that person still remember old friends he made back when he was a nobody? There is a man without social rank in my village whose family is extremely poor. One of his childhood friends became an official with high rank and salary. The poor man thought, 'If I trust to his generosity, surely he'll take good care of me.' So the poor man packed his belongings and made the arduous journey across a thousand *li*, only to be disappointed. After spending all of his money and selling his horse, he returned home.

"His joker of a brother wrote a *yueling* that mocked him: 'This month, my brother returned, his fur cap lost, his umbrella no longer working, his horse exchanged for a donkey, and he won't be traveling again until his boots stop squeaking.' Read it for a good laugh."

Shikeng village, in Zhangqiu Country: In modern Jinan district.
Yueling: A short poem which contains seven elements to form a record of what has happened during the current lunar calendar month (e.g., recounting news or politics).
Until his boots stop squeaking: An aphorism that means he's not going to make any other trips solely on the hope of friendship being reciprocated.

13. Stealing Peaches

Back when I was a teenager, I went to our administrative district to take an examination at the time of the Spring Festival. It's an ancient custom that on the day before the new year's eve, every working site and every business shop is decked out in colors and musicians parade to the provincial governor's office—this is always called "Performing Spring." I followed some friends to watch the festivities. That day the streets were virtually jammed with wandering people.

At the head of the court of justice were four officials, each dressed in red, sitting across from each other, two on the east and two on the west. Back then I was still very young and hence wasn't aware who the officials were. All I could hear was the buzz of people speaking and the clamor of the musicians in my ears.

Suddenly a man appeared, with a long-haired boy following him to convey his possessions on a carrying pole, and stepped up onto the stage, apparently having something to say. There were myriad uproarious sounds in that place, so I couldn't hear what he was saying. Yet I could see people at the head of the court smiling and

---

Spring Festival: Also known as the "Spring Festival of Purity" (*qingming*), celebrated at about the same time as Easter, and interestingly features the coloring and eating of boiled eggs. Also a "feast of resurgent life, dedicated to remembering the dead" as "family graves were cleared of weeds, burial mounds were repaired, and sacrificial vessels laid thereon" (Eberhard 103).

49

laughing.

At once, a dark-robed person with a loud voice ordered them to give a performance. As the man prepared to deal with this mandate, he inquired, "What shall I perform?" Those at the head of the court conferred with each other. A clerk came down and announced that they wished to see his best. He answered, "I can transpose living things." The clerk then related this to the officials. Almost immediately, the clerk came down again and directed him to obtain some peaches.

The performer promised to do so, removed his outer garment and laid it over his bamboo basket, audibly muttering an apparent complaint: "These officials aren't exactly long on intelligence! The ice hasn't even started to thaw yet, so how can I get any peaches? If I don't lay hold of some, I fear these officials will be angry. What now?"

His son said, "Father, you've promised them, so how can you back out?

The conjurer seemed pretty melancholy for a long time before finally declaring, "I've calculated and keep coming back to the same conclusion. It's spring, but the first snow's still on the ground—so how's someone supposed to go about searching for something like this? Only in the orchard of the Queen Mother of the West, where the four seasons never change and nothing ever withers or drops its leaves, might there be some. One would have to steal them from heaven above. It's the only way."

These officials: The performer literally calls them southern lords, for "facing the south" here (*nanmian*) is an allusion to the monarch's throne, which faces the south, and hence a term of respect (and obsequiousness) for the officials here. The term also refers generally to the officials heading a court of justice (Zhu 35n10).

Queen Mother of the West: The *xiwangmu*, or Western Queen Mother, "is supposed to hold sway over a fairy realm" (Eberhard 98) in the Kunlun Mountains, near the border with Tibet (see Cahill).

His son blurted, "Huh! You going to climb a stairway to heaven?"

"I have certain skills," he replied.

Then he opened his bamboo basket, took out a coil of rope about a hundred feet long, held an end, looked up and flung it skywards; at once the rope stood suspended in mid-air, as if it were hanging from something. Nor was that all, for the more he flung, the higher it went, until it disappeared into the clouds and the rope in his hands also came to an end. Next he shouted to his son, "Get over here! I've old and worn out, my body's too heavy and clumsy. I can't go up there, so you'll have to be the one." Consequently he passed the rope to his son and said, "Hang on to this and up you go."

The son took the rope with a disgruntled expression, grumbling, "Old man, you must be totally crazy! With this excuse for a rope, you want me to hang on and climb several thousand feet to high heaven. If it happens to snap somewhere along the way, not even my skeleton will survive!"

Sobbing violently and patting him, his father said, "I made a slip of the tongue and I regret I can't withdraw it. Don't make it worse—just go. If you steal one and bring it back, surely they'll grant us hundreds in gold, enough for you to marry a beautiful woman." His son then grabbed onto the rope and twisting in a circle, he climbed up, hands sliding and feet following like a spider on its silk, till gradually he passed through some clouds and could no longer be seen.

After a while, a peach the size of a large bowl fell from the sky. The joyful conjurer held it on display for the officials there. At the head of the hall they studied it for a very long time, unable to determine whether it was genuine or a fraud.

All of a sudden the rope fell to the ground from above and the conjurer, alarmed, cried, "How terrible! Up there, someone's cut our rope, so there's nothing for him to hang onto!" A moment later, something else fell from above. One glance told them that it was the son's head. Cradling it in his arms and sobbing, he said, "It must have been for stealing the peach, when some guard became aware of what he'd done. It's the end of my boy!"

As more time passed, a leg dropped from above; nor was that all, as the limbs of his dismembered body fell down until there were no more left to recover. Overwhelmed by grief, the conjurer picked up the pieces one by one, put them in his bamboo basket and shut it, then said, "I'm an old man and had only this one son, who followed me everywhere I traveled. Now having carried out my strict orders, he's suffered this bizarre and cruel fate! I must carry this away and bury him."

Then he walked up to the officials' table, knelt, and cried, "For that peach, my son was killed! If you have pity for a working man and will help me bury him, I'll pledge to repay your kindnesses even after death." The shocked officials sat there, stunned, and each one bestowed some gold on him.

The conjurer received their gifts, wrapped them up and bound them around his waist, then rapped on his bamboo basket and shouted, "Beloved son, you should come out and give thanks for these gifts. What're you waiting for?" Suddenly a boy with disheveled hair pushed up the lid of the basket with his head and bowed it in the direction of the officials—thus revealing himself to be the conjurer's son.

Such was that strange feat of magic, it still comes back to me in my memory. Afterwards I heard that the White Lotus Cult had the ability to practice such skills. Is it possible that the conjurer was one of their practicing descendants?

White Lotus Cult: The secret society dates back to the Song dynasty (960-1279), when it was organized in opposition to tyrannical rulers.

14. Sowing Pears

A certain villager was selling his extremely sweet, fragrant pears in the marketplace at sky-high prices when a Daoist priest wearing a worn-out scarf and cotton clothing came before his cart and begged for one. The villager cried out angrily at him, but couldn't drive him away; incensed, the villager cursed him even more strongly.

The Daoist priest replied, "There are several hundred pears in your cart—I'm only begging for one, a modest request that would cause you no great harm, so why become angry?" The bystanders encouraged the villager to give the Daoist one of his pears that'd gone off and then send him away, but the villager refused to go along with the suggestion. In the midst of this a hired laborer, unable to endure the noisy conflict, took some of his money and bought a pear, then handed it over to the Daoist.

The priest bowed his thanks and declared to the crowd, "We Daoists don't understand miserliness. I now have a nice quality pear and will bring it out to share with all of you here."

Somebody asked, "Since you've got a nice pear, why don't you eat it yourself?"

He replied, "I needed this fruit's seeds to grow others." Thereupon he held the pear in both hands and devoured it. When he finished, he took the seeds in his hand, rearranged his clothing so he could use a spade, dug into the soil to a depth of several inches, inserted the seeds and then covered them with earth. Facing the people in the marketplace, he asked for some warm water to irrigate them and to make them fertile. Some mean-spirited volunteer thereupon approached a nearby shop to get some boiling water—which the priest received and poured over the hole he'd made.

The eyes of the gathered crowd looked on, witnessing sprouts poke out and gradually get larger; in an instant, they formed a tree with branches supporting lush foliage; suddenly there were flowers, and just as suddenly, enormous and incredibly fragrant fruit filled the entire tree. The Daoist priest then reached to the top of the tree and plucked them off, bestowing them on the observers so they ran out in no time at all.

Next he vigorously chopped away at the tree, contending with it for quite a while, eventually cutting it down; then he put the leafy load over his shoulder, and slowly walked away with it.

Throughout this exercise of the Daoist's arts, the villager had been standing in the midst of the assembled crowd, craning his neck and straining his eyes, meanwhile forgetting all about his business. Once the priest was gone, he turned to look into his cart and found it completely empty of pears. He then realized that the pears that had been so generously distributed in that place had all been his.

Upon inspecting his cart carefully he found one of its handles gone, having been recently sheared through and cut off. His heart filled with anger and hatred.

Eager to catch up with the priest, he tore past the corner of a wall and found his handle discarded at its base, at that moment recognizing it as the trunk of the pear tree that had been chopped down. There was no

---

Completely empty of pears: The central action of this story was first recounted by Gan Bao, historian of the Eastern Jin Dynasty, in his *sou shen ji (Anecdotes about Spirits and Immortals)*, volume one, chapter 24, though the fruit in question there is a melon and the duping of the melon-seller is mentioned as only one example of the magical talents of a sage named Xu Guang.

sign of the Daoist priest anywhere. Everyone in the marketplace smiled broadly.

The collector of these strange tales remarks, "The villager was so incredibly stupid, his foolishness was almost something you could consider endearing. No surprise, then, that he saw the marketplace people grinning at him. One often sees that when villagers who have no official titles, and are considered rich locally, are asked by a good friend for some rice, they won't do what's right—indeed, calculating before replying, 'That's several days' earnings there.' Or if they're encouraged to help those threatened by disaster, or to prepare a meal for a lone, solitary person, again resenting what is right, calculatedly say, 'That's enough food for five or ten people.'

"At the worst, fathers and sons, elder brothers and younger brothers, all exhaust themselves in the settling of trifling money matters. When their hearts are driven mad with gambling lust or sexual desire, however, in an instant they're no longer stingy; or when the sword is about to come down on their necks, they'll pay to buy their own lives back without hesitation. But individuals in such categories are too numerous to list separately, so the example of such a foolish villager is anything but a surprise."

15. The Daoist of Laoshan

A scholar named Wang lived in our county, the seventh son in a large, wealthy family. From the time he was small, he'd admired the magical arts of Daoism, so hearing news that there were many immortals living on Laoshan, he set out wandering with a bamboo bookcase on his back.

Ascending to the summit, he saw a monastery there, very remote and serene. A Daoist priest was sitting cross-legged on a mat of rushes, his white hair hanging down his neck, wearing a look of radiant openness. Wang kowtowed and spoke with him, the priest's words proving both wise and mysterious. He asked if the priest would become his teacher.

The Daoist answered, "I'm afraid from your fragile and indolent appearance that you'd be unable to bear the necessary suffering."

Wang insisted, "I can do it."

The Daoist had many disciples who came together at twilight. Wang kowtowed to all of them and succeeded in being allowed to stay at the monastery.

As the morning sun rose, the Daoist priest called for Wang to get an axe, sending him out with the many

---

Laoshan: Mt. Lao, in Shandong province near the Yellow Sea and the city of Qingdao. A Daoist center since the Western Han dynasty, it was the site at one time of nine palaces, eight temples and over seventy convents/monasteries.

others to select and collect firewood. Wang solemnly listened, doing as he was instructed. After a month of this, he developed thick calluses on both hands and feet, could no longer endure his hardships, and began nurturing a private desire to return home.

One evening he returned to see two visitors drinking together with his master. Though the sun had already given way to dusk, still no lamps or candles had been lit. The master then cut paper with scissors to form a mirror shape and pasted it to the wall. In an instant the room glowed with the bright splendor of the moon, a brightness sufficient to reveal even the finest hairs or corn silks. All the disciples heard about this and rushed to the room.

One of the visitors said, "It's a fine night to enjoy the sublimely beautiful together." The Daoist reached for a wine jar on the table and gave it to his disciples, urging them to drink all they could. Wang considered to himself: how can seven or eight people all get enough from just one wine jar?

Then each of them looked for something suitable to drink from, vying to be the first to drain a goblet for fear that the wine would run out; but as they kept pouring from it time and time again, it didn't seem to be reduced even a little. Wang felt this was very strange.

Suddenly one of the guests spoke up: "Thank you for granting us the bright, shining light of the moon—it's just that it's kind of lonesome drinking wine by itself. Why not call the moon goddess to come down here?" Taking a chopstick, the Daoist proceeded to fling it into the center of the paper moon.

The moon goddess: Sometimes considered a Prometheus analogue, Chang'e (or Heng'e) stole the "elixir" (Allan 33), "drug, or dew" (Mercatante 310) of immortality from her husband, Archer Yi, and fled to the moon. Eberhard describes a variant in which the curious goddess swallows some of Yi's elixir (given to him by *xiwangmu*, the Queen Mother of the West) and simply "found herself floating up to heaven" (1952:103), where she became goddess of the moon.

They saw a beautiful lady emerge from the midst of the rays. At first not even quite a foot tall, by the time she reached the ground she was equal in size to a regular person. With her tiny waist and elegant neck, she lightly performed the "rainbow skirt dance." And then she sang,

> As I dance airily,
> I must either return to the mortal world
> Or remain secluded in the icy Moon Palace!

Her voice was exceedingly clear, as resonant as the notes of a xiao flute.

Having finished her song, she spun around and rose up, jumping up onto the table, and with everyone looking at her in surprise, she turned herself into a chopstick again.

The three men roared with laughter. Again one of the visitors spoke: "This evening has been perfectly enjoyable, but the wine's potency is getting to me. Would you agree to have a farewell drink with me in the Moon Palace?"

Rainbow skirt dance: A Tang dynasty entertainment, supposedly first performed for the emperor Xuanzong (685–762 C.E.) by Yang Yuhuan, one of the four great beauties of ancient Chinese tradition (Zhu 42).

Xiao flute: An end-blown flute, the "main accompanying instrument" (Blunden and Elvin 202-3) in the aristocratic *kunqu* operas of the sixteenth century. See *The New Grove Dictionary of Music and Musicians* (27:614-15).

Moon Palace: According to folklore, the Tang emperor Xuanzong ("mysterious ancestor") who ruled 712-736 C.E., posthumously known as Minghuang ("brilliant emperor"), asked a Daoist mage. on the day of the mid-autumn festival (fifteenth day of the eighth month in the Chinese calendar) in 713, some questions about the moon—and the master created a bridge from his girdle, allowing the two to walk upon the moon, where they met the moon goddess, Chang'e. Upon returning home, the emperor "took his flute and played the melody he had heard in the palace of the moon" (Eberhard 99), initiating the tradition of musical theater in China.

The three men relocated their banquet, gradually, to the center of the paper moon. The crowd of disciples gazed upon them sitting there, drinking, their beards and eyebrows totally visible as if images in a mirror.

After some time, the moon grew dark; a disciple, however, brought a candle. The Daoist priest was discovered sitting alone as normal, the guests long gone. The leftovers from earlier were still in dishes on the table, but the moon on the wall was now just a piece of paper shaped like a circular mirror.

The Daoist asked his disciples, "Have you had enough to drink?"

"Quite enough," they replied.

"If so, then you'd better get to bed—you won't be able to collect firewood if you're not rested." The group promised they would do so and withdrew. Wang was secretly both happy and jealous, so he stopped thinking about going back home.

But a month later, the suffering was once again more than he could bear, and the Daoist priest hadn't passed a single magical technique on to him. Feeling he could wait no longer, he resigned his duties and said, "As a pupil, I journeyed a hundred *li* to study with you, an immortal teacher, so even if I can't obtain the skill of being immortal myself, perhaps there's some small technique you could pass on to me. This would also ease my mind of its desire for instruction. Looking over these last two or three months, it's no exaggeration that the only thing I've done as a pupil in your school is to collect firewood from dawn till dusk, the kind of hardship I never knew at home."

The Daoist smiled, saying, "I originally said you wouldn't be able to handle the suffering, and now it seems I was right. Tomorrow morning I think I will release you to go."

"I've toiled as your pupil for many days," Wang replied. "Master, if you teach me a bit about one little trick, it won't all have been a waste."

The Daoist asked, "What skill do you seek?"

"I've seen that when you walk, walls cannot stop

you," Wang said. "Merely to obtain the method for this would be enough." The Daoist smiled his permission. He provided a rhyming chant for Wang to use, commanded him to repeat the incantation, and then shouted: "Enter the wall!"

Wang faced the wall, but didn't dare attempt to enter it.

Again the priest exclaimed, "Try it now." Wang, though determined and unhurried, came up to the wall and then stopped.

The Daoist said, "Put your head down and plow into it, don't shrink from it!"

Wang resolutely moved back from the wall several steps, then ran right at it; when he reached the wall, it was as if nothing were there. He turned back to inspect it, and consequently found himself on the other side of the wall. Greatly pleased, he went back through the wall to the other side and thanked his teacher.

"When you return home," the Daoist said, "maintain an appropriate purity of action, or the incantation won't prove effective." Thereupon he provided Wang with some money to pay for his return journey and sent him on his way.

Arriving home, Wang bragged that he'd met an immortal, and solid walls were no longer able to stop him.

His wife didn't believe him.

Wang made ready to perform, backing away from the wall several steps, then sprinted, his head striking the wall—bouncing off, however, and causing him to fall.

His wife pulled him up and looked him over, found a bump swelling on his forehead, and informed him of the large, egg-sized lump there. She ridiculed him. Wang was ashamed and angry, and cursed the old Daoist priest for being so mean to him.

The collector of these strange tales remarks, "Those who hear of this episode can't help but roar with laughter; but if so, they must not be aware of all the scholar Wangs in this world, who are not exactly few in number. Take, for instance, a crude official, the kind who's happy to choke down poison but afraid of taking medicine: suddenly some brown-noser boisterously proclaims the power of the official's skill in order to flatter him, repeating the official's advice to 'Stick to what's worked in the past and you can use it to run wild with impunity.' When first practiced on some naïve individual, this kind of approach might have no small effect. So then the official would claim it could be applied to affairs worldwide. This kind of person will inevitably meet an impassable wall somewhere and fall heavily to the ground."

Brown-noser: Pu's description is, literally, "some pus-licking hemorrhoid sucker."

16. The Changqing Monk

In Changqing, there was a Buddhist monk who had followed the Way in admirable purity. Though more than seventy years old, he was still quite healthy. One day he fell down and couldn't get back up. The monastery's other monks rushed over to help him, but he had already passed away. The old monk, however, didn't realize he was dead, and so his soul began floating away until it finally reached Henan.

It happened that the son of certain Henan gentry was riding at the head of more than ten mounted servants, who were carrying hawks for rabbit hunting. His horse suddenly broke away and threw him, killing the man. The monk's soul passed by just about that time, and merged with the young man, who thereupon began to revive.

The servants anxiously asked him how he felt. He opened his eyes wide, wondering, "How did this happen?" The group then helped him get home.

Once he was inside the door, a frenzied crowd of powdered and painted ladies surrounded him, examining and asking about him. Greatly startled, he cried, "I'm a Buddhist monk! How did this happen?"

Changqing: A county in western Shandong province, home of a number of Buddhist sites including fifth-century C.E. (Northern Wei dynasty) Divine Cliff Temple in Divine Cliff Ravine.
Henan: An eastern province with northern borders touching Shanxi, Hebei and Shandong provinces.

His family members thought he'd gone crazy and together tried to bring him to his senses. The monk didn't try to explain himself, simply shutting his eyes without answering them. If they brought him millet he would eat, but if it was wine or meat, he'd refuse. At night he slept alone, not accepting the favors of wives or concubines.

Several days later, he suddenly decided to take a little walk. Everyone was cheered by this. As soon as he stepped out, however, a group of servants with financial account books immediately crowded around him, prevailing upon him to look them over. Using the excuse of being sick and tired, he managed to avoid dealing with them.

He then asked the servants, "Do you know if there's a Changqing county in Shandong?"

"Certainly," they all replied.

"I'm depressed here with nothing to do," he said, "so I'd like to take a trip. Assemble everything I'll need at once." They tried to tell him that since his condition had only recently improved, he shouldn't try to deal with traveling to such a distant place. He wouldn't hear of it, so they set out the next day.

Arriving at Changqing, the monk found things to be as they previously had been. He hadn't even been bothered by having to inquire how to find his way there, en route to the monastery. A number of his former disciples noticed this was an honored guest and bowed to him most respectfully.

He then asked them, "What happened to the old monk who used to be here?"

"Our Master's shell has returned to nature," they told him.

He inquired about the grave. The group led him to a grave there that was mounded about three feet high, where the wild grass had not yet grown over it. The monks had no idea what his intentions were.

Soon he called for his horse so he could return home, instructing his former disciples, "Your Master lived piously as a monk. The personal items he left behind should be guarded faithfully. You must not allow anything to harm them." The monks assured him they would do so, and he left.

Once he was back home, he sat, pale and lethargic, refusing to take charge of any of the family's business.

Living this way for several months, finally he slipped out the gate to escape and went straight back to the old monastery where he called out to his disciples, "It's me, your Master." The monks were extremely skeptical, exchanging glances with each other and scoffing. So he related to them how his soul had returned, then described what his life with them in the monastery had been like, till it all fit together. With his disciples convinced at last, he occupied his old dais once again and resumed his daily routines.

Afterwards, the young master's family sent horses and sorrowful requests that he return, which he refused even to acknowledge. When more than a year had gone by, the young master's wife sent a responsible servant with many gifts to leave there. He turned away the gold and silk, keeping for himself only a simple cloth robe. Some of his friends once went to Changqing and paid him a respectful visit, discovering that he had become quiet and sincere. Though he appeared to be only about thirty years old, he often spoke of events that had taken place over eighty years earlier.

The collector of these strange tales remarks, "When a person dies, the soul scatters, and though a thousand *li* apart from the body, it doesn't just disperse if its owner was an individual of devout character. Concerning the monk, I'm not at all surprised that he returned to life again, though what *is* surprising to me is that he entered into a life of splendor and luxury and was unable to refuse or to escape from it. A single glance can bring about a seduction, or one can find a seduction impossible to achieve despite one's most vigorous efforts—think where this leaves the monk!"

17. The Snake Man

In East Prefecture, there was a certain fellow who trained snakes to perform for a living. He once raised and trained two snakes together, both entirely green: he called the larger one Big Green, the smaller one, Green the Second. Green the Second had a red-spotted forehead and was especially clever and cooperative, invariably winding and swaying just as he wished it to do. The snake man took a special fancy to it, favoring it over his other snakes.

After a year passed, Big Green died, and though the trainer thought about trying to fill its vacancy, he could never find the time to do so. One night, he stayed at a monastery in the mountains. At daybreak, he opened his bamboo basket and Green the Second was nowhere to be seen. The snake man was so bitterly disappointed, he wanted to die.

He searched high and low, calling out for Green the Second, but there was no sign of the snake. Previously, whenever they would pass through a grove with abundant grass, he always let it out so it could enjoy itself, and it would return again when he went to look for it; on this occasion, he hoped, of course, for the same result.

He sat and waited until the sun was high in the sky and he was worn out from watching, then, dispirited, he finally left. He'd only gone a few steps out the monastery's door when he distinctly heard something inside a pile of kindling, making the sound of a snake's hissing.

He froze in his tracks, startled, and looked back at it: there was Green the Second. He was overjoyed—it was

like he'd found a huge piece of jade. He stopped to set his load down at the side of the road and Green the Second also stopped suddenly. The snake man noticed that a little snake was also following behind them. Petting Green the Second, he said, "I was afraid you'd gone for good. Is this your little buddy?"

The snake man took out some treats for it and for the little snake as well. The little snake, however, wouldn't move towards them, being so timid and frightened that it wouldn't venture near the food. Green the Second took some in its mouth to feed it, in the same way that a host might offer some to a guest. The snake man also offered it some more, and it ate that, too. Once it had been fed, it followed Green the Second into the basket.

He carried it back with him and taught it to gyrate and sway, and always to be well-behaved. Soon it was no less trained than Green the Second, and for that reason he named it Little Green. Showing off their talents everywhere he went, he raked in more money than he could count.

Generally speaking, snake men work with snakes only until the creatures are about two feet long, for any larger than that they become too heavy and require substitutes. Since Green the Second was so well-trained, the snake man was reluctant to replace him. In another two or three years, it grew well over three feet long and when coiled would fill the entire bamboo basket, and hence he determined to let it go.

One day, standing at Zibo's East Mountain, he fed it some especially nice treats, wished it all the best, and then released it. He turned around an instant later and found it had come back and was coiled around the bamboo basket. The snake man waved at it and cried, "Go on! Everything in the world comes to an end, even if it's lasted a hundred years. If you conceal yourself in the valleys here, surely in time you'll become a dragon spirit.

Zibo: A city in north central Shandong province, close to Pu Songling's home village in Zichuan.

A bamboo basket can't hold you forever, can it?"

Green the Second then left indeed. The snake man watched until it was gone. Then it came back again and wouldn't leave despite his attempts to shoo it away, but kept bumping its head against the bamboo basket. Little Green was inside, and it was also upset and agitated.

The snake man became aware of the problem and asked, "Didn't you get to bid Little Green farewell?" Then he let him out, and Little Green went straight to his friend. They put their heads together and flicked their tongues out, apparently speaking to each other. In no time the snakes were crawling off together, side by side. Just when he was beginning to wonder whether Little Green was coming back, it returned, slithering in by itself, until it had entered all the way into the bamboo basket and curled up.

From that point he began searching for a snake of comparable quality, but couldn't find one so excellent. And then Little Green began growing steadily until it was unable to perform any longer. Eventually he did find one that was quite docile, though it certainly wasn't as talented as Little Green. And Little Green had become as thick as a child's upper arm.

At first, Green the Second settled in the mountains and firewood gatherers often spotted it there. Over the years it grew several feet long and as big around as a bowl; it also began to chase after people and for that reason travelers started warning each other not to venture into its territory.

One day, the snake man was passing through that vicinity when a snake suddenly and violently came after him like a gust of wind. The snake man was quite scared and fled. The snake was swift in its pursuit. When he turned back to look at it he saw it was about to catch him. But when he glanced at its head, he noticed those familiar red spots and quickly realized it was Green the Second. He put down his belongings and cried out, "Green the Second! Green the Second!"

The snake came to a sudden halt. It held its head high for a long time, then wound its body around the snake man, as it had in the past when they were performing. He sensed that it wished him no harm whatsoever, but the human body can only take so much weight, so all its winding wasn't very pleasant; he fell to the ground, gasping and praying, and thereupon he was released.

Then it bumped its head against the bamboo basket. The snake man understood what it wanted, opened the bamboo basket and out came Little Green. The two snakes exchanged glances, then wrapped themselves around each other like candy confections and stayed that way for quite some time before parting.

The snake man then gave his blessing to Little Green: "For a long time I've been thinking about setting you free, and now here's your buddy."

To Green the Second, he said, "You first led him here, so you should also lead him away. And there's one more thing I have to say to you: deep in the mountains you have no shortage of food and drink, so don't go troubling people—it offends heaven and you'll be condemned for it." The two snakes were crestfallen, as though they had both received the rebuke. Then they hastily slithered off, the big one in front and the little one behind, through the forest which parted for them as they passed. The snake man stood there for a long time, watching them until he could no longer see for sure which way they'd gone.

Since then, people go there all the time, but no one knows where the two snakes went.

The collector of these strange tales remarks, "Snakes, which may seem like stupid creatures, as it turns out feel affection and have human-like reasoning behind their actions. In addition, they can take criticism and listen to advice readily. Thus it seems hard to justify that there are people who take ten years to become friends with someone else, or several lifetimes to show humble gratitude toward a superior, most of the time thinking badly of those friends and superiors, either adding to the troubles they've already suffered or treating them with crazy hostility. They should feel themselves shamed by these two snakes."

18. Chopping the Python

In Hutian village there were two brothers named Hu who set out to collect firewood in a deep, secluded ravine. They ran into an enormous python while the elder brother was going first, so it began swallowing him; the younger brother was so terrified that he wanted to run away, but seeing his elder brother being devoured, he roused himself in anger, took up their woodcutter's axe and chopped at the snake's head. Although he wounded it there, it wouldn't stop its swallowing.

Although the elder brother's head had already been swallowed, it was his good fortune that the snake was unable to get past his shoulders. The younger brother, at wit's end and unable to come up with a better plan, then grabbed the elder brother's two feet in his hands and with all his force dragged his elder brother out of the python's mouth.

Due to its own suffering, the python went away.

Upon inspecting the elder brother, the younger brother discovered that his nose and ears had been entirely digested and he could barely breathe. He carried him away on his shoulders, having to stop along the way ten times or more before arriving home.

Medicines were administered to the elder brother for half a year before he recovered. To this day one can still see every scar on his face and the holes where his nose and ears used to be. Alas!

Unexpectedly, it was among farm folk that there was such a good younger brother! One could even say, "The python didn't consume the elder brother because it was touched by the younger one's virtue and righteousness." Believe it!

19. The Adulterous Dog

In Qingzhou, there was a merchant named Jia who traveled out away from home, and was frequently gone for a whole year at a time before returning. His household owned a white dog which his wife trained to have sex with her, and the dog made a habit of doing it with her constantly.

One day, Jia arrived home and that night he and his wife went to lie down in bed together. The dog suddenly rushed in, jumped up on the bed, and mauled the merchant to death.

Afterwards, word got out to other village residents, who were collectively outraged and reported it to their local official. The official shackled the wife, who refused to acknowledge her guilt, and imprisoned her. He ordered the dog tied up and brought in, then summoned the woman to appear as well.

When the dog saw her, it came right up and ripped off her clothes, ready to start humping her. There was no longer anything the woman could say except to confess her guilt. Two servants were sent to transfer them to the divisional court, one to accompany the woman and the other the dog. There were onlookers who wanted to see the two perform sexually, and hence they collected money to bribe the servants, who then would lead the dog over to the woman so they could have sex together. Wherever they stopped, they routinely attracted hundreds of people to watch, netting the servants a hefty profit.

Ultimately, the woman and the dog were executed by being dismembered an inch at a time. Alas! With the

73

world as big as it is, even the weirdest things can happen somewhere. But was this woman alone in her desire to have intercourse with an animal?

The collector of these strange tales remarks, "Those who engage in illicit sexuality in a notorious place must expect to be censured for it; but even a rendezvous in such a place is to be scorned. This was a woman who couldn't bear to live without sex and thought about intercourse all the time. At night the one lying on her turned out to be an animal from her own household. She made the dog her lover, and it mounted her under the covers.

"At the place of their lovemaking, the dog's tail wags back and forth. With the beast inside her warmth and softness, the woman moves her waist sweetly. The truth eventually comes out when she opens her thighs and uncovers its tool—then gives in as it returns the shaft to its target, which swallows its length to the root. To take to the idea of bestiality suddenly is really warped.

"The dog, which should guard against adulterers, turned out to be an adulterer itself. Then it became a murderer because of its jealousy. It's difficult to apply the laws of the government to punish its guilt. The woman, who was not an animal, turned out to have a truly bestial mind and engaged in filthy, stinking copulation with it.

An inch at a time: This torturous form of execution is designed to reflect the heinous nature of the crime being punished.
A notorious place: The Bu River in Shandong province passed into the vernacular as a "place notorious for profligacy" since it became a popular site for romantic trysts (see Zhu 51n6).
Truth eventually comes out: Pu delicately adapts the proverb that the awl will eventually pierce through the leather bag holding it, which is conventionally construed as meaning that one's true qualities will eventually come to light. The *ying*, or "tool" in this translation, is literally the "sharp point of the awl," to extend Pu's euphemistic proverbial analogy.
The shaft . . . to the root: More of Pu's euphemistic references to the male and female genitalia and the sex act. The penis is referred to here in the original as an awl, an arrow/javelin, and a feather.

Even the jackals and the tigers would refuse to eat her flesh.

"Alas! As the human being involved in this adultery, the woman should be cut an inch at a time; but when it comes time for the adulterous dog to be punished, there's no way to sentence it with the laws of the mortal world. Since a human being transgressed, the law should ideally punish that person by turning her into a dog; but when the dog transgressed, even the underworld couldn't find a way to punish it. It would be better to dismember the dog and leave its spirit unable to rest—then its spirit could be arrested and brought before the Hell King for sentencing."

The jackals and the tigers: Here Pu sets up his subsequent argument that the nature of one's crime should dictate the circumstances of one's punishment. Tiger and jackals, carrion eaters who would ordinarily be glad to feed on a human carcass, here prove too genteel to devour anything as depraved and obscene as Jia's wife.

20. The Hail God

Wang Mengzhen, whose style name was Yuncang, arrived to take up an official appointment in the area of Chu. He planned first to hike up Longhu Mountain to visit a Daoist master. When he came upon a lake, no sooner had he stepped into a boat than a smaller boat came near and the man piloting it requested to see the official. Wang met with him, noting his lean and muscled appearance.

The boatman took a name card out of his robe and gave it to Wang, explaining, "The Daoist master heard news that someone in an official's position was approaching, so I was dispatched to deliver an invitation to him." Wang was surprised that they knew in advance, like the gods, of his coming, but he took this in good faith and so they departed.

The Daoist master treated everyone with equal respect. His servants, who all had broad faces and long

---

Wang Mengzhen . . .Chu: Wang Mengshen was a Qing dynasty official who shared Pu Songling's hometown of Zibo/Zichuan. During the Spring and Autumn Period (772-481 B.C.E.), Chu, in south-central China, was one of about 170 feudal states (Perkins 486). The name customarily refers to Hunan and Hubei provinces, which were part of the Chu kingdom during the Spring and Autumn Period.
Longhu Mountain: Situated in the prefecture of Guangsin in the province of Jiangxi, Mayers identifies this as the abode of Daoist patriarch Zhang Daoling "and of his reputed descendants" (153).

beards, weren't dressed like common people. The servant who had been dispatched to meet Wang also served there and stood at the master's side. He paused, faced the Daoist, and spoke to him in a low, confidential, tone.

Referring to the servant, the Daoist then said to Wang, "This gentleman is your fellow countryman—don't you recognize him?"

The official asked who he was and the Daoist replied, "He's the one your world calls the Hail God, Li Zuoche." The official was so stunned he couldn't control the change in his facial expression. "Just now," the Daoist master commented, "he received an edict from heaven to make it rain and hail, so he'll have to say goodbye to you right away."

"Where's it going to fall?" Wang asked.

"At Zhangqiu," was the reply.

Concerned about the safety of Zibo, which was near Zhangqiu, Wang left his place at the table and begged for his hometown to be excused from the Hail God's mission.

The Daoist master explained, "This is an edict from the Jade Emperor above. The amount of hail is fixed in quantity—who has the authority to reduce it?" Wang was beside himself with worry.

The Daoist master pondered this for a very long

Li Zuoche: During the conflict between the Zhao and Han armies that would eventually result in the triumph of Liu Bang (who subsequently became the Emperor Gao), Li Zuoche, a counselor and nobleman for the Zhao, proposed taking 30,000 troops to block the grain shipments to the Han forces through the Taihang mountains, a suggestion that the Zhao prime minister, Chen Yu, refused to take, leading to the loss of the decisive Battle of Jingxing in the early 3rd century B.C.E. Li has been honored by heaven for his wisdom by being made an elemental deity.

Zhangqiu: A county in Qinan district, Shandong province.

Jade Emperor: The supreme deity in Chinese folk religion and mythology, ruler of the heavens, perhaps the most venerated of Daoist entities, associated with jade because of the magical qualities attributed to it, including healing and longevity.

time, then turned to his servant and advised him, "You could channel the rain and hail into the gorge without hurting the corn in the fields." He further noted, "The guest of honor is already seated; when you leave, try not to be so disruptive."

The god then went out into the courtyard, where mist suddenly materialized around his feet, spreading magically over the ground. Soon he flew up into the sky to the height of the trees in the courtyard; continuing, he soared up past the rooftops of its buildings. Then a thunderclap sounded as the god flew swiftly to the north, shaking the court so violently that bamboo mats and other items waved liked fans.

"His departure's making it thunder!" cried out the startled Wang.

The Daoist master replied, "This was a mild departure, since I warned him; otherwise, he'd disappear just as the wind was making an enormous sound."

Resigned, the official left to return home, recording the date and sending someone to Zhangqiu to inquire about the hail there. It turned out to be true that there was a huge rain and hail storm on that date that filled every irrigation canal and ditch—while in the farm fields, barely any accumulated at all.

21. The Fox Marries Off His Daughter

Minister Yin of Licheng, a high-level official, was impoverished in his youth, but had a reputation for boldness. In his hometown there was an estate owned by a formerly prosperous family that spread over several *mu*, with multi-story buildings joined together at the eaves into quite an expanse. But because weird things kept happening there, no one had occupied the premises in a long time; it gradually became so overgrown with wormwood that even in the daytime no one would risk going in there.

It happened that Yin was joining some scholar friends for a drink when someone playfully said, "If anyone has the nerve to spend a night there, we'll all pool our money to put on a feast for him."

Yin jumped up and said, "It can't be that tough!" He snatched up a mat and walked out.

They all accompanied him to the entrance and then taunted him, "We'll wait here for a little while, so if you see anything, you can just cry out to us."

He smiled. "If there are any ghosts or foxes, I'll catch them as proof for you."

Upon entering, he noticed tall weeds obscuring the paths and dense growths of wormwood and mugwort.

Licheng: Now Jinan, the capital of Shandong province.
Mu: A Chinese acre, equal to .0667 hectares (and one hectare is equal to 2.471 acres).

It was the time of the first quarter of the moon, which fortunately projected a dim yellow light, enabling him to distinguish the locations of doors. Feeling his way with his hands, he proceeded past several doors until he arrived at the furthest building. He stepped up to the moon-viewing platform, which was so bright and clean that he decided to stop right there. To the west he saw the moon shining, though it graced the hill with only a single thread of light.

He sat there a long time, noticing nothing strange, laughing in secret at the ridiculous rumors that had been circulated. Putting his mat down on the platform and resting his head on a stone, he lay down to gaze at the Cowherd and the Weaving Maid.

At nearly ten o'clock, as he was feeling drowsy and about to fall asleep, he heard the sound of someone walking around noisily in the building below, then coming upstairs. He surreptitiously peeked while pretending to be asleep, seeing a person in dark clothing carrying a lotus lantern, who suddenly noticed Yin with fright and quickly withdrew. This person said to someone standing behind him, "There's a stranger here."

From below came the question, "Who is it?"

"I don't know," he replied.

Presently an old man came up, proceeded to take a good look at him, and said, "This is Master Yin, a governmental secretary, who's fallen fast asleep. We can go about our business and since he's an easy-going, unpretentious gentleman, he won't make any trouble for us." So they came in together and opened up all of the doors.

The Cowherd and the Weaving Maid: The Cowherd constellation is recognized in Chinese astronomy as the beginning point of the *tian di zhi shu*, or astronomical record of the universe (Sterckx 17). The folktale of the cowherd and the weaving maid (see Eberhard 1986:272-73) explains how the two became constellations and also accounts for the conjunction that occurs once a year, when the two meet on the seventh night of the seventh month.

In a little while, increasing crowds of people were bustling about. The buildings were illuminated by so many lamps that it looked like daytime. Yin rolled over on his side briefly, sneezed and coughed. The old man heard him wake up, came over to him and knelt, saying, "I have a daughter who's getting married this very evening. Since I didn't mean to offend you, your honor, I hope you won't look too harshly on my disturbing you."

Yin stood up, helped the old man up, and replied, "I had no idea that such a joyous ceremony would be held tonight, and I'm ashamed I have no gift to offer in congratulations."

The old man said, "It's our good fortune that your honor's very presence here will drive away any evil spirits. If I could trouble you to come and participate with us, I'd feel doubly favored by your generosity." Yin happily agreed to do so.

Upon entering the building, he saw that it was exquisitely decorated. Then a woman, about forty years old or so, came out to pay her respects to him. The old man explained, "This is my wife." Yin bowed respectfully to her, clasping his hands together.

Instantly, they heard the sound of a sheng's boisterous music, and someone rushed in, crying, "He's here!" The old man hastened out to meet the arrival while Yin also stood up to wait for him. In a few minutes, a cluster of people carrying gauze-covered lanterns led in the bridegroom. He was seventeen or eighteen years old, graceful and handsome.

The old man directed him first to pay respects to their wedding's honorable guest. In deference, the young man looked over at Yin, who responded graciously with the manner of an attendant representing the host. Next the old man and the son-in-law exchanged bows, and once they were finished they took their seats. Soon some beautiful maidservants came to serve them with wine and steam-covered meat dishes, presented in jade bowls

---

A sheng's boisterous music: Made by a Chinese reed instrument.

and golden cups, till the entire table was glowing.

Once the wine had made several rounds, the old man sent one of the maids to usher in the bride. The girl then went into an inner room, but a long time passed while no one came out. The old man himself got up, drew back a curtain, and made a plea. Presently a number of maidservants and older women came out accompanying the bride, whose ornaments and jewelry tinkled, and whose perfumes gave off the fragrances of musk and orchid.

The old man directed his daughter to face her elders and pay her respects to them, then he had her go over and sit beside her mother. Even a quick glance at her wearing her brilliant jade phoenix headdress revealed her to be a paragon of beauty.

Not long afterwards, wine was poured into golden cups large enough to hold what seemed like several *dou.* Yin figured that something like this would provide effective proof to his fellows, so he secretly slipped one up inside his sleeve. Pretending to be drunk, he slumped over on the table, relaxed, and seemed to fall asleep.

Everyone said, "Look, Master Yin's drunk." Soon the bridegroom wanted to take his leave, so the music suddenly struck up again, and one after another they all went downstairs and left.

Once they were gone and the servants began collecting the wine cups, they found they were short one and carefully hunted for it without success. One privately suggested that perhaps the sleeping guest had taken it; the old man, however, anxiously warned them not to say so, for fear that Yin might hear.

After some time, all was quiet inside and out, so Yin stood up. It was dark since there weren't any lamps lit, but the smell of cosmetics, perfumes, and wine still filled every portion of the room. He looked to see that in the

---

Phoenix headdress: As a symbol of joy, the phoenix would be an ideally auspicious wedding emblem.
Dou: A measure of capacity equal to ten liters.

east it was just getting light, then calmly took off, checking in his sleeve to be sure the gold cup was still there.

When he reached the entrance, his friends were already present. The students had arrived early to wait, suspicious that he might have left the house at night in order to reenter it in the morning. Yin took out the golden cup to show them. The group, astonished, interrogated him, so he gave them an account of what had happened. They all agreed that this cup was something no impoverished scholar could afford, so they believed him.

After all this, once Yin had passed the examination to earn the title of *jinshi*, he was appointed as magistrate for Feiqiu. There the head of an aristocratic family named Zhu threw a banquet for the new official, ordering his servants to bring out their largest wine cups—but quite some time passed and the servants didn't return.

Finally one of the lowly servants came in and whispered a report to the host, whose looks revealed him to be quite angry. After a while, a golden wine cup was offered to the guest and he was encouraged to drink up. Yin carefully examined the cup and found its patterns of refined engraving to be no different than the one he had taken from the fox. Quite curious, he inquired where the cups were made.

The host replied, "There were only eight in all after one of my ancestors, who was a minister in the capital at the time, hired a skilled artisan to supervise their crafting. Thus they've been heirlooms for generations, stored away like treasure for a long, long time. In honor of your presence, I wished them brought out, and just as they were to be taken from their chest, it was discovered that there were only seven. I would suspect that one of the servants had stolen it—except that ten years' worth of undisturbed dust on the seals suggests otherwise."

Jinshi: This, the highest level of the civil service examination, was achieved by passing an examination held at the imperial capital.
Feiqiu: An unspecified place name.

Yin laughed and said, "The gold cup must have sprouted wings and flown away. Certainly in this age one must guard hereditary treasures so they don't become lost. As it happens, I have a cup quite similar to yours, that I should like to give you as a present."

Once the banquet was ended and Yin returned to his official residence, he picked up his own cup and speedily had it delivered. His host scrutinized it and was extremely shocked.

Personally paying Yin a visit in gratitude, Zhu asked him how the cup had come into his possession. Yin then told him the details from beginning to end. Thus one learns that though a thousand *li* away, a fox has the power to take possession of something but may not dare to keep it permanently.

22. Jiaona

Kong Xueli, a descendant of Confucius, was a refined and cultivated man, accomplished in poetry. A close friend of his who was a magistrate in Tiantai sent him an invitation to visit—but while Kong was traveling to stay with him, the magistrate happened to die. This left Kong without the financial means to return, so he went to live at the Putuo Monastery, where he was employed as a scribe for the monks.

To the west of the monastery, just over a hundred paces away, there was a residence belonging to a Master Shan. Although originally the son of a rich family, Master Shan had found himself in financial straits because of an extensive litigation, so he took the few members of his remaining household and moved to the country, leaving the house near Putuo untenanted.

One day, a heavy snow fell and no one was out traveling. Coincidentally, Kong was passing the house's gate as a young man came out, attractive and quite elegant. Noticing Kong, he hurried over and greeted him politely, and after briefly making courteous acquaintance with him, humbly requested the privilege of receiving him as a visitor. Kong immediately liked his pleasant manner and happily followed him inside.

The rooms were lovely though not very large, with brocade curtains hanging everywhere, while many of the ancient masters' calligraphy and paintings were

---

Tiantai: A county in Zhejiang province.

85

displayed on the walls. On the table lay a volume with the title, *Trivial Records from Langxuan*. As he glanced through its pages, he found the volume filled with things he'd never read before.

Because the young man was living in the Shan residence, Kong believed him to be its owner and hence didn't inquire into his family background. The young man skillfully examined Kong in depth about his own background, feeling a genuine sympathy for him and advising him to set himself up as a teacher.

Kong sighed and said, "A wanderer like me? Who'd even agree to recommend me?"

The young man replied, "If you won't reject a worthless person like myself, I hope you'll allow me to be your student." Kong was very pleased by this, but didn't dare presume to act as the young man's instructor, requesting instead that they be friends.

Then he asked the young man, "Why has your house been closed up for so long?"

"This mansion belongs to Master Shan," he responded, "who used to live here before he moved to the country and hence it has been empty a long time. My family name is Huangfu and our home used to be in Shaanxi. Because our family home was burned down in a wildfire, we've arranged to take refuge here temporarily." It wasn't until this point that Kong realized the young man was not Master Shan. That same night, they laughed and chatted very merrily till finally Kong was invited to stay and share the young man's bed.

At dawn, a servant boy came in to light a charcoal fire in the room. The young man had risen earlier and gone into an inner room while Kong remained there, sitting with the bedspread hugged around him. The boy then entered again and announced, "The master has arrived."

Trivial Records from Langxuan: The Yuan dynasty (1279-1368) collection of fairy tales, *langxuan* [or *langhuan*] *suo ji*, by Yi Shizhen, the title of which is reminiscent of Pu's own collection of tales from his pseudonym, *liaozhai* (literally, "studio of leisure").

Surprised, Kong stood up.

An older man, the hair on his temples showing white, came in, turned towards Kong and eagerly thanked him, saying, "Sir, you've been kind enough not to abandon my dullard son, and have even agreed to offer him instruction. The youngster is just beginning to work on his poor composition skills, so don't treat him as a friend, but instead as your student." With these words he presented Kong with a brocade suit, a sable hat, stockings, and a pair of shoes.

He watched while Kong finished washing his face and combing his hair, then called for wine and food to be set out. Kong didn't know what the table, bed, and clothing were made of that gave them their eye-dazzling luster. The wine went around a number of times, then the old man sat up and took his leave, departing with the aid of his walking stick.

When the meal had ended, the young master submitted the lessons he'd prepared in the characters and phrasings of antiquity, not one of them written in the contemporary style. When Kong asked him about this, he answered, laughing, "I'm not trying to win any official recognition." With the sun beginning to set, he poured out more wine, saying, "This evening we'll make merry till we're exhausted—because tomorrow it'll no longer be permitted." He called out to the servant boy, "See if the master's asleep or not; if he's sleeping, sneak over and call for Xiangnu." The boy went out, and then came back in with an embroidered bag that held a pipa.

In no time at all, a maidservant entered, stunning in her gorgeous make-up. The young master had her play

---

The contemporary style: That is, the essay model of Ming and Qing civil service examinations, consisting of a rigidly precise eight-paragraph structure that limited or precluded creativity and introspection.
Pipa: A four-stringed instrument with a short neck and round body, held vertically in the lap and plucked or strummed.

"The Two Wives of Emperor Shun." Xiangnu used an ivory pick to strum the strings, arousing resonant feelings of desolation, with a rhythm unlike anything Kong had ever heard before. The young master then told her to take some huge cups and fill them with wine, and they didn't stop until the third watch.

The next day, the young master and Kong rose early to study together. The young master was exceptionally bright, being able to recite accurately what he had looked over only once, and in just two or three months, could construct an excellent composition expressing wise opinions. They agreed to drink together every five days, making certain that Xiangnu was always summoned.

One evening, when his joyful drinking had begun to make him feel horny, Kong started staring at Xiangnu. The young master was able to guess his intentions and said, "This maid was raised by my aging father. Elder brother, since you've been alone for a long time and have no wife, I've been planning day and night for a long time to find someone for you. I'll be sure she's a beautiful mate."

Kong replied, "If you really mean it, that'd be a great favor—as long as she's just like Xiangnu."

The young master laughed as he observed, "You're proof indeed that 'what the experienced see as commonplace, the inexperienced find extraordinary.' If

---

"The Two Wives of Emperor Shun": One of the legendary sage-kings, Shun, a farmer advanced to the throne for his filial devotion, was believed to have become emperor circa 2255 B.C.E. and "was credited with inventing the writing brush" (Perkins 460). Emperor Yao, who abdicated in Shun's favor, gave him his two daughters in marriage. The melancholic description of the song suggests that it depicts the wives' mourning for their husband. Giles comments that at the death of Shun, "these ladies are said to have wept so much that their tears literally drenched the bamboos which grew beside their husband's grave; and the speckled bamboo is now commonly known as the bamboo of Shun's wives" (22).
Third watch: Approximately 11:00 p.m.-1:00 a.m.

she's your idea of a beauty, your wish will be easy to satisfy."

After he'd been there half a year, Kong decided one day to explore the countryside, but when he arrived at the gate, he found it bolted shut from the outside and went to inquire about it. The young master explained to him, "My father worries that if I get involved with too many people I'll be distracted from my studies, so that's why he's discouraging visitors." That made sense to Kong.

At that time, the sweltering summer weather was heating up, so they moved their study to a garden pavilion. Kong noticed a swelling on his chest that grew to the size of a peach and overnight became as big as a bowl, the pain of which made him groan aloud. The young master watched over him constantly, going without sleep and food.

After several days, the affliction became so severe that Kong could no longer eat or drink. The old master also came to look in, so the father and son lamented together. The young master said, "Last night, thinking about Master Kong's ailment, I realized that younger sister Jiaona might have the skills to heal him. I sent someone to grandmother's to ask her to come—what could be taking her so long?"

Suddenly the servant entered and reported, "Miss Na is here; Auntie and Miss Song have also come." Father and son quickly hastened them inside. Shortly after, the young man led his sister out to take a look at Kong. She was about thirteen or fourteen years old, her lovely eyes sparkling with intellect and her willowy figure making her even more attractive. When Kong stared into her face, he forgot to groan and no longer looked distressed, his spirit improving remarkably.

The young master then explained, "This gentleman is my dear friend, as close to me as if we were brothers. Sister, do your best to cure him." The girl then set aside her shyness, and with her long sleeves trailing behind her, approached the bed to examine him. As she reached out to take his pulse, he perceived a fragrant aroma surpassing that of orchids.

With a smile, she said, "It's no surprise you have this condition, since your heart rate has accelerated. Although the illness is life-threatening, it can be cured; however, this lump of tissue is already dead, so we simply must trim away the skin and cut off the flesh." Then she took a gold bracelet from her arm and calmly placed it over the troubled area, steadily pressing down on it. The swelling puffed up about an inch, poking up through the bracelet, until the base of the swelling was contained entirely inside it, so it was no longer the size of a bowl in diameter.

With one hand, she opened the front of her thin gown and unfastened the knife she was wearing that had an edge as thin as paper, then while holding the bracelet in place, she took the blade, gently set it at the base of the lump, and began cutting it. A flood of purple blood began to flow, soaking into and staining the bed mat, but Kong was so eager for the beauty to be near him that he not only didn't feel the pains—he was even afraid that she might finish the surgery too quickly, preventing him from being close to her for a longer period of time.

Not long after, a piece of the rotten flesh that had been cut broke off, rolling away like a gall that had been trimmed from a tree. Jiaona then called for some water to cleanse the site of the cut. From her mouth she spat out a sizeable red pellet, then touched it to the wounded flesh, pressed it down and rolled it around and around: after the first revolution, it began to feel hot enough to turn water to steam; after the second revolution, this turned to a gentle itching; after she finished the third revolution, his body began to relax and cool off all over, penetrating to his very bones and marrow.

The girl then returned the pellet to her throat, announced, "You're cured!" and hastily walked away. Kong jumped up and ran to thank her; it was as if his illness had vanished. But whenever he thought about her shining beauty, he couldn't stop his pangs of longing. From then on, he ignored his books and sat around in a daze, as though he had nothing to live for.

The young master, who'd already observed this

behavior, encouraged him, "Elder brother, I've scouted out a beautiful mate for you."

"Who?" Kong asked.

He replied, "She's also a member of my family."

Kong thought hard about this for a good long time, and then replied, "No need." With his face to the wall, he recited, "To one who's already passed through the great seas, other waters are nothing difficult; / Except for those surrounding Wushan, there are no other clouds."

The young master recognized his meaning and responded, "My father admires and respects your significant talents, and has often wished for you to marry into the family. But I only have one little sister and she's just too young. There's my cousin, Song, who's eighteen and far from coarse or crude. If you won't believe unless you can see for yourself, Song's daily routine takes her to a pavilion in the garden—you can be waiting there in a side-room to take a look at her."

Kong did as he was instructed and as a result saw Jiaona arrive in the company of a real beauty, her painted black eyebrows curved like moth antennae, her tiny feet adorned in phoenix slippers, in appearance Jiaona's equal. Kong was greatly pleased, and invited the young master to serve as his go-between in the marriage plans.

The next day, the young master came outside and congratulated him: "It's a match." Then he cleared another courtyard for Kong's wedding ceremony. At sunset, court music filled the air, shaking the dust loose everywhere, and as he looked at the fairy maid snuggled

---

To one . . . other clouds: The words of Tang Dynasty (618-907) poet, Yuan Zhen (779-831), who was also known as the author of short stories like "The Story of Yingying," which was one of the most renowned *chuanqí* (prose narratives of the Tang and Song Dynasties). He was "involved in many obscure adventures and had a checkered career as a bureaucrat" and was lauded for "his virtuoso use of rhyme" (Idema and Haft 129).

Wushan: Witch/Wizard Mountain, located in the east of Sichuan province.

beside him under a large quilt and canopy, he began to wonder whether the goddess' palace wasn't necessarily located in the heavens. They were very happy indeed.

One day the young master informed Kong, "I have learned much from your benevolent instruction, and I'll never forget about it. Recently Master Shan resolved his litigation and is returning, anxious to move back into his home, so we intend to leave this place for Shaanxi. Under the circumstances, it will be difficult for us to meet again, and the sadness of being apart from you is very much on my mind."

Kong expressed his desire to leave with them. The young master advised him to return to his hometown, which put Kong in a rather awkward position since he lacked the money to pay for the trip. "Don't worry," the young master comforted him, "I'll ensure that you get there right away."

Soon, the old gentleman led Song out, and presented Kong with a hundred gold taels. Then the young master grasped Kong by his right hand and his wife by her left, instructing them to shut their eyes and to keep them shut. They began to float as though walking on air, sensing only the sound of the wind in their ears, until after a long time their comrade said, "We're here." They opened their eyes and could see they were in Kong's old neighborhood. At that moment he realized that the young master was something other than human.

Joyfully, Kong knocked at his family's door. His mother, thrilled, came out to meet his beautiful wife, and they rejoiced that they were together again. When they turned around to look for him, the young master had vanished. Song proved to be a filial daughter to her mother-in-law; word of her glamour and her virtue spread far and wide.

The goddess' palace: Pu names the Vast Coldness Palace (*guanghan gongdian*) here, the moon home of the goddess Chang'e/Cheng'e.

Afterwards, Kong became a *jinshi* and was appointed to a judge's position in Yan'an district, so he brought his family along to his post. His mother stayed behind since it was such a long distance for her to travel. Song became mother to a son, who was named Xiaohuan.

Kong then opposed a superior and was dismissed from his appointment, finding himself forced to stay there without being able to return home. Coincidentally, while out hunting in the countryside, he came across a handsome young man, riding a black horse, who kept turning around again and again to look at him. Scrutinizing him carefully, he realized it was young master Huangfu. He grabbed the reins to stop his horse, experiencing mixed feelings of grief and joy.

The young master invited Kong to go home with him and they arrived at a village where the trees were planted so densely that they made it dark, their luxuriant growth blocking out the sky and sun. Entering the young master's house, he noticed the door's decorative gold nails, the sure sign of a powerful family with generations of influence.

He inquired about Jiaona and learned that she had married; his mother-in-law had died, and the men commiserated together, moved by her loss. He stayed overnight and then departed, returning together later with his wife. Jiaona also arrived, hugged Kong's son, picked him up and carried him around, teasing Song, "Elder sister, you've mixed up our species." Kong again paid his respects to Jiaona, thanking her for her former cure of him.

Smiling, she replied, "Brother-in-law, you're an important person now. Your wound is long healed, but you haven't forgotten its pain?" Jiaona's husband,

---

Jinshi: Literally an "advanced scholar," a successful candidate in the highest level civil service examination held in the imperial capital.

Mixed up our species: Since Song and Jiaona, as relatives of young master Huangfu, are also not mortals like Kong Xueli and Kong Xiaohuan.

Master Wu, also arrived to visit them. They stayed two nights and then departed.

One day, the young master, with a worried look, told Kong, "Heaven is about to drop catastrophe on us—can you help to save us?" Kong didn't know what this was all about, but he spiritedly volunteered his assistance. The young master quickly stepped out, beckoning his family to come into the hall, kneel down around him, and show submission to Scholar Kong. Astonished by this, Kong anxiously asked for an explanation.

The young master answered, "We're not human beings, but foxes. We're about to be destroyed by thunder and lighting. Sir, if you agree to risk your life to face this disaster, there may still be hope for our survival. If not, please take your son in your arms and go, and you won't be involved."

Kong swore that he would live or die with them. Thus they directed him to stand at the door with a sword, warning him, "When thunder and lightning crack and strike at you, you must not move!" Kong took his place as instructed. Sure enough, as he watched, dark clouds blocked out the light of day, the sinister darkness as black as basalt.

When he turned around to look at where they'd been living, the gate was no longer there—in its place he saw a towering grave mound and a cavernous, bottomless pit. Just as he was standing there startled, there came the sound of a thunderclap that shook the lofty mountains like a fan; the pelting rain and violent winds uprooted even long-established trees. Kong was dazzled and deafened, but stood like a mountain, unmoved.

Suddenly from within an expanding column of thick, black smoke, he saw an evil spirit, with sharp beak and long talons, emerge from the pit with a person it had seized, following the smoke straight upwards. He caught a glimpse of the person's clothes and shoes, recognizing them as Jiaona's. Anxiously he leapt up and attacked the thing with his sword, fortunately bringing Jiaona back down.

All of a sudden a violent burst of thunder exploded,

and Kong fell to the ground, dead. In a short time, the sky cleared up and Jiaona began to revive. When she found Kong dead at her side, she cried piteously, lamenting, "Master Kong has died for me, so how can I still live!" Song also emerged from the pit, and together the women carried Kong back.

Jiaona had Song hold her husband's head up while the young master used a golden hairpin to pry open his teeth; she then pinched his cheeks, used her tongue to push her red pellet into his mouth, then joined her lips to his and blew. The red pellet was forced into his throat by the breath and his throat made a gurgling sound. In a little while, he returned to life. He saw his whole family in front of him, as if he'd just awakened from a dream. The family all gathered around in a circle, their initial fright dissipated and now filled with happiness.

Because of the pit's connection to the underworld, Kong decided they couldn't live in their residence any longer, and proposed that they all return to his village. Everyone offered their support except for Jiaona, who seemed unhappy. Kong requested that she and her husband, Master Wu, join the rest of them, but upon thinking it over, she worried that her husband's parents would miss their grandchildren, so they discussed the matter all day long without settling it.

Suddenly a Wu family servant arrived, sweating profusely and gasping for air. Alarmed, they immediately began to ask him questions and it came out that Master Wu's household that same day had also met with disaster, and that the entire family had been wiped out. Jianona was completely heartbroken, unable to stop crying. Together, they consoled and encouraged her.

And thus the return to Kong's hometown was planned and approved. Kong went into the city for a number of days to take care of matters, then he joined the others as they hastened to load everything for a journey by night. Upon their arrival, an isolated garden, which remained bolted from the outside, became the young master's residence; only when Kong and Song appeared was the bolt removed. Kong passed the time with the young master and Jiaona, playing chess, drinking wine, chatting and dining, as if they were all members of one family. Xiaohuan grew up to be quite accomplished, with very handsome features and a trace of the fox in him. When he went out for a walk in the city, everyone could tell he was the son of a fox.

The collector of these strange tales remarks, "Regarding Scholar Kong, I envy him not because he married a gorgeous wife, but because he found a true friend. Looking into the face of such a friend can make one forget hunger; listening to such a friend speak can make one smile. To gain such a good friend, with time to chat and to eat together, is much more pleasing to the spirit than 'clothing attractively disarrayed.'"

'Clothing attractively disarrayed': An excerpt from a poem by Qi Feng from the *dongfang wei ming* (Zhu 67n74), referring to the sexual relationship between a man and a woman.

23. The Buddhist Monk's Sin

A man named Zhang suddenly died, so he complied with a ghost envoy who came to take him to see the Hell King. The king examined his book of death records and became furious with the ghost envoy for accidentally having brought him the wrong person, reproachfully ordering that he be taken back.

As Zhang walked out of the king's presence, he secretly asked a favor of the envoy, begging for a look at Hell's prisons. The ghost guided him through the various levels of the underworld, past the Mountain of Swords and the Grove of Daggers, pointing out each spot one by one. At last they arrived at a place where there was a Buddhist monk, hanging by a rope that had been inserted into a hole bored through his thigh, howling in pain and begging to be cut down.

Approaching to take a closer look, Zhang could see it was his elder brother. The sight left Zhang terrified and distressed as he asked, "What crime has deserved this?"

The ghost replied, "He was a monk who traveled widely to solicit large monetary donations which he

---

Various levels of the underworld: Eberhard explains that the Chinese hells "are ten in number: the first is the court-room where sentence is passed, the last is the place where, after punishment, sinners are reborn as human beings or as animals, according to their merits" (143).

Mountain of Swords: The *daoshan* is a proverbial signifier of quintessential threat or punishment. It might be compared with Sisyphus's stone or Ixion's wheel in Greek myth.

spent on whoring and gambling—and that's the reason for his punishment. If he wishes to be free of this torment, he must repent for what he has done."

Once Zhang had been restored to life, he figured that his elder brother must have died already. He left for his brother's residence at Xingfu Monastery to find out what had happened. Upon entering the doorway, he could hear the sound of his brother howling in pain. Coming into his room, he could see a sore spot on his thigh which was oozing pus and blood—his leg, elevated, was hanging from the wall, reminiscent of its suspension in that place in the underworld.

Astonished, Zhang asked him what was going on. He explained, "Suspending it helps; otherwise, the pain's overwhelming." Zhang informed his brother about what he'd seen in the underworld. The monk was so profoundly startled, he consequently gave up meat and alcohol and began piously chanting sutras. In half a month he began healing. Thereupon he became a completely sincere monk.

The collector of these strange tales remarks, "The ghosts' prison appears insubstantial and far off, so all sinful persons use this to excuse their guilty acts; but they don't realize that the punishment in the underworld comes as a result of wicked behavior in the mortal world. How can one not be afraid of it!"

Xingfu: In Suzhou, south of the Changjiang River, in Jiangsu province.

24. Sorcery

Master Yu was generous and chivalrous as a young man, fond of boxing, and fearless, possessing sufficient strength to hold a colossal kettle and dance with it, spinning like a whirlwind. During Chongzhen's reign, while Yu was taking the imperial examination in the capital, his servant fell ill and couldn't even raise himself, which troubled Yu a great deal.

A certain skilled fortune-teller, able to forecast a person's life and death, happened to be working in the marketplace, so Yu went to make inquiries on behalf of his servant. When he arrived, he didn't say a word, so the fortune-teller said, "Doesn't the gentleman wish to ask about his servant's illness?"

Startled, Master Yu acknowledged that he did. The fortune-teller replied, "The servant's illness will not harm him—it is his master who's in danger." Master Yu then had his own future divined. The fortune-teller consulted the Eight Diagrams and said in a shaken voice, "The gentleman will be dead in three days!" Master Yu stood stunned for quite some time. The fortune-teller then

---

Chongzhen: The last of the Ming emperors, reigning from 1628-1644.
Eight Diagrams: The eight patterns of triple lines, broken and unbroken, that are joined with a commentary, traditionally attributed to Confucius, to form the foundation of the *Book of Changes*' (*yi jing*'s) system of divination.

added with unhurried calm, "I possess a bit of magic and if you'll requite me with ten taels of silver, I'll avert the evils for you."

Master Yu considered to himself that since the times of one's birth and death are fated, magic was unlikely to be able to change that; hence he declined and stood up, intending to leave. The fortune-teller declared, "Spare this little fee, or you'll be sorry. You'll be sorry!" All those who cared about Master Yu were worried about him after they heard this news and advised him to empty his money bag so the fortune-teller would save his life. But Master Yu wouldn't hear of it.

Very quickly the three days elapsed while Master Yu sat at his inn, calmly waiting to see if the time for his death had come. The whole day, he was quite safe. When night fell, he shut his door, turned up his lamp, and leaned upon his sword to await the pending peril. When the first watch had already passed, there was still no sign of his death. He was just thinking about going to bed when he heard a rustling sound at a crack in his window.

He anxiously watched as a tiny man entered, carrying a halberd over his shoulder; upon touching the ground, he instantly grew as tall as a normal person. Master Yu grabbed and raised his sword, striking swiftly, but it fluttered away and so he missed it. Then it hastily shrank again, turned and made for the window, intending to escape through the crack. Master Yu quickly chopped at it, cutting it down. He brought over the lamp, which revealed it to be a paper man that had been cut in two at the waist. Master Yu didn't dare lie down, so instead he just sat and waited.

After a bit, something pushed through the window and entered, some horrible kind of monster. Just as soon as it touched the ground, he leapt to attack it, cutting it in two, though each half continued to squirm about. Fearing that it might rise again and reconnect itself, he

---

First watch: The first of the five two-hour periods into which the night was divided. Approximately 7:00-9:00 p.m.

made every sword thrust count, yet it didn't sound like he was hitting something fleshy. On careful inspection, he found it to be a figure made of earth, now broken into many fragments.

Master Yu moved to sit next to the window, his eyes concentrating on the crack there. Quite a bit of time elapsed, then outside the window he heard something like an ox breathing heavily and something began pushing against the window lattice, making the entire wall of the room shake so powerfully that it threatened to collapse. Master Yu feared he might be crushed, and calculated that he'd have a better chance by fighting outside, so he slammed open the bolt on his door and rushed out.

There he saw a giant of a demon, as tall as the eaves of the house; in the dim moonlight he could tell that its face was black as coal, its eyes flashing with a bright yellow light; it wore neither clothing nor shoes, but held a bow, while carrying arrows at its waist. As Master Yu stood there astonished, the demon drew its bow and shot at him. Master Yu deflected the arrow with his sword and it fell to the ground; just as he was about to strike back, it shot another arrow. Master Yu deftly dove out of its way, the arrow hitting a wall with a reverberating sound.

The demon, infuriated, pulled out a knife it wore at its waist, whirled it like the wind, and with its force aimed a blow that was meant to gut Master Yu. Yu jumped out of the way like a monkey and the blade came down on a stone in the yard, splitting it. Master Yu then scrambled between the demon's legs and slashed at its ankle, which made a metallic clanging noise. The demon became even angrier, roaring like thunder and twisting its body around to attack again. Master Yu crouched and again ducked through its legs; the knife came down and sheared off some of his gown. Master Yu came up under its armpit, delivering a violent thrust that also made a clanging sound, and the demon fell to the ground, motionless. Master Yu struck wildly at it, the sound echoing like a watchman's woodblock.

By the light of a lamp, he found it to be a wooden

idol, the size of a man. The bow and arrows were still tied at its waist and its features had been carved and painted to appear hideous; blood seeped out from those places where his sword had struck. Consequently, Master Yu kept the light in hand and waited for daybreak, now aware that the monsters had all been sent by the fortune-teller who wanted Yu dead to prove his magic was real.

The next day, he told everyone he knew to join him in paying a visit to the fortune-teller's place of business. From a distance the fortune-teller saw Master Yu, who was looking his way—but saw nothing there. "That's his magic to fool the eye," somebody said, "but dog's blood ruins it."

Master Yu followed this advice, working covertly to prepare it, and then he came back. The fortune-teller disappeared like before. Yu quickly poured the dog's blood on the place where he'd been standing, revealing the fortune-teller's head and face, dripping with blood, his eyes burning there like a ghost's. Then he was handed over to the authorities and executed.

The collector of these strange tales remarks, "As I have said before, paying for fortunes is a silly thing to do. In all the world, how many people are there who can accurately identify when someone will be born or die? The purchased fortune turns out either to be inaccurate or not really to be a fortune at all. In addition, even if someone unerringly tells me when I can expect to die, isn't there anything I can do to change my future? What a horrible situation it is for someone to abuse fate and his own supernatural magic just for the sake of proving his fortune-telling ability!"

Dog's blood: The blood contaminates the magic being practiced, nullifying it; the folk practice appears, for example, in both the *sanguo yanyi* [*Romance of the Three Kingdoms*] and the *shuihu zhuan* [*The Water Margins*].

25. The Feral Dog

It was during Yu Qi's uprising, which slaughtered a numbing quantity of people, that Li Hualong, a villager, was trying to return home, fleeing from the mountains. It was just at the time when soldiers were patrolling and Li feared that he might suffer disaster for being mistaken a rebel. Anxiously finding no place to hide, he lay down stiffly among the dead bodies crowded together, pretending to be one of the corpses. Once the soldiers had finished passing through, he was still too frightened to try to get away.

Suddenly he saw the corpses, missing heads and limbs, rise and stand up like a forest. From the mouth of one of them, whose nearly severed head was still connected to its shoulder, came the words, "If the feral dogs surround us, what then?" The mob of corpses joined in chorus, crying, "What then!" Shortly afterward, they all collapsed, and their voices were still.

Li, justly terrified and trembling, longed to get up—but then a grotesque creature, with a beast's head and a human body, appeared and started chewing open human

---

Yu Qi's uprising: During the reign of Shunzhi, the first Qing emperor (1644-1661), Yu Qi led a peasant revolt in Shandong province. In 1648, he guided a peasant uprising that seized Juchishan; in 1650, his forces attacked Ninghai and left many dead. Eventually he was mollified by being given control of Qixia county, Shandong, which he held until 1661, when he was unable to suppress yet another uprising. His power was finally completely broken in 1662. See Zhu (1:73-74n1).

heads, sucking out the brain of each one. The horrified Li hid his head under a corpse. The thing poked at Li's shoulder, trying to get at his head. Li used all his might to stay hidden so it couldn't get to him, but the creature shoved away the corpse covering him till it could see Li's head.

His fear increasing, with one hand Li searched underneath his waist, until he found a stone as huge as a bowl and grabbed it. The thing stooped, intending to bite into him. Li suddenly rose up and with a big shout struck it right in the mouth. The creature cried like an owl, covered its mouth in pain, and fled, spitting blood as it went.

Moving over to look, he found two teeth in the blood, with twisted middles and sharp ends, over four *cun* in length. He decided to take them back with him to show people, but nobody knew what kind of thing it was.

Cun: A measure equal to 1/3 decimeter.

26. Three Lives

A *juren* named Liu had the ability to recall details from previous incarnations. He was always narrating them for my elder brother, Wenbi, who'd become a *juren* the same year he had.

In a previous life, Liu had been an official who was responsible for many transgressions. When he reached the age of 62, he died. He went immediately to see the Hell King, who received him courteously as a scholar and an official, inviting him to sit and sip some tea. Stealing a glance at the inside of the Hell King's cup, Liu noticed that his tea appeared entirely clear, while in his own small cup it was muddy, like wine with the dregs still in it. Puzzled and deeply suspicious, he wondered: was it really some infernal brew? Taking advantage when the Hell King looked away, he poured his cup down the corner of their table, making a show of having finished it all.

Shortly afterward, the Hell King turned to an account of the evils associated with Liu's life; furious at what he found, he ordered a group of demons to hold him down and punish him by sending him back as a horse. Grim demons bound him and took him away at once.

Juren: Designates a graduate of the provincial-level civil service examination. Miyazaki rationalizes Pu Songling's failure to pass the examination at this level as an example of his becoming lost in the shuffle of bureaucratic paperwork: "at best one in a hundred candidates was passed, and the sheer number of papers made it most difficult to select, say, a hundred papers out of ten thousand" (59).

They traveled and arrived at a particular home, the entrance to which was up so high that Liu was unable to go any further. Just as he faltered there, the demons vigorously flogged him, causing him so much pain that he unconsciously raised his leg.

When he looked around, he found himself on the ground in a stable. Then he heard someone say, "The black horse's given birth to a pony, a colt." In his heart he understood this all too well, but was unable to speak. He felt starved, but couldn't find anything to stop his hunger, so he followed a mare around, begging for milk.

After four or five years, Liu grew quite powerful. Nevertheless, he was terrified of the pain of the whip, and upon even seeing it would flee in dread. When his master rode him, he always added some padding to ease the load and would gradually slacken the reins as they went, so it wasn't all unpleasant; but when it was the servants or groom, they'd go without outfitting him with any extra saddle cloth, digging their heels into his sides until the pain penetrated to his very bowels. Eventually, in a fit of anger, he went without eating for three days and succeeded in dying.

Liu arrived again in the underworld, where the Hell King determined that he had not fulfilled the terms of his punishment, reproaching him for plotting to get out of it—so he had Liu's skin peeled off and sentenced him to become a dog. Liu felt depressed and didn't want to go. A group of demons flogged him wildly till his pain was so extreme that he fled out into the wilds. Thinking to himself that it would be better to try to end it all, he flung himself off a cliff, and after the jolt of impact he was unable to stand up.

Looking around, he found himself curled up inside a burrow, with a female dog licking and protecting him, and then he realized his body had been reborn into the world. As time passed, he came to recognize that urine and feces were dirty—even though they smelled good to him—and hence he refused to lap them up.

After he'd been a dog for a year, Liu found himself constantly angry and wishing to die again, though also afraid he'd be found guilty of trying to evade his punishment. In addition, his owner was feeding and supporting him, and would never agree to kill him. For that reason he decided to bite his owner, tearing some flesh from his thigh. The owner, furious, beat him to death with his cane.

The Hell King, checking over his case again, furious at his bestial stubbornness, had him whipped several hundred times and then sent him back as a snake. Liu found himself a prisoner in an isolated room where it was so dark he couldn't even see daylight. He became so bored that he found a wall and went up it, spotted a hole in the wall and got out through it. When he looked around himself, seeing his body lying in the lush grass, it became clear he really was living as a snake. Thereupon he made the determined vow not to harm any living thing and to eat only vegetarian foods.

As the years went by, he was always brooding over the fact that he couldn't commit suicide, nor could he harm other people so they'd kill him; he longed for an acceptable strategy for dying, but was unable to come up with one. One day, while laying in the grass, he heard a cart approaching and hastily crawled over to the road; the cart sped right over him, slicing him in two.

The Hell King was surprised by his speedy return, so Liu prostrated himself and revealed what had happened. The Hell King ruled that he could see no crimes associated with his death, so he pardoned him, declaring that he had fulfilled the terms of his punishment and could return as a man—which is how he became Master Liu.

Master Liu was born with the ability to speak, and could recite compositions, letters and books after having read them only once. In the first year of the reign of Tianqi, he qualified as a *juren*. His advice to others was always the same: when riding a horse, be sure to give him a nice

---

Tianqi: Son of the Ming emperor Taichang, Tianqi (ruled 1621-1627) was "a sorry figure" (Paludan 183) who managed to grow up at court illiterate and whose five children all died in infancy.

thick saddle blanket; and digging one's heels into the sides of a horse inflicts a punishment more painful even than flogging.

The collector of these strange tales remarks, "Among the animals there are former noblemen; at the same time, some noblemen were once animals. When a humble person does a good deed, it's like planting a tree in order for it to flower later; when a great person does a good deed, it's like nurturing the roots of the tree that has already been brought to flower: such a person should grow a bigger tree and nurture longer roots. Otherwise, one is merely pulling a salt cart, enduring the bridle as a horse does; or else one is just lapping up urine and feces like a dog until it's killed and cooked; or if not, one is just throwing on a scaly armor in order to end up buried in the belly of a crane or stork, like a snake."

27. The Fox Hides in a Jug

In Wan village, a man named Shi's wife was haunted by a fox, which caused her considerable suffering, because she hadn't been able to drive it away. They kept a jug behind a door, and whenever the fox heard the husband arrive, it would escape by hiding itself inside it. The wife maintained surveillance of the fox doing this, and secretly hatched a scheme without saying a word about it.

One day, it fled once again and entered the jug. The wife then quickly stuffed a stopper in its mouth, popped it into a cauldron, and heated the water in it until it was boiling. The jug's temperature soared and the fox cried out, "It's too hot! Don't be so mean." The wife, meanwhile, said nothing.

Its howls became increasingly urgent, but after a long while there was finally no more sound. She pulled out the stopper and looked inside, finding a pile of fur and several spots of blood.

28. The Weeping Ghosts

At the time of the Xie Qian rebellion, many officials' houses were taken over by the rebellious mob. Wang Xueshi's house in Qixiang was especially plundered by the assembled crowd. The city was pacified once national soldiers occupied the city and proceeded to slaughter the renegades, whose corpses were piled along the city steps, and whose blood filled the streets and flowed through every gate.

Master Wang reentered the city as the corpses were being carried out and the blood washed away, and took up residence once again. His family began seeing spirits all the time, even during the day; at night, ghostly lights flew under their beds and sat in the corners of their rooms, weeping.

One day, Wang's underling, Hao Di, stayed overnight with Master Wang's family, and from the end of his bed he heard a small voice crying, "Hao Di! Hao Di!" It ceased and then gradually became louder, moaning, "I died wrongfully!" The weeping and wailing filled the entire courtyard.

Master Wang heard this, took up his sword and entered, boasting loudly, "Don't you know that I'm Wang

---

Xie Qian rebellion: Xie Qian lived in Gaoyuan, Shandong province, and in 1646 led a revolt at the time that Dorghon, uncle/regent of eight-year-old Shunzhi, the first Qing emperor (reigned 1644-61), was attempting to strengthen the Qing imperial power by bringing rebel provinces Zhejiang and Fujian under its control (Paludan 191).

Xueshi, the public official?" Despite this, he heard a hundred voices sneering and jeering, mocking him.

Master Wang consequently established an altar for performing religious rituals to help the ghosts make their departure peacefully. When he left out some cooked rice for the ghosts that night, he saw many glowing lights flit around here and there, so he followed them. He was led to a gatekeeper, also named Wang, who had become seriously ill, remaining confused and unable to recognize people for a number of days.

That night, he suddenly yawned and stretched as if just waking up. His wife then got him to eat. The gatekeeper explained to her, "While I don't know why, the master left some cooked rice out in the courtyard, and I joined a crowd of others who were gobbling it up. Basically, then, when I was finished eating, I returned here, and now I don't feel hungry at all." Henceforth, the ghosts stopped appearing there any more. Wasn't this likely the positive result of inviting Buddhists to perform their religious rituals there?

The collector of these strange tales remarks, "Demons and ghosts exist, but only virtue can stop them. At the time the city was taken over by the mobs, Master Wang's influence was so strong and powerful that people would tremble just at the mention of his name; but the ghosts didn't fear him at all. Maybe that's because the ghosts didn't realize that Master Wang wouldn't let them stay there. This demonstrates the limited power of public officials: when human faces are unable to scare away ghosts, let's hope the ghosts don't use theirs to frighten away people!"

29. The Zhending Girl

In the vicinity of Zhending, there was an orphan girl, just six or seven years old, who was being raised by her future husband's side of the family. She had been living with them for a year or two when her husband-to-be seduced her into having sex with him and she became pregnant.

Her belly began to swell, so she thought she was ill and told her mother-in-law about it. The mother-in-law asked her, "Do you feel any movement inside?"

The girl replied, "I sure do."

The mother-in-law was quite puzzled about this. Since the girl was so young, no one dared to imagine that she was pregnant. Not long after, she gave birth to a baby boy.

The mother-in-law sighed and said, "Who could've thought it possible for such a small, underaged mother to give birth to a little baby!"

Zhending: In Hebei province.

30. Jiaoming

The household of the official Dong Moan was being harassed by a fox spirit, for out of nowhere, rubble, bricks and stones would suddenly fall like hail. The family members had to hurry and run for cover, then wait for the fox to stop before venturing out to go on with their activities. Master Dong was so upset over this that he borrowed the house of Sun Sima, another official, and moved into it to escape the fox. Meanwhile the spirit continued to make trouble.

One day, while waiting for an imperial meeting to begin, Dong began chatting with the other officers about the strange events. A great courtier told him that there was a Daoist priest named Jiaoming, from Guangdong, who now lived in the capital. He possessed the magical skill to control evil spirits.

Master Dong traveled to the Daoist's cottage and requested his assistance. Jiaoming created a red amulet for him and sent him back home to paste it up on one of his walls. The fox, however, didn't fear the amulet and subsequently began to throw down even more things.

Master Dong went back again to inform the Daoist. Jiaoming was furious, so he personally paid a visit to Dong's household, piling up earthenware jars and exercising his magic on them. Instantly they were able to see an enormous fox lying prostrate next to the jar. The family members had endured its ceaseless cruelties for a long time, harboring an extremely deep grudge, so one of the maid servants drew close to strike it.

The maid servant suddenly fell to the ground, unable to breathe.

Jiaoming declared, "This thing is on a rampage— even I haven't been able to frighten it, and the woman shouldn't have attacked it recklessly." Then he added, "We might use her body to hear what the fox has to confess."

Making a hand gesture over his halberd, he directed an incantation to the fox through the maid, and the maid-servant suddenly rose till she was kneeling upright. The Daoist then grilled the fox about where he lived. The maid servant, speaking as the fox, declared, "I was born in the western regions, then entered the capital where I have already lived for eighteen lifetimes."

The Daoist exclaimed, "How dare you live in the imperial capital for so long? We need you to leave now!" The fox made no reply. Jiaoming struck a table in anger, demanding, "Are you trying to resist my command? If so, you'd better think twice—my magic won't forgive you!"

Terrified, the fox then crouched and changed his facial expression, honestly and sincerely expressing his respect for the priest's warnings. Jiaoming again told him to go away quickly. The maid servant fell forward again, breathless, and after a long time began to regain consciousness.

Immediately, they saw a group of four or five round white lumps, rolling like balls, come near the edge of the roof's eaves before moving away, one following after another, and in an instant they were all gone. As a result, the place was peaceful thereafter.

31. Scholar Ye

In Huaiyang, there was a scholar named Ye—I've lost track of his first name. He was gifted in the writing of compositions and poetry, which were always first-rate by the time he'd finish them; but he didn't have good fortune and always failed in the official examinations.

Then he became associated with Ding Chenghe, who'd arrived from Guandong to take charge of their political district, and who'd looked at Ye's writing and been quite impressed by it; Ye was invited to speak with him, and the resulting exchange absolutely delighted Ding. He immediately provided Ye with an office in the government building and lights to study by; at times, he even gave him money and food to provide for his family.

On the occasion of the preliminary examination that preceded the triennial imperial examinations, Magistrate Ding roundly praised Ye's learning to the imperial examiner and consequently he was considered the best of a group of examinees. The magistrate expected he would surely produce an excellent examination.

After Ye had taken the county examination, Ding asked to see what he'd written and read it aloud, beating out the cadences and praising them. But expectations are often frustrated, and his compositions were fated to be rejected, so when the list of successful candidates was released, as usual he had failed again.

Ye was demoralized and returned home, ashamed that his dear friend had trusted him to succeed, so his appearance began to deteriorate until he was reduced almost to bones and looked as senseless as a wooden figure. Magistrate Ding received news of this, summoned him, and upon his arrival attempted to console him. Ye's tears fell like rain that would not cease. Ding, pitying him, suggested that when the time came for him to go to the capital to give a full account of his own work, he could bring Ye along to take part in everything there.

Ye was very moved and grateful. Taking his leave and returning home, he closed his doors and refused to venture out. In no time he was confined to bed by illness. Magistrate Ding continually sent inquiries and help; Ye took over a hundred doses of Chinese traditional medicines, but they had no effect at all.

By chance, for being defiant to an official above him, Magistrate Ding was to be removed from office and was about to vacate his official position. He sent a letter to Ye, which, in brief, said, "The day for my return to the east has come; I've been slow to do so because I've been waiting for you to join me. If you will arrive this morning, you and I can leave this evening together." It was delivered to Ye while he lay in bed. He held the letter, sobbing piteously.

Ye entrusted these words to Ding's envoy: "My illness has become too severe for me to recover so hastily; please go on ahead." When the envoy returned and delivered the message, Ding couldn't bear to leave, and patiently waited for Ye to recover.

When a number of days had passed, the man at the gate suddenly made way for Scholar Ye, who had just arrived. Elated, Ding welcomed him and inquired about his condition. Ye replied, "Since I was taken ill, I've troubled you into waiting for me a long time and I've been extremely concerned that I've caused you worry. Now it's my good fortune to be able to accompany you, sir." Ding accordingly packed his clothes to be ready to depart early at daybreak.

When they arrived at Ding's hometown, he ordered his son, Zaichang, to work as Ye's student, so from morning till night Ye was always accompanied by the boy, who was sixteen years old but still unable to compose a literary essay. Yet he was peerlessly bright, and whenever he'd read over a piece of literature just two or three times, he could always recall it, without forgetting a thing.

Once Ye had been living with them for a year, Zaichang proved able to begin writing accomplished literary essays. With this improvement and his father's influence, he was able to become a *xiucai*. Ye intended to teach the boy as much as he could, writing down everything he knew for Zaichang to review. In the examination hall, Zaichang wrote on seven topics without missing any of them, and finished second from the top.

Ding said to Ye one day, "You only used the leftovers of your wisdom, and they were enough to help my boy succeed in the examination. Yet your outstanding talents continue to be ignored—there must be something we can do!"

Ye replied, "I'm afraid it's fated. But because you've lent me some of your good fortune, my writings will finally receive an audience and make everyone understand that while half of my life has been profitless, it's not because I lacked the talent to succeed—that will be enough to wish for. What's more, if a scholar obtains even one person who knows and appreciates him thoroughly, there should be no trace of regret at all. There's no point in bothering to take off the white clothes of the *xiucai* only to chase after degrading fame and profit."

Since Ye had been staying with them for such a long time, Ding, fearing he might miss the yearly examination, strongly advised him to return to his home province. Ye, saddened by this, felt miserable. Ding couldn't bear to force Ye to leave, so he asked his son to buy an official title for Ye when Zaichang went to the capital for the examination there.

Zaichang was successful once again in the examination at the southern palace and was conferred the administrative head of a department there. He

---

Xiucai: A scholar who's passed the imperial civil service examination at the county level.

brought Ye along to his imperial office, where they were together from morning till night.

The following year, Ye took part in the civil service examination in the capital and surprisingly won the title of *juren*. Just at that time, Zaichang was assigned to take charge of the Southern Yellow River District's affairs, and said to him, "This posting will take me to a place not far from your home town. Master, you've been promoted to an esteemed position, so your glorious return will be a happy event." Ye was equally joyful and chose an auspicious date for them to journey on their way. When they reached the borders of Huaiyang, Zaichang ordered an attendant to take a horse and accompany Scholar Ye home.

Upon his return, he saw his house and noticed how dreary it looked, which made him very sad. While he walked around to the courtyard, his wife came out carrying a dustpan, saw Ye, threw the utensil down and backed away. Ye said to her, "I'm a respected individual now. Even though it's been three or four years since we've been together, how can it be that you suddenly don't recognize me?"

Keeping her distance from him, his wife replied, "You've been dead already for a long time, so what's this talk about being respected? We'd have buried you in your coffin a long time ago, but the family was too poor, and our son was too young to bury you. Now our son's finally establishing himself and is about to consult a diviner about a suitable gravesite. Don't do anything strange at this point to scare those who're still alive."

Ye was puzzled and saddened to hear all this. Wavering at first, he entered the house, saw a dignified coffin containing a corpse, then threw himself to the ground and vanished. His wife, alarmed, inspected his remains and found only his cap, gown, and shoes, as though they'd been peeled off and abandoned there. Powerfully grieved, she held his clothes in her arms and

Juren: A successful examinee in the imperial civil service examination at the provincial level.

wept.

Their son, returning from school, saw a team of horses tied up at the gate, found out where they'd come from, and ran, amazed, to inform his mother. She wiped away her tears and told him what had happened. They carefully made inquiries of Ye's attendant, and only then did they get the whole story.

The attendant returned to give Zaichang the news, and his tears ran till they dripped down his chest. At once he gave the order that they should travel, all of them weeping, to Ye's house; from a purse he took out money to cover the funeral costs, and they buried Ye with a ceremony befitting a *juren*. Zaichang was similarly generous in giving support to Ye's son, and he hired a tutor to instruct him in his studies. Zaichang praised Ye's son, and the next year he successfully passed the lowest level civil service examination to become a *xiucai*.

The collector of these strange tales remarks, "Is it possible that a man could follow his closest friend even after he's already died, and not realize the fact of his death? Although someone hearing Ye's story might doubt this, I am firmly convinced of it. At heart, it's the same as the story of Qian Niang, whose soul left her body behind, resting on a pillow, to following her lover; though 1,000 *li* separated the good friends, it seems that they could stay connected through the roads in their dreams.

"Naturally, for scholars, their compositions and hand-written drafts are their most cherished treasures. Whether these are truly excellent or not, they constitute the heart and life of a scholar! That's just the way it is!

"It's hard to know when you'll meet someone who'll appreciate you or when you'll experience good fortune on the way to achieving official fame. Often a scholar faces his own shadow with a sigh, alone with the fact of his lack of success. He wants to stand straight and

---

Qian Niang: According to R.H. Mathews, the story of *qian niang* tells of a young woman "whose soul fled with her lover and left her body behind" (128).
Li: A distance equal to 1/3 mile.

proud despite his skinny figure, for only he knows what emotions he has felt. He sighs about his shabby appearance when snobbish officials and wicked persons come to tease him. If he fails in his examinations time after time, others will regard every white hair on his head to be ugly. If he fails to become the top examinee, his compositions will be criticized unceasingly.

"Among the people past and present who have had ample reason to weep, Ye was just like Bian He. When the white is mixed with the black, who then can serve as the Bole? Nowadays no one cherishes intelligent people, so there's no use expecting your mind to amount to anything. Look around yourself, there's no place to settle down. In this life, there's no need for a man to be serious and clear-minded all the time. You just close your eyes and walk your own way. Let heaven dispose of everything.

"There are a lot of people in the world like Scholar Ye. But how can they find a friend like Ding, who'll follow them regardless of life and death? Alas!"

Bian He . . Bole: According to Zhu Changwen's eleventh century history of the Qin dynasty, Bian He discovered a fabulous jade stone and offered it to the King of Chu, who ordered his feet cut off for trying to swindle him; subsequent investigation proved Bian's honesty and he later wrote an account of his loyalty to his sovereign. The Bole was a Zhou dynasty man who was famed for being extraordinarily adept at evaluating the qualities of horses.

32. Forty Thousand

In Xincheng, there was a steward who served in the wealthy household of the primary army minister there. While he was asleep and dreaming, a man unexpectedly rushed in and said to him, "You're 40,000 short, and now you have to pay up." He asked what this was about, but there was no reply from the man, who went directly into the household's inner rooms.

Immediately, the steward woke up and found that his wife had given birth to a son.

He recognized that this boy must be the consequence of some misdeed from a previous life, so he proceeded to bundle together 40,000 copper coins and set them aside in one of the rooms of the house, put the boy in the same room, and provided him with clothing, food, and medicine for illnesses.

Three or four years passed by, and when he checked on the money remaining from what he'd set aside in the room, there were only 700 coppers left. Just then the boy's old wet-nurse arrived and hugged the boy, trying to make him laugh as she stood beside him. Then the steward cried, "The 40,000 is just about used up, so it's time for you to go."

Once these words had been spoken, the color suddenly drained from the boy, his neck contorted and

---

Xincheng: A county in Shandong province.
40,000: That is, 40 strings of cash, each holding 1,000 copper coins.

his eyes bugged out. As the steward tried to check on him, the boy just stopped breathing. So they took the last of the surplus cash to cover the cost of his funeral preparations and then buried him. This was a good warning for those men who owe others money.

Long ago, there lived an old man who had no children, so he asked a learned Buddhist monk what he should do about it. The monk said, "You don't owe anyone, and no one owes you—how come you have no son?" Then an excellent boy was born to him as a consequence of some good deed from a previous life.

If I'm born a good man, it's a recompense that I'm fated to receive; if I'm born a wicked man, it's because I've incurred that debt. Just as being born is no cause for rejoicing, dying is no cause for grieving.

33. Cheng the Immortal

In Wendeng, there was a man named Zhou, who in his younger days had been a student, sharing pen and ink-stone with a fellow named Cheng, with whom he became a sworn brother in friendship, regardless of wealth or lack of it. But Cheng was destitute, so he always had to depend upon Zhou. Since Zhou, the older of the two, acted as his elder brother, Cheng called Zhou's wife his sister-in-law. During the annual festivals, the Chengs went to visit the Zhous as if they were all part of the same family.

Zhou's wife gave birth to a son, but contracted a sudden post-natal illness and died. Subsequently he married a woman named Wang, and Cheng, because she was younger than him, didn't formally request to meet her.

One day, her younger brother came to see her and was being banqueted in an inner room. Cheng arrived just then. A servant reported Cheng's presence and Zhou ordered that he be invited in. But Cheng didn't want to intrude, so he left. Zhou moved the banquet outside, sending someone to fetch him, so he returned. They had barely been seated when someone suddenly reported that a servant of the family had been seriously caned at the order of the local magistrate.

What had happened was that a servant of the Huang family had been herding cattle when he crossed over into Zhou's fields. The servants of both families had

---

Wendeng: In modern Shandong province.

exchanged insults as a result of this. The cattle herder had hurried away to inform his master, who'd had the Zhou family servant arrested and sent to the magistrate, and after being declared guilty, he'd been caned as punishment.

Zhou ferreted out the details of the incident, blew up and exclaimed, "That Huang family's pig and cattle herder—how dare he do that! Huang's ancestor served my grandfather before; because of this, his family prospered, now no one else is as important in his eyes!" Anger filling his throat and chest, he stood up to go in search of Huang.

But Cheng restrained him, delaying him long enough to say, "Bullies run the world, giving no heed to what's wrong or right. Furthermore, aren't half of the officials in power nowadays bloody thieves who can't even handle a spear or bow?" Zhou refused to listen. Cheng advised him another three times to stop, but it was only when his tears began falling silently that Zhou finally gave in. His anger, however, didn't end there, so he tossed and turned all night long.

The next day he called his family members together and said, "The Huang family has taken advantage of us and made us enemies, but let's not talk about that. The magistrate is supposed to handle administration of this district, free of the influence of powerful families, and wherever there is a dispute, he must also work with both parties—so how could he simply respond like a dog being ordered to do something? I'll file a complaint against Huang's servant, too, and we'll see how the magistrate deals with the other side."

His family members were all up in arms, encouraging him at that moment, so he put his plans into action. He wrote out his accusation and went to see the magistrate, who tore it up and threw it away. Zhou, furious, verbally attacked the magistrate. The official, humiliated and angry, ordered him to be seized and tied up.

In the morning, Cheng went to visit Zhou, and found that he'd gone into the city to manage the lawsuit. He swiftly ran after him to persuade him to desist, but by the time he'd arrived, Zhou had already been jailed. He stamped his foot in frustration at not being able to offer some help.

At the time, three pirates had been arrested, so the magistrate and Huang decided to bribe them to claim that Zhou was a member of their gang. Seizing on their words, the magistrate appealed to his superiors to strike Zhou's name from the list of successful civil service examinees and had him cruelly beaten.

When Cheng entered the prison to see him, they just looked at each other, miserable and sad. Cheng thought about appealing directly to the royal court. Zhou declared, "My body's bound and imprisoned like a bird in a cage; though I do have a younger brother, it's all he can do just to supply me with rice."

Cheng, stepping up to take the responsibility on himself, said, "It's my duty. If a friend won't help when times are hard, what use is he?" With that, he left. Zhou's younger brother gave Cheng a fee sufficient to cover his costs, and he traveled a long time before reaching his destination.

Once he'd arrived at the capital, he found no way to submit his appeal. However, it was reported that the emperor would participate in a hunt outside the palace, so Cheng hid himself ahead of time in the woods; when the emperor passed through, he prostrated himself, crying piteously, and succeeded in submitting his appeal. The emperor accepted his request. It was delivered to a courier's station, which sent it on to a judicial department, where it would be reviewed.

It was ten months afterward that it was reviewed, by which time Zhou had already confessed to the false accusations and received a death sentence. The court officials were quite shocked to receive the emperor's comments, and determined to hear the case again personally. Huang was also shocked, and made plans to kill Zhou. With this in mind, he bribed the jailers to cut off Zhou's food and drink; when his younger brother arrived with supplies and asked about him, he was callously turned away.

Once again for Zhou's sake, Cheng went to public officials to make the injustice known, and by the time his suffering was discovered and investigated, he was already so starved he was unable to stand. The investigating officials, furious, had the jailers caned to death. Huang, terribly frightened by this, paid out thousands in gold to be let off, and due to softened descriptions of his guilt, he was exempted from punishment. The magistrate, however, was banished for bending the laws. Zhou was set free to return home, feeling closer than ever to Cheng.

After enduring the justice system, Cheng's feelings for mundane concerns were reduced to ashes, and he invited Zhou to join him in withdrawing from the world. Zhou, powerfully attracted to his young wife, consequently laughed at the absurdity of the notion. Leaving everything behind, Cheng went missing for several days.

Zhou sent someone to find out from Cheng's family how he was, but his family members were just as much in the dark as Zhou; since neither family had seen him, it began to look suspicious. Zhou thought to himself about Cheng's odd suggestion and sent people to search for traces or clues of his whereabouts in all the area monasteries and temples. From time to time he also provided money and clothing out of compassion for Cheng's son.

It was eight or nine years later that Cheng suddenly returned, wearing a yellow scarf and robe, with the dignified appearance of a Daoist. Zhou, overjoyed, grasped his arm and asked, "Where did you go, sir, for I've sent people everywhere looking for you?"

Laughing, Cheng answered, "The lone cloud and the wild crane stay in no single place. Since I left all this behind, it has been my good fortune to become healthy and strong." Zhou ordered some wine for them and summarized all that had happened since they'd been separated for so long, hoping to get Cheng to drop his Daoist appearance. Cheng smiled but didn't speak.

Zhou exclaimed, "Don't be so foolish! How can you

throw away your wife and child like a pair of worn-out sandals?"

Cheng smiled and answered, "That's not correct. It is other men who wish to throw me away, not I who wish to throw away others." Zhou asked him where he'd been living, and he explained that he'd taken up residence on Mt. Lao in the Palace of the Sublime Silence.

After drinking together, as the two of them went to sleep with their feet side-by-side, Zhou dreamed that Cheng was naked and lying on top of his chest, making it so he couldn't catch his breath. Nervously, Zhou asked him what he was doing, yet he didn't respond. Suddenly he woke up in alarm, calling out to Cheng without receiving an answer; he sat up and reached over for him, but he'd disappeared, and Zhou had no idea where he'd gone.

Once he'd had time to settle down, he became aware that he was on Cheng's side of the bed, and, surprised, declared, "I wasn't drunk last night, so through what craziness did I get over here?" Then he called for his household servants. The servants brought a light and revealed that he looked just like Cheng. Zhou had worn a beard for a long time, so he went to stroke it with his hand but found only a few thin hairs.

He grabbed a mirror and looked at his reflection, exclaiming in wonder, "This is Cheng alright—so where did *I* go?" He stopped, finally grasping the situation, and realized that Cheng had used magic to try to lure him into leaving the world behind. He wanted to go back inside his room, but his younger brother saw that he didn't have his brother's familiar face and forbade him to enter, refusing to listen to him as before. Zhou was also unable to verify his own identity. At once, he ordered a servant to bring a horse and accompany him in search of Cheng.

Several days later, they came upon Mt. Lao. The horse was making such good time that the servant was unable to keep up. Zhou stopped under a tree and watched a great many Daoist priests coming and going. Among them was one Daoist who kept his eye on Zhou, so Zhou decided to ask him about Cheng. The Daoist priest smiled and said, "I've heard his name—he's probably in the Palace of Sublime Silence." When he finished speaking, he proceeded on his way.

Zhou kept an eye on him, watching him the distance of an arrow's flight, until he stopped to speak to another person, also exchanging just a few words before heading off again. When the person who'd been spoken to approached him, Zhou realized he was from the same community of students of which Cheng and he had once been part.

When he saw Zhou, the man remarked, "I haven't seen you face-to-face for several years, but people maintained that you'd come to the mountain to study Daoism—so why are you still playing around in the mundane world?" Zhou told him about his strange experience. Alarmed, the man replied, "I just met and spoke with a fellow I took to be you. He left just a little bit ago, so he probably hasn't gone far."

Zhou was really shaken by this and exclaimed, "That can't be! How could I meet myself and not recognize my own face?" His servant caught up with him and they anxiously rushed off, but finally there were no traces or signs of Cheng. As they looked out over a vast expanse, they couldn't make their minds up whether to go forward or back. But Zhou thought about the fact that he no longer had a family he could return to, hence he resolved to continue his pursuit. The road, however, was quite dangerous, and he couldn't ride around it, so he handed his horse over to his servant and sent him back, taking the winding path himself.

In the distance he saw a boy sitting by himself, so he hastened to approach and explain his purpose, introducing himself and his objective. The boy identified himself as Cheng's pupil, lifted Zhou's clothes and provisions onto his back, and led them on their way. They ate by starlight and slept in the open, traveling high and low while covering great distances, until after three days they arrived—but this place they call Sublime Silence isn't like a place called Sublime Silence in the world. Although it was already into the tenth month of the year, mountain flowers lined the road, not at all like the beginning of winter.

The boy entered to announce his guest, and Cheng at once hurried out; only then did Zhou recognize his own body. Cheng clasped his hand and together they entered a place where there was wine and food, then began a conversation. Zhou had observed a number of strangely colored birds, so docile that they weren't frightened by people, with voices like pan-pipes, that would land at times on a seat and begin singing. He found this very unusual. This mortal life, however, cut into his thoughts. and he had no intention of asking to stay and join in.

On the ground there was a pair of kneeling mats made of rushes, placed there so they could sit side-by-side. The two sat there for four hours until all of their thoughts were stilled, when suddenly Zhou thought he'd take a short nap and felt his body change places with Cheng's. Curious, he stroked the bottom of his chin and found his beard there as before. By dawn, all he could think about was returning. Cheng, however, insisted that he stay.

After three days he declared, "Get yourself some sleep, and in the early morning I'll see you off on your way."

Just as he'd shut his eyes, Zhou heard Cheng call to him, "Go get dressed, we're all ready." So he got up and followed him.

They went along a different road than the one he'd previously taken. Zhou was aware that although little time had passed, he could already see his village and home in the distance. Cheng sat to wait by the side of the road in order that Zhou could go on by himself. Zhou tried earnestly, but couldn't get him to accompany him, so he walked on alone to his family's gate.

He knocked but received no answer, so he determined to climb over the wall, suddenly feeling as though his body could float like a leaf—and with a single leap he was over it. Altogether, he passed over several walls this way, only then arriving at the sleeping quarters, where he noticed the lamp still shining and heard the people inside, not yet asleep, murmuring to each other. Making a hole in the paper window to spy through it, he saw his wife drinking together with a male servant in quite improper, even indecent, condition.

This made him burn with anger; he calculated to himself and was about to mount a surprise attack to catch them, but then worried that, alone, he might not be able to overcome the two of them. Hence he surreptitiously unbolted a door and slipped out, rushing off to tell Cheng and to ask his assistance.

Agreeing to accompany him, Cheng followed as they went inside, straight to the bedroom. Zhou picked up a rock and beat on the door, while inside they were extremely panicked; as the pounding became more and more insistent, they worked all the harder inside to barricade the entrance. Cheng made a motion with his sword, and with a stroke promptly broke the door open. Zhou rushed inside, then the servant burst through the doorway, running. Cheng was waiting outside and struck the servant with his sword, cutting off his arm and shoulder.

Zhou held the wife so he could interrogate her, and learned that she had been having an intimate relationship with the servant since he had been imprisoned. Zhou borrowed Cheng's sword and cut off her head, then strung up her intestines between trees in the courtyard. After all this, he followed Cheng outside, where they searched for the road and made their return.

All of a sudden, he woke up and found his body still lying in bed, terrified, and declared, "What a strange dream I've just experienced, enough to really startle a person!"

Cheng, laughing, replied, "Your dream, elder brother, you've treated as truth, when clearly you regard the truth as only a dream." Zhou, still shaken, asked what he meant. Cheng took out his sword and showed him that it was still spattered with blood. Zhou, frightened and distressed, was ready to end it all—though he still privately suspected that it was just Cheng trying to persuade him again with his magic. Cheng knew what he was thinking and hastened to send him back home.

In no time at all, they arrived at the village gate, where Cheng said, "Outside here I waited for you that night, and relied upon my sword! Wasn't this the place? It disgusts me to look upon the evil and filth of the place, so please go on, sir, while I wait for you here; if you have not returned by afternoon meal time, I will leave by myself."

Zhou then walked up to his home and found it deserted, as if no one was living there. Then he went and entered his younger brother's house. When the brother saw him, he immediately broke down in tears, crying, "After you left, elder brother, thieves in the night killed your wife, then ripped out her guts and left—such grievous cruelty. To date, the officials haven't caught them."

To Zhou, it was as if he was waking from a dream again, so he explained his situation to him, warning him not to pursue the matter any further. The brother was shocked speechless for quite some time. Zhou asked him about his son, then ordered an old woman to bring him to them. Zhou explained to his brother, "This infant is our clan's connection to posterity, so look after him well. Your elder brother longs to take his leave of this mortal world." Then he stood up and went away.

The younger Zhou, in tears, raced to catch up with him, but Zhou continued without looking back. When they got to the outskirts of the village, he watched Cheng leave with his brother. In the distance, Zhou turned back to look at him and called out, "If you just bear with things, you'll be the most happy." The younger brother wanted to have a few words with him, but Cheng raised one of his broad sleeves and instantly they were gone from sight. Disappointed, he stood there for some time, bitterly crying, before turning back.

Zhou's younger brother was simple and dull, not very good at managing the family's property, and over the next several years the family became increasingly impoverished. Zhou's son by then was growing up, and Zhou's younger brother wasn't able to hire a teacher for him, and for this reason Zhou's son taught himself to study.

One morning, his uncle entered his study room, and at the head of a table he saw that there was a letter, sealed very securely, inscribed "To be opened by our clan's second born." He examined it, noting that it was written in his brother's handwriting; upon opening it to inspect its contents, he found it was empty except for a fingernail, about as long as two fingers. He found this quite odd. He put the fingernail down on the ink-stone, then went out to ask other household members where it had come from, but no one knew.

When he returned to look at it, the ink-stone on the table was gleaming magnificently, having been changed into pure gold. He was utterly amazed. He tried another piece of metal on it, and it also turned into gold. As a result of this, they became very wealthy. Therefore he bestowed 1,000 taels of gold on Cheng's son, for which reason, word got around that the two families had learned the magic of transmuting gold.

Magic of transmuting gold: Chinese alchemy, a Daoist pursuit, sought to recreate the workings of nature in a compressed, highly efficient manner, so the workings of a thousand years, for example, might be replicated in a thousand hours. The preparation of gold and a great variety of elixirs is discussed in Chinese alchemical literature, although gold "is a matter of relatively minor concern in the central tradition," with "its emphasis on individual self-cultivation" (Sivin 257).

34. The Bridegroom

In Jiangnan, there was a virtuous person named Mei Xiaolian, whose courtesy name was Ouchang. He said that his countryman, Sun, being the magistrate formerly in Dezhou county, had once investigated an extraordinary case.

It all began with a village man who arranged a marriage for his son, and when the bridegroom arrived and entered the gate, his neighbors and relatives all joined in to celebrate his wedding, lavishing their congratulations on him. They drank together until midnight, when the bridegroom briefly stepped outside and saw his bride, dazzlingly dressed, turn and hurriedly dash behind the house. This made him suspicious, so he tailed her.

Behind the residence, there was a long creek with a small bridge over it. He saw his bride cross the bridge and slip away quickly, increasing his suspicions. He shouted to her, but she didn't answer.

In the distance, she beckoned to her husband with her hand; he ran anxiously to follow her, but there remained a distance between them so he couldn't reach her. He pursued her for several *li* till he came to a village. The wife stopped and said to her husband, "Your family

---

Jiangnan: A large province, divided under the reign of the first Qing emperor into Jiangsu and Anwei provinces.
Dezhou county: In modern Shandong province.
Li: A distance equal to 1/3 mile.

is dull and too quiet, and I'm not used to it. Please take up temporary residence as the master of my family's household for a few days, then we can return together after a visit."

When she finished speaking, she took the pins out of her hair and knocked at a door, pounding until a small girl servant came to answer it. The wife entered first. Without any other choice, the husband followed her. Once inside, he found his father-in-law and mother-in-law waiting for him in the household's central hall.

They called out to the son-in-law, "Our daughter's been spoiled, never experiencing a quarter hour away from her parents, so when she left for your home, we all felt sad and missed her. Now that she and her lord have arrived, our missing her has been eased and consoled. Stay with us for several days, then we'll see you two off properly for your return." Certain rooms were appointed for them then, a bed and mattress was prepared, and so they settled in.

When the family and guests of the bridegroom noticed that he hadn't returned, they went out to look for him. They checked in the house where the bride had been staying, but no one there knew where the husband had gone. Because of this they made inquiries about him far and near, but were unable to gather any news of him. The groom's aged parents shed tears, believing he must be dead.

Meanwhile, after about half a year had passed, the wife's family was grieving that their daughter had lost her spouse, so they went to consult his father, the village man, wishing him to determine whether their daughter could remarry. The father made them even more upset by exclaiming, "No clothes or a skeleton of my son have been identified, so how can you supposedly know that he's already died! But even if he'd died suddenly,

---

Pins out of her hair: Symbolically suspending her married status, by reverting to the loose, flowing hair of the single adolescent from the pinned-up hair of the married woman.

waiting a year before getting married again isn't too much; you're acting recklessly to be so impatient!"

The wife and her father became angrier when they heard the village man's words, and they brought the case to the magistrate and sued him. Magistrate Sun was quite skeptical and wished not to mishandle his authority, so he made his ruling and ordered them to wait for three years, then put it on public record and sent them away.

Meanwhile, the villager's son was still dwelling with his wife's family, and the family members treated him very well. Every time he proposed to take his wife and leave, the wife would give her consent for him to do so, but then procrastinated so they never actually got around to leaving. After more than half a year, he became more agitated in mind about having stayed there too long. He wanted to return home alone, but his wife insisted that he stay.

One day, the whole family appeared scared, as if some kind of disaster was impending. The father-in-law hastily told his son-in-law, "The original plan was in two or three days to send you and your wife together on your way. Despite our expectations, things haven't been prepared properly, because our family has suffered some hardships. We have no choice but to send you back home alone first."

Thereupon, he accompanied the husband as he left through the gate, and following his hasty farewells, he returned quickly in no time at all. Afterwards, the villager's son wanted to retrace the route he'd followed, and when he went back to look at the house and yard, they were no longer there: in their place he saw a tall grave mound. Terribly frightened, he located his path and hurriedly came back.

Upon his arrival at home, he told about everything that had happened to him, from beginning to end, and for that reason was encouraged to send the magistrate his statement. Master Sun detained the bride's father, issuing a decree that he send his daughter back to the man she'd married, so they could finally join their nuptial winecups in a toast.

35. The Magistrate of the Heavenly and Mortal Worlds

At a Daoist temple named Chaotian, there was a Daoist priest who was fond of practicing the traditional method of breathing. There was also an old man who lived temporarily in the temple till he found that he had the same hobby as the priest, so they became good friends. The old man ended up living there for several years, and on each memorial day honoring people's ancestors, he would leave ten days early, and then come back once the memorial activities were concluded. The Daoist priest became curious and asked him about his reason for doing so.

The old man replied, "We two have no secrets from each other, so I can tell you honestly: I'm really a fox. When memorial day arrives, all sorts of gods come out to clean away evil things. I have no place to stay then, so I run somewhere and hide myself."

After another year, the memorial day arrived again and he went out, but after a long time he didn't return. The priest became concerned.

Traditional method of breathing: Traditional Chinese breathing involves inhaling fresh air through the nose and exhaling through the mouth because people believed that the air exhaled was unclean and harmful if returned through the nasal chambers. According to the ancient Chinese doctrine of correspondences, the nose "is the bodily orifice corresponding to the lungs" (Eberhard 208).

One day, the old man suddenly returned. The priest asked him what had happened. By way of answer, he explained, "I almost didn't make it back to see you! I'd been wanting to keep my distance from them but was quite careless about it, so when I spotted a covering over a cavity that was very well concealed, and was satisfied that it was out of sight, I hid in a small jug underneath it.

"I didn't expect the magistrate of the heavenly and mortal worlds to come here to take part in the cleaning. When he looked in my direction and caught sight of me, he became so angry that he wanted to thrash me. I was so scared that I tried to run away. The magistrate came after me then, with great speed.

"I arrived at the head of the Yellow River and he was just about to catch me. Under enormous pressure, on the spur of the moment, I decided to dive into the shit in a toilet. The magistrate's spirit couldn't stand to get itself dirty, so he immediately returned to his body and left.

"Once he was gone, I was soaked in the toilet's smelly foulness and couldn't return to the mortal world again, so I just went on. I jumped into the water and washed repeatedly, then went into seclusion and hid in a cave for many, many days, filthy and greasy, only eventually able to get clean.

"Now that I've arrived to say farewell to you before departing, you'd also better become a hermit somewhere else: a calamity's about to arrive here and this is not a blessed place." His speech finished, he took his leave and moved on.

The Daoist priest complied with his words and went elsewhere. Soon afterwards, Jia Shen's unexpected turn of events occurred.

Jia Shen: General who died during a rebellion in 1644 led by the "Dashing General" Li Zicheng, during the reign of the last Ming emperor, Chongzhen (Paludan 187).

36. Wang Lan

In Lijin, Wang Lan suddenly took sick and died. When the Hell King checked his record of Wang's death, he determined that one of his demon minions had mistakenly crossed out Wang's name and that's why Wang died suddenly. The demon was reprimanded and charged to return Wang's spirit to his body, but his corpse had already decomposed.

Fearing he'd be punished for his mistake, the demon spoke to Wang: "For a person to die and become a spirit is bitterly sad, but for a spirit to become an immortal is cause for celebration. And if one is happy, what's the need to return to the mortal world?"

Wang thought there was some truth in this. The demon continued, "There's a certain fox who has succeeded in producing an immortality pill. You can steal the pill and gulp it down, then your spirit won't dissipate and you'll be able to live forever. No matter where you go, you can do as you wish. Won't you agree to accept this advice?"

Wang followed his suggestions. The demon led him out and they entered a vast mansion where they could see grand pavilion towers, but it was silent and no people were around. A fox was there sitting under the moon, his head raised, looking up into the sky. He exhaled a

---

Lijin: In modern Shandong province.
Immortality pills: "Medicines of immortality" are a common feature of early Chinese occultist texts (Sivin 257), particularly those addressing Daoist alchemy.

142

breath, till a pill came out of his mouth and rocketed straight up to the moon; when he inhaled, the pill fell back down, and the fox took it into his mouth, practicing this over and over again.

The demon hid at the fox's side, waited for him to spit the pill out, then swiftly grabbed it in his hand and turned it over to Wang to swallow. The surprised fox, exploding in rage, turned to face them. Seeing there were two of them, the fox, realizing that the difference between his strength and the others' would guarantee that he would lose a fight, expressed his rancor and left.

Wang took his leave of the demon and rejoined his family, but when his wife and son saw him, they were thoroughly frightened and ran away. Wang announced what had happened to him, and then gradually they assembled around him. After this, the family was finally able to rest easy, and things got back to normal.

When Wang's friend, Zhang, heard the news and came to visit him, they exchanged their normal greetings. Afterwards Wang said to Zhang, "Our families have been poor for as long as I can remember, but now I have some magic and can make us rich. Would you be able to go on a trip with me?" Zhang said he could. Wang explained, "I can cure maladies without using medicine, and ascertain the future without resorting to fortune-telling. I wanted to appear in my own body, but I'm afraid that those who know me would be terrified by the strangeness of it. I could attach my spirit to your body—would you approve of that?" Zhang again gave his consent. That same day they hastened to pack and traveled west till they arrived at the border of Shanxi Province.

In a wealthy home, they found a daughter who had become sick suddenly, and after feeling dizzy had then slipped into a coma. Her family had already tried everything from medicine to sacrifices aimed at averting evil, so Zhang went up to the house, bragging about his magic. The rich old man only had this one daughter, whom he considered very precious, so he announced his desire to give anyone able to cure her a thousand taels.

Zhang asked to examine her. He followed the old

man into the house and saw the daughter, her eyes shut, lying in bed; when he lifted the large quilt from her and rubbed her body, the comatose daughter showed no sign of feeling it. Wang privately told Zhang, "This shows that her spirit has been lost, so I should go hunt for it."

Zhang then informed the old man, "Though her illness is life-threatening, I can save her."

"What medicine do you need?" the old man asked.

Zhang's words made it clear that this wasn't necessary. "Your daughter's spirit, sir, has gone to another place, so I've already dispatched a deity to locate it."

About an hour later, Wang suddenly returned, reporting that he'd already found her. Zhang then requested that the old man allow him back into the daughter's room, and he massaged her body again. In a little while, the daughter yawned and opened her eyes abruptly. The old man was overjoyed, hugging her and asking how she was.

The daughter explained, "I'd been playing in the garden when I saw a young gentleman holding a slingshot and shooting at sparrows; several others leading fine horses followed behind him. I nervously wanted to run away from them, but they stopped me from doing so. The young gentleman then handed me his slingshot and taught me how to shoot it. Just as I was feeling shy and was about to complain to him, he pulled me up onto his horse and we rode off.

"Laughing, he said, 'I'm happy to have you to play with, so don't feel shy.'

"Several *li* later, we entered the mountains, but from horseback I howled all kinds of abuse at him; this made the young gentleman angry, so he pushed me off and I fell down beside the road, wanting to go home but not knowing the way.

"Just then a man arrived, grabbed me by the arm, and we sped away, till in the blink of an eye I was home so quickly that it's as though I just awoke from a dream." After hearing his daughter's words, the old man treated

---

Li: A distance equal to 1/3 mile.

Zhang like a supernatural being, and handed over the thousand taels.

Wang discussed things with Zhang that night, suggesting that they keep two hundred taels for their use while traveling, then he took the remainder home, knocked on the door, and handed them over to his son; he also directed his son to give three hundred taels as a gift to Zhang's family, then he returned. The next day, when they took their leave of the old man, he couldn't see where they could've stored all the money, which only added to the strangeness of it all, so he generously gave them other gifts as well, and then saw them off.

Several days later, Zhang was in the suburbs when he ran into a fellow villager named He Cai. Cai was a drinker and gambler who wouldn't work, and hence was as poor as a beggar. He'd heard that Zhang had obtained some rare magic and had used it to make money without working for it, so he'd rushed off to look for him. Wang suggested that Zhong give him some small amount of money, and then send him back.

Cai didn't modify his usual pattern, so in just ten days of debauchery, he'd spent it all and came looking again for Zhang. Wang had anticipated this and said, "Cai is undisciplined and contrary, so you shouldn't try to support him very much—just give him a suitable bribe and send him away, and though this makes you party to his activities, your guilt is pretty minimal."

The following day, Cai arrived as predicted, intrusively following Zhang everywhere. Zhang declared to him, "I knew from the start that you'd be back. Your daily routine is drinking and gambling, so why should even a thousand taels fill your bottomless pit? If you're sincere about changing your ways, I'll offer you a hundred taels as a present."

Cai promised he would change.

Zhang emptied his money bag and conferred the contents on him. Cai left with the hundred taels in his own bag, and gambled even more unrestrainedly; in addition, he visited the brothels, squandering money like it was as common as dirt.

In town, the constables became suspicious and arrested him, taking him before the local magistrate, where he was subjected to flogging and other brutal cruelties. Cai told them the truth about the source of his money. Subordinates were then dispatched to take Cai with them and arrest Zhang. In a few days, due to his wounds, Cai died while en route. His spirit still wouldn't leave Zhang alone, returning to follow him around as he had previously, which is how he came to meet Wang.

One day, while they were all drinking together on a mound in the mist, Cai got crazy drunk and started shouting, and though Wang tried to stop him, he wouldn't listen. By chance, an imperial representative, making an inspection, was passing through when he heard the shouting, and went to investigate, discovering Zhang alone. Zhang, frightened of the man's power, told the truth about everything. The imperial representative was furious at this tale, had Zhang flogged, and sent a memorial to the gods.

That night, the imperial representative dreamed that a person dressed in gold armor appeared to him and said, "We have examined the case of Wang Lan, who was innocent but died anyway and now has become an immortal spirit. The practice of medicine is a benevolent use of magic, and should not be punished as an evil or demonism. So now I'm presenting the Heaven King's command: he is to be granted the posthumous title of Minister of Street-Sweeping. He Cai is evil and debauched, so for his punishment his spirit will be exiled to Tiewei

---

Returning to follow him around: With the implication that Cai's spirit attaches to Zhang as Wang had done earlier.

Minister of Street-Sweeping: Guards routinely cleared the way for the sedan chairs of high officials and magistrates, alerting people to their pending passage or arrival.

Tiewei Mountain: In ancient Buddhism, Tiewei, or Ironclad, Mountain surrounds the four continents that exist to mark the four directions, so its location "outside" the world of the four directions makes it an appropriate place to exile He Cai's wicked spirit.

Mountain. Zhang is certainly not guilty, and hence should be pardoned." The imperial representative woke up and marveled at the dream, then released Zhang.

Zhang packed his belongings and returned to his village. In his bag he still had a few hundred taels, and he respectfully offered half of them to Wang's family. From this point forward, the Wang clan's children and grandchildren grew to be wealthy.

37. The Eagle and Tiger Gods

Dongyue Temple stood just south of the city wall in a particular prefecture. On the left and right sides of its large gate stood two deities, each over ten feet tall; hideously awe-inspiring, they were commonly known as the "Eagle and Tiger Gods." In the temple there was a Daoist by the name of Ren, whose daily routine started with the rooster crowing, at which time he would wake up, burn incense, and begin chanting.

There was a robber who had hidden himself ahead of time in an adjoining hallway, waiting until the Daoist got up, then stealthily entered his bedroom to steal his belongings. Once in the room, he found no property except for thirty coins under a straw mat, which he tucked into his waist, then he removed the bar from the door and took off. He aimed to ascend Qianfo Mountain.

Southward he fled, and shortly arrived at the base of the mountain. There he saw a gigantic man descending the mountain with an eagle sitting on his left arm, and in a moment they met up with each other. Looking closely at him, the thief noticed that the man's face was the color of weathered bronze, like one of the gods he was accustomed to seeing beside the temple's gate. Terrified, he cowered on the ground, trembling.

Qianfo Mountain: Qianfo ("Thousand Buddha") Mountain, about 1.5 miles south of Jinan in Shandong province, has been the site of thousands of stone-carved effigies of the Buddha since the time of the Sui dynasty (581-618 C.E.).

Roaring, the god demanded, "After stealing the money, where can you go?" The thief was even more frightened, and began kowtowing nonstop. The god grabbed him up, took him back, and once they entered the temple, he made the thief pour out the money he'd stolen and then kneel on the ground to wait.

The Daoist priest, having finished his devotions, turned to see him and was amazed. The thief confessed in great detail about what he had done. The Daoist accepted the money, and then sent him on his way.

38. Wang Cheng

Wang Cheng, son of a venerable family in Pingyuan, was by nature extraordinarily lazy. His limited resources declined until he had nothing left but a ramshackle house with a couple rooms, and he had only a coarse blanket to lie beneath with his wife, who complained that she couldn't bear it.

At the time, it was summer and very hot, and outside the village was the Zhou family's old park, where the walls had all collapsed, and only a pavilion remained; many other villagers were going there to spend the night, so Wang joined them.

When daybreak came, the other sleepers all left; the sun had been up about three hours when Wang finally got up and sluggishly went along his way. In the grass, he spotted a gold hairpin, and when he picked it up to examine it, he noticed some delicate characters on it that read, "made by the family of the imperial son-in-law." Wang's grandfather had married into the imperial family, hence his family had owned such things, many with the same inscriptions, so his thoughts were preoccupied as he held the hairpin.

Suddenly an old woman showed up, looking for the hairpin. Even though Wang was poor, he was honorable by nature, so he promptly took it out and gave it to her. The old woman was pleased and magnanimously praised him for his great virtue, saying, "The hairpin's value is modest, except that it was something left behind by my late husband."

He asked her, "Who was your husband?"

"He was the former imperial son-in-law, Wang Jianzhi," she replied.

Wang, startled, sputtered, "My own grandfather. How did you two meet?"

The old woman, equally surprised, wondered aloud, "So you're really Wang Jianzhi's grandson? I'm a fox fairy. A century ago, I was the beloved of your noble grandfather. When he died, I went into seclusion. Passing through this place, I lost the hairpin, which fortunately fell into his grandson's hands, so it must have been fated!"

Wang had already heard about his grandfather having had a fox for a wife, so he trusted her words and invited her to come for a visit. The old woman followed him.

Wang called to his wife to come out and see her, and she came out wearing ratty clothing, looking emaciated. The old woman sighed, "Oh! That a grandson of Wang Jianzhi should have arrived at such a state of poverty!" She also noticed no smoke coming from their decrepit stove, and asked, "With your household in such a condition, how do you manage just to stay alive?" Wang's wife then quietly narrated the facts of their poverty, accompanied by choking sobs of deep sorrow.

The old woman took out the hairpin and gave it to her, bidding her to exchange it for money at the market to buy rice, and revealed that in three days she would return to see them. Wang begged her to stay. The old woman replied, "You're unable to keep your own wife alive; if I were to remain, dependent on your house and home, how would that make things any better for you?" Having had her say, she went off on her way.

When Wang told his wife who she was, she became alarmed. But Wang was insistent in reciting her generous qualities, and asked her to treat the old woman as her own grandmother, so she agreed to do so.

In three days, consequently, the old woman returned. She took out some money so they could buy a large weight each of millet and wheat. That night, she shared a small bed with Wang's wife. At first the wife was afraid of her; but upon considering how extremely supportive she had been of them, she abandoned her doubts.

The next day, the old woman told Wang, "Don't be lazy, grandson; you should conduct a little business to make a living, earn your keep and grow up!" Wang reported that he had no money to do this. She responded, "In your grandfather's time, there was gold and silk for the taking; but since I wasn't human, I had no need for such things, so I didn't take much. I accumulated forty taels in gold from my gleanings, but up till now it's just been stored away. For a long time I've been hoarding it, since there was no use for it, but I'm going to give it to you so you can go to the market and buy lightweight cloth, then take it to the capital where you can make a modest profit on it."

Wang obeyed her, purchased over fifty units of the cloth, then returned. The old woman directed him to make haste and load up, calculating that in six or seven days he could easily reach the capital. By way of advice, she also admonished him, "You must be diligent, not lazy; expedient, not tardy—if you're a day late, you'll regret that you stopped for the night!" Wang respectfully took her advice, packed his merchandise into bags, and then hit the road.

Along the way, he ran into a rainstorm that soaked his clothing and shoes. In all his life, Wang had never undergone such hardship and was so worn-out that he couldn't bear it, so he took a short break from his travels at an inn. Unexpectedly, the rain kept pouring through the night, cascading off the eaves like ropes.

By the next day, conditions outside had become extremely messy. He watched people going and coming, dragging themselves through mud up to their shins, and knew he couldn't face such suffering. He decided to wait to go out until it stopped, and about midday it began to

---

Lightweight cloth: The character *ge* signifies kudzu (*Pueraria thunbergiana*), a vine with fibers that "can be made into linen-like cloth" (*Far East Dictionary* 1312).

dry up—but dark clouds returned to shut out the daylight, the rain again coming down heavily. He stayed one more night and then left.

As he was getting close to the capital, he overheard that the price for lightweight cloth had skyrocketed, so he felt privately thrilled. Upon entering the capital, he stopped to register at an inn, where the host explained it was a great pity that he'd arrived late. Earlier on, before the southern route had opened up, very little lightweight cloth had been getting through. An affluent, influential prince had been extremely anxious to buy some, so its price suddenly soared to three times its norm. On the previous day, the prince's family had purchased all they needed, and everyone coming since then had been disappointed. Thus the host broke the news to him. Wang's beautiful merchandise would not bring in the money he'd hoped for it.

Each day, more and more lightweight cloth arrived, so its price continued to plummet. Wang could make no profit, but he refused to sell it at a loss. He waited for ten days, until the expenses for his boarding were calculated, greatly increasing his depression. His host encouraged him to sell, even at a loss, to make a change and formulate another plan. Wang followed his advice. He lost another ten taels this way as he unloaded his stock.

At sunrise, just as he was planning to leave, he looked into the bag holding his money and found his taels were gone. Alarmed, he told the host, but there was nothing he could do about their loss. Others there encouraged him to file an official complaint, making it the responsibility of the host to compensate him. Wang sighed and said, "This is just my fate, so why should it involve the host?"

The host, hearing this and admiring his ethics, offered him five taels as a present, enough to allow him to be sent home. But Wang couldn't stand the thought of facing his grandmother, so he paced back and forth, inside and outside, advancing and retreating, stuck in his predicament.

Just then, he noticed that a fellow who managed fighting quails was raking in money from all the betting on them; each bet brought in a thousand coins, but the cost of buying a quail was just over a hundred coins. The notion suddenly struck him to use the money now in his bag, which was just enough to begin dealing in quails, and so he discussed his idea with the host. The host earnestly supported his plan, and in addition arranged to "loan" him room and board without taking anything directly from him.

It was a happy Wang who went out then. He bought a load of surplus quails, then reentered the capital. The host was pleased for him, congratulating him and suggesting he sell them quickly. It rained heavily all that night until dawn. By first light, the thoroughfares were like rivers, and it was still raining without sign of letting up. Wang stayed inside, waiting and watching. It continued like this for several days, without ceasing.

When he went out to look inside his bamboo baskets, he discovered that some of the quails had been gradually dying. Wang was very upset, but didn't know what to do about it and finally left them. By the following day, several more had died; only a couple of them remained alive, so he combined them in a single basket and fed them. When the night had passed, he went out to look in on them and found only a single quail still alive.

He told the host what had happened, unable to stop his tears from falling. The host shared his disappointment. Wang, realizing that since he'd spent all the money he couldn't afford to go home, just wanted to die, so the host did his best to console him. Together they went to check on the quail, and upon carefully examining it, the host said, "This seems to be a superior specimen. The other quails all died not through misfortune, but because this one killed them. Sir, since you're currently free and have no other pressing affairs, I'd encourage you to train it; once he's ready, you can make a living by gambling with him." Wang acted as advised.

As soon as the quail had been trained, the host directed him to take it out to the streets, first to gamble just for drinks and snacks. The quail's body was strong and it always won. The host, pleased, gave Wang some money, sending him back out to gamble with some local young men; in three bouts, he scored three wins. After about half a year, he'd accumulated twenty taels. His mind was greatly relieved, and he began to think of the quail as his livelihood.

It just so happened that one of the princes loved quail fights, and each year during the Lantern Festival he would bring local quail trainers together at the palace to hold a competition. The host told Wang, "Now, with his great wealth, he should be able to set you up; but what's unclear is what is going to happen thanks to your unlucky fate." He then explained to him all about it, directing Wang to go with him. He advised Wang, "If you lose, let everyone hear how despondent you feel. If instead you're the fortunate one, and your quail achieves victory, the prince will surely wish to buy it—but sir, do not agree to do so; if he's firm in his insistence, check to see if I'm nodding my head, and wait for my nod before you answer him."

Wang said, "I promise."

When they arrived at the palace, the quail-handlers were already bumping into each other's shoulders at the foot of the palace steps. In an instant, the prince stepped forth from the palace. To his right and left, heralds proclaimed, "Let those who wish to fight come up." At once, a man holding a quail hastened to advance. The prince ordered his own quail released and the challenger also released his; at the first contact, the challenger's quail was stopped cold. The prince laughed heartily. In no time, he went on to defeat many other handlers.

The host told Wang, "You can do it." Then they went up together.

The prince remarked to them, "Its eyes pulse with anger, its feathers are robust—we mustn't treat this enemy

---

Lantern Festival: New Year celebrations officially end with this festival on the fifteenth day of the first lunar month, known as Superior Principles or Three-Principles Day, "for it commemorates the Three August Ones who taught humans the first principles of civilization" (Palmer 200; see also 15).

lightly." He ordered his quail, Iron Beak, to be brought in for the match. Once, and then a second time, they leapt at each other, till the prince's quail had its feathers knocked out. He had it replaced with a better bird, and after that exchange, it, too, was defeated.

The prince impatiently gave the order for his Jade Quail to be brought from inside the palace. A short while later it was brought out, displaying white feathers like a snowy heron's, an extraordinary creature of outstanding appearance. Wang Cheng was terribly disheartened, so he kneeled and begged for the contests to end, pleading, "Great prince, your quail is a wonder—I fear it will wound my bird, depriving me of my livelihood."

The prince smiled and said, "Get up. If it's beaten in this contest and dies, I'll compensate you appropriately."

Wang then released his bird. The Jade Quail rushed straight for it. But when the Jade Quail came in close, Wang's bird, like an angry chicken, was waiting for it; the Jade Quail had a strong beak, while Wang's quail rose up like a soaring crane to strike; advancing and retreating, stiff-necked, they grabbed each other and struggled for some time.

The Jade Quail began to tire, which made Wang's quail angrier and fiercer, so he fought with even greater intensity. It wasn't long before snowy feathers began to fly, and with its wings hanging limply, the Jade Quail ran away. The myriad spectators couldn't help but praise the display.

The prince himself then demanded to hold the bird, looking it over from beak to talons, scrutinizing it carefully, and then asked Wang, "Is this quail for sale?"

He answered him like this: "Since I'm a petty person without much permanent property, I've come to depend upon it as my livelihood, so I wouldn't want to sell it."

The prince replied, "I could give you a significant price, a middleman's expected wages. Wouldn't that be quite sufficient?"

Wang bowed and thought about this for a long time, then said, "I'm not happy about selling it; but if the great prince has already become fond of it and will give me in exchange the amount of money to obtain clothing and food, what more could I ask?"

The prince invited him to name his price, and he proposed a thousand taels. Laughing, the prince exclaimed, "Silly man! You think the quail's a precious gem, but how can it be worth a thousand taels?"

"The great prince doesn't think it a gem," Wang answered, "but I think it worthy of a Liancheng gem."

The prince asked, "What makes it so valuable to you?"

Wang explained, "When I take it to the market district, every day it earns me a certain amount of money which I exchange for millet, enough to feed a family of more than ten, and to keep them from worrying about freezing, so is that not a precious thing?"

The prince answered, "You won't sacrifice any of that with what I'll give you—so I'll make it two hundred taels." Wang shook his head no. The prince increased his offer by another hundred. Wang looked at the host, whose expression hadn't changed.

Then he said, "Keeping in mind the great prince's prestige, please feel free to reduce my asking price by a hundred."

The prince cried, "Stop fooling around! Who'd be willing to pay nine hundred taels for a single quail?" Wang put his quail into his bag and began to leave. The prince blurted, "Come back, and I'll actually give you six hundred—you can agree to sell it or not, but that's it." Wang again glanced at the host, who remained unchanged as before.

Wang was absolutely elated, but he feared that they might let the opportunity slip past, so he replied, "For this price I'll sell, though in my heart I'm truly sad; I'm distressed to give up my quail, but not to do so might increase my hardships even further. Rather than end up with nothing, I'll take the prince's offer." The prince was

---

Liancheng gem: A *lianchengbi* is proverbial (from ancient Chinese history) for any gem of inestimable value.

delighted and had payment turned over to Wang at once. Wang put the taels in his bag, paid his respects for the prince's generosity, and left.

The host chided him, "I told you what to do, so why were you so anxious to sell? If you'd resisted a bit longer, you'd be holding eight hundred taels in your hands."

Wang returned with him to the inn, tossed the taels on a table, and invited the host to collect his share, but he wouldn't take anything. Wang made the offer more insistently, so the host checked his tab, figured up the cost of Wang's meals, and accepted that amount.

Wang packed his bags to return, and when he arrived home, he described everything he'd done, then took out the money to show them—and they all celebrated together. The old woman directed him to purchase three hundred *mu* of good farmland, to build a house, and to make some implements, and upon doing so, his family soon rose to prominence.

The old woman got up early each morning and sent Wang out to supervise the cultivating while his wife oversaw the weaving; if they ever behaved rather lazily, she roundly scolded them. Husband and wife lived peacefully together, no longer attempting to blame things on each other. Three years passed by with the family becoming increasingly more wealthy.

The old woman finally expressed the desire to take her leave of them. Wang and his wife together tried to dissuade her, until it brought them to tears. The old woman agreed to stay. But by sunrise the next morning, she had already vanished.

The collector of these strange tales remarks, "Riches are the consequence of living a zealous life; only in this case were they the consequence of laziness, which makes it an unprecedented situation. Wang didn't know what to do about his extreme poverty, but he still retained his honest nature, which is why heaven at first abandoned

---

Three hundred mu: This would amount to about fifty acres, since one *mu* equals 0.0667 hectares, or about 1/6 acre.

him, and then, feeling pity, rescued him later. Thus wealth actually can come from being lazy!"

39. Qingfeng

The Geng family of Taiyuan, because they were a powerful family, lived in a resplendent mansion. But once their affluence declined, half the house's network of linked corridors were abandoned and neglected. From this sprung up weird accounts of hallway doors often opening and closing by themselves, and of family members constantly startled by noises in the night. This so troubled Geng, that he moved his household to a country villa and retained an old man to serve as watchman at the mansion's gate.

Afterwards, the estate fell into further neglect. At times, the sounds of laughter, talking, singing, and playing the flute came from inside. Geng had a nephew, named Qubing, wild and incorrigible, who instructed the old watchman to run and tell him if he heard or saw anything. One certain night, the old man saw lantern lights up in the house, appearing and then vanishing, so he ran to tell Qubing. He wanted to slip inside to spy on this strange activity. The watchman tried to stop him, but he wouldn't listen.

The estate's gates and doors were familiar in Qubing's memory, but he had to follow a round-about path, poking through thickets of wormwood and fleabane before he could enter. He climbed to one of the upper floors without noticing anything particularly odd, then began to hear people speaking softly when he passed from one building into another. He stealthily peered around a corner and saw a tremendous pair of candles

160

burning, shining as brightly as daylight.

An old man with a scholar's cap sat at the south end of the room, together with an old woman opposite him, both well past their forties. On the east side, there was a young man, maybe about twenty; on his right was a young woman, whom Qubing judged to be about fifteen. Their table was loaded with meats and wine, and the group sat laughing and chatting. Qubing abruptly walked in, laughing, and cried, "Your uninvited guest has arrived!" The terrified group ran away to hide.

By himself, the old man came back, and in a scolding voice demanded, "Who do you think you are, entering people's private rooms?"

Qubing answered, "These are my family's rooms that you're occupying. You're drinking this excellent wine by yourselves without inviting the home's owner—so why are you being so stingy?"

The old man, glancing cautiously at him, replied, "You're not the owner."

Qubing countered, "I'm the irrepressible scholar, Geng Qubing, nephew of the house's owner."

The old man respectfully exclaimed, "For a long time I've admired your impressive efforts!" Then bowing with hands clasped, he led Qubing to the table, calling to his servants to bring out different food. Qubing stopped him. The old man then poured wine for his guest.

Qubing remarked, "Our families have much in common, and those guests who were seated here have no reason to fear being seen, so I implore you to invite them to return and drink."

The old man called out, "Xiao'er!" Instantly a young man reentered. "This is my son," the old man explained. Xiao'er bowed respectfully to Qubing, and they sat down together, briefly surveying their families' histories. The old man commented, "My surname was Hu."

Hu: Although this second-tone character is a family name (and also means "foolish"), it sounds exactly like the character that means "fox," more accurately suggesting the old man's supernatural identity.

Qubing was his conventionally extroverted self, conversing of opinions and unusual customs, with Xiao'er also displaying a casual elegance and charm; pouring out their hearts to each other, they quickly became close friends. Qubing was twenty-one, making him two years older than Xiao'er, so he called him his "younger brother."

"I've heard," the old man observed, "that your grandfather compiled *The Stories of Tushan*—do you know about that?"

Qubing replied, "I do know indeed."

The old man reported, "I'm a descendant of the Tushan family. I can trace our family's genealogy all the way back to the Tang dynasty; but from the Five Dynasties and earlier, we have no records. It would be my good fortune, sir, if you could share some of your knowledge about it."

Qubing briefly described how the lady of Tushan had skillfully aided Emperor Yu, making up many poetical phrases as he went, his excellent narrative bubbling forth like a spring. The old man was overjoyed, telling his son, "Now we have the good fortune to hear what we've never heard before. This young gentleman is not just anyone, so please ask your mother to bring Qingfeng along and we can listen to him together, so they will also learn of our ancestors' virtue." Xiao'er slipped past the curtain that divided the room.

Soon, the old woman reappeared with the young lady. Qubing looked her over carefully—her delicate form was exquisite, her bewitching eyes infused with intelligence—and nowhere was there a more beautiful creature. The old man pointed to his spouse and said, "This is my venerable wife." Then pointing to the young

---

Tushan: A legendary nine-tailed fox, supposedly from Tushan, in Anhui province.
Tang dynasty: 618-906 C.E.
Five Dynasties: 420-618 C.E.
Emperor Yu: Legendary founder of the Xia dynasty (2200-1750 B.C.E.).

woman, he added, "This is Qingfeng, who's been like a niece to me. She's quite kind, and whatever she hears or sees, she remembers and never forgets, so for that reason I've summoned her to listen."

Qubing finished his oration and began drinking, turning first just to watch Qingfeng, then openly staring at her, transfixed. She felt his glance, and simply kept her head bowed. When Qubing covertly rested his foot upon her tiny slipper, she quickly pulled away her foot, but also didn't appear upset. Qubing lost all discretion, and, unable to control himself, he rapped on the table, announcing, "If I could get a wife like this, I'd never exchange her, even to become a king!"

The old woman saw that as Qubing became more and more intoxicated, he also became more uninhibited, so she stood up with Qingfeng, hastily pulled aside the curtain, and left. Qubing, disappointed, took his leave of the old man and went out. His heart was so tightly bound, he couldn't stop thinking about his passion for Qingfeng.

When the next evening came, he returned, finding the place still fragrant with orchid and musk, so he waited there all night without moving, but amidst his loneliness, he didn't so much as hear a cough.

He went back home and proposed a plan to his wife, expressing his desire to move their household to the Geng mansion, in hopes of achieving another meeting. His wife wouldn't go along with it, so he went there by himself and did some reading on one of the mansion's lower floors. When evening came, just as he was leaning over a desk, a ghost with streaming hair entered, its face black as lacquer, and stared at Qubing, wide-eyed. Qubing just laughed, dipping his fingers in some fresh ink and smearing it on himself, staring back in response with his eyes shining. The ghost, humiliated, vanished.

The next night, quite late, after extinguishing his candle to go to sleep, from the back of the house Qubing heard a bolt being withdrawn and a door opening. He quickly rose to take a look and found a door leaf open. Instantly, he heard the sound of a delicate tread, then candlelight began shining from inside the house.

On further inspection, he discovered it was Qing-feng. When she suddenly noticed Qubing, she was shocked and drew back, hastily closing the double-leaved door. Qubing knelt there for quite some time before speaking these words: "It was for you that I faced what was perilous—honestly, darling, that was the reason. We're lucky no one else is around, and if you'd give me the pleaure of holding your hand, I could die without regret."

Qingfeng said, "Don't you think I know about your sincere, deeply-felt passion? But my uncle taught me a strict standard of family behavior that I dare not disobey."

Qubing maintained his abject begging: "I don't dare hope for the intimate feel of your flesh, but just to gaze into your eyes would be enough." She agreed to permit this, opened the door and came out, whereupon he clutched her arms and drew her to him. Qubing was giddy with delight and they went downstairs together, where he took her in his arms and then sat her on his lap.

She said to him, "It was fate that brought us together; but once this night is over, there's no use thinking we can stay together."

"Why not?" he asked.

Qingfeng explained, "My uncle is afraid of your unpredictability, so he changed into that vicious ghost to try to scare you away, but he didn't even faze you. Now he's already found another place for us to live, the family's just moved all of our various possessions there, and I've been left to guard this place, but tomorrow I have to leave." When she finished these words, she stood up to go, adding, "I'm afraid my uncle might return."

Qubing stopped her, wanting to make love to her. They continued their debate until the old man unexpectedly walked in. Qingfeng, ashamed to face her uncle, lowered her head and leaned against the bed, tugging nervously at her sash without speaking. The old man angrily declared, "Your cheap behavior is a disgrace to my household! If you don't leave here quickly, a flogging will help you along!" Hanging her head, Qingfeng ran out, then the old man also departed.

Tailing them and eavesdropping, Qubing caught a wide range of scolding and abuse. The sounds of Qingfeng's plaintive sobbing cut him to the heart and in a loud voice he yelled, "Why are you treating Qingfeng this way when the fault is mine? If you'll forgive her, punish the crime with sword or any other kind of blade and my body will willingly bear it!" Everything went silent for a very long while until Qubing returned and went to sleep. Subsequently, there were no more sounds—not so much as a breath—from inside the mansion.

Qubing's uncle, hearing all about it and finding it bizarre, agreed to sell the place without dickering. Qubing, delighted, brought his household to the mansion and moved them in. They lived there quite comfortably for over a year, but Qubing never forgot about Qingfeng for even a moment.

He went to the family tomb on Pure Brightness Day, and while returning home, he spotted two little foxes being relentlessly pursued by hounds. One of them fled by dashing into the underbrush, but the other was so agitated that it continued running along the road. When it saw Qubing, it cried pitifully, cowering and ducking its head submissively, as though begging him for help. The scholar took pity on it, opened his coat, took it in his arms and carried it home.

When he'd shut his door, he put it down on his bed—and it became Qingfeng. Beside himself with joy, he told her how sorry he was, and asked her how she'd been. She replied, "I was just out playing with a maidservant when we were confronted with that great misfortune. Without you, I'd surely have ended up in a dog's stomach. I hope that even though I'm not like you, you won't look on me

---

Pure Brightness Day: Known as Qingming, this celebration on the 5th or 6th of April is a day of respect spent at family graves or tombs.

with disgust."

Qubing told her, "Every day I'm filled with thoughts of you, both in my conscious mind and in my dreams. Seeing you is like finding a rare gem, so how can you speak of disgust!"

"Heaven has been acting in all of this," she replied, "for if you hadn't been revealed to me, how could we have been brought together? Fortunately, the maidservant must surely think me dead, so we can easily stay together forever as appointed." The happy scholar lodged her in a part of the mansion separate from his family's portion.

More than two years went by until Qubing was reading one night, and Xiao'er suddenly entered. The scholar stopped reading, surprised, and asked him why he'd come. Xiao'er prostrated himself on the ground, and with great gravity said, "My father has experienced a horrible disaster, and no one but you can save him. He was about to visit you himself to make his plea, but he was afraid you wouldn't agree to it, which is why I've come."

He asked, "So what's the matter?"

"Do you know the third son of Master Mo?" inquired Xiao'er.

Qubing answered, "That's the son of one of my classmates."

Xiao'er elaborated: "Tomorrow he's going to come through here, and if he's carrying a fox that he's caught, I hope you'll ask him to let you keep it."

Qubing declared, "He made me feel ashamed in my own home, so I've given it a lot of thought and I don't want to hear any more about his affairs. And as for your imploring—if you wish me to exercise my feeble efforts, I cannot unless Qingfeng comes to me!"

Through a shower of tears, Xiao'er cried, "Younger sister Feng died out in the wilds three years ago!"

Qubing shook his sleeve disdainfully and exclaimed, "Since that's the case, my resentment is that much more!" He held up his book and loudly began to recite, careful

---

Younger sister Feng: That is, Qingfeng.

not to look up from it. Xiao'er rose, sobbing until he lost his voice, then covered his face and left.

Qubing then went to Qingfeng's quarters, to inform her of the incident. She went pale and inquired, "So are you going to rescue him or not?"

He said, "I'll save him for sure; not consenting to it was just a way of paying him back for being harsh and unreasonable earlier."

Qingfeng then happily remarked, "I was orphaned when quite young, and I depended on my uncle, who took care of me. Though he offended you in the past, it was to defend the family standards of behavior."

"Even so," Qubing responded, "it's hard for a person not to take that kind of thing to heart. If you were really dead, I certainly wouldn't come to his aid."

Laughing, Qingfeng said, "Why are you so obstinate!"

The next day, Third Son Mo did arrive, bearing a bowcase engraved with tigers and followed by an impressive array of servants. Qubing met him at his gate. He noticed that Mo had shot quite a number of birds, and that in amongst them was a black fox, its pelt dark with blood; he ran his hand over it, the flesh underneath the fur still feeling warm. As he supported it with his hand, he commented that he had a worn fur coat and asked if he might have the pelt to sew on as a repair. With great deference, Mo untied it and offered it as a present.

Qubing immediately handed it over to Qingfeng, then offered his guest a drink. Once Mo had departed, Qingfeng hugged the fox to her chest, and in three days it revived, then expanded and metamorphosed into her uncle. When he raised his eyes, he saw Qingfeng, which made him think that he was no longer among the living. She narrated the details of what had happened to him. The old man then bowed to pay his respects to Qubing, expressing remorse for his former actions. Happy, he then turned to Qingfeng and said, "I always insisted you weren't dead, and now here's proof."

She then told Qubing, "If you care for me, I ask that you will still allot us a portion of your mansion, to allow

me to care in private for one who has cared for me."
Qubing promised he would do so. The old man, blushing,
thanked him and took his leave.

When evening came, he returned with his entire
family. Thereafter, they were like blood relatives, father
and son, no longer suspicious of each other. Qubing lived
modestly in the house and passed the time with Xiao'er,
sharing conversation over wine. The scholar's wife bore
him a son, who gradually grew up and accordingly was
sent to Xiao'er to be tutored patiently on the right path,
in order to imitate his teacher's behavior.

40. Painted Skin

In Taiyuan, a scholar named Wang was out walking one morning, when he met a young woman carrying a bundle of belongings by herself as though running away, and having a very difficult time with it as she went. Moving more briskly to catch up with her, he noticed she was about sixteen and quite beautiful. Enjoying the sight of her as his heart filled with love, he asked, "Why are you walking alone so early in the morning?"

The young woman replied, "A passerby can't solve my unhappiness, so there's no point bothering yourself to inquire."

"What's making you so upset?" Wang asked. "If I can do anything in my power to help, I won't say no."

Despondent, the young woman explained, "My parents, in their greediness, sold me as a concubine to a rich, influential family. The first wife was so jealous, all day long she insulted me and humiliated me with beatings, to the point that I couldn't take it any longer, so I'm heading for someplace far away."

"Where to?" he asked.

"An escapee," she said, "alas, has no certain destination."

Wang then declared, "My home isn't far, and if it wouldn't trouble you too much, you might join me there." The young woman, delighted, agreed. Wang picked up her bundle of belongings and led her home.

Seeing there was no one else in the room, the young woman inquired, "Sir, why isn't your family here?"

"This is just my study," he explained.

She observed, "This place is really nice. If you pity me and want to save me, you must keep my presence here a close secret, and not let it out." Wang promised not to tell. Then they slept together.

He set her up to hide in a secret room, and several days passed without anyone knowing she was there. Then Wang mentioned it privately to his wife, Chen. She suspected that the girl had been given as a concubine to some family, so she advised Wang to send her away. Wang wouldn't hear of it.

In the market one day, Wang met a Daoist priest who turned to stare at him in amazement, and asked, "What have you gotten yourself into?"

"Nothing," Wang replied.

The Daoist declared, "There's an evil presence wound around you—how can you say it's nothing?" Wang reasserted his innocence.

The Daoist then left, muttering, "Idiot! Some people just refuse to recognize when death is coming after them." Wang thought his words strange, and entertained brief doubts about the young woman; then he considered that since she was obviously such a beauty, she couldn't possibly be an evil spirit, meaning that the priest must have been hoping to offer his prayers for averting evil in exchange for the price of a meal.

Not much later, arriving at the door of his study, he found it barred from the inside, so he couldn't get in. This made him think that something was going on inside, so he clambered over a ruined wall. The door to the inner room was also barred, so he crept quietly to a window and peered inside, spotting a hideous demon, its face bluish-green, its teeth as jagged as a saw's. It spread a human skin out on the bed, holding a brush, and began to paint on it; when it was done, it tossed the brush aside, held up the skin, and shook it out like it was a cloak, then wrapped it around its body, immediately transforming it into the young woman.

When he saw it take her shape, Wang, terrified, scurried away like a wild animal. He anxiously sought out the Daoist, but didn't know where to find him. Looking all over for traces, he finally found him outside the city, and went down on his knees to beg for rescue. The priest said, "Let me drive it away for you. This thing must be suffering pretty significantly, and just found a way to rest itself—so for that reason, I couldn't be hard-hearted enough to take its life."

Then he gave Wang a fly swatter, ordering him to hang it above the door of his bedroom. As Wang was about to leave, the Daoist arranged for them to meet at the Qingdi Temple. Wang left, but didn't dare enter his study, so he slept in the inner room and hung the swatter above the door there.

About the time of the first watch, he heard something rubbing at his door, but he wouldn't venture to sneak a look for himself, so he sent his wife to take a peek. She simply saw the young woman draw near, stare at the swatter, and then come no closer; she stood there grinding her teeth for a very long time, then left. A short time later she returned, growling, "The Daoist hopes to scare me off. But I can't spit out what I haven't yet put in my mouth!" She grabbed the swatter and broke it into pieces, wrecked the bedroom door, and in she rushed.

Leaping directly onto Wang's bed, she ripped open his chest, took his heart in both hands, and fled. His wife screamed. A maid servant rushed in with a candle, but Wang was already dead, his chest cavity a bloody ruins. Chen, horrified, wept, but dared not make a sound.

The next day, she sent her husband's younger brother to inform the Daoist. The priest, furious, fumed, "I originally took pity on this demon, then it dares to do this." He left immediately, following Wang's brother home. The young woman was already gone, but the priest raised his head to look in all four directions, and said, "We're lucky—she hasn't gotten very far!" Then he asked, "Whose home is that in the southern courtyard?"

The young brother replied, "That's my place."

Qingdi: Literally, "Green Emperor."
First watch: Approximately 7:00-9:00 p.m.

"That's where she is right now," said the Daoist. Wang's brother was dumbfounded, and didn't think it even possible. The Daoist then asked, "Haven't you recently had a stranger show up there?"

The brother answered, "Early this morning I left for Qingdi Temple, so I don't know. Let me go and find out." He went out and shortly returned, reporting, "Someone's there, alright. This morning an old woman showed up, hoping to be hired as a household servant, and my wife hired her, so she's still there."

The Daoist said, "That's the monster." Consequently, he went there with the younger brother. Brandishing a wooden sword, he stood in the middle of the courtyard, shouting, "Accursed demon! You owe me for my swatter!"

The old woman froze in the house, pale with fright, then ran out the gate, hoping to escape. The priest thereupon struck her. The old woman fell, her human skin peeling up and flaking off, changing her back into a horrible demon that lay on the ground, squealing like a pig. With his wooden sword, the Daoist beheaded the abomination; its body turned into a dense smoke, spread over the ground, and then collected into a single pile.

When the priest took out a bottle gourd, pulled out the stopper, and placed it in the smoke, there was a sucking sound, like someone drawing in a breath, until in the blink of an eye, the smoke was sucked into the gourd. The Daoist replaced the stopper and put the gourd back in his bag.

Together they looked at the human skin with eyebrows, eyes, hands, and feet painted on, all ready to be worn. The Daoist rolled it up, with the sound someone would make rolling up a scroll painting, also put it in his bag, then took his leave of the others and went on his way. Chen knelt respectfully to him at the gate, weeping and begging him for a way to bring Wang back to life. The priest explained that he lacked the ability to do so. Chen increased her pitiful pleading, throwing herself on the ground and refusing to get up.

The Daoist then pondered carefully and said, "My

magic is superficial, so I really can't raise the dead. But I can point out a man who probably can do it, so if you go and make your request of him, he'll surely try to help you out."

She asked, "What man?"

The priest replied, "In the marketplace, there's a mad beggar, who's always resting on dungheaps. Try kowtowing, and then make your plea to him. If the madman insults you or your husband, don't give way to anger." Wang's younger brother had heard of the man. He and his sister-in-law bid farewell to the Daoist and headed off together.

They found the beggar singing agitatedly beside the road, long strands of snot hanging from his nose, stinking so foully that it was almost impossible to force oneself near him. Chen crawled before him on her knees.

The beggar, laughing, cried, "Is this beauty here because she loves me?" Chen then informed him why she'd come. Again he laughed, and said, "There are plenty of men who can be your husband out there, so why do you want this one alive?" Chen remained steadfast in her pleading. Then he exclaimed, "How strange! A man dies and she comes to beg his life from me. What am I, Yama, the Hell King?"

Furious, he struck Chen with his stick. Chen endured the pain patiently. Bystanders began gathering like a wall around them. The beggar coughed up phlegm, spit a large glob of it into his hand, then raised it in the direction of Chen's lips, demanding, "Eat it!" Chen turned red in the face, refusing to do it; but once she recalled the Daoist's advice, she successfully choked it down. She felt it enter her throat like a wad of cotton being forced there, extremely resistant to going down, until it finally stopped to form a knot in her chest.

The beggar roared in laughter, exclaiming, "The beauty really loves me!" He then stood up and walked off, without even glancing at her. She pursued him until he entered a temple. Chasing after him to beg his assistance, she couldn't tell where he'd gone; she hunted everywhere yet there was no sign of him, so she left, ashamed and angry. Already mourning her husband's death, now she also regretted having eaten the phlegm, and felt humiliated, hanging her head as others watched her crying pitifully, just wanting to die.

Then she decided to lay out her husband's corpse and drain the blood from it, while household members stood by, looking on, without daring to approach. Chen held the corpse in her arms, and placed the intestines back in it, sobbing all the while.

Just when she had gone hoarse from the wretched extremes of her crying, she suddenly felt the urge to vomit. She became aware of that knotted thing in her chest suddenly forcing its way out, and before she could turn her head, it dropped into Wang's chest cavity. She was stunned, for it was a human heart. There it sat in the cavity, rhythmically beating, warm vapors rising off it like mist. It was astonishing.

Anxiously, with both hands, she closed the cavity, using all her strength to squeeze it shut as she held him in her arms. If she relaxed even a little, a dense cloud of vapors would seep through the edges of the wound. Thus she tore up some silk and wrapped it tightly around Wang. With her hands, she warmed his body, which gradually began responding. She covered him then with a large quilt. In the night, when she looked under it, she found faint breath coming from his nostrils.

By daybreak, Wang was whole and alive. He told her, "It was oddly like a dream, but I could feel some mysterious pain in my chest." When she examined the place where he'd been torn open, she found a scab had formed there the size of a coin—and soon he recovered.

The collector of these strange tales remarks, "How foolish some people are! What are obviously demons they take for beauties. How deluded such fools are! What is obviously devotion, they treat with disregard. When men are lured by the appearances of love, their wives are obliged to eat what others have spit out. The way of heaven is to repay love, yet the foolish and deluded are oblivious to this. What a pity that there are such men!"

41. The Merchant's Son

In Chu, there was a certain old man who was off engaged in foreign trade. His wife, who'd been left alone in the house, dreamed that someone was there with her; when she woke up and reached out her hand, she found a little man there. Scrutinizing him, she thought him an odd creature, before she realized that it was a fox. A moment later it ran under the bed and vanished, though the door to the room hadn't been opened.

When the next night came, she asked the old woman who was her cook to sleep there and keep her company. The wife had a ten-year-old son who ordinarily slept in his own bed, and he was also invited to join them. Late that night, as the old woman and the son slept, the fox returned. The wife began murmuring, like she was speaking in her dreams. This woke the cook, who cried out to her, and the fox ran away. From then on, the wife felt agitated, as though she needed to escape from something.

When the evening arrived, she didn't dare blow out the candle, and warned her son not to sleep too deeply. As the night progressed, the son and the old woman leaned against the wall to catch a few winks of sleep. Then when they woke up, the wife was gone, so they figured she must have stepped out to relieve herself; they waited a long time, but she didn't return, so they began to worry. The old woman was frightened, and didn't dare go out to look for her.

The son grabbed a burning candle and looked

everywhere in the house, till in one room he found his mother lying naked; he drew near to offer her assistance, and she didn't seem to feel at all bashful or self-conscious. She became progressively more aberrant, singing, sobbing, shouting and cursing each day, in many different ways.

At night, she'd become disgusted at the idea of other people being in the room, so the son slept in a separate bed and the old woman was also kept out. The son always listened till he heard his mother's caustic voice, then he'd get up with a light to investigate. The mother would angrily scold her son, but he didn't let it get to him, and everyone admired his courage.

However, he also indulged himself in playing, pretending each day he was a block layer, piling up tiles and blocks against a window, ignoring calls for him to stop. When someone removed one of the blocks, he rolled around on the ground in a crying tantrum, so no one ventured to provoke him further by touching them. After several days, two windows had been completely covered up, so no light could shine through. When this was done, he smeared on mud to close up any gaps in the wall, applying it all day long without complaining about the labor.

Once he was finished spreading it on, he had nothing to do, so he grabbed a kitchen knife and quickly began sharpening it. Observing this, everyone became disgusted with his foolishness and refused to pay any further attention to him.

That night, the son concealed the knife in his clothing, and with a large dipper covered his lamp. He waited until his mother began to rave in her sleep, then swiftly uncovered the lamp, shut the door, and began shouting. Time passed without anything odd happening, so he feigned moving away from the door, pretending that he wanted to leave the room and relieve himself outside.

Suddenly, something like a fox appeared, abruptly seizing the opportunity to run for the door. The son struck quickly, neatly cutting off two inches of its tail though it got away. Blood dripped from the segment like water. Subsequently, when he carried his lamp over and lifted it up, his mother as usual began cursing him, but the son just acted as though he hadn't heard her. He hadn't hit the thing where it mattered, and, profoundly disappointed about it, he went to rest. Thinking it over to himself, he realized that even if he hadn't killed it, at least he'd been able to stop it from getting back in.

At daybreak, he noticed that there were traces of blood beyond his wall, so he followed them. The blood led him into a garden belonging to the He family. When night arrived and it became clear that the thing hadn't come back, the son was privately overjoyed. Nevertheless, his mother inexplicably remained still, lying there like she was dead.

Not long afterwards, the merchant returned home, rushed to his wife's bed, and asked what had happened. The wife began insulting him, treating him like an enemy. The son then gave his account. The old man, horrified, sent for medicine for her. The wife, however, poured out the medicine, while berating and swearing at them. Secretly, they put the medicine into her soup and assorted beverages, so over the course of several days, she gradually settled down. The father and son were extremely pleased.

One night they were sleeping when the old man woke up to find his wife missing; father and son went looking for her, and discovered her in another room. Henceforward. she was continually agitated, and the old man found her unwilling to be in the same room with him. As the evenings arrived, she inevitably fled from her room. When he tried to hold her back, she heaped even more abuse on him.

The old man had no plan to offer, and hence he locked her in the room. But whenever his wife rushed to make her escape, the door opened all by itself. In his suffering, the old man tried to expel the evil with prayers aimed at driving it out, but nothing seemed to have any effect.

At dusk, the son stealthily entered the He family

garden and laid down in the bushes, to see if he could determine the fox's whereabouts. As the moon began to rise, he suddenly heard someone speaking. Quietly pushing aside a gnarled branch, he saw two persons having a drink while a servant with a very long beard poured a jug for them, wearing an old, brown-colored garment. Their words were muttered softly and confidentially, so he wasn't able to make out what they were saying.

After awhile, he heard one of the people say, "Tomorrow you can bring some wine here." An instant later, they were gone, and only the long-bearded servant remained behind, taking off his garment and lying down upon the stones of the courtyard. Carefully examining him, the son noticed that while his four limbs were human, he had a tail hanging down behind him.

The son wanted to rush home, but was afraid the fox might become aware of his presence, so he stayed there until the night passed. Just before daybreak, he heard the two men return again, one after the other, murmuring before they all three entered a bamboo grove. The son then ran home.

The old man asked him where he'd gone and he answered, "I slept at uncle's house." Then he followed his father into the marketplace, where he spotted a hat with a fox tail hanging garishly from it, and begged the old man to buy it for him. The old man wouldn't turn around. The son tugged at his father's clothing, noisily acting spoiled. The old man couldn't put up with this— and hence to stop his shenanigans, he bought it for him.

While the father carried on an amicable trade in one of the shops, the son played beside him, and then took advantage while he was turned away to grab some of his money and buy some wine, which he left on deposit with the owner of the wine shop.

He had an uncle from his mother's side of the family who owned a house in the city, and whose business was hunting. The son ran off to his house. His uncle, however, had stepped out. His aunt inquired about his mother's infirmity, to which he replied, "Each successive day she's a little better. However, some rat has been chewing at her wardrobe, and she's so angry that it's brought her to tears that she can't get rid of it, so that's why she sent me to ask for some poison."

The aunt picked up a box, took out a lump of the compound the size of a coin, wrapped it up, and gave it to the boy. The son felt there was too little. The aunt wanted him to have a seat while she went to prepare some soup and pancakes. The son scanned the room to make sure no one was around, before he took out the box of poison, stealthily scooped up two handfuls of it, and stowed it away. Then he hurried to tell his aunt not to trouble herself cooking for him, since "Father's waiting for me in the marketplace, so I don't have the leisure to stay and eat."

He then retraced his steps and secretly slipped the poison into the wine. He wandered about the market-place until dark, and then returned home. His father asked him where he'd been, and he reported that he'd been at his uncle's house. For days, the son repeated this habit of wandering between shops.

One day, he spotted the long-bearded man mingling in the crowd. The son scrupulously verified it was the same man, then covertly stayed close to him. Eventually, he actually spoke to him, asking him where he lived.

The man answered, "North of the village."

He inquired the same of the boy, who lied, "In a burrow."

The long-bearded fellow allowed as how it was strange that he lived in a hole for his home. The son, laughing, exclaimed, "That burrow's been our home for generations—and yours as well, right?"

The man was alarmed by this, and flatly demanded to know his name. The boy replied, "I'm a son of the Hu family. Some time ago, I stopped at the He family's garden, and there I saw you serving two gentlemen, so how could I forget you?"

The man then carefully examined him, half believing and half doubting him. The boy proceeded to open his

---

Hu family: Playing on the fact that *hu* is also the sound of the character meaning "fox."

robe ever so minutely, little by little, until he revealed his purchased tail, and said, "We folk can pass ourselves off as humans except for our tails, which bring us unlimited resentment."

The man asked him, "So why'd you want to come to the marketplace?"

"Father sent me to buy wine," the son explained. The man told him that he, too, had come to buy wine. "So have you bought any or not?" asked the boy.

"We folk are quite poor," the man answered, "hence I usually steal it when I get the opportunity."

The son noted, "That kind of venture's very hazardous, a risky exercise."

"I received my masters' orders," the man declared, "so I can't disobey them."

"Just who are your masters?" the son asked him.

The man explained, "What you saw were two brothers. The one's been having intimate relations north of the village with a lady named Wang, the other's been lodging east of the village with a certain old man's family. The old man's son is very cruel, and actually cut off enough of his tail that it took ten days to heal, but now he's back at it like before." When he finished speaking, he wanted to leave, explaining, "I don't want to expose my intentions."

The son declared, "Stealing it's hard, but buying it's easy. I bought some earlier that I stored in the wine shop, and I'd respectfully like to offer it to you as a present. My bag still has some money in it, so it's no problem for me to buy more."

The long-bearded man was so embarrassed, he didn't know how he could repay the boy. The son reassured him, "We're the same kind of folk, so why be stingy about such a little thing? When I get some time, I'll come accept a hearty drink from you." So they went to the shop together, the son picked up the wine and gave it to the man, then he went home.

When night came, his mother eventually fell into a peaceful sleep and didn't try to run off. The son knew in his heart that something was up, so he told his father;

they went to take a closer look, and found two dead foxes outside the garden house, one of them dead on the grass, blood still streaming from its mouth. The wine jar remained there, so they picked it up and shook it, determining it wasn't yet all gone.

The father, shocked, demanded, "Why wasn't I informed about this earlier?"

His son replied, "This thing was extremely clever— once I'd told you, it would have known everything."

Delighted, the old man said, "My son, to defeat a fox makes you another Chen Ping." Thereupon, father and son slung the foxes over their shoulders and went home. They saw that one fox had a blunted tail, just as if it'd been scarred by a knife.

From that time on, all was tranquil again. But the wife remained very, very thin, and though her mind gradually became coherent, she nevertheless developed a persistent cough, constantly having to get up to vomit or to spit while still trying to get well.

North of the village, the woman named Wang had also been afflicted by a fox; it was said of her that when the foxes were killed, she also began to recover from her illness.

Because of all this, the old man thought his son most rare, so he taught him to ride and to shoot. Later on, he became a distinguished general in the army.

Chen Ping: Sima Qian's *Records of the Grand Historian* devotes an entire section (number 56) to Chen Ping, the Han dynasty statesman who assisted Liu Bang by offering him six tactics that preserved his life and mission, including "making thousands of women dress up as Han soldiers to be slaughtered by the Chu army so that Liu Bang could escape; sowing distrust between Xiang Yu and his most important generals; deceiving Han Xin to capture him" (Wang 32), and bribing the wife of a leader to allow Liu Bang to escape a siege.

42. A Craving for Snake

In my home town, Wang Puling had a servant named Lu Fengning, who, by nature, loved to eat snake. Every time he found a small snake, he'd swallow the whole thing, like he was gobbling down a green onion. With the big ones, he'd take his knife and cut them into small chunks, then grabbing the bits with both hands, he'd eat them. When he chewed, it sounded like crunching metal and his cheeks were smeared with blood.

He was also skilled at sniffing them out, so one time he smelled a snake behind a wall and ran over to it hastily: it turned out to be over a *chi* long. At the time, he wasn't wearing his knife in his sash, so after he bit its head off, the tail was still wriggling from the corner of his mouth.

Chi: A measure of length equal to 1/3 of a meter, so Lu Fengning's snack was a little over a foot long.

43. Jin Shicheng

Jin Shicheng lived on Mt. Chang. He was a completely unconventional character. He'd abandoned his family to pursue Buddhist contemplation. He became like a madman, eating unclean things and thinking them quite tasty. If he came upon some dog or goat shit, he'd bend down and gobble it up. He even nicknamed himself Buddha.

Ignorant men and women observed his aberrant antics, and then thousands of them followed him as disciples. Jin ordered them to eat shit and no one dared disobey him. He established a temple on Changshan, sparing no expenses, and people were happy to donate to the project. Master Nan detested his bizarre behavior, grabbed and flogged him, telling him to go build a Confucian temple.

The disciples then surprised everyone by announcing, "The Buddha has fallen on hard times!" They quickly made donations to save Jin's life. The money was collected so speedily that the temple was constructed in little more than a month, even faster than if cruel officials had been chasing and shouting at the people.

Master Nan: Nan Zhijie, styled Yiyuan, was appointed to serve at a Buddhist school on Changshan when it was known for ten years as Tan, or "the clouds," during the reign of Qing emperor Kangxi (Zhu 1:134).

Sparing no expenses: Perhaps in part a pun on the fact that the character representing Jin's family name also means "gold."

The collector of these strange tales remarks, "I've heard of Jin the Buddhist, or as people call him, 'Jin Shicheng, the Buddha.' His moral character was abased to its lowest extreme. Flogging him wasn't disgrace enough, and in looking for a proper way to punish him, Master Nan did so much good! However, having to ask this abnormal monk to be the one to construct a Confucian temple there is also a shame to all the nation's scholars."

44. Scholar Dong

Scholar Dong, whose style name was Xiasi, lived in the westernmost portion of Qingzhou. Around sunset on a particular winter's day, he spread a quilt over his bed and stirred the coals in his room. He was just about to put a cover over his lamp when a friend invited him over for drinks, so he locked his door and went out.

Over at his friend's house sat a doctor who was very knowledgeable about the fundamentals of reading the pulse, and was busily examining all of the guests. At last he turned to Wang Jiusi and Dong to say, "I've read a great many pulses, but none so strange as yours, gentlemen: one with the pulse of the wealthy, but containing signs of pending bankruptcy, and one with the pulse of the long-lived, but with the possibility of sudden death. This anomaly exceeds my humble knowledge. Certainly, Master Dong, yours is particularly unusual."

Alarmed, everyone asked him to elaborate. He replied, "That's the limit of my medical skills, I couldn't venture any other opinions with certainty. I hope you two gentlemen will be very careful." Upon hearing this, the two men were quite startled, but since the doctor's diagnoses were so contradictory, they didn't put much

---

Qingzhou: In Shandong province.
Fundamentals of reading the pulse: *The Yellow Emperor's Inner Classic of Medical Basics* (*huangdi neijing suwen*) describes, for example, "six aspects of examining the pulse with regard to the four seasons" (66). For types of normal/abnormal pulses, see pp. 30-32, 70-82.

186

faith in them.

At midnight, Dong went home, where he noticed his door was half open, and became extremely suspicious. Trying to recall in his drunken state, he decided that he must have been in such a hurry to leave home that he'd forgotten to lock it. He went inside and before hurrying to light a fire, first stuck his hand under the quilt to find out if it was still warm or not. Upon doing so, he felt the smooth flesh of someone lying there. Greatly stunned, he drew back his hand.

He quickly lit a fire and to his surprise found a beautiful girl there, with a child's flawless complexion, looking like one of the celestials. He was deliriously happy. He figured he'd have some naughty fun, and explored the lower part of her body further, only to find a long, fuzzy tail there. Terribly frightened, he started to run away.

The girl woke up just then, put out her hand, and grabbed Dong's arm, saying, "Where are you going?"

Dong, who became even more frightened, pitifully begged, "I hope you'll pardon me, beautiful fairy!"

The girl, laughing, asked, "What have you seen here, to be afraid of me?"

Dong answered, "I don't fear your hand—it's your tail that scares me."

The girl laughed again and said, "You're mistaken. What tail would that be?" Guiding Dong's hand, she forced him to explore with it, and he felt the smooth flesh of her leg and rump. Laughing, she asked, "What do you think now? You're so ridiculously drunk, you can't even see straight, yet you're accusing me falsely of whatever it is."

Dong remained excited that she was so beautiful, and was even more attracted to her, so he began to berate himself for having been wrong before. Yet he still had doubts about the reasons for her showing up. The girl explained, "Don't you remember your neighbor to the east, the small girl with the light-colored hair? As I count on my fingers, it's been ten years since we moved away. Back then, I wasn't yet fifteen, and you were also just a youngster."

Dong suddenly realized who she was, and said, "So you're the Zhou daughter, A-Suo?"

"That's me," the girl answered.

Dong declared, "Your talking about it helped me to remember. I haven't seen you for ten years, and now, slim and lovely, here you are! But why have you suddenly come back?"

The girl explained, "I was married to a foolish man for four or five years, then my parents-in-law both died, and it was my further misfortune to become a widow after that. I became the last surviving member of the family, all alone with no one to depend upon. In recalling my childhood, the only person I could remember was you, so for that reason I came here to see you. I entered your gate at sunset, but you'd been invited out for drinks and were just leaving, so I secretly hid and waited for you to return. Since I was waiting for a long time, my feet felt icy and my skin had goosebumps, thus I borrowed your quilt to warm myself; please don't greet me with suspicion."

Dong was hoping to hear this, so he undressed and they slept together, with the scholar feeling very satisfied about it all. Carrying on like this for over a month, he began to lose weight, and when his family members asked him about it, he always told them he didn't know why it was happening.

Over a period of time, he became increasingly e-maciated, until, in dread, he went to see the man who was skilled at reading pulses again. The man informed him, "This pulse is bewitched. Now the death prediction I gave you that day a while back has been proven by this illness." Dong broke into tears and wouldn't leave. Since the doctor couldn't avoid his pleas, he applied acupuncture and moxibustion, and offered him some medicine as a present. He also advised Dong, "If you meet any women, force yourself to avoid becoming intimate with them." Dong recognized how dangerous his situation had become.

He went home and the girl, giggling, wanted him to make love to her. Dong grew angry and exploded,

"We're not going to be doing anything together any more, because I'm going to die!" He stormed out without turning back to look at her.

The girl felt terribly humiliated, and with equal fury, exclaimed, "So, you still want to live!"

When evening arrived, Dong took his medicine, went to bed by himself, and had just shut his eyes when he began dreaming of making love to the girl. He woke up suddenly, and found the bedclothes wet with his ejaculation. More fearful than ever, he moved and went to sleep in the central portion of the house, while his wife made a fire and stood by to defend him.

Dong went on having such dreams. Whenever he woke up to see the woman, she just disappeared. After several days, Dong vomited blood, fighting against it as long as he could, and then died.

Wang Jiusi was in his study when he saw a young lady walk in, and overwhelmed by her beauty, he made love to her. When he asked about her background, she replied, "I was involved with your neighbor. I was faithful to him as his lover, never suspecting that he'd get involved with some fox and die. That kind of evil spirit can easily be angered—scholars in particular should be cautious and guard against them." Wang adored her even more for this, so they became lovers.

Once this had gone on for quite some time, his mind began to wander, he became ill and emaciated, and he had a dream in which Dong said to him, "You've gotten involved with a fox. She killed me and now she wants to kill my friend. I've made a complaint against her in the underworld in order to achieve revenge. On the seventh day of the month, you must burn incense outside your room—don't forget to do it!" Wang woke up, thinking this odd.

He called out to the girl, "I'm very sick and I'm afraid I'm about to fall into the great abyss, so I've been persuaded not to get close to any women."

The girl answered, "Those who are destined to have long lives can still live a long time even when they're involved with women; those who are doomed to die at a young age will die all the same, even if they avoid wo-men." She sat there making fun of him and laughing. Wang was unable to concentrate on holding out, so again he had sex with her. When they were finished he regretted it, but he just couldn't stop himself.

That evening, he inserted a stick of incense above his door. The girl showed up, pulled it out, and threw it away. In the night, he dreamt once again that Dong had come to him to admonish Wang for having ignored his advice.

Once it was dark the next night, he enjoined his family members to delay going to bed until after they'd secretly burned some incense for him. The girl crawled onto his bed and, suddenly frightened, demanded, "Has someone put out more of that incense again?" Wang said he didn't know.

The girl got up and found the incense, once again broke it in two and extinguished it. She reentered and asked, "Who told you to do that?"

Wang replied, "It was probably one of my household members, concerned about my illness, who took the advice of some exorcist and has been offering prayers to avert evil." The girl became unsettled and dour. When his family members stealthily spied that the incense had been snuffed out, they started some more burning.

The girl suddenly sighed and exclaimed, "You're a lucky one, alright. It was a mistake for me to harm Xiasi, and then come running to you—that was definitely excessive. I'm about to have it out with him in the underworld. If you can still think fondly about the love between us, don't let anything happen to my remains." She withdrew from the bed to make her journey below, then fell to the ground and died.

He lit a candle and found a fox lying there. Still fearing for his life, he shouted for his family members to skin it, and to hang its hide up. Wang remained very sick till he saw the fox return and say to him, "I made my appeal to the underworld judges. They ruled that Dong had been aroused by lust, so death is what his guilt deserves. As far as my own blame in the matter, they said

I shouldn't beguile people, and demanded that I forfeit my pill of immortality, then ordered me to return among the living. So where'd you put my remains?"

He told her, "My family members didn't know any better, so they skinned it."

The fox, mortified, cried out, "I've killed so many people, my death now is hardly premature; but for it to come suddenly at your hands—!" Filled with hate and resentment, she went away. Wang was so sick that he nearly died, though he recovered in about half a year.

Pill of immortality: Cf. the other fox stories involving the *jindan*.

45. Chomping on Stones

In the city of Xin, the family of aged and respected Wang Qingwen had a young horse groom also named Wang, who, while still young, left to go to Laoshan to study the Dao. After a while, he no longer ate cooked food, but merely nibbled pine nuts and white stones, while hair began growing all over his body.

After he had already been there several years, he began to miss his elderly mother and returned to his home town, where he gradually resumed eating prepared food, while continuing to eat stones as before. As he held the stones to the sun and looked at them, he could tell whether they would taste sweet, bitter, sour, or salty, like the flavors of different root crops.

When his mother died, he went back once more to the mountain, and he's been there now for seventeen or eighteen years.

Qingwen: The coutesy name of Wang Yuchi, father of the Qing poet, Wang Yuyang (Brown 140).
Laoshan: Mt. Lao, near Qingdao, in Shandong province, is one of the sacred mountains of Daoist belief.

46. The Temple Demon

There was a scholar in the city of Xin, Wang Qihou, whose courtesy name was Zhongyu, the grandson of provincial governor Wang Xiangkun. One day he saw a woman, plump and dark-looking, enter his room. Laughing, she drew near and sat on his bed, her intentions clearly indecent. Wang resisted her, but she wouldn't leave.

Thereafter, whether Wang was sitting or was lying down, she was always in his sight. However, he was so determinedly stoic that the woman couldn't seduce him. She became angry with him and slapped his cheek loudly, but his face betrayed no sign of it having been at all painful.

The woman then tied a belt to an overhead beam, and grabbed him, to hang the two of them together. Wang unconsciously flung himself under the beam, and craned his neck so she could hang him. Anyone could see that his feet weren't on the ground, suspended there in the air, though it was also the case that he seemed unable to die this way.

Others considered him to have gone mad.

Suddenly he cried, "She's going to take and throw me in the river." Staring into the distance toward the river, he wildly rushed off towards it until someone tugged at him to stop. It was like this in all matters: daily, again and again, medical skills and medicine had no effect.

One day, unexpectedly, he watched as a warrior knight bound her in chains and then came forward, furiously shouting, "How dare you trouble such an honest and sincere man like that!" Having made a prisoner of the woman, he dragged her out through a window.

Once the knight took her outside, the woman no longer appeared like a normal person, for her eyes flashed with lightning while her mouth, bright red with blood, gaped as large as a basin. Wang remembered that on the gate of the temple of the city god, there were four clay demons that had been broken off—looking just like the one in front of him. Thereupon he recovered from his madness.

47. Official Lu

In Lingyang, there lived a scholar by the name of Zhu Erdan, whose style name was Xiaoming. His personality was vigorous and unrestrained. However, he was basically rather stupid, and though he sincerely studied hard, he still wasn't very widely known.

One day, a crowd of scholar's society members were drinking. Undoubtedly to make fun of him, one of the members said, "You have a reputation for being heroic, so if you dare to go to the Temple of the Ten Kings in the middle of the night and bring back here the fierce-looking afterlife official from the gallery on the left, the group of us will pool our money and treat you to a feast."

This Temple of the Ten Kings, built at Lingyang, featured gods and demons carved entirely from wood, decorated so convincingly that it seemed as though they were alive. Standing in the eastern corridor, there was a *panguan* with a green face and red beard, whose looks were especially ferocious and horrible. Sometimes in the night, one could hear the sounds of torture and interrogation in the corridors. Entering them caused the hair on one's head immediately to stand on end. With this in mind, the group of scholars meant to challenge Zhu.

Zhu smiled, got up, and left directly to go there. In no

Panguan: An official whose job is record management and decision making. See Hucker (363).

time, a great cry came from outside the gate: "At my invitation, here he is—the venerable bearded master!" The waiting scholars all rose to their feet.

Suddenly Zhu burst in, carrying the carved *panguan* on his back, put him down on the table, served him a cup of wine, and respectfully poured out three libations. The scholars watched him, shrinking back in fear that they weren't safe, and remained standing, having upset their seats. They begged him to take the official back.

Zhu poured another cup of wine on the ground, praying, "Though my rash actions were ignorant, your honor, I hope you'll forgive them rather than hold them against me. My modest home is not far from here, and if it pleases you to come and share some drinks there, I hope you'll let nothing stand between us." Then he picked up the carving and carried it back.

The next day, the scholars really did invite him out for drinks. By the time dusk arrived, Zhu was half drunk and went home, but figured he wasn't finished yet, so he grabbed a lamp and poured himself some more wine. Suddenly someone entered through the dividing curtain, and when Zhu looked closely, he could tell it was the *panguan* himself.

Zhu stood up and exclaimed, "I imagine this means that I'm about to die! Last night I brazenly showed disrespect for you—so have you arrived now to chop off my head?"

With a small chuckle, the official spoke through his thick beard: "Not at all. Yesterday your bit of high-jinx was concluded between us justly with your offer, and since this evening I'm unexpectedly at leisure, I've come to honor your invitation."

Zhu was greatly pleased and tugged at the *panguan*'s robe, urging him to sit, while he got up to wash some cups and light a fire. The official suggested, "The weather's warm and mild, so let's drink the wine cold." Zhu followed his suggestion, setting a wine jar on the table, then rushed off to tell his servants to prepare a variety of dishes.

When his wife heard about the *panguan*'s arrival,

she was astonished, and warned Zhu not to go back. But Zhu, refusing to listen, stood waiting while supervising the dishes' preparation, then left with them.

After they had amiably toasted each other with cups of wine, Zhu asked the *panguan* his name. He replied, "My family name is Lu, but I don't have a first name." They spoke about the classics, the official responding instantly to Zhu's questions.

"Can you compose in the style of the imperial examinations?" Zhu inquired.

Official Lu responded, "I can distinguish what is elegant from what is terrible. The compositions that we underworld officials have to recite are pretty similar to what's produced in the world of the living."

Official Lu proved to be a prodigious drinker, draining ten cups in a single round. Since Zhu had been drinking all day long, he soon passed out with an elegant gesture, falling onto the table into a drunken sleep. When he woke up, the last of the burning candles was sputtering a dim yellow, and his ghostly guest was gone.

After that, *panguan* Lu always put in an appearance every two or three days, so their camaraderie increased to the point that the official at times would even sleep there. Whenever Zhu showed him his essays, Lu would always mark them in red, with words to the effect that they weren't so good.

One night, Zhu became drunk and went on to bed while Lu continued drinking. Suddenly, in the midst of a drunken dream, he became aware of a slight pain in his guts; when he woke up and looked around, he saw Lu sitting up on the bed next to him, pulling Zhu's intestines and stomach out of a gaping cavity, and then carefully rearranging them. Stunned, he cried, "There's been no hate or resentment between us, so why are you trying to kill me?"

Lu laughed and said, "Have no fear, I'm just exchanging your heart for a wiser one." He then unhurriedly replaced the intestines and closed him up, wrapping him around the waist with the kind of bandages used for binding women's feet. When his objective had been accomplished, there were no traces of blood on the bed. Zhu's belly simply felt a little numb.

He saw Lu put a piece of flesh on the table. When Zhu asked him what it was, he explained, "This is your heart. Since it wasn't very adept at writing compositions, I knew that the channels of writing ability in your heart had become blocked. Just now, in the underworld, from out of ten million hearts I chose a superb one for you, inserted it in place of yours, and will keep yours to make up for the one that's missing." Then he stood up, shut the door behind him, and left.

At first light, Zhu loosened the bandage to take a look, and found the wound had sealed itself, leaving a bright red line of scar to mark it. From thence forward, his writing improved tremendously, and he remembered everything he read.

After several days, he brought another essay to the official. Lu said, "Now you can do it. Unfortunately, your luck's a bit shaky, so you won't be able to achieve great success, though you'll succeed at the local and provincial examinations."

Zhu asked, "When will that happen?"

"This year you'll certainly be the best," Lu replied.

Not surprisingly, Zhu finished at the top of his cohort in the local examinations, and when the results of the provincial examinations were posted that fall, Zhu also finished in first place. The same group of scholars who had always played tricks on him happened by; upon spotting the compositions of the successful candidates, they gawked in disbelief and inquired into the details until they learned what strange things had happened.

Together they begged Zhu at his earliest convenience to set up a meeting for them with *panguan* Lu. Lu agreed to the meeting. The scholars made big plans for receiving him. During the first watch, Lu arrived with his red beard waving and his eyes flashing like lightning. All color drained from the scholars and their teeth began chattering; one after another, they all ran off.

Zhu then took Lu home with him for some drinks and once they were intoxicated, Zhu remarked, "You've

washed my intestines and rearranged my stomach, so
I've already received many favors from you. Still, there's
one piece of business that I'd like to trouble you with, but
I don't know—may I?"

Lu plainly invited him to make his request.

Zhu replied, "Since you can change a person's heart,
I suppose you can also change a person's looks. My wife,
whom I married when we turned adults, has a body you
can't help but like, but from the neck up she's just pretty
ugly. So I'd like to trouble you to use your blade again—
how about it?"

Lu laughed and said, "Very well, but permit me some
time to carry it out."

After several days, Lu arrived at midnight and
knocked at the door. Zhu anxiously got up and invited
him in. Lighting a candle, he could see that there was
something wrapped up under Lu's robe. When he asked
about it, Lu answered, "Not long ago you urged something
of me, and a most difficult matter it was. But I've just
obtained a beautiful woman's head, which I'm offering
to you as you requested."

Zhu poked at the bundle, and upon inspection found
the neck still wet with blood. Lu urged him to go inside
quickly, without rousing the poultry and dogs. Zhu was
worried that the door to the sleeping quarters might have
been bolted for the night. When Lu pushed at it with one
hand, the door opened up all by itself.

Zhu led him to his wife's bedroom, where they saw
her lying on her side, asleep. Lu gave the head to Zhu to
hold, then from his boot he took a blade sharp enough
to cut off a head, and pressed it at the nape of the wife's
neck, as though he was cutting beancurd—the blade
easily sliced and severed, till the head rolled off the side
of the pillow; Lu urgently grabbed the beauty's head that
Zhu had been clutching to his chest and fitted it to the
wife's neck, thoroughly checking that it was lined up
straight, then pressed it into place. With that concluded,
Lu propped her shoulders up with the pillow, directed
Zhu to bury his wife's head in a peaceful spot, and then
left.

Zhu's wife woke up, her neck feeling rather numb and her face rather strange; when she rubbed it, some dried blood flaked off, which really shook her up. She called to her maid to bring in a basin of water for washing; the maid saw the bloody mess on her mistress' face and was utterly terrified. The wife washed it off, the water in the basin turning completely red. When she raised her face, the maid was utterly astonished once again to see that it was entirely unfamiliar to her.

The wife examined herself in the mirror, stunned by the image and unable to explain it. Zhu came in and told her what had happened; when he looked her over, he noticed long eyebrows with ends disappearing under the bangs of her hair, and dimples that formed in her cheeks when she smiled, just like a beauty from some painting. He loosened her robe to get a better look and found a red line circling her neck, with flesh above and below it that was certainly of two different shades.

Before all this took place, there was an official named Wu, who had a beautiful daughter who'd never married, having lost two prospective husbands to death, for which reason she was nineteen and still single. On the occasion of the Lantern Festival, she visited the Temple of the Ten Kings. At the time, there was a large assortment of people milling around, among whom was an unscrupulous thug who spied on her lustfully, followed her, and made inquiries about where she lived.

That night, he used a ladder to enter the house, made a hole in her bedroom door, killed a maidservant at her bedside, then attempted to rape the daughter; she used all her strength to resist him and screamed, which made the thug furious, so he killed her, too.

Wu's wife, who'd heard some of the noise, called for a maid to go check on it, and when she spotted the daughter's corpse, she was further mortified to find it

---

Lantern Festival: The final celebration of the Chinese New Year, held on the fifteenth day of the first month in the lunar year calendar.

decapitated. Once the whole family had been startled awake, they put the daughter's body in the main room of the house and laid her head beside the neck, while the entire household wept and howled all night long.

At dawn, when they lifted the daughter's shroud, they found the body as they'd left it—but her head was gone. All of the serving women were flogged for not being vigilant in their duty, since it was assumed that the head had been eaten by dogs.

Wu then reported the events to the prefecture's officials. They set a strict timetable for the capture of the criminal, and three months elapsed, but they couldn't apprehend the murderer. Over time, word got back to Master Wu about the strange exchange of heads in the Zhu family.

Wu became suspicious and sent an old woman to find out what the family had been up to; as soon as she walked in and saw Zhu's wife, the old woman ran off, startled, to inform Master Wu. He verified that his daughter's corpse was still there, so, alarmed and apprehensive, he just couldn't figure out what had happened. He began to speculate that Zhu had employed some kind of magic to kill his daughter, so he left to interrogate Zhu.

Zhu told him, "My spouse's head was switched in a dream, but I really have no idea how it was done; to say that I killed her would be an injustice."

Wu didn't believe him, so he initiated legal action. Zhu's servants were rounded up and their stories proved to be the same as his. Hence the prefectural officials were unable to prove Zhu guilty.

Zhu went home and begged Lu to advise him. Lu declared, "This is no problem, for I'll just send his daughter to explain it to him herself."

Wu dreamt that night that his daughter said to him, "Yang Danian of Suxi is the criminal who did this to me, not the scholar, Zhu. He wasn't happy with his wife's looks, thus *panguan* Lu took my head and exchanged it—so although my body is dead, my head lives on. I hope you won't treat him like an enemy." Upon awakening, he informed his wife, who revealed that she'd had the very same dream.

They then reported the information to the authorities. The officials' investigation discovered that there was indeed a Yang Danian; after being arrested and shackled, he confessed to his crime. Wu then paid a visit to Zhu, requesting to see his wife, and afterwards began treating Zhu like his son-in-law. The head of Zhu's wife was subsequently joined with the body of Wu's daughter and interred together.

Zhu made three more tries at passing the next examination level, but each time he was punished with forfeiture of his candidate's position because he disobeyed the rules of the examination. As a result, he became discouraged and gave up, and went on with his life for the next thirty years.

One night, Lu remarked to him, "You know, you can't live forever." Zhu asked him how much time he could expect, and the answer was that he had five days.

"Can you save me?"

Lu replied, "It's heaven's decree, so how can a common person privately hope to resist it? Moreover, a wise man perceives that life and death are a single continuum. Why must life necessarily be a cause for celebrating, and death a cause for lamenting?" Zhu took this to be quite right. Without delay, he obtained appropriate burial clothes, a shroud, and a coffin; once this was done, he dressed himself in his funeral robes and died.

The next day, while his wife was weeping beside his coffin, Zhu suddenly drifted in from outside. His wife was quite shaken. Zhu acknowledged, "I'm a ghost, that's for sure, but otherwise no different than I was during my lifetime. I've been thinking about you, a widowed mother with an orphaned son, and the loving reluctance to part that I feel for you." His wife was deeply moved, sobbing

---

He disobeyed the rules of the examination: Zhu's fate is a perfect parallel of Pu Songling's own examination experiences; he was failed for being independent.

till the tears dripped onto her chest; Zhu did his best to console her.

She pleaded, "In ancient times, there were spirits who returned to life, and since you still possess your spirit, why can't you live again?"

Zhu answered her, "What has been predestined may not be evaded."

"What do the officials of the underworld have you doing?" she asked.

He explained, "*Panguan* Lu recommended me for a position supervising case records, and conferred an official's title on me, so it's not unpleasant."

His wife wanted to speak with him further, but Zhu said, "Official Lu has come along with me, so I hope you can provide us some wine and food." Then he hastened away.

His wife complied with his request, managing to get everything ready. When she heard them laughing and drinking, making high-spirited sounds, it was just like the way things used to be. At midnight, she peeked in and was sad to discover that they'd both vanished. But from that time forward, every three days or so, they'd come back, and occasionally Zhu would even stay all night and make love to her, giving her useful advice on managing the family's affairs whenever he passed through.

His son, Wei, was five years old, so when Zhu arrived, he always hugged him; when Wei was seven or eight years old, Zhu taught him by the light of a lamp to read. His son was also very bright, able by the age of nine to compose essays, and at fifteen entered a county school, never realizing that he had no father. After this, Zhu's visits became more infrequent, no more than one day per month.

One evening he arrived and said to his wife, "It's time now for me to say farewell to you forever."

"Where will you go?" she asked.

He replied, "The underworld emperor has asked me to serve as the mountain god in Taihua, and I must travel far away to go there. There will be a great distance between us, and I'll have lots of business to conduct there, so for those reasons I cannot return." The mother and son clung to him, weeping, so he told them, "Don't be like that! My son has distinguished himself, the family's livelihood will allow you to survive, and even a couple who remain married for a hundred years must sometimes be apart!"

He turned to his son and said, "Be a good man, and don't neglect your father's estate. Ten years from now, we'll see each other again." He walked directly out through the gate and then disappeared.

After Wei turned twenty-five, he succeeded in qualifying as a *jinshi* and was made an official inspector. He was directed to offer sacrifices at Xiyue while traveling through Huayin, when suddenly a carriage appeared, entirely covered by plumes, galloping frantically to intercept them. Wei was quite surprised.

Upon careful scrutiny, he spotted the person inside the carriage and realized that it was his father. He climbed down from his own carriage and prostrated himself, weeping, by the side of the road.

His father stopped his carriage and declared, "Your reputation as an official is excellent, so now I can die without regret." Wei remained on the ground, not getting up; Zhu urged his chariot to go quickly and didn't look back.

Before he'd gone very far, he did turn back, untied the sword fastened at his waist, and sent one of his men to present it to Wei. His words sounded as though from far away: "Wear this and you will always be esteemed." Wei, wishing to chase after him, saw the carriage, horses, and his father's followers all flutter away suddenly as if scattered by the wind, and in the space of a breath there was nothing left to see.

Wei grieved sorrowfully for quite a long time; then he drew the sword and looked closely at it, noting its superior craftsmanship and a phrase carved in characters upon

---

Jinshi: A successful candidate in the metropolitan (held in the capital) civil service examination.

it: "Desire to be brave when making decisions, but prudent in considering them; tactful in wisdom, but equitable in actions." Wei afterwards became an official comparable to the Simas. He had five sons, called Chen, Qian, Tang, Hun, and Shen.

One evening, he dreamt that his father told him, "The sword you wear should be given to Hun." Wei followed his wishes. Hun became an official, a court examiner with a reputation for administration.

The collector of these strange tales remarks, "To cut off the leg from the crane in order to connect it to the duck is to commit an act of absurdity; but to graft a flower from one tree to another is to do something extraordinary; this is even more true when chopping through guts and applying knives to the napes of necks! Official Lu can be said to have been ugly on the outside, but beautiful on the inside. From the Ming dynasty to the present day is not a great distance in time—but does Lingyang's Official Lu still exist? Is his spirit still around or not? To wield the lash merely as his carriage driver would be my greatest delight."

The Simas: The Three Kingdoms-era founders of the Jin dynasty (265-420 C.E.).

48. Yingning

Wang Zifu lived in Luodian, in Ju county. His father had died when he was very young. Being quite clever, at the age of fourteen, Wang qualified as a *xiucai*. His mother was extremely fond of him and normally didn't allow him to stray beyond the city limits. He had been engaged to a daughter of the Xiao family who died before they could wed, so to date he'd been unsuccessful at obtaining a bride.

When the Lantern Festival arrived, his cousin, Wu, invited him to do some sightseeing. When they'd just reached the village outskirts, a servant from Wu's family ran up, summoning Wu to return home. Wang saw that there were groups of girls out wandering around, so he decided to continue strolling by himself.

Accompanied by a maid, there was a young woman holding a branch of plum blossoms, a matchlessly gorgeous beauty, whose smiling face captivated him. Wang glued his eyes on her, without a second thought concerning proper behavior. The girl walked past him several paces, then turned to her maid and said, "That

---

Ju county: In modern Shandong province.

Xiucai: A scholar who has passed the county level of the imperial civil service examination.

Leaving the plum blossom branch behind: Pu is playing with semantic ambiguity here—*yí*, to leave behind, can also be read as *wei*, to send or present as a gift, suggesting that perhaps Yingning (despite her later comments to the contrary) is entirely aware of the "token" she has left for Wang to find.

young man has eyes that blaze like a thief's!" Leaving the plum blossom branch behind on the ground, laughing and chattering, she walked away.

Wang picked up the branch, disappointed, feeling as if he'd lost his very soul, and then sadly returned home. Once in the house, he slipped the blossoms under his pillow, laid down and went to sleep, refusing thereafter to speak to anyone or to eat anything. His mother became very worried about him. Priests were summoned to put a stop to his decline, but only made things worse. His flesh toughened like hide, and he dropped an alarming amount of weight. Doctors examined him, prescribing medicines that only worked to bring the internal causes of his condition to surface on his skin, and he lay there as if in a trance. His mother caressed him and asked what was causing his condition, but he remained silent, offering no answer.

Right at that time, Wu arrived, so Wang's mother urged him secretly to find out what was going on. Wu went to his cousin's bedside, and Wang's tears fell when he saw him. From the edge of the bed, Wu sought to put him at ease, little by little working toward the source of the problem. Wang revealed the matter and begged Wu to help him plan what to do.

Wu laughed and said, "Your overreaction is ridiculous! What's so tough about fulfilling your desire? I'll go locate her. Since she was out and about on foot in the countryside, she must not be from an influential family. If she's not already betrothed, surely we can come to an agreement; and even if she is, we'll go all out with a heavy bribe and surely that'll settle the matter. But you have to take care of yourself, while I take care of everything else." When Wang heard this, his face relaxed into a smile.

Wu went and informed Wang's mother that the issue was a girl who lived in the vicinity, and though he subsequently searched and inquired thoroughly, he could find no trace of her. The mother was terribly worried, but there was simply nothing else to try to do. However, just after Wu had left to search, Wang's outlook brightened, and he began to eat and move around.

Several days later, Wu came again. Wang asked him how his plan was working. Wu fibbed, "I found her. I was curious who she was, and it turns out she's my aunt's daughter—so she's also your cousin, and she's still waiting to be married. Even though you're closely related and there is resistance to allowing cousins to marry, when we tell her how you feel, surely anything is possible between the two of you."

Wang's happiness spread over his face as he asked, "Where does she live?"

Wu made something up: "In the hills to the southwest, about thirty *li* or so." Wang repeatedly begged him to settle the matter, so Wu vigorously swore he would take care of it and left.

Hence Wang began drinking and eating again, getting better gradually, each day bringing him closer to recovery. When he looked under his pillow, he found the plum blossoms had dried up, though the petals hadn't dropped off. He took pleasure from concentrating while holding them, imagining he could almost see her.

He thought it strange that Wu hadn't come back, so he sent a note inviting him to visit. Wu put him off by claiming that he had a prior invitation to honor. Wang was indignant, and became depressed. His mother was afraid that his illness would return, so she anxiously discussed the possibility of another marriage; this strategy was unproductive as Wang simply shook his head, unwilling to talk about it, and spent his days waiting for Wu.

All the while, Wu sent no report of his efforts, merely increasing Wang's anger. He began thinking about those thirty *li*—that wasn't so far, was it? Why wait for news from someone else? Stowing the plum blossoms inside his sleeve, he went off in a huff by himself, without his family knowing anything about it.

Traveling alone, with no one around to give him directions, Wang nevertheless made a beeline for the

---

Li: A distance equal to 1/3 mile.

southern hills. After covering about thirty *li*, he found himself disoriented, with mountains on all sides, but awed and energized by the landscape's lush greenery, till finally he came across a precipitous path. Looking into the distance, at the bottom of a valley he saw a thicket of flowers and trees, and he could just barely make out a small village nestled there.

Coming down from the mountain, he entered the village, noticing that while there weren't very many huts, each had a thatched roof that was, in Wang's opinion, of sophisticated construction. One hut faced north, with willow trees in front of its gate, while inside its wall, peach and apricot trees were in full blossom, alternating with pruned bamboo; he heard wild birds singing there. Figuring this for a family garden, he didn't dare just barge in.

When he turned to go, opposite the entrance he found a gigantic stone, smooth and clean, so he decided to sit down and take a little rest. Instantly from the other side of the wall he heard a girl calling, "Xiaorong," her voice lovely and delicate. As he sat there listening, he noticed a girl walking back and forth, holding an apricot blossom, who lowered her head to fix it in her hair. When she raised her head and saw Wang, she didn't fasten it with her hairpin, but instead picked up the blossom and ran laughing with it into the garden.

Carefully scrutinizing her, Wang realized it was the girl he'd encountered in the road during the Lantern Festival. His heart was filled with joy. But he couldn't think of a rationale for entering; he longed to cry out his aunt's name, but they'd never been introduced and he feared he might be misconstrued as some swindler. There was no one nearby he could question, either. Restlessly sitting, reclining, and pacing back and forth, he watched until late in the day, waiting expectantly, forgetting both hunger and thirst. From time to time, he spotted the girl's profile when she'd sneak a glance at him, as though surprised that he hadn't left.

Suddenly, an old woman who walked out supporting herself with a stick, turned to look at Wang and asked,

"Where is it you live, since I hear that you got here this morning and you're still here now? What is it you're after? Aren't you feeling hungry?"

Wang nervously stood up and bowed respectfully, replying, "I'm here to look for my relatives."

The old woman, who was rather deaf, didn't hear him. He repeated his words more loudly. Then she asked, "What's their family name?" Wang was stuck for an answer. The old woman laughed, "That's pretty strange! If you don't know their family name, how can you hope to find these relatives? By looking at you, I'd guess you're a bookworm, too. Come on, follow me in—you can eat a little something and there's a modest bed you can sleep in. Tomorrow you can head home, find out the family name, and then come back here."

Wang's stomach rumbled at the thought of eating, and besides, accepting would bring him closer to the beauty, so he gladly agreed. Following the old woman inside the gate, he saw a walkway paved with white stones and lined by red flowers whose petals had fallen across the path's steps; winding to the west, they came to another entryway, where bean trellises and flower frames filled a courtyard.

Wang respectfully entered the hut, with its flour-white walls as bright as mirrors; outside the window, a great many wild plum branches were in flower, some of them extending into the room; the mats, stools, and bed were all clean and fresh. As soon as Wang sat down, he felt that there was someone outside the window spying on him.

The old woman called out, "Xiaorong! Go fix some millet quickly." From outside, the maid answered in a high voice. As he sat there, Wang laid out the details of his family tree. The old woman asked him, "Was your mother's grandfather by any chance named Wu?"

He replied, "He was, indeed."

Amazed, the old woman declared, "You're my nephew! Your mother is my younger sister. For years now, our family has been poor, and since we also have no son, we lost all contact with your family. Nephew, you're all grown up, yet we've never met for me to get to know you."

"I came here to find my aunt," said Wang. "In all my anxiety, I forgot your name."

The old woman explained, "My family name is Qin, but I never gave birth to a child; my adopted daughter, Yingning, was the daughter of a concubine. When her mother remarried, she was left behind for me to raise. While she's certainly no simpleton, she's received little proper teaching, so she's always having fun and never worrying about anything. In just a bit, I'll send for her to come and meet you."

Not much later, the maid served a meal of tender chicken, with plenty to accompany it. The old woman encouraged Wang to eat his fill, and afterwards the maid cleared away the dishes. The old woman instructed her, "Tell your mistress, Ning, to come here." The maid answered affirmatively and left to do so.

After a good long while, they heard the sound of muffled laughter outside the door. The old woman called out, "Yingning, your cousin's here." The giggling and laughter outside the door didn't stop. The maid pushed her into the room, Yingning still covering her mouth since she couldn't stop her laughter.

The old woman gave her a stern look and said, "We have a guest here; is this any way to behave, with derisive snickering?" The girl restrained her laughter and stood still while Wang bowed respectfully to her. The old woman explained, "This is Master Wang, your aunt's son. We're part of the same family, yet we've never met each other—now *that's* enough to make a person laugh."

Wang asked, "How old is my cousin?" The old woman didn't catch his question. Wang voiced it a second time. The girl started laughing again so hard that she couldn't even raise her head up.

The old woman said to Wang, "I told you she's had little by way of teachings and admonitions, as you can readily see. She's sixteen years old and as foolish in judgment as a baby."

Wang noted, "One year younger than I am."

She replied, "If you're seventeen, weren't you born in the Year of the Horse?" Wang nodded in response.

She asked again, "Who is your wife?"

"There isn't one," he answered.

"Someone with your talent and looks," she said, "how can you be seventeen and still unmarried? Yingning isn't betrothed yet either, and the two of you would be well matched; it's a pity that your being close relatives makes it unlikely." Wang was speechless, not taking his eyes off Yingning even to blink.

The maid turned to the girl and whispered, "His eyes are still blazing—the thief hasn't changed his tune!"

Yingning burst into laughter again, turned to the maid and said, "Shouldn't we check to see if the peach blossoms have opened?" She quickly got up, covering her mouth with her sleeve, and with tiny, quick steps, hurried away. Once she was outside the gate, she let loose her laughter.

The old woman also got up and called for the maid to prepare a bed so Wang could spend the night. She told him, "It wasn't easy for you to get here, so it's only right you should stay for a few days and relax, then we'll send you home. If you grow tired or bored with the quiet, there's a garden behind the hut, with various ways there for you to pass the time; or there are books you can read."

The next day, Wang went out behind the hut and found a garden there about half a *mu* in size, along with a ground cover of grass as soft as felt, plus tree blossoms and catkins; there were three thatched huts in a row, with flowers and trees on all sides of each. As he walked through the flowers, he heard a rustling sound from a treetop, and glancing up, he saw Yingning there. When she saw Wang appear, she laughed so hard she almost fell down.

Wang cried, "Don't do that, you'll fall!"

The girl climbed down, laughing all the way, unable

Mu: A measure of size equal to .0667 hectare, or 1/6 acre.

to stop herself. Just as she was about to reach the ground, she almost lost hold and fell down, her laughter finally coming to a halt.

Wang helped her up, taking advantage of the moment to fondle her wrist. This started Yingning laughing again until she had to lean against a tree for support, unable to go on, and it was a good long while before she could stop. Wang waited for her to finish laughing, then took the plum blossoms from his sleeve to show her.

Yingning accepted them from him and exclaimed, "They're all dried up. Why keep them?"

He answered, "During the Lantern Festival, cousin, you left them behind—that's why I've kept them."

"If they're not fresh, what's the point?" she asked.

Wang explained, "To show my love, and that I'd never forget you. Since we first met, I've thought about you so much that I became ill, and it caused so much turmoil inside me that I almost died, faced with the possibility of never seeing your face again; I hope you'll take pity on me."

"It's no big deal," Yingning said. "For a relative, what price is too great to pay? When the time comes for you to go, I'll call on an old servant to pick a big bunch of flowers from the garden so you can take them with you."

"Are you crazy?" Wang demanded.

She asked, "What's crazy about that?"

Wang explained, "It's not the flowers I care about, but the person who was holding them."

"Naturally, since relatives love each other," said Yingning.

Wang said, "I'm not talking about the love between relatives, but between a husband and wife."

"There's a difference?" Yingning wondered.

"At night, they sleep together," he explained.

Yingning bowed her head and thought about this for a very long time before remarking, "I'm not accustomed to sleeping with strangers." Before her words were finished, the maid quietly appeared and Wang fled in embarrassment.

A little later, they met back at the old woman's place.

She asked them, "Where'd you go?" Yingning replied that they'd been in the garden, talking together. The old woman said, "The meal's been ready for a long time—you spoke to each other for so long, there must have been plenty to cover."

Yingning said, "Elder brother wants to sleep with me."

She'd barely spoken the words when Wang, horribly embarrassed, anxiously gave her a silencing glance. Yingning giggled and said no more. Fortunately, the old woman hadn't heard, so she kept on chattering, pursuing her questions.

Wang swiftly spoke up to gloss over the comment, then whispered a rebuke to Yingning. She asked, "Isn't it proper I should mention it?"

Wang told her, "It's the kind of thing you only say behind a person's back."

"Behind someone else's back, maybe," said Yingning, "but surely not behind my aged mother's back. Everybody has to sleep somewhere, that's always the case—so what's there to avoid?" Wang was frustrated with her naïveté, since he was unable with his attempts to make her understand. Just as they finished eating, a member of Wang's household arrived with a pair of donkeys, searching for him.

Apparently, when Wang didn't come home after a long time, his mother had become worried; a search party hunted for him repeatedly in the village, failing to turn up the slightest trace of him. Hence she went to consult Wu. Wu recalled the words he'd spoken to Wang, and directed her to search for him in the hills southwest of the village. The servant looking for him had gone to several villages before coming to this place. Wang had walked outside the gate just as he happened past, so he went back inside to tell the old woman and to beg her to let him take Yingning home with him.

The old woman gleefully said, "I've desired this myself, for some time. But my decrepit old body can't make such a journey, so if you'll take your cousin to meet her aunt, that will be splendid!" She called for Yingning.

Ning came in, laughing. The old woman demanded, "What's so funny that you can't stop laughing all the time? If you weren't always laughing, you'd be a perfectly proper person." Because she was angry, she glared at Yingning. Then she said, "Elder brother wants to take you home with him, so hurry and get your things packed."

Meanwhile, she offered Wang's servant some wine and food, then walking them out later, she told Yingning, "Your aunt's family owns a great deal of land and goods, so they can afford to support an extra person. You should stay with them rather than returning home, learn a bit of poetry and proper conduct, and also practice caring for your future in-laws. Also plead with your aunt to help you select a good husband."

Wang and Yingning then started off. Once they got to the foot of the mountain, they turned around and could just barely see the old woman leaning on the gate, looking northward in their direction.

When they arrived at Wang's home, his mother was astounded at the beautiful girl accompanying him, and asked who she was. Wang answered that she was his aunt's daughter. His mother said, "What Wu told you before was all a fabrication. I don't have a sister, so how can I have a niece?"

She asked this of Yingning, who replied, "I'm not my mother's child by birth. My father belonged to the Qin family, but he died when I was still a baby in swaddling clothes, so I can't recall the details."

Wang's mother said, "My elder sister did marry into the Qin family, but she was barren; she died a long time ago, so how could she have come back to life?"

Hence she carefully interrogated Yingning about the features of her sister's face, and the location of moles, and one by one they matched exactly. Still suspicious, she stated, "That's all well and good. But she died many years ago, so how can she be alive now?" Just as she was mulling over her doubts, Wu arrived, and Yingning slipped away to her room.

Wu requested all the details and became very quiet for some time. Suddenly he asked, "This girl—is her name

Yingning?" Wang affirmed it was. Wu earnestly noted that this was a strange business. Asked how he knew her name, Wu replied, "After my aunt, who joined the Qin family through marriage, died, uncle lived as a widower in his house until he was seduced by a fox, grew ill, and died. The fox gave birth to a daughter named Yingning, who was wrapped up and laid on a bed, as witnessed by every member of the family. After uncle died, the fox still kept coming around; after we requested that a Daoist charm be pasted up on the wall, the fox took her child and left. Couldn't this be the daughter?" They mutually discussed their suspicions.

But from inside her room, they could hear the sound of Yingning's chortling laughter. Wang's mother remarked, "That girl is just too silly."

Wu asked to meet her. Wang's mother entered her room, where Yingning was still roaring in laughter and didn't even notice her at first. Wang's mother urged her to go out to see Wu, so she used every bit of her strength to resist laughing, turning her face to the wall several times, and then finally came out.

As soon as she finished greeting the others respectfully, she quickly ran back inside and let loose a hearty guffaw. All the women in the house joined in her laughter. Wu suggested that he go and discreetly investigate the mystery surrounding Yingning, in order to make arrangements for the marriage.

By the time he arrived at the village, the huts and everything else had disappeared, with only the fallen petals of the mountain flowers remaining. Wu remembered that the place where his aunt had been buried was not far away. However, the grave had become entirely overgrown, making it impossible to determine precisely where it was located, so with a sigh of frustration, he went back.

Wang's mother was convinced that Yingning was a ghost. She went in and informed her of Wu's report, but Yingning wasn't the least bit startled; Wang's mother sympathized with her for having no family, but not only did Yingning show no sign of sorrow, she kept on laughing naively. No one there could make sense of it.

Wang's mother arranged for Yingning to share sleeping quarters with her youngest daughter. Each morning at daybreak, Yingning dutifully paid her respects to Wang's mother, and the exquisite precision of her needlework was unsurpassed. But even when it was forbidden, her friendly laughter couldn't be stopped; and there was a charming quality to it, so even when it was wildly uninhibited, her laughter didn't damage her attractiveness, and it made everyone else feel good. Both the girls and the women in the neighborhood competed for opportunities to welcome her.

Wang's mother chose an auspicious day for the wedding, but she still fretted that Yingning might be some kind of evil spirit. She covertly spied on her in the daylight, but she didn't see anything unusual in the shape of her shadow.

When the wedding day arrived, they had her magnificently dressed for the marriage ritual; but Yingning was laughing so hard that she was unable to kneel properly, so they gave up that part of the ceremony. Because of all her foolishness, Wang feared she might divulge the details of their sexual intimacy; but Yingning was especially careful, and didn't give anything away with her words.

Whenever Wang's mother became worried or angry, Yingning would appear, and even a single laugh would make her feel better. If the servants or maids ever went a little too far and feared they might suffer a whipping for their actions, they'd beg Yingning to visit Wang's mother and speak on their behalf; the guilty maids who trusted themselves to her mediation were usually excused.

But she had a persistent craving for flowers, searching high and low for them, from relatives and friends; she even pawned a gold hairpin to purchase the seeds for especially beautiful varieties, until after several months there wasn't a stair, pathway, fence, or outhouse that wasn't surrounded by flowers.

In the rear of the courtyard, there was a trellis of banksia roses that had been planted by the family of the neighbor to the west. Yingning often climbed up it to pick some flowers to wear in her hair for fun. Wang's mother would scold her whenever she saw her doing so. Yingning, however, would never change her ways.

One day, the neighbor's son saw her and couldn't take his eyes off her, he was so smitten by her beauty. Yingning didn't try to avoid him, but just laughed. The neighbor's son thought she was making herself available to him, so his heart filled with desire. Yingning pointed to a place at the base of the wall, laughed, and then climbed down, while the neighbor's son, thinking she was proposing a rendezvous there, was deliriously happy.

Once night fell, he went to the spot, and Yingning was already waiting there. He pulled her close and thrust himself into her, but felt something like an awl stab his privates with a pain that penetrated to his very heart, and after screaming madly, he stumbled and fell. On closer examination, he saw that it wasn't Yingning, but a rotten log leaning against the wall, and the place he'd thrust into was a soggy knothole.

When his father next door heard him yell, he hurriedly rushed over to find out what had happened, but his son merely groaned and wouldn't say anything. Once the man's wife appeared, however, the son told them everything. When they lit a torch and examined the knothole, they saw that inside it was a huge scorpion, the size of a small crab. The old man split the log open, then caught and killed the scorpion. He hoisted his son onto his back and carried him home, where he died in the middle of the night.

The neighbor brought a suit against Wang, alleging that Yingning was a demon spirit. The county magistrate, who thought of Wang as an admirable man of talent and knew he was a scholar of sincere and honest intentions, determined that the old neighbor was making a false accusation, and was about to have him beaten as punishment. Wang interceded to have the sentence dropped, so the matter was cleared up and the neighbor released.

Wang's mother told Yingning, "This idiocy has gone

far enough, and I knew that this excessive frivolity was covering up something worth worrying about. It's lucky for you that the magistrate didn't implicate you; if he'd been a muddle-headed official, you'd certainly have been arrested and tried in court—how could my son and I face our relatives and neighbors then?"

Yingning wore a serious expression and swore she'd never laugh again. Wang's mother said, "People don't have to stop laughing, but they mustn't do it all the time." But because of all this, Yingning never laughed again, and even if she was teased, she still wouldn't laugh; but she also never, ever looked sad.

One night, Yingning's face was streaked with tears. Wang found this very strange. "In the past," she said, choking back sobs, "because we'd only been together a short while, I was afraid you'd be shocked if I told you something. Now that I see how much you and your mother have gone through for me without resentment or suspicion, being frank with you can't possibly harm our relationship, can it? The concubine who gave birth to me was a fox. When my mother was about to go away, she left me to be raised by the ghost of my father's wife, and we've depended upon each other for more than ten years, which is why I've come to you now. I have no brothers, so I can depend upon no one but you.

"My old mother lies alone in the mountains, with no one to pity her or to bury her properly, so she wanders the underworld in grief and sorrow. If the trouble and expense wouldn't be too great for you, you could take away the pain of someone's suffering down below and also make the point that adopted daughters are not useless, and shouldn't be drowned or abandoned." Wang promised he would take care of it, but he was concerned that the grave might be so obscured by undergrowth that they couldn't find it. Yingning assured him he didn't need to worry.

On the designated day, they set out with a cart and a coffin. Yingning directed them to a desolate spot in the mists and tangled growth, pointed to show them the gravesite, and indeed they found the old woman's corpse, her leathery skin still intact. Yingning caressed the body, weeping piteously from the pain of her grieving. They carried the body away, sought for and located the family graves, and buried her there.

That night, Wang dreamt that the old woman came to thank him, and when he woke up, he told Yingning. She informed him, "I saw her last night, but she insisted that I not bother you." Wang was sorry that she hadn't been invited to stay. Yingning replied, "She's a ghost. There are so many mortals here that the *yang* force is overwhelming, so how could she stay here for long?"

Wang asked her about Xiaorong, and she explained, "She's also a fox, and exceedingly crafty. My fox mother asked her to look after me, and she always gave me cakes and other treats, so I owe her a lot and always think about her. Yesterday I asked mother about her, and she said Xiaorong is already married."

Every year on the day of the Cold Food Festival, husband and wife would visit the Qin family graves, paying their respects and sweeping them clean. When a year had passed, Yingning gave birth to a son. Even while he was still a baby in his mother's arms, he was never afraid of strangers, and laughed at every person he saw, much like his unpredictable mother.

The collector of these strange tales remarks, "Observing her endlessly silly laughter, it seemed like she was no great prize; and it would be hard to come up with something more cunning than the nasty trick at the base of the wall. But considering the pity and love shown her ghostly mother, that turned her laughter into weeping, I believe her laughter nearly covered up the real Yingning. I've heard that in the mountains there is an herb called

---

Yang force: *Yang* is the male essence, just as *yin* is the female essence.
Cold Food Festival: The 105th to 107th day after the winter solstice, "a period set aside in memory of Chieh Tsu-tuei," when food "is supposed to be eaten cold" (*Far East Dictionary* 366).

'Xiaoyihu.' One sniff of it and you can't stop laughing. If some of this was grown in a home, then neither silk trees nor day lilies could match it for appeal. Even the 'flower that understands words' is only a pretender compared to Xiaoyihu."

'Xiaoyihu': Literally, "laugh and shout."
'Flower that understands words': Tang Emperor Xuanzhong (reigned 712-56) called his concubine, Yang Yuhuan, his "flower that understands words."

49. Nie Xiaoqian

Ning Caichen was from Zhejiang. Generous and open-hearted by nature, he comported himself scrupulously. He was always telling people, "In my life, there's no woman for me but my wife." Traveling to Jinhua one time, he arrived just north of the city and stopped to rest in a Buddhist monastery. The temple's halls and pagodas were quite splendid; however, the grounds were covered by weeds and thistles, there was no one around, and furthermore, there were no signs that anyone had walked through there. On the east and west sides of the monks' housing, there were pairs of doors casually closed; yet the door of the small hut on the south side had been secured with a new lock.

When he turned to look into the east corner of the hall, he noticed a dense stand of bamboo; down some steps from it, there was an enormous pool filled with wild flowering lotuses. He felt very happy about the quiet and seclusion of the place. Since scholars were assembling to take the imperial examination in town, the price of lodgings there had skyrocketed, so he thought it might be better to stay at the monastery, and he took a walk while waiting for the monks to return.

At the end of the day, there was a scholar who arrived and opened the locked southern door. Ning immediately greeted him courteously and informed him of his decision to stay. The scholar replied, "The place has no master, so I'm staying here as a visitor, too. If you can stand the place being overgrown and dilapidated, it would be my very good fortune to learn from you during

223

your stay." Ning was delighted and proceeded to use some straw to make himself a bed, also setting up a board to serve as a small table, since he planned to be there for some time.

That night, the moon was shining high and bright, its light as clear as water, as the two men sat on the verandah of the hall and spoke like close friends, revealing their family names to each other. The scholar reported, "My family name is Yan, my courtesy name, Chixia." Ning figured that he must have come to take the imperial examination, but as he listened to Yan's accent, he realized he couldn't be from Zhejiang.

He asked about this, and Yan replied, "I'm from Shaanxi." His words were quite frank and sincere. Once they no longer had anything else to discuss together, they bowed to each other and parted company to go to bed.

Since Ning was in an unfamiliar place, for a long time he couldn't fall asleep. He began to hear the sound of low voices north of where he was staying, like there was a family there. He got up and hid himself just below a stone-lined window on the north side of his room, spying out from his place of concealment.

He saw a courtyard outside a short wall, where there was a woman in her forties; with her was an old woman, hunchbacked and frail, wearing a gown that had once been dark red, but was now quite worn and faded, the two conversing together by the light of the moon. The woman asked, "What's taking Xiaoqian so long to arrive?"

The old woman answered, "She must be almost here."

"She hasn't been complaining to you, has she, granny?" the first woman asked.

"Not that I've heard," the other replied, "though she looked like she was upset."

The younger woman remarked, "That girl doesn't appreciate what she has now." The words were hardly out of her mouth before a seventeen- or eighteen-year-old girl showed up, a peerless beauty.

The old woman laughed and noted, "One shouldn't

talk about a person behind her back—we two were doing just that when you, you little goblin, quietly sneaked up on us without making a sound. Fortunately, we weren't saying anything mean about you." She added, "Young lady, you're so lovely, you're like a beauty from a painting, and if I were a young man, you'd have attracted and stolen my very soul."

The girl replied, "Granny, if you don't praise me, who else is going to?" The woman and the girl then exchanged words that Ning couldn't make out. Thinking that they must be members of his neighbor's family, he decided to go to sleep without turning back to listen further.

Time passed and there were no more sounds. Just as he was about to drift off to sleep, he sensed that someone had entered his room. He hurriedly got up to investigate, and discovered it was the girl from the courtyard on the north side. Surprised, he asked her what she was doing there.

Laughing, the girl told him, "With the moon so bright tonight, I can't sleep, so I want to make love to you."

Ning solemnly declared, "You should protect yourself against public censure, for I'm afraid of what people might say; lose your footing even just once, and you'll end up living in shame."

The girl insisted, "It's late at night, so no one will know."

Ning loudly scolded her again. The girl backed away, then returned as if she had more to say. Ning cried, "Leave me alone! If you don't, I'll call and tell the gentleman in the south room." The girl, frightened, quickly retreated. Once she was outside the door, however, she turned around and came back, placing an ingot of gold on his straw bed.

Ning picked up the gold and threw it out into the courtyard, saying, "This filthy thing would defile my moneybag!"

The girl left, ashamed, picking up the gold and commenting, "This man is as unmovable as stone."

At daybreak, a scholar from Lanxi arrived with his servant to wait to take the examination, setting up quarters in the temple's east side, and that same night he died suddenly. On the sole of his foot there was a small hole, as if it had been pierced by an awl, a tiny bit of blood seeping from it. No one there knew what to make of it.

The next night, the servant also died, his symptoms the same as the scholar's. Later that night, when Yan returned, Ning asked him about it, and Yan thought that evil spirits were responsible. Ning had always stood for the right, so this didn't faze him.

At midnight, the girl came back to see him, saying, "I've encountered many men, but none of them as uncompromising as you. You're truly a sage, so I don't dare deceive you. I'm Xiaoqian, my family name is Nie—I died when I was only eighteen, and was buried beside this monastery, where I'm constantly coerced by demons to carry out their foul demands. It's actually not my own will to turn to people and seduce them. Now that there's no one left in the monastery to be killed, I'm afraid the evil spirits will come to destroy you."

Horrified, Ning begged her to help him find a solution. The girl declared, "If you stay in Yan's room, you can escape them."

He asked, "Why can't they attack Yan?"

"He's one of those rare people," she explained, "whom they don't dare approach."

Then Ning inquired, "What do you do to the men who become infatuated with you?"

"While he makes love to me," Xiaoqian replied, "I secretly drill a hole in the sole of his foot, and then when he loses consciousness, I extract his blood for the demons to drink; sometimes I use gold—which isn't really gold, but the bones of a *luosha* demon—and anyone who kept it would have his heart and liver cut out: these two tactics ordinarily work on everyone."

Luosha demon: Transliteration of a Buddhist term (Zhu 165n25); on the Chinese conception of demons and spirits, particularly as expressed in the first century C.E. writings of Wang Chong, see Bonnefoy (254-55).

Ning was grateful for the information. He asked when he should prepare himself for their coming, and she told him they would come the following night. As she was about to leave, Xiaoqian began weeping and exclaimed, "I'm sinking into a bottomless sea, grasping for land where there isn't any. Your righteous spirit towers above the clouds, so surely you can find a way to rescue me from my torments. If you're willing to do this, collect my bones and then bury them in a quiet place—you'd be giving me more than a second life."

Ning pledged to do so for her. When he asked where she was buried, she replied, "Just remember that you'll find me at the base of a white willow where there's a crow's nest." With these words, she walked out the door and mysteriously vanished.

The next day, fearing that Yan might go somewhere, first thing in the morning Ning paid a visit to invite him over. By just after 9:00, he'd prepared them wine and food, and he carefully scrutinized Yan as they ate. Afterwards, he suggested that he stay in Yan's room that night, but Yan declined, explaining that he was unfit for company and was used to being alone. Ning wouldn't hear of it and peremptorily carried his bedding over to Yan's quarters.

Since Yan couldn't get him to stop, he moved his bed over to make room, advising him, "I know you are a moral man, and I respect your innate goodness. I have some important things on my mind, and I'm not in a position to divulge them just now. Please don't poke around and peek into my chest or clothing, for we'll both suffer if you disobey my request." Ning sincerely swore to honor Yan's words.

Then they both went to bed, Yan placing his chest on the window sill, and the moment he laid his head to rest, he began to snore like rolling thunder. Ning, however, was unable to get to sleep.

Near midnight, he saw the shadow of some indistinct figure outside the window. Immediately it came near the window and peered inside, its eyes flashing with light. Ning was terrified, but just as he was about to cry out for Yan, suddenly something dazzlingly bright like white silk split open the chest and burst out, broke through the stone surrounding the window, and shot out, then quickly reentered the chest like a bolt of lightning.

Yan sensed this and got up, while Ning pretended to be asleep, in order to observe him secretly: Yan picked up his chest to examine it, drew something out, then in the moonlight sniffed and inspected it as it gave off a lustrously bright white light, a thing two inches long and about as narrow as a chive leaf. When he was finished, he wrapped it thoroughly in several layers, and put it back inside the now-damaged chest. He said to himself, "What a thing that old demon is—coming here like that took some nerve, and now it's ruined my chest." Then he lay back down to sleep.

Ning was astonished, so he got up to ask Yan about it, telling him everything he'd seen occur. Yan stated, "Since we've come to know each other pretty well, I can risk sharing the secret with you. I am a swordsman. If not for the stone around the window, the evil spirit would have been killed instantly; though it was certainly wounded."

Ning asked, "What is that thing you keep sealed up?"

"My sword," Yan replied. "When I sniffed it, there was the scent of demon on it." Ning wanted to have a look at it. Yan generously took it out to show him, revealing a tiny, luminous sword. From that time forward, Ning's respect for Yan was considerably increased.

The next day, he looked outside the window and found traces of blood there. Then he walked around to the north side of the monastery, where he found countless overgrown graves, and sure enough there was a white willow with a crow's nest at its top.

Once he'd discovered the object of his search, he hurriedly gathered his things, since he wanted to go home. Yan set up a farewell dinner for him to show his great respect for Ning's upright nature. Afterwards, he offered Ning a worn leather bag as a present, explaining, "This is a sword bag. If you keep this close, no evil spirits will be able to come near you."

Ning wanted Yan to instruct him in his art of the

sword. The swordsman told him, "A faithful person like you, outspoken and upright, would certainly be able to practice this art. But you're a gentleman of wealth and rank, so this is not the path for you."

Ning then provided a pretext for his subsequent actions by saying that he had a younger sister buried there—so he dug up Xiaoqian's bones, wrapped them up in a winding-sheet, hired a boat, and left for home.

Ning's study overlooked the open country, so he set up a tomb there and buried Xiaoqian's remains outside his study. He spoke this benediction there: "I felt pity for you, lonely spirit, so I've buried you near my home, where we can hear each other, whether singing or weeping, and your grave will no longer be troubled by powerful demons. Here's a bowl of wine to drink, and though it's neither refined or delicious, I hope you won't dislike it!"

Finished expressing his benevolent wishes, Ning turned to go home. From behind him, a person cried out, "Slow down and wait for me to catch up!" When he turned around to look, he saw it was Xiaoqian, laughing merrily and thanking him, saying, "You're true to your word, and if I were to die for you ten times, it wouldn't be enough to repay you. Please let me accompany you home, so I can pay my respects to your mother and father; even if you make me your servant, I won't regret it."

Examining her carefully, he noted her skin was like a mirror of rosy clouds drifting overhead, her feet like tender bamboo shoots, and as they stood together later in the daylight, he found her even more extraordinarily lovely. Consequently, they went back to Ning's study. Urging Xiaoqian to sit there and wait a bit, Ning first went in to inform his mother. She was stunned at the news. For a long time, Ning's wife had been ill, so his mother warned him not to say anything to her, for fear that the news might worsen her condition.

As they were discussing this, Xiaoqian lightly swept into the room and prostrated herself on the ground, to show her respect. Ning said, "This is Xiaoqian." His mother was alarmed, not daring to look at her.

The girl said to her, "I was drifting all alone, far from

parents and brothers. Young master Ning rescued me when I was exposed to horrible influences, and to express my gratitude even superficially for the aid he's given me, I'd be glad to serve him with dishpan and broom to repay his great kindness."

Ning's mother, seeing that she was both prudent and lovely, felt emboldened to speak with her and said, "Young lady, I appreciate your offer to look after my son, as my old body just isn't up to it. But he's my only son and I need him to carry on the family line, so I dare not let him take a ghost wife."

"Truly, I could never be disloyal to him," Xiaoqian replied. "Though you're worried about the honesty of a person from the underworld, please let me stay with you, his mother, and consider him my elder brother, treating you like my own parents, serving you from dawn till dusk—how would that be?" Ning's mother, sympathetic due to her sincerity, allowed her to stay.

Xiaoqian wanted to pay her respects to her sister-in-law. Ning's mother rejected the idea, due to the illness of Ning's wife, so nothing came of it. Xiaoqian then went into the kitchen where she took the mother's place and prepared a meal. She entered rooms and located beds like she was familiar with all of them.

At the end of the day, Ning's mother, still fearful of Xiaoqian, said goodnight and sent her home to sleep rather than setting up a bed for her. Xiaoqian understood what Ning's mother was feeling, so she finally left. Passing Ning's study, she wanted to enter, but instead backed away and began pacing back and forth outside his door, as though scared of something.

Ning called out to her. She answered, "There's a sword presence in your room that frightens me. It's in the way, so that's why I can't come in and see you." Ning realized that the leather bag was the problem, so he grabbed it and hung it up in a different room. Xiaoqian then came in and sat down near his candle. For some time, she was utterly silent.

After a long while, she asked him, "Do you read at night or not? When I was little, I used to recite the

Surangama sutra, but now I've forgotten more than half of it. If you'd let me borrow a copy, at your leisure in the evenings, you could help me to get it right again." Ning agreed to do so. Once again, they sat in silence until the second watch had passed, not speaking of her leaving.

Finally, Ning urged her to go. Turning pale, she exclaimed, "It's a strange land that a lonely spirit inhabits—a desolate grave is awfully frightening."

Ning remarked, "There's no other bed in my study for you to sleep on, and besides, even brothers and sisters should keep their distance, to avoid suspicion."

Xiaoqian stood up, her brows furrowing into a sorrowful look, as though she were about to start crying; dragging her feet and moving sluggishly as she slowly walked out the gate, she made her way to the steps and disappeared. Ning privately pitied her and wished he could let her stay the night on another bed, but he feared this would anger his mother.

Each dawn, Xiaoqian appeared to Ning's mother, bringing a basin for her to wash in, then turned to managing other activities in the household, never failing to carry out the mother's will. At dusk, she'd announce her intention to retire, then walk over to Ning's study, where by candlelight she'd recite from the sutra. Once she could tell that Ning was ready to go to bed, she would leave, miserable once again.

Before all this, when Ning's wife first fell ill, Ning's mother became fatigued, unable to handle the load; the arrival of Xiaoqian was a great relief to her, and in her heart she esteemed the girl. As she became more familiar with her day by day, she came to love Xiaoqian like she was her own child, forgetting meanwhile that she was a ghost; she couldn't bear to send her away at night any longer, so she invited her to stay and sleep in her room.

Surangama sutra: In Mandarin, the *lengyanjing*. For an online translation, see http://www.buddhanet.net/pdf_file/surangama.pdf.

The second watch: The second of five two-hour periods in the night (approximately 9:00-11:00 p.m.).

When she first arrived, Xiaoqian never ate or drank, but after half a year, she began to sip a bit of congee. Mother and son were extremely fond of her, and they treated as off limits the subject of her being a ghost, since no one else could tell it by looking at her.

It wasn't long before Ning's wife died. His mother secretly wanted to accept Xiaoqian as his wife, but she was afraid that no good would come to her son from it. Xiaoqian, sensing this, took the opportunity to inform Ning's mother, "Since I've been living with you for more than a year, you should know what's going on inside me. I didn't want to continue bringing disaster to travelers, hence I followed the young master here. I had nothing else in mind, for the young master is straightforward and upright, someone upon whom both heaven and mortals look with respect, so my honest desire was to follow and to support him for three years or so, hoping thereby to win myself some kind of recognition that would confer honor in the world of the dead."

Ning's mother knew Xiaoqian wasn't evil, yet she dreaded not being able to extend her family's line. The girl declared, "Only heaven can grant us children. The young master's listing in the *Registry of Fate* says he will have three notable sons, and his taking a ghost wife will not change that."

Ning's mother believed her, so she discussed the possibility with her son. Ning was elated and arranged for a feast where he could inform his relatives of the news. Someone there asked to meet his new wife—Xiaoqian gladly consented, and came out in a splendid trousseau while everyone stared in astonishment, not because they thought she was a ghost, but because they thought she might be a goddess. Hence the family's female relatives all presented her with congratulatory gifts, competing with each other to make an impression on Xiaoqian so she'd remember them.

Xiaoqian was a talented painter of orchids and plum blossoms, so she returned the favor by making small paintings about a *chi* in size, and those who were given them, feeling greatly honored, kept them as treasures.

One day, sitting with her head bowed in front of a window, Xiaoqian seemed worried and depressed. Suddenly she asked Ning, "Where's that leather bag?"

He explained, "Since you were afraid of it, I folded it up and put it away somewhere else."

"I've been breathing again with life for quite a while now," she said, "and I won't be afraid of it any more so ,you should get it and hang it up at the head of our bed." Ning asked her why she wanted him to do so, and she replied, "For the past three days, I've been continuously nervous and apprehensive because the demons at Jinhua monastery hate me for having escaped, and I'm afraid day and night that one of them is going to come looking to get me."

Ning consequently brought the leather bag out to her. Xiaoqian turned it over repeatedly, examining it very carefully, and then said, "This is what the sword god used to hold the heads of his victims. It looks worn out and tattered, so imagine how many murders it's responsible for! Just looking at it now makes my flesh crawl." So they hung it up.

The next day, Xiaoqian directed Ning to move it and hang it on their door. That night, they sat near the candle, and Xiaoqian made sure that Ning wouldn't fall asleep. Suddenly something appeared, like a bird falling out of the sky. Xiaoqian was so terrified, she hid herself behind a curtain.

Ning got a good look and the thing appeared to be a yaksha, with lightning in its eyes and a bloody tongue—flashing and slashing, it roared up to the front of the house. When it got to the door, it stepped back a pace; hesitating for a long time, it finally came close to

About a chi in size: One *chi* is equal to 1/3 of a meter.
Yaksha: In Buddhism, these nature spirits are sometimes portrayed as malevolent creatures that devour their victims. See story #100, in volume two, "The Yaksha Kingdom."

the leather bag and snatched it like someone plucking a melon, as though it was about to rip it apart. The bag suddenly made a loud noise, and became as large as a pair of baskets combined; like something from a dream, there was a monster that leapt halfway out of the bag, grabbed the yaksha, and pulled it inside, replacing noise with silence, while the bag instantly shrank back to its normal size. Ning was quite shocked.

Xiaoqian came out, overjoyed, exclaiming, "The plague is over!" Together they looked inside the bag, finding nothing more than a large quantity of clear water.

Several years later, Ning succeeded in passing the imperial examination as a *jinshi*. Xiaoqian gave birth to a son. Afterwards, Ning added a concubine to his family, who along with Xiaoqian gave birth to two more sons, and all three brothers became influential officials with good reputations.

Jinshi: A successful candidate in the highest level of the imperial civil service examination.

50. The Faithful Mouse

Yang Tianyi claims that he was watching two mice come out of the ground when one of them was swallowed by a snake; the other one's eyes blazed like red-hot peppers, it was so enraged, but it could only look on from afar, rather than approach. The snake's belly was stuffed, so it began slithering into its den; but just as it was about halfway in, the other mouse rushed at it and bit the snake's tail with all its might.

The snake, furious, withdrew its body and came back out. The mouse, because it was just plain fast, swiftly scampered away. The snake chased after it, but couldn't catch it, gave up, and returned. Just as it entered its den again, the mouse reappeared, biting the snake just as it had before. The snake went in and out, back and forth, for quite some time.

At long last the snake reemerged and vomited the dead mouse out onto the ground. The other mouse went over and sniffed at it, squeaking like it was grieving, then picked the first mouse up with its mouth and carried it away. My friend, Zhang Liyou, composed a poem about this that he calls, "The Conduct of the Faithful Mouse."

Zhang Liyou: For more on Pu's friend, see Zhu (167n6).

51. An Earthquake

In the seventh year of the reign of Emperor Kangxi, on the seventeenth day of the sixth lunar month, between seven o'clock and nine o'clock at night, there was a tremendous earthquake. I was visiting in Jixia, and just then I was with one of my first cousins, Li Duzhi, drinking by candlelight.

Suddenly, we heard a sound like thunder rolling in from the southeast and heading northwest. Everyone was surprised, unable to identify what was making the noise. An instant later, the table started fluttering and our wine cups toppled over; the room's beams, rafters, and posts made sounds like they were going to split. We looked at each other and went pale.

After some time, we realized it was an earthquake, so we quickly hurried outdoors. We could see that houses, pavilions, and such had been shaken, and were now stabilizing; but there were the sounds of walls collapsing and rooms caving in, of children crying and women wailing, the noise boiling up like a huge cauldron. People were so dizzy that they couldn't stand up, so they just fell to the ground while the earth contorted beneath them. The river's waters shot up a *zhang* over my head, to the accompaniment of squawking ducks and barking dogs.

When about an hour had passed, things began to

Seventh year . . . Kangxi: Kangxi reigned 1661-1722, hence the earthquake would be dated 1668.
A zhang: A distance equal to about 3.3 meters.

settle down a bit. We noticed that naked men and women had gathered in the street, talking agitatedly to each other, completely forgetting that they had no clothes on.

Later on, I heard that the walls of a particular well had fallen in, so water couldn't be drawn from it; that a certain family's pavilion, previously facing south, had shifted to face the north; that Qixia Mountain had been torn open; and that the Yi River had drained into an enormous fissure several *mu* across. This was a genuinely extraordinary and rare occurrence.

In my town, there was a man whose wife got up to urinate one night, and when she was walking back, she came upon a wolf holding her infant son in its mouth. The wife immediately began struggling with the wolf. When it opened its jaws, the wife snatched her child back and escaped, carrying it in her arms. The wife then gave a mighty scream. The neighbors came running in response, so the wolf trotted off.

Once she was no longer terrified, the wife became jubilant, pointing here and there to describe the incident, drawing pictures in the dirt, relating the story of the wolf holding her baby in its mouth, and how she'd grabbed him away through sheer force. It was a considerable length of time before she suddenly became aware that she didn't have a stitch of clothing on her body, and frantically ran off.

This was the same thing that happened after the earthquake, when men and women similarly lost track of themselves. When people are frightened and anxious, they don't think clearly—which is good for countless laughs!

Several mu across: Each *mu* is equal to approximately .0667 hectare, or 1/6 acre. Pu is thinking of something close to an acre here.

52. The Lord of the Sea

In the East Sea, on Guji Island, there's a five-colored flower called Winter's Survivor, that lives through all four seasons without withering. Since ancient times, no one's lived on the island, and people rarely visit there.

In Dengzhou, there was a scholar named Zhang, who loved encountering the unexpected, enjoying both traveling and hunting. When he heard that Guji Island was a place of natural beauty, he packed some wine and food, found himself a boat, and set off.

When he arrived, he noted the multitudes of flowers, their fragrance carrying for several *li*; and there were trees so large that more than ten people could be fitted around their perimeters. Returning to the sights again and again, reluctant to leave any of them, he felt very contented, enjoying the place tremendously. He opened up his wine, sorry that there wasn't anyone traveling with him.

Suddenly, a beautiful woman appeared among the flowers, dressed in a red skirt that dazzled the eyes, and to put it briefly, she was simply beyond compare. She saw Zhang, smiled, and said, "I figured my interest in this place was unusual, so I didn't expect there would be someone who shared my enthusiasm."

Zhang, surprised, asked, "Who are you?"

She replied, "I'm a courtesan from Jiao prefecture. I traveled here with the Lord of the Sea. He took off to

---

Li: A measure of distance equal to 1/3 mile.

238

view the scenery, but I was too exhausted to walk any further, so I decided to stay here." Zhang, who'd been feeling rather lonely, was very pleased to be joined by this beauty, so he invited her to sit and share his wine.

The woman spoke with words that were warm and enticing, that could turn a man's thoughts to licentiousness. Zhang consequently was attracted to her. Worried that the Lord of the Sea might return and that they wouldn't be able to indulge in their mutual pleasure, he suggested they seize the moment and make love. The woman cheerfully agreed.

Their coupled bodies were showing no signs of slowing down, when suddenly they heard an awe-inspiringly powerful wind, accompanied by the sound of trees cracking and falling. The woman, worried, forced Zhang to get up and cried, "The Lord of the Sea has come." Zhang threw on his clothes and turned back around, stunned to see that the woman was already gone.

Then he whirled around to see a huge snake coming out from among the trees, its body as thick as an enormous pipe. Zhang was terrified, so he slipped behind a large tree, hoping the snake wouldn't see him. The snake came right up close to him, then wound its body around both Zhang and the tree several times; his arms were both bound stiffly at his waist, so he couldn't bend them even a little.

The snake raised up its head and flicked its tongue repeatedly at Zhang's nose. Distracted by the blood that began streaming from the nose, which collected in a shallow pool on the ground, the snake then lowered its head and drank from it. Zhang was sure he was going to die, when suddenly he remembered he was wearing a bag at his waist that contained poison for dealing with foxes, so with two fingers he pulled it out, and from the worn bag he was able to take some poison into his palm; then he turned his neck so he was able to look at the palm and the blood from his nose began to drip onto the poison until soon there was enough to fill his hand. The snake consequently came near to drink the blood from his palm.

Before it could finish drinking, its body abruptly stiffened, then it began thrashing its tail, making a noise like thunder crashing, and every tree that it struck was broken in half, until the snake toppled to the ground like a mighty pillar and died.

Zhang felt so dizzy that he couldn't stand up, and it took some time for him to recover. He collected the snake and went home, where he fell ill for more than a month. He suspected that the woman must have been a snake spirit.

53. Ding Qianxi

Ding Qianxi lived in Zhucheng. He was wealthy, both in terms of cash and of grain. A champion of justice, he was an admirer of Guo Xie, a truly upright man. A particular corrupt government official began searching for ways to censure him. Ding, consequently, was forced to live as a fugitive.

When he arrived in Anqiu, it had begun to rain, so to stay dry he had to give up traveling any further. By noon, the rain still hadn't let up. A boy came, offering him comfortable lodging and ample food. Since it was already dark, Ding stopped to lodge with the boy's family; the boy fed some hay and beans to his horse, then considerately served Ding his meal.

Ding asked his name, and the boy replied, "The host here is named Yang, and I'm his nephew. The master, who loves to travel, is out now, and of the other family members, only my aunt stayed behind. We're poor, so we can't offer a visitor everything he might wish, and we hope you'll forgive us for that." Ding asked the boy what his uncle did for a living, and discovered that the family had neither money nor possessions, so during the day they set the place up for gambling, and in that way paid for their food.

Zhucheng: In modern Shandong province. Anqiu is also in modern Shandong.
Guo Xie: A Han dynasty figure; see Zhu (174n3).

The following day, it rained as before, without stopping, and the boy was never idle in keeping Ding supplied.

When night arrived, he gave the horse more hay; but Ding could tell that the sheaf of hay was soaked; it was also cut to many different lengths. He thought this odd. The boy declared, "To tell you the truth, my family's so poor that we have no livestock to feed, so my aunt took down some thatch from our home's roof for your horse." Ding found this stranger yet, figuring the boy was just hinting to him for some extra pay.

At first light, Ding offered him some money, but the boy wouldn't accept it; then when he offered it more insistently, the boy took it inside. When the boy came back out, he returned it as before, reporting, "My aunt said that we don't make our living by serving customers. When the master goes out, even for several days, he doesn't take along any cash; so when someone comes to stay with our family, how can we demand compensation?"

Ding expressed his admiration and commendation of the master, then prepared to take his leave. He instructed the boy, "I'm known as Ding, from Zhucheng—please inform Master Yang that I should like to have him visit me. When he has the leisure to do so, it would be my good fortune to welcome him."

Years passed, and he heard no news of his former host. Then it happened one year that there was a great famine, and the Yang family became desperate in their poverty. Yang's wife persuaded him to pay a visit to Ding, so he went.

Once he arrived, he gave his name at Ding's gate, but Ding didn't remember him; once Yang repeatedly explained, however, Ding remembered everything. He slipped on some sandals and ran outside, bowing to his visitor and ushering him inside. When he noticed Yang's raggedy clothing and worn-out shoes, he brought him to a warm room, laid out a feast, and entertained him with extraordinarily lavish generosity.

The next day, Ding had a cap and a set of clothes

made for Yang, to keep him warm. Yang was grateful; but he worried about his family more and more, anxious that he couldn't know how they were doing, since he was so far away.

After Yang been staying there for several days, Ding still hadn't said anything particular about offering him assistance once he decided to leave. Yang's thoughts remained extremely troubled, so he told his host, "When I first saw you, I didn't dare reveal the facts: when I came here to prostrate myself before you, we didn't even have a *sheng* of rice left. Now, due to your kind treatment, I'm fine. But what about my family!"

Ding reassured him, "Don't let it prey on your mind, for I've already taken care of the details. I hope you'll allow yourself the leisure of staying a little longer, so I can help provide you with some traveling expenses." Then he sent his servants out to summon various gamblers, so Yang could sit there and ask them for a share of their profits, till by the end of the evening he had collected a hundred taels, and Ding saw him off for his return trip.

Once he was back home, Yang spotted his wife dressed in brand new clothing and shoes, with a young maidservant waiting on her. Startled, he asked what had happened. His wife explained, "The day after you left, servants with carts came to offer us cloth, silk, and grain, piling it all up until they filled a room, saying it was a present from Ding, who was once a guest here. Even this maid was sent to serve me." Yang couldn't express how moved he was by all this. Hence his family became moderately wealthy, and Yang never had to resort to his old way of making ends meet.

The collector of these strange tales remarks, "Poor yet hospitable to visitors—even drinkers and gamblers can be moved to do good; the unusually insightful person here, however, was Yang's wife. For who *could* receive assistance and not return the favor? By rightly refusing to forget a single meal he'd received, Ding demonstrated his virtue."

Sheng: A measure equal to approximately one liter.

54. The Whales Surface

Along a certain stretch of the seashore, there were no mountains. One day, however, people suddenly observed an entire mountain range there that stretched for many *li*, and the crowds were utterly astonished. But on the following day, the mountains suddenly began to shift and dissolve, until there was nothing left.

There was an old legend which said that whales would come to the surface during the Pure Brightness Festival, and then people afterwards took their families to pay their respects at their ancestral graves, so it was also very common to see this happening during Cold Food Day.

Li: A measure of distance equal to 1/3 mile.
Pure Brightness Festival . . . Cold Food Day: The early April celebration of the *qingming*, or Pure Brightness Festival (aka Tomb-Sweeping Day), honors family ancestors. Part of the celebration includes not cooking on this day, instead serving only cold food. *Hanshi*, or Cold Food Day, begins on the evening before the Qingming Festival.

55. Old Master Zhang

An old gentleman named Zhang lived in Shanxi province. When it came time for him to marry off his daughter, he took his family to Jiangnan, and personally purchased his daughter's trousseau. Once their boat arrived at Gold Mountain, Zhang disembarked, advising his family to stay in the boat and not to fry any fish or meat.

Now there was a monstrously large sea turtle living in the river that would surface whenever it smelled something tasty, wrecking boats and gulping down travelers, and it had been wreaking havoc on the people there for quite some time. When Zhang left, his family members forgot about his warning, and started roasting some meat in the boat.

Suddenly, a gigantic wave capsized the boat, drowning his wife and daughter. Zhang returned to the site, mourning sorrowfully and wishing he were dead. Subsequently, he climbed Gold Mountain to visit a Buddhist monastery, in order to inquire about the monstrous turtle that had become the object of his hatred.

Shocked, a monk who heard his story, replied, "We live near it daily, and fear that it endangers people's lives, so we serve it as a god, and I pray it hasn't been angered; at regular times we sacrifice livestock, throwing the body segments into the river—then something surfaces, swallows them, and submerges again. Who could hope to survive the enmity of such power!"

When Zhang heard this, a plan suddenly occurred to him. It was easy to enlist some blacksmiths, who had set up a forge on the mountainside, to smelt some red iron weighing a few hundred *jin*. When they had learned where the thing most frequently hid itself, they directed two or three strong men to use large tongs to lift the hot iron up and throw it into the river. The monster turtle came up, quickly swallowed it, and went back down.

Shortly, waves the size of hills began surging. An instant later, the billows ceased and the monstrous turtle, dead, floated to the surface.

Travelers and monks quickly united and built a temple to old Master Zhang, placing an effigy of him inside it—where they revere him as a water deity, and when they supplicate him, he answers them.

A few hundred jin: One *jin* is approximately .5 kilograms.

56. The Shuimang Herb

Shuimang is a poisonous herb. It's a creeping vine like the kudzu; it also has purple flowers, similar to lentils. Those who eat it by mistake immediately die, and become shuimang ghosts. Popular belief holds that such a ghost will not be reincarnated, and can only be returned to the cycle of life if someone else dies from the poison and can serve as a substitute. For this reason, there's considerable suffering in the area around Peach Blossom River, where these ghosts are particularly prevalent.

A scholar named Zhu was going to see a "same-year," a friend who'd been born the same year he had, which involved paying a visit with one's name-card, calling each other "elder brother" and "younger brother," and their sons being called "nephews" and calling them "uncles," a popular custom. As Zhu was heading off to see his same-year, Mou, he felt violently parched along the way, his throat longing for an immediate drink.

Suddenly he spotted an old woman at the side of the

Shuimang: While *illicium verum*, or Chinese Star Anise, produces seeds pods that are used both as a flavoring and as a medicine, *illicium anisatum*, or Japanese Star Anise, features cardamom-scented fruits and leaves which are poisonous (and the flowers are not scented), though the fruits are used externally as medicine. The second and third characters of the story's title, *mangcao*, is the Chinese designation for *illicium anisatum*, which grows as a small evergreen tree, rather than as a vine.
Peach Blossom River: Taohua Jiang, in Hunan province.

road, in a hut, apparently giving out tea to drink, so he hurried over. The old woman welcomed and conducted him into her hut, and hospitably offered him a cup of something that was very dark. He sniffed at it and noticed a peculiar smell, not like tender tea leaves, so he wouldn't drink it, put it down, and got up to leave.

The old woman anxiously stopped her guest and shouted, "Sanniang, fetch a cup of the good tea out here." In a few moments, a young woman, carrying a teapot in her hands, came out from behind the hut. She seemed about fourteen or fifteen years old, looking breathtakingly lovely and captivating, with rings on her fingers and bracelets on her arms, glittering and gleaming, casting varied shadows.

Zhu accepted a little cup from her, his thoughts fixated on Sanniang; he sniffed his tea, finding it heavily fragrant and energizing. He drained it and asked for a second cup. He watched the old woman until she turned around, then playfully grabbed the girl's wrist and took one of her rings off a finger. Sanniang blushed and gave a slight smile, which made Zhu become even more smitten.

He had intended to ask her where her family was from, but just then the girl told him, "If you come tonight, I'll still be here." Zhu begged her to give him a small pinch of her tea leaves, which he put together with her ring, and then he went on his way.

When he arrived at the home of his same-year, he began to feel an awful pain in his heart, and suspecting that there was something wrong with the tea, he informed his friend, Mou, of his experience.

Horrified, Mou exclaimed, "You're in grave danger! They were shuimang ghosts. My late father died of that. Nothing can save you, so what shall we do?"

Zhu was terribly afraid, and took out the leaves to examine them, verifying that they were from the shuimang herb. Then he took out the ring, revealing everything about the girl.

Mou thought for quite some time, then replied, "She must be Kou Sanniang."

Zhu, surprised that he was familiar with her name, demanded, "How'd you know that?"

Mou explained, "In a village to the south, a wealthy family named Kou had a daughter who was known as a great beauty, until she mistakenly ate shuimang and died—undoubtedly she was the malevolent spirit you encountered."

Someone there revealed that to deal with such spirits, if one could learn the ghost's family name and then beg the family for some of the ghost's former undergarments, the clothing could be boiled and the result could be drunk as an antidote. Mou anxiously paid a visit to the Kou family, fully and accurately informing them of Zhu's entire story, kneeling for a long time in earnest sorrow, begging for help; but the Kous realized that Zhu was about to serve as a substitute for their daughter who had died, and consequently they turned stingy, refusing to grant his request.

Mou returned in anger, and broke the news to Zhu. Grinding his teeth in frustration, Zhu cried, "If I'm to die, it's certainly not going to be just so their daughter can be reincarnated!" Mou then saw him home in a sedan chair, but just as they were almost at his front gate, Zhu died.

Zhu's mother wailed and wept as she buried him. He left behind him a son who had just turned one year old. His wife was unable to remain a widow, so half a year later, she remarried and moved out. Zhu's mother cared for her fatherless grandson and fed the little boy all by herself, which was too demanding for the beleaguered grandmother to stand, so she sobbed piteously day and night.

One day, just as she was holding the child and crying, Zhu suddenly and silently entered the room. His mother, aghast, wiped away her tears and asked him why he had come. He answered her, "I heard your weeping from the underworld, and it made me so grievously sad that I've come to serve you, at least paying my respects in the mornings and evenings. Though I am dead, I've already taken a new wife, and we're both going to take over your toil, mother, so don't be so sad."

"What kind of person is your wife?" his mother asked.

Zhu replied, "The Kou family just sat by and let me die, which I resented violently. After I died, I wanted to find Sanniang, but I didn't know where to look for her; recently I met with an uncle, who pointed out for me how to locate her. Sanniang had been reincarnated into the family of an official named Ren; I sped there, grabbed her spirit back forcibly, and brought her with me. Now she's become my wife and we actually get along well together, so she's suffered no hardship."

A little while later, a young woman entered through the gate, gorgeously attired and absolutely beautiful, and prostrated herself on the ground to show her respect for Zhu's mother. Zhu explained, "This is Kou Sanniang." Though Sanniang was no longer a living person, when Zhu's mother looked her over, she found herself feeling rather pleased with the girl.

Zhu then sent Sanniang to perform the household chores. Though the girl wasn't accustomed to doing such work, she was so obedient that she nevertheless made it her responsibility wholeheartedly, earning everyone's love and appreciation. Hence once they moved in with Zhu's mother, they stayed there and never deserted her.

Sanniang requested that Zhu's mother inform her family about everything that had happened. Zhu didn't want his mother to do so; but she obliged Sanniang, and in the end reported everything. The head of the Kou family and his wife were greatly astonished by the news, and quickly ordered a carriage to take them back with her.

When they saw the girl, they knew it was Sanniang. They hugged her, silently weeping, till she encouraged them to stop their crying. Sanniang's mother noticed that the Zhus were quite impoverished, which made her all the more upset. Sanniang remarked, "I'm already a ghost, so what difference does it make if they're poor? Zhu and his mother care about me, generously and faithfully loving me, so I feel entirely at ease here."

They asked her then, "Who was the old woman who

gave out the tea?"

"Her surname was Ni," explained Sanniang, "and since she was ashamed of being unable to trick any passersby, she begged me to assist her. Now she's already been reincarnated into a family that runs a sour-liquor shop in town." Then she turned to Zhu and said, "You're already my husband, but you still haven't yet paid your respects to my parents—how's that supposed to make me feel?"

Zhu abruptly flung himself down to show respect for his parents-in-law. Sanniang then went into the kitchen to act for Zhu's mother by preparing a meal, which they offered to the Kous. Sanniang's mother felt wretched about this. She returned home and sent two maidservants back to serve them, plus a great quantity of currency and many bolts of fine cloth and silk; she also had wine and meat delivered frequently as tokens of their good will toward Zhu's mother, attempting to improve her life a bit.

The Kous also periodically invited Sanniang to return home and visit them. After several days, she would always say, "There's no one at home to keep house, so you'd better let me head back before long." Sometimes when the parents intended to urge her to stay with some kind of excuse, Sanniang would simply fly away home herself. Her father then built a grand house for Zhu, and oversaw that it was furnished with all the best before he left. Nevertheless, Zhu never paid a visit to his father-in-law's home.

One day there came word of a villager who'd been poisoned by shuimang, had died, but had then come back to life, with everyone commenting on the strangeness of it all. Zhu remarked, "I'm the one who revived him. He was killed by a person named Li Jiu, but I drove Li's spirit away from him and eliminated it."

"Why didn't you take over the man when you had the chance?" asked his mother.

Sour-liquor shop: A shop that sells a mixture of alcohol and vinegar.

He replied, "I despise that kind of behavior, and since I've prevented others from acting like that, how could I stoop to it! Besides, my greatest happiness is is to wait upon my mother, so I have no desire to be reborn." Henceforth, whenever anyone was poisoned by shuimang, they'd prepare a lavish supplication feast and beg Zhu for rescue, which he always granted them.

When just over ten years had passed, Zhu's mother died. Zhu and Sanniang were grief-stricken, became listless and debilitated, and refused to receive any visitors, only directing their son to put on rough mourning garments and express his sincere sorrow, instructing him in the proper rites, nothing extravagant and wasteful.

About two years after they'd buried Zhu's mother, the parents arranged their son's marriage to the granddaughter of Ren, the government official. Previously, Master Ren had had a daughter by a concubine, and the girl was only a few months old when she died. After hearing the strange stories about Zhu, he ordered that he be driven to Zhu's home, where he treated Zhu as his son-in-law and arranged a granddaughter's marriage to Zhu's son. Once the granddaughter became the son's wife, relations between the families were always cordial

One day, Zhu called his son to him and said, "The gods feel that I have performed meritorious deeds for the common people in the world, so they've appointed me as the Dragon Master of the Four Great Rivers, and now it's time for me to take up my position."

A daughter . . . only a few months old when she died: That is, Ren's infant faughter was the reincarnated Sanniang before Zhu "grabbed her spirit back forcibly."

Dragon Master of the Four Great Rivers . . . scaled shells: Chinese dragons are water creatures, inhabiting the oceans and large rivers surrounding China. Rather than a coat of mail, then, the horses deputed to carry Zhu and Sanniang to the Dragon Lords are covered with scales, like other denizens of the deep. The four rivers are the Zhujiang (Pearl) in the extreme south; the Changjiang (Long, also known as the Yangzi), just south of central China; the Huanghe (Yellow) in central China; and the Heilongjian (Black Dragon) in the extreme north.

Shortly afterward, in the courtyard they saw four horses appear, pulling an immaculate yellow coach, the thighs of each horse covered with scaled shells. Husband and wife came out, grandly attired, and stepped up into the coach together. The son and his wife tearfully prostrated themselves, and in the space of a breath, the coach had vanished.

That same day, the Kou family saw their daughter arrive, and she lovingly took her leave of her father and mother, explaining Zhu's advancement to them. Sanniang's mother, weeping, pleaded with her to stay, but she simply replied, "My dear Zhu has already gone on ahead." She walked out the gate then, and was never seen again.

Zhu's son, who was named E, his courtesy name Lichen, begged Sanniang's father to give her bones to him, and he subsequently buried them alongside his father's remains.

57. Creating Livestock

There are plenty of ways to bedevil people magically, like tossing out some kind of tempting bait for people to follow when they're sleepwalking, which is popularly known as "attacking with a fistful of fluff," and is called "bluffing with fluff" south of the Yangzi River. Children don't know about such things, so they're constantly vulnerable to such harm.

There's also another enchantment one can cast that changes people into beasts, called "creating livestock." The spell is little practiced north of the Yangzi, though it's quite common in the south. At an inn in Yangzhou, a man leading a five-headed donkey came in and tied it up at the inn's stable, declaring to the innkeeper, "I'll be right back." He quickly added, "Don't let it eat or drink." Then he went away.

The donkey was out in the sun and became agitated, raising a ruckus with its kicking and biting. The innkeeper led it away from the stable to cool off. When the donkey spotted some water, it rushed towards it and indulged itself in guzzling. A moment later, it changed into a woman. The innkeeper was astonished and asked her what had happened, but she was tongue-tied and couldn't speak. Then he hid her inside the inn.

Not long afterwards, when the donkey's master returned with five sheep and entered the courtyard, he nervously asked where his donkey had gone. The innkeeper dragged him over to a seat and offered him food, earnestly saying, "For now, sir, enjoy your meal—

your donkey will show up quite soon."

The innkeeper then stepped out, fed the five sheep with water, and in seconds they turned into five children. The innkeeper secretly sent a message to prefectural headquarters, from whence servants were dispatched to arrest the man, who was subsequently shackled and executed.

58. The Scholar from Fengyang

A scholar from Fengyang county hoisted his bamboo bookcase on his back, and prepared for a long journey. He told his wife, "After six months, I'll return." More than ten months later, to her dismay, she'd heard nothing from him. The wife anxiously kept a vigil for him, hoping for his return. One night, while she was resting on her pillow, the moon shining through their cloth-covered window projected a wavering image that made her restless with thinking about being separated from her husband.

Just as she was tossing and turning, a fairy with pearls in her coiled hair, and a crimson cape over her shoulders, pulled aside a curtain and entered, smiling, as she asked, "Big sister, don't you want to see your husband?" The wife immediately got up and repeatedly said that she wanted to see him. The fairy invited the wife to come with her. The wife was concerned about the difficulties of traveling very far, but the fairy persuaded her not to worry.

She quickly offered the wife her hand and led her outside, the two walking together in the moonlight for a short while. Then the wife became aware that the fairy was walking quite fast, her pace so brisk that the wife was having a hard time keeping up with her, so she called for the fairy to wait for her while she went back home to put on some other shoes that would enable her to travel faster.

Fengyang: In modern Anhui province.

The fairy led her to sit by the side of the road, took off her own shoes, and gave them to the wife. She gratefully put them on, and fortunately they were a perfect fit. She got up and continued following the fairy, her pace so rapid that she felt like she was flying.

After a while, she saw her husband riding towards them on a white mule. When he saw his wife, he was quite surprised, so he anxiously got off the mule and asked, "Where are you going?"

She replied, "I came to find you." Then he turned around to look and asked her who the fairy was.

Before his wife could answer, the beauty hid her laughing mouth behind her hand, and remarked, "Don't ask anything. Your wife had to rush here frantically and it hasn't been easy for her; you've also traveled urgently for half the night, so the two of you and your mule must be exhausted. My home isn't far away, so it wouldn't be too late for you to take a rest from your travels there, and in the morning you can be on your way."

They noticed that there was a village not too far away, so they proceeded to enter it. After walking into a courtyard, the fairy urgently woke up a sleeping maidservant to serve her guests, saying, "Tonight the moonlight is so bright that there's no need for candles, and we can sit on the stone chairs around this little table."

The scholar tied his weary mule to a pillar under the house's eaves, then sat down. The fairy commented to his wife, "My shoes aren't comfortable for your feet, so weren't you exhausted on the way? You'll be able to ride on your way home, so I'd like to ask you to return them to me." The wife expressed her thanks and handed them over.

Soon wine and fruits were set out, and the fairy poured wine for them, saying, "The married couple have long been apart, but tonight they are reunited; I'd like to drink this cup of wine in honor of congratulating you two." The scholar also held up his cup and offered his own toasts with more wine.

The hostess and guests laughed and chatted, becoming quite uninhibited. The scholar stared at their stunning hostess, repeatedly directing glib comments to her as they flirted together. In contrast, the husband and wife hadn't shared even a single word of intimacy since they'd been reunited. The fairy's alluring eyes communicated passion while she spoke in suggestive double entendres. The scholar's wife sat there silently, pretending not to understand their innuendos.

As they gradually became more and more intoxicated, the words of the two became more explicitly seductive. The fairy encouraged the scholar to drink from an enormous wine cup, but the drunken scholar declined, insisting that he'd already overindulged. Laughing then, he exclaimed, "Sing me a song and I'll accept your drink."

The beauty offered no resistance, strummed a qin with an ivory plectrum, and began to sing:

> Dusk wipes away all my make-up,
> The cool west wind penetrates the cloth of my
>   window.
> I listen to the sound of broad leaves strike,
> Drizzle falls in fits and starts.
> Where and with whom can I gossip as I used to do?
> I have a burning desire to see him
> But there's no response.
> I weep continually, my tears trailing like ropes.
> Thinking of him often,
> Hating him often.
> I hold my red embroidered slipper in my hand
> To divine my future from the spirits.

When the song was finished, she smiled and said, "This is just a ditty that people sing in the streets, and not worth your listening. But it's very popular around here, so this is just my version of it." Her tone of voice was soft, her movements indecently intimate. The scholar was so excited, he could hardly control himself.

Qin: A zither-like stringed instrument.

Before long, the fairy pretended to be drunk and left her seat; he also got up and followed her out. A long time passed and they didn't come back. The maidservant grew tired and laid down to sleep on the porch. The wife sat there alone, abandoned, with no one to talk to, her heart raging with unbearable anger. She considered fleeing for home, but the darkness was intimidating and she couldn't remember the route that they'd taken.

With her thoughts churning around and around, she couldn't come up with a definite plan, so instead she got up to spy on the two. As she crouched near the window, there came the unmistakable sounds of lovemaking, faintly audible. She perked up her ears, hearing her husband whispering all the sweet nothings he had always used to please her in the past, pouring out all those words to the fairy.

By this point, the wife's hands were trembling, her heart pounding in her throat, and she decided to run out through the gate, jump into a ravine and die. She had just run outside angrily, when suddenly she saw her second younger brother, Sanlang, ride up on a horse, hastily dismount, and ask what was going on. She told him everything.

Sanlang, outraged, returned to the house with his sister, barged inside, and found the door to the fairy's room bolted shut, with the bedside whispers still coming from inside. Sanlang hefted up a tremendous stone like he was going to use it as a weapon, then pitched it through the window lattice, breaking the window to pieces.

From inside a voice screamed, "His brain's split open! What am I going to do!"

When the wife heard this, she panicked and wept hysterically to her brother, "I didn't mean to conspire with you to kill him, so now what can we do?"

Sanlang opened his eyes wide and declared, "You called for me to hurry and aid you; now that I've addressed your complaint, you begin to protect your husband and blame it on your own brother—I'll never listen to you again!"

When he turned with the intention of leaving, the

wife grabbed at his clothing, pleading, "If you don't take me along with you, where can I go?" Sanlang pushed his sister to the ground, shook off her touch, and left. The wife suddenly awakened in terror, only then realizing that it had all been a dream.

That very day, the husband really did return home, riding a white mule. His wife thought this was strange, but didn't mention it. The scholar, too, had had a dream the previous night, and when he described what he'd seen and experienced in it, the details tallied exactly with everything that had happened in her dream, which scared them both.

Not long afterwards, Sanlang heard that his elder sister's husband had come home from his travels, so he also visited them to make inquiries. During their conversation, he told the husband, "Last night I dreamt that you'd come home, and now sure enough you have, which is really strange."

The scholar laughed and replied, "Fortunately, your boulder didn't kill me." Sanlang, stunned, asked him why he'd said that, so the husband told him about his dream. Sanlang found this utterly bizarre. That same night, he'd dreamt that he had found his sister weeping out her accusation, and in violent rage he'd flung the stone. They had three identical dreams, but no one knew from where the fairy had come.

59. Geng Shiba

Geng Shiba, from Xincheng, fell gravely ill and realized that he was never going to get up again. Hence he told his wife, "It's not too long from now that I'll have to leave you. After I die, either marry someone else or remain loyal to me and take care of my parents—please let me know what you'll do." His wife sat silently and wouldn't speak. Geng remained adamant in his request, adding, "Remaining loyal to me is a fine gesture, but marrying again would be equally acceptable. Tell me the truth about what you intend to do! If you remain loyal to me, it'll ease my mind; if you marry someone else, I won't worry about you any longer."

His grieving wife then replied, "Our family couldn't bear your loss—you're still alive and you mustn't give up, so how can I answer such a question?"

Geng heard this, hastily grabbed his wife's arm, and with an edge in his voice, cried, "You're so cruel!" His words trailed off, and he died. The hand grasping her arm wouldn't release it. His wife began wailing. Family

---

Shiba: Literally, "eighteen." At first glance, an auspicious name, since there are so many significant "eighteens" in Chinese culture—e.g., the eighteen weapons developed by Sun Pin and Wu Chi during the Warring States period; the eighteen immediate disciples (*arhat*) of the Buddha—but in the context of this story, his name recalls the extremely inauspicious eighteen "places of torment" in the underworld (see Mayers 75).

members came in, two of them reaching for Geng's fingers, and, using all of their might to pry them off, finally succeeded in opening them.

Geng didn't know he was dead, so when he walked out past his gate, he saw over ten small carts, each cart carrying ten people, and noticed pieces of paper with names written on them attached to their sides. When one of the cart drivers saw Geng, he urged him to climb on up. Geng observed that previously there had been only nine people in this particular cart, but counting him, there were now ten. Then he examined a list posted on the cart's side and found his name at the bottom of it.

The cart traveled along quite noisily, with a vibrating sound that jarred the ears of everyone inside, so Geng was unable to find out where they were going. After a while they stopped, and when he asked where they were, he was told, "Think of this as your your new home town." Geng became suspicious upon hearing this.

Then he overheard a conversation involving the cart driver, who said in a low voice, "Today they chopped up three people." Geng was shocked.

When he heard these whispered words, he realized that they were talking about the underworld, and demanded, "Have I become some kind of ghost?" He immediately began thinking about his family, and found nothing to worry about except his aged mother, for if his wife wanted to remarry, there'd be no one to take care of her; and as he thought it, he couldn't stop his tears from flowing.

As time passed, he noticed that there was a very high platform and many people wandering around it, with cangues over their heads and shackles on their feet, sobbing as they climbed down and climbed up it, and he heard someone say something about "visiting the village stage." All the people came there, plodding along with restraints on, chaotically vying with each other to climb

---

"Visiting the village stage": An archaic euphemism for the underworld.

up. The cart driver would either flog them or detain them, and it was only when it was Geng's turn that he urgently directed him to start climbing.

He went up about ten flights of steps, finally arriving at the very top. When he raised his head to look around, he saw a large gate and grand hall. Yet once he was inside, the rooms were barely visible, as though thick with the steam rising from a bamboo cooker. Miserable, he felt crushed.

When he looked back, there was a fellow wearing a short, cotton-padded jacket, standing just behind his shoulder, and he promptly inquired if his last name was Geng. Geng confirmed that this was, indeed, his name. The man then told him that he was a craftsman from Donghai. Seeing Geng shedding tears, he asked, "What unfinished business is troubling you?" Geng then told him his story.

The craftsman hatched a plan for Geng to jump down from the platform and escape with him. Geng was afraid that he'd be pursued through the underworld, but the craftsman firmly insisted that there would be no problem. Geng was also worried about falling and hurting himself from such a height, but the craftsman persuaded him to follow him. He then took the lead and leapt ahead, with Geng determinedly following after him.

When they reached the ground, Geng surprisingly no longer felt ill. He was overjoyed not to be noticed. Then he saw that the carts were still parked beneath the platform. The two men anxiously dashed away. After several steps, Geng suddenly recalled that his name was posted on the side of a cart and feared that if he didn't remove the name, someone would come after him again, so he turned back and crept close to the cart, spit on his fingers, rubbed out his name, then ran away till he was gasping for breath, but didn't dare stop for an instant.

In a short time, Geng reached the gate of his house and the craftsman sent him on inside. Suddenly he saw his own corpse there, which then stirred and returned to life.

He felt exhausted and terribly thirsty, so he hurriedly cried out for some water. His family members, though horribly frightened, brought him plenty of water which he gulped down. Then all of a sudden he stood up, bowed respectfully, and prostrated himself on the ground as though showing someone his gratitude; he walked out the gate with his hands folded together in thanks, then returned.

When he went inside, he laid down stiffly and was unable to turn over. His family members thought his actions were pretty odd and began to wonder whether he was really alive; but when they started keeping an eye on him, they found that he wasn't really acting all that strangely. Coming closer, they wanted to know what had happened to him, so he vividly described everything to them, from beginning to end.

"Why did you walk out through the gate?" they asked him.

He answered, "Because the craftsman was leaving."

"Why'd you drink so much water?"

"At first it was only me drinking," he replied, "but after that the craftsman had some to drink."

They brought him some broth, and after several days, he recovered. Because of this, he grew bitter and mean towards his wife, and never again shared bed or table with her.

60. Zhu'er

In Changzhou, there lived a man named Li Hua, who was a wealthy landowner. He was over fifty years old, yet he had no son. There had been a daughter named Xiaohui, possessed of an elegant beauty, whom her father and mother loved dearly. But when she was fourteen, she became violently ill and passed away, causing a chill to settle over their home as their greatest delight in life was taken from them.

Li then took a concubine, and when over a year had passed, she gave birth to a son who was valued like precious jade and was named Zhu'er. The boy gradually grew into a husky fellow of sweet temperament. However, by nature he was also hopelessly dense, so when he was five or six years old he still couldn't tell the difference between beans and wheat, and he also experienced great difficulty with speaking. Li, however, loved him and refused to acknowledge his inadequacies.

It so happened then that there was a monk, blind in one eye, who came to the city to solicit donations, and always knew what was going on in the privacy of people's homes, so everyone was rather scared of him, like he was some kind of spirit; in addition, he asserted that he was able to control a person's life or death, misfortune or happiness. He persisted in his seemingly limitless demands for money from the people, and no one dared

---

Zhu'er: Literally, "the pearl boy."
Beans and wheat: These are paired proverbially as edible items that are distinctly different and hence easily distinguishable.

to hold out on him.

He paid a visit to Li, hoping to collect a hundred strings of coins. Li was in no position to give him that much. He presented him with ten strings, but the monk refused them; eventually Li increased the amount to thirty. The monk gave him a severe look and said, "It has to be a hundred strings and not a jot less!" Li, equally furious, picked up the proffered strings of coins and left. The monk abruptly stood up, exclaiming, "You'll be sorry, you'll be sorry!"

Not long afterwards, Zhu'er experienced violent heart pains for no apparent reason, and began clawing at his mattress, looking as pale as dust and ashes. Frightened for him, Li took eighty strings of coins to the monk and begged him to save his son.

Laughing, the monk declared, "It's not easy to earn this kind of money! What could a mere hermit possibly do for you?"

Li returned home and learned that his son had already died. He was profoundly grieved, so he filed a complaint with the county magistrate. The magistrate had the monk arrested and interrogated, accepting none of his impassioned pleas. The magistrate then called for him to be flogged, but it sounded like a drum was being beaten rather than a man. The magistrate ordered someone to search his body, where they found two wooden men, a small coffin, and five small flags. Outraged, the magistrate began repeating certain magical gestures with his hands. The monk then became frightened and knocked his head against the ground countless times in contrition. But the magistrate wouldn't listen to him, and had him beaten to death. Li kowtowed his gratitude and returned home.

Sometime after sunset, Li and his wife were sitting on their bed. Suddenly a frightened-looking little boy rushed into the room and said, "Papa, why'd you go so fast? I tried my hardest, but couldn't catch up with you." Li examined his body and face, figuring him to be about

---

Strings of coins: Each string held 1,000 copper coins.

seven or eight years old.

Shaken, Li was just about to ask him some questions when he looked over and found him there one moment but gone the next, suddenly turning to a smoky fog that wound and twisted around them, then rose and climbed up onto their bed. Li pushed him off and he fell to the floor without a sound.

The boy cried out, "Papa, what did you do that for!" He glanced shyly at Li, and then climbed back up. Li was frightened, as was his wife, so they both ran away. The boy cried for his papa and mama, moaning ceaselessly.

Li led them into his wife's room, hurriedly slamming the door shut; but when he turned around, the boy was suddenly there beside them. Shaken, Li asked him what he wanted. The boy replied, "I'm from Suzhou, and my name is Zhan. At the age of six I became an orphan, but my elder brother and his wife wouldn't take me in, sending me instead to my maternal grandfather's household.

"Unexpectedly, while I was playing outside the gate there, a mad sorcerer killed me beneath the mulberry tree, turning me into a wandering ghost, unjustly barred from the underworld, unable to be reincarnated. It was my good fortune that you redressed that wrong, papa, so now I wish to stay here as your son."

Li told him, "People and ghosts must follow different paths, so how can we live together?"

The boy answered, "If you could allow me just a small room, to set up a bed and mattress, and each day prepare me a cup of cold congee, I wouldn't need anything more." Li agreed to this. The boy was jubilant and laid down to sleep in one of the other rooms.

When morning arrived, he got up and walked into the family's private quarters, just like he'd grown up in the house. He heard the sound of Li's wife weeping and asked, "How many days has it been since Zhu'er died?" Li told him that it had been seven days. The boy declared, "Since the weather's quite cold, his body won't have decayed. Send someone out to open his grave and look inside, for if his body hasn't been damaged, we should be able to bring him back to life."

Li was overjoyed, so he accompanied the boy, opened the grave, and examined the body, discovering it completely unchanged. Amazed by this, he turned to look at the boy, but found him nowhere in sight. Finding this strange, he lifted his son's body and carried it home.

Just as he was laying the body onto a bed, Zhu'er's eyes opened, looking in Li's direction, and less than a moment later he was calling for hot water—the hot water made him sweat, and after sweating it out, he was able to get up.

Everyone was elated that Zhu'er had returned to life, and in addition he was clever and capable in ways curiously different than before. Yet at night he would lay there utterly stiff, not breathing in the least, and when they turned him over on his side, he didn't move, just like he was dead. This frightened everyone, who said he must've died again; but at the crack of dawn, he began to stir like he was waking from a dream.

The household members drew near and asked him all about it. Zhu'er replied, "When I was with that sorcerer, there were two boys, one of whom was named Gezi. Yesterday, I couldn't catch up with Papa because I was saying goodbye to Gezi. In the underworld, he's now been adopted by Jiang Yuanwai, living a free and happy life. Last evening, he heartily invited me to play with him. Afterward, he sent me home on a yellow horse with a white nose and black mouth."

His mother then asked him, "In the underworld, did you happen to see Zhu'er?"

The boy replied, "Zhu'er had already been reincarnated. He and papa were never fated to enjoy a father and son relationship. He was reincarnated into Yan Zifang of Jingling, who had come to collect a debt of a thousand and eight hundred coins." In the past, Li

---

With that sorcerer: This reveals that Zhan is speaking through Zhu'er's body.

Yellow horse: Eberhard notes that the color yellow is associated with "fame, progress, and advancement" (322), here perhaps foreshadowing Zhu'er's later success.

had indeed done some trading in Jinling, and he'd owed money to a man named Yan, who had died, but no one else knew about the debt. When Li heard this, he was terribly startled.

Zhu'er's mother asked him, "Did you see your elder sister?"

"Nope," the boy replied. "But I'll go back and search for her."

Two or three days later, he reported to his mother, "Happily, elder sister is quite content in the underworld, since she's married to Chu Jiangwang, son of a minor official, and has pearls and jadeite aplenty to adorn her hair; whenever she goes out the door, there are always hoards of servants to announce her departure from the hall."

His mother wondered, "Why doesn't she come back to see her folks?"

"When a person's dead," he explained, "she no longer has any bones or flesh, so there's not much to be concerned about any longer. But if someone reminds her even a little of her former life, then she can be put back in touch with her old emotions. Yesterday, I asked Master Jiang if he would arrange for me to see elder sister, and she called for me to sit with her on a bed made from coral, where I told her that father and mother were very worried and concerned about her, which she took in like someone who was asleep.

"So I said to her, 'Elder sister, when you were alive, you took pleasure in embroidering stemmed flowers side-by-side—then one time, when you were trimming your fingernails with the scissors, some blood dripped onto the fine silk of your work, so you simply turned it into some reddish running water. Even now, mother has it hanging on the wall at the head of her bed so she can see it and always think of you. Sister, have you forgotten her?'

"Sister was moved to tears and declared, 'I have to explain to my husband, then I can return home to visit mama.'" His mother asked him when to expect her, and Zhu'er replied that he had no idea.

One day he suddenly told his mother, "Elder sister's on her way with a large entourage of servants, so we'd better set out a generous supply of wine." Shortly thereafter, he rushed back in to tell her, "Sister's here!"

He moved a seat for her into the hall, saying, "Sister, please sit down and rest yourself, till you can stop your crying." No one else who was there saw anything at all. Zhu'er directed the others to burn some hell money and offer libations of wine outside the gate, then returned and said, "I've commanded her escort to retire temporarily. Sister told me, 'There used to be a green brocade quilt that already had a burnt spot in it the size of a pea—is it still around?'"

Zhu'er's mother replied, "It's still around." At once she opened a basket and took out the quilt.

The boy reported, "Sister has requested her old bedroom. She's exhausted and would like a little rest. Then tomorrow, mama, you can talk to her."

Their neighbor to the east, named Zhao, had a daughter who used to embroider with Xiaohui. One night, she suddenly dreamt that Xiaohui, dressed in a scarf and purple robe, had come to visit with her, chatting and laughing like they always had before.

After quite a while, Xiaohui said, "I am dead now, and though my father and mother are face-to-face with me, we might as well be far apart. Little sister, I'd like to borrow your body so I can speak with them; please don't be alarmed."

When the next morning arrived, she was all ready to speak with her mother. Then she fell to the ground suddenly, unconscious. After she'd been in this state for about fifteen minutes, she started to come around, turned to her mother and said, "Auntie, while we've been apart for oh so many years, something has happened to make your hair turn white!"

Her mother, astonished, wondered, "Are you insane, child?"

The daughter broke off her visit and left at once. Her mother, thinking this odd, followed her. Xiaohui made a beeline for the Li household and tearfully hugged her mother. Mrs. Li didn't know what to think. Her daughter remarked, "When I came home yesterday, I was quite exhausted and couldn't manage a single word. I'm not a filial daughter, to have left my parents behind, troubling my father and mother with grieving over me—what can I do to redeem such a crime!"

Her mother, suddenly realizing what was going on, started crying. When she was able to stop, she inquired of her, "I've heard that you're well off now, which certainly takes a load off my mind. But you're living in a powerful household, so how were you able to leave and come here?"

Her daughter replied, "My husband is extremely loving, and my in-laws are also very affectionate, so they said nothing against my coming."

Not long afterwards, Zhu'er ran in and reported, "Sister's entourage is ready to depart."

Xiaohui then stood up, bowed farewell while weeping, and said, "I must leave." When she finished speaking, she fell down again, and for a time, the Zhao daughter remained motionless before reviving.

After several months, Li became deathly ill and neither doctors nor medicines had any effect on him. Zhu'er cried, "I'm afraid that soon we won't be able to save him! Two demons sit at the head of his bed, one holding an iron staff, the other a coil of hempen rope about 4 or 5 *chi* long, but I've stayed day and night to ask them to leave, and they won't listen to me." Mrs. Li wept, then began to prepare her husband's burial clothes.

At dusk, the boy hurried in and declared, "Everyone must leave, for sister's husband has come to see papa." Instantly he clapped his hands and laughed. His mother asked him why, and he replied, "I'm laughing at the two demons, who heard that sister's husband had arrived and hid themselves under the bed like turtles."

Shortly thereafter, he was staring into empty space when he began to exchange a few words of greeting,

---

Chi: A length equal to 1/3 meter.

asking his sister about life at home. Then he clapped his hands and said, "Although the two lackey demons regrettably wouldn't leave, it's actually turned out to be a good thing!"

Then he stepped outside the door, returning soon thereafter to announce, "Sister's husband has just left. The two demons were chained up and strapped over his horse's back. Papa should immediately get over his sickness. Sister's husband told me that when he gets home, he'll speak with the king and ask that both father and mother receive a hundred years of life." The family was overjoyed. That night, Li's illness was gone and in just a few days, he was completely healed.

They hired a tutor to teach the boy his lessons. Zhu'er proved to be very intelligent, and at the age of eighteen, he entered the county school, all the while still capable of discussing matters with denizens of the underworld. Whenever he saw anyone ill in his village, he'd always point out where there were demons and evil spirits in the place, apply moxibustion to clear them out, and thereby effect a cure.

Later, however, he personally became violently ill, his skin turning black and blue, and he explained that he was being attacked by demons and spirits because he had revealed their presence—hence it was that he never spoke of them again.

61. The Tiny Gentleman

There once was a certain court historian, whose name I've forgotten. While he was laying down for a daytime nap in his study, there suddenly appeared a miniature honor guard, emerging from a corner of his room. The horses were only as large as frogs, and the people no bigger than fingers. The little troop included some ten squads; an official in a black silk cap, wearing a ceremonial gown, was riding in a sedan chair as droves of figures passed into the room and went out through the doorway.

The historian found this pretty strange, but figured since he'd been sleeping, it was all just his imagination. Suddenly he saw a little man reenter the room, carrying a stuffed cloth bag, the size of a fist. Eventually he made his way to the historian's bed and set it down. Then he announced, "My master respectfully wishes to offer this modest gift to you, sir."

When he finished speaking, he stood facing the historian, but without delivering whatever was in the bag. After a bit, the little man laughed and said, "I imagine a historian wouldn't have any use for such a tiny, tiny thing, so it'd probably be better to give it to me."

The historian nodded his approval. Joyfully, the little man picked up the bag and departed. It's a pity that in his shock, the historian didn't think to ask where the little man was from.

62. Fourth Sister Hu

Scholar Shang lived in Taishan. He spent his time alone in the quiet of his study. One autumn evening, with the Milky Way twinkling from on high and the moon shining bright in the sky, Shang was pacing back and forth through some moonlit flowers, indulging himself with a beauty in his imagination.

Suddenly a young lady emerged from the other side of the wall, and with a smile, asked, "What could a *xiucai* be thinking about so deeply?"

Shang came over for a closer look, and found she had the stunning beauty of a goddess. Pleasantly surprised, he embraced her and led her inside, where they immediately became very intimate. She told him, "My name is Hu, Third Sister Hu." When he asked her where she lived, she merely smiled and said nothing. Shang didn't repeat his question, wishing nothing more than for them to be together always, in love. From that time forward, there were no more empty evenings for him.

One night, while he sat beside her, chatting under the lamplight, Shang became so obsessed with her that he couldn't stop staring at her. Third sister laughed and said, "Why are you staring at me like that?"

He replied, "I'm looking at my darling, who's like the red peony and the peach blossom, and I could gaze like this all night long and never grow tired of it."

Xiucai: A rank of scholar achieved by passing the county level imperial civil service examination system.

Third Sister remarked, "I'm homely and simple, yet you're so taken with me; if you were to see my family's Fourth Sister, you'd really stare." Shang became even more aroused, expressing his regret that he hadn't yet seen her face, and knelt in sincerity for a long time, abjectly begging for the opportunity.

The next evening, consequently, she brought Fourth Sister to meet him. She was only about fifteen, a pink lotus dripping with morning dew, an apricot blossom moistened by morning mists, with a captivating smile on her lips—the fascinating beauty was peerless. Shang, wildly happy, led them to sit down. Third Sister shared laughter and chit-chat with him; Fourth Sister simply played with her embroidered sash, her head bowed and silent.

A bit later, Third Sister stood up to leave, and her sister wanted to follow her out. Shang grabbed her and wouldn't let go, turned to Third Sister and said, "Sweetie, please help me out by saying something."

Third Sister then laughed and said, "This crazy fellow's so impatiently passionate! Sister, you'd better stick around for a little while." Fourth Sister said nothing, so her elder sister departed.

Shang and Fourth Sister proceeded to make love exuberantly, till afterwards Fourth Sister stretched out her arm for Shang to lie upon, and she began honestly to disclose everything about herself, without holding anything back. Fourth Sister explained to him that she was a fox. Shang had become so attracted to her beauty that he didn't find this at all strange.

Hence, Fourth Sister revealed, "Third Sister is ruthlessly cruel, and has already killed three people. No one misled by her will can avoid dying. It's my good fortune to be the object of your love, and I couldn't bear to see you die, so you must stop all contact with her as soon as possible." Shang was fearful, and pleaded with her to help him out. Fourth Sister explained, "Though I am a fox, I was taught the secrets of the celestials, so I'll make a talisman for you to paste up on your chamber door, and it can keep her away." Then she copied down the talisman.

At dawn, Third Sister arrived, saw the talisman and drew back, crying, "The girl has lost all loyalty, falling all over herself for her new lord without recalling who served as her matchmaker. You two may be meant to be together, but I've never opposed that, so why're you acting like this?" Then straightaway she left.

A few days later, Fourth Sister found Shang and made arrangements to see him the following night. That day, Shang unexpectedly went outside to enjoy the view, and at the foot of a hill where there was a stand of trees, from out of the mist, there emerged a young woman who was also quite charming. She approached Shang and said, "*Xiucai*, why are you so lovesick over those Hu sisters all the time? They can't even offer you a single string of cash as a present."

At once she gave him a string of coins, advising him, "Take this right home and buy some nice wine; I'll bring some little tidbits along directly and we can have some fun." Shang took the money and went home, doing just as he'd been instructed.

A little later, the young woman showed up, laid a roast chicken and a shoulder of salt pork on the table, took out a small knife, and deftly cut the meat into thin slices; then they poured the wine and began teasing each other, chatting with giddy gleefulness. Afterwards they extinguished the candles, went to bed, and made passionate love.

The sun was already up by the time they rose. They were sitting at the end of the bed, playing with each other's feet and exchanging their slippers, when suddenly they heard someone's voice; they were listening closely when the Hu sisters entered through the curtains. When the young woman saw them, she panicked and fled, leaving her slippers behind on the bed.

The two sisters followed after her, shouting, "Fox bitch! How dare you sleep with this man!" They chased her out, and were gone for some time before returning.

Fourth Sister berated Shang: "You're not scoring many points, getting together with that fox bitch, so don't try to snuggle up to us again!" In a huff, she prepared to leave. Aghast, Shang flung himself to the ground and begged her forgiveness with penitent words. With Third Sister working on the other side to explain and to dismiss his actions, Fourth Sister's anger began to abate somewhat, and hence the two of them were reconciled.

One day, a Shaanxi man, riding a donkey, came up to Shang's gate and said, "I've been searching for this evil thing day and night, and now I've finally caught up with her." Shang's father found his words odd, and inquired where the man had come from. He replied, "I've been traveling on the lakes daily, combing all four directions for ten years and some months, often away from my home for eight and nine months at a time. That's why this evil thing had the chance to kill my younger brother.

"At home, profoundly sad, I swore an oath to find and exterminate her. Pursuing her for several thousand *li*, I could find no sign of her. Now she's in your home. If she's not destroyed, others like my brother will die."

Though Shang had tried to keep his intimacy with the women a secret, his father and mother had begun to suspect the situation, so when they heard the visitor's words and found themselves greatly afraid, they encouraged him to come in and try his magical solution.

He pulled out two bottles, lined them up on the ground, then worked on talismans and incantations for a good long time. Four columns of black fog materialized, then were sucked inside the bottles. The visitor joyfully exclaimed, "That's the entire family." Then he stuffed pig's bladder into the mouths of the bottles, sealing them airtight. Shang's father was very happy, and eagerly encouraged the guest to stay for dinner.

Shang, however, felt pity, and drew near the bottles to steal a glance, where he heard Fourth Sister say from inside one of them, "You sit there and watch us without coming to our rescue—don't you have any feelings?"

Shang was stung by her words. He anxiously tried to remove the bladder, but couldn't untie the knot holding

---

Li: A distance equal to 1/3 mile.

it in place. Fourth Sister called again, "Don't bother; just lay the charms down, then poke a needle into the bladder and I'll come out at once." Shang did as she requested. The result was a thread of white fog that came out through the needle hole, rose up into the sky and vanished.

When the guest from Shaanxi came out, he saw the charms lying flat on the ground, and, greatly alarmed, cried, "She's escaped! It has to be the young master who did this." He shooked the bottles and inclined his head to listen to them, then said, "Fortunately, only one of them got away. That one apparently wasn't meant to die, so she can be forgiven." Then he took the bottles that were still sealed and departed.

Quite some time afterwards, Shang was out in the fields, supervising his servants as they were harvesting wheat, when in the distance he spotted Fourth Sister sitting under a tree. He came over to her, taking her hand, and expressed how worried he'd been about her.

She explained, "Ten springs and autumns have passed, and now I've succeeded in producing my immortality pill. Yet I can't get you out of my mind, so I've come back to pay my respects and find out how you are." Shang wanted to take her back home. She replied, "I'm no longer the individual I used to be, so I can't allow myself to develop feelings for this mortal world, but we will see each other again some day." Once her words were finished, she disappeared.

Another twenty years passed, and Shang was alone at home when he saw Fourth Sister come in from outside. Jubilant, Shang tried to speak to her. She interrupted to declare, "I've now become one of the celestials, and shouldn't have returned to walk this mortal world. But moved by your thoughtfulness to me, I've respectfully come to announce when you will die. You can settle all of your affairs ahead of time; don't be sad, I'll help you pass on to become an immortal spirit, so you won't suffer." Then she took her leave and left him.

When the day she'd named arrived, Shang did, indeed, die. Shang was a relative of my friend, Li Wanyu, who actually saw him in person.

63. Old Man Zhu

In the Jiyang village of Zhu, there was an old man, also named Zhu, well over fifty years old, who became ill and died. His family members had just gone into the house to put on their mourning hats and robes when suddenly they heard the old man abruptly cry out.

The bunch of them ran out and gathered around his body, where they saw that Zhu had returned to life. All of them, happy and relieved, asked him what had happened. Zhu, however, spoke only to his wife: "When I recently left, I determined not to return again. But once I'd traveled several *li* from here, I turned to the thought of having left you behind, elderly skin and bones placed in the hands of young relatives, forced to rely upon others and no longer able to lead a meaningful life, a poor alternative to following me and departing. For that reason, I've come to take you along on my journey." Everyone attributed his words' strangeness to the fact that he'd just revived, and hence didn't take them seriously.

Zhu repeated his words to her. His wife replied, "Such sentiments are very nice. But you've just come back to life, so how can you think about dying?"

Zhu waved his hands and insisted, "It's not difficult. Please finish arranging your affairs quickly, and come with me."

Jiyang: Located in modern Shandong province.
Li: A distance equal to 1/3 of a mile.

His wife laughed and made no move to leave. Zhu pressed her again. She didn't want to go against his wishes, so she walked out the door and reentered about fifteen minutes later, trying to fool him by remarking, "I've taken care of settling everything." Zhu ordered her to hurry up and put on her make-up. His wife didn't react, so he urged her even more anxiously. She couldn't bear to deny him what he wished, so she put on a skirt and some make-up, and then came out.

The younger members of the family tried to conceal their giggling. Zhu laid his head on his pillow and clapped his hands for his wife to join him. "That's completely weird," his wife said, "having us lay together like a pair of corpses—is that what you want our young relatives to see?"

Zhu beat the bed with his fists and cried, "How can you find death something to laugh about!" The younger family members saw that Zhu was quite impatient, so together they encouraged their auntie to go along with what he wanted. Zhu's wife did as she was told, and laid stiffly next to him. The family members once again began snickering among themselves.

Shortly afterward, they observed that the wife was no longer grinning, and gradually had closed both of her eyes, and for a long time there was no sound, just as though she'd fallen asleep. When the others drew close to take a look, they found her skin cold as ice, and determined she wasn't breathing. They also examined Zhu, who was in the same condition, and then realized the horrible truth.

This happened in the twenty-first year of the reign of Kangxi, and the wife of Zhu's younger brother, who was working in the household of an official named Bi, told me all she knew about it.

Twenty-first year of the reign of Kangxi: A reference to 1666, since this Qing emperor's reign, the longest of his dynasty, spanned 1645-1722.
An official named Bi: Possibly Bi Jiyou (see Zhu 206n11), friend and employer of Pu Songling (Zeitlin 132).

The collector of these strange tales remarks, "Maybe old man Zhu had always behaved strangely. The road to the underworld is vast, so how rare it is for him to leave, and then to come back like that! Though that white-haired head wanted the two of them to leave, even shouting and finally demanding that they leave, what unhurried restraint he showed! When a person is going to die, the hardest thing to endure is saying goodbye to one's dearest companion. If we can spread old man Zhu's magic, when it comes time for us to die, we won't need to make arrangements for our family in advance."

64. The Alligator

Alligators used to live in the west bank of the Yangzi River's lower reaches. Their appearance was like a dragon's, though shorter, and they were able to move about quite speedily; they often went out to submerge themselves along the shore of the river, waiting to spring up and feed on the geese and ducks. Sometimes they were hunted, their flesh sought as a commodity by the Chen and Ke clans. Both of these families were descendants of Chen Youliang, and had a tradition of eating alligator meat, though other clans didn't have the courage to eat this kind of thing.

A visitor from Jiangyou came, caught one, and bound it up in his boat. One day, he anchored his craft in the Qiantang River, but had tied the alligator up rather carelessly—suddenly it leapt into the river. In an instant, enormous waves were stirred up, causing the boat to capsize and sink.

Chen Youliang: Chen (1320-1363) was "one of several unsuccessful warlords contending for power with the first Ming emperor around the time of the collapse of the Mongol Yuan dynasty" (Clunas 98-99; see also Zhu 207n3).

65. *A Certain Gentleman*

In Shanxi, during one of the *xinchou* periods, there was a certain gentleman, a *jinshi*, who could recall his former lives. He often said that in a former life he'd been a scholar who died in his middle age. After he'd died, he met with the Hell King to settle his debts and noticed a three-legged cauldron, used for punishing people by boiling them, just as people had talked about when he was still alive. In the eastern corner of the Hell King's palace, a number of scaffolds had been set up, and hanging from each were the skins of pigs, sheep, dogs, and horses.

The Minister of the Registry called out his name, announcing that as his punishment he would be made something like a horse or a pig; then the people there were all stripped entirely bare to be hung up, seized, and skinned.

After a while, it was the scholar's turn, and the Hell King declared, "This man should be made a sheep." Demons grabbed hold of a white sheepskin and spread it over the man's body.

"He once saved a person from dying," the Minister cried out.

Xinchou periods: The thirty-eighth year of the Sexagenary Cycle (part of the traditional system of numbering dates in China). Zhu identifies the particular *xinchou* in Pu's story as the year 1661 in the western calendar (208n2).
Jinshi: A successful candidate in the highest level of the imperial examination.

The Hell King checked his register, scouring it carefully, then commanded, "Let him go free. Even if he's been evil many times, this kindness could redeem him." The demons then prepared to peel off his furry hide. However, the hide had already become attached to his body, so they couldn't make it budge.

Two demons pulled at his arms while pressing down on his chest, trying their best to pull him apart from the skin, the pain driving him crazy as his skin split and tore away in pieces, until it was completely off. Though other parts were all stripped clean, near his shoulder there was a place where a patch of sheepskin remained attached, as big as one's palm.

The man was reincarnated—and growing thickly on his back was sheep's wool, which had to be trimmed with scissors on a regular basis.

66. The Sharp Sword

At the end of the Ming dynasty, Jinan was overrun by thieves. Every town mustered its soldiers, who always executed the thieves when they caught them. In Zhangqiu, the thieves were especially plentiful.

There was a soldier there who wore an exceptionally sharp sword, that could slice off a head with a single stroke. One day, more than ten thieves had been arrested and were being escorted to the execution grounds.

One of the thieves in the group, who knew the soldier, hung back and said to him, "I've heard that your sword is so exceptionally sharp, when you behead someone, you never need two strokes. I beg you to kill me!"

The soldier replied, "Alright. Stay near me, and don't wander off."

Once the thieves arrived together at the place of execution, he drew out his sword, flourished it once and suddenly the thief's head fell off. Several paces away, it was still rolling and loudly declaring, "Truly a sharp sword!"

Jinan: Capital of Shandong province.
Zhangqiu: A division of Jinan.

67. The Swordswoman

Scholar Gu lived in Jinling. Despite his being rich in talent and skills, his family was quite poor. Since his mother was aged and he couldn't bear to leave her behind to make his fortune, he devoted his days to producing calligraphy and paintings for people, using what he received in exchange to care for his mother. At the age of twenty-five, he still had not married.

Across from their house was a residence that had long been empty, until an old woman and a girl moved in to rent it. Since it was apparent that there were no men in the family, Gu didn't ask them who they were.

One day, as he was coming in from outdoors, he noticed the girl, who appeared to be about eighteen or nineteen, emerging from his mother's room, elegantly beautiful and utterly refined, a rare combination indeed; she made a big detour to avoid Gu when she saw him, though she seemed quite brave and serious at the same time.

He went to ask his mother about her. She explained, "She's the young lady from the family across the way, who came to borrow my scissors and tapeline. She explained that she, too, has only her mother for family. This girl isn't the product of some poor family. I asked her why she isn't married, and she replied that her mother's too elderly for her to leave her. Tomorrow I should pay my respects to her mother and observe what she thinks; if her hopes for the girl aren't too extravagant, you could marry her and take over supporting her mother."

The next day, Gu's mother paid a visit to their home, discovering that the old woman was virtually deaf. She looked around the house and found that there wasn't any food left over from the previous night. She asked what they did for a living, and the old woman replied that she depended upon the sewing work of her daughter's ten fingers.

When Gu's mother had a dinner with the mother and daughter, she eventually proposed her plan for their families' coming together. The old woman seemed willing to accept it, but then she turned to consult her daughter; the girl was speechless, but seemed displeased nonetheless. Gu's mother then returned home.

She gave Gu the details of what had transpired and wondered aloud, "Is the girl worried that we're too poor? She neither speaks or smiles, she's as beautiful as peach and plum blossoms but as cold as ice—what an odd person!" The mother and son speculated and sighed, then let the matter drop.

One day, as Gu was sitting in his studio, a young man arrived and requested a painting from him. The fellow was extremely good-looking, and rather irreverent. When asked where he was from, the young man responded, "A nearby village." He subsequently visited Gu every two or three days.

Over time, they became better acquainted, and gradually began to tease each other; Gu lasciviously embraced the young man, who put up no resistance, and they indulged in sexual pleasures. Hence their contact became intimate indeed.

Once when they ran into the girl, who was passing by, the young man followed her with his eyes and asked who she was. Gu answered, "The neighbor girl."

The young man commented, "As gorgeous as all that, why's she look so unapproachable?"

After a little while, Gu went inside. His mother informed him, "That girl just came over to borrow some rice, and admitted that they haven't built a cooking fire for a day or so. This girl is very filial, but so poor that one has to sympathize, so it's only proper that we show a little compassion."

Gu obeyed his mother's words, carrying a *dou* of rice on his back to the neighbors' door and delivering his mother's sentiments. The girl accepted the rice, but without expressing any thanks.

Henceforth, she often visited Gu's home, and when she saw his mother making clothing or shoes, she would take her place and do the sewing; she went in and out of their rooms, doing the manual labor of a wife. Gu grew progressively more appreciative of her. Any time someone brought him some cakes or dainties as a present, he made sure to give some to her mother, though the girl also failed to acknowledge this.

Gu's mother subsequently developed an ulcerous sore near her genitals that caused her to cry out in pain all through the night. The girl came to the old lady's bedside at every opportunity to look in on her, washing her sore clean, and applying medicine to it three or four times a day. Gu's mother didn't feel right about this, but the girl was not in the least put off by the putrescence.

"Ah me," sighed Gu's mother, "how can I find a young woman like you for my son, to care for me till I die!" After speaking these words, she began to sob, choked with emotion.

The girl comforted her, asserting, "Your son is extremely filial, which is ten, even a hundred times better than being like us, a widowed mother and her lone daughter."

"But how can even a filial son remain on call by my bedside like a servant?" Gu's mother wondered. "Besides, this body is moving towards its end, and in a short while I shall die of an illness, so I'm deeply troubled that our ancestral line may not be continued."

While she was speaking, Gu walked in. Weeping, his mother said to him, "Your mama owes this young woman a great deal, so you must not forget to repay her kindnesses." Gu immediately prostrated himself to

---

Dou: A measure equal to approximately ten liters.

signify his gratitude.

The girl declared, "You showed compassion for my mother, yet I did not thank you; so why should you thank me now?" At this, Gu became even more respectful and fond of her. She, on the other hand, continued her distant behavior, having nothing in the least to do with him.

One day, as the girl walked out through their gate, Gu found his eyes glued to her. Suddenly she turned her head and smiled at him seductively. Gu, rapturously happy at this unexpected turn of events, hurried to follow her into her house. He began caressing her, and she didn't resist, so they joyfully made love.

When they were finished, the girl warned Gu, "This was a one-time affair—it can never happen again!" Gu gave no reply and returned home.

The next day, he tried to arrange another rendezvous with her. With a severe expression on her face, the girl refused to look at him and left. When she appeared each day and Gu encountered her, she refused to respond, verbally or facially. Even his slightest effort at teasing her was met with cold words that chilled him.

Once, when they were alone, she suddenly asked him, "Who is that young man who comes here every day?" Gu answered her. She replied, "His manner is insulting, and his behavior toward me is always impertinent. Since he's your intimate companion, I've let the matter lie. Please be sure to give him this message: unless he wants to die, he'd better not act like that again!"

When night came, Gu gave the young man her message, and insisted, "You've got to be careful, she's not someone to mess with!"

The young man retorted, "Since she's not to be messed with, what've you two been doing in private?" Gu quickly denied having done anything. The young man demanded, "If you haven't been involved with her, then how did those filthy insults manage to reach your hearing?" Gu found himself unable to respond.

"I'll trouble you," the young man said, "to tell her this: stop the pretentious posing; otherwise, I'll spread the story everywhere." Gu was furious, his anger reflected as his face flushed, so the young man went away.

One night, while Gu was sitting by himself, the girl suddenly came in, smiling, and said, "My relationship with you apparently isn't fated to end just yet, so it must be heaven's doing." Insanely happy, he clasped her tightly in his arms.

Suddenly they heard the sound of footsteps noisily approaching, so the startled pair sat up just as the young man pushed the door open and burst in. Gu, shaken, demanded, "What are you doing here?"

Laughing, the young man replied, "I've come to see what a virtuous, chaste person looks like." He turned to the girl and sneered, "What, no rebukes for me today?"

The girl's eyebrows shot up and her cheeks reddened, but she remained silent, uttering not a word. She quickly rummaged inside her clothing and brought out a leather bag, then withdrew a long, glittering, translucent blade. When the young man saw it, he turned and ran.

The girl chased him out the door, but when she looked around for him, he was gone. When she then cast her blade up into the air, there was a piercingly sharp sound as it sailed in a luminous arc, till suddenly something fell to the ground with a thud. Gu anxiously brought a candle over, and was astonished to discover a white fox, its body and head sliced asunder.

"This is your boyfriend," explained the girl. "I had genuinely forgiven him, but there was no alternative since he just didn't want to live any longer!" She then retrieved her sword and placed it in her bag. Gu tried to draw her back inside. She replied, "That evil spirit has spoiled the mood, so if you please, I'll come another night." She went out the door and in no time was gone.

The next evening, the girl did indeed return to him, so they lay together, twined in perfect harmony. When he asked her about her swordcraft, she answered, "This is not something for you to know. Indeed, you must keep this a secret, for revealing it, I fear, would bring you misfortune."

Gu then proposed marriage, to which she replied, "I've been to bed with you, I've carried water for you—if that's not being a wife, what is it? Since we're already husband and wife, what's the point of talking about marriage?"

"Is it because you despise my being poor?" Gu asked.

"Of course you're poor," she responded, "but am I wealthy? I'm staying with you tonight precisely because I sympathize with your being poor." When it came time for her to leave, she advised him, "These indiscretions of ours cannot continue. When it's right for me to come, I will come; when it's not, even the strongest coercion won't succeed."

Thereafter, whenever they ran into each other, Gu always wanted to lead the girl somewhere to talk privately, but she would simply walk the other way, avoiding him. Nevertheless, she tended to clothes that needed mending, collected the fuel for cooking fires, and set everything in order, no differently than a wife would do.

Several months later, her mother died, and Gu spent everything he could muster to bury her properly. The girl thereafter lived alone in her house. Gu thought that since she was by herself, he might be able to sleep with her again, so he climbed over the wall and called repeatedly outside her window, but she gave no response.

Then he looked over at her gate, and noticed that while the house was empty, the gate was bolted shut. He began to suspect that the girl had someone else there with her. When he returned the next night, things were just the same. So he left a jade pendant on her window sill and went home.

The following day, he met her in his mother's room. As soon as they stepped outside it, the girl, trailing behind him, asked, "Do you suspect me of something? Each person keeps certain things in the heart that are not for others to know. Although I don't want you to be suspicious, I have nothing to tell you. But there *is* a troubling matter that I'm anxious to have you settle for me."

He asked what it was and she explained, "I'm eight months pregnant, and worry that I may give birth at any time. Since 'my body isn't clearly my own,' I can bear you a child, but I can't nurse it for you. You can confide this to your mother, so she can search for a wet nurse and act as though you're adopting the child, but don't say anything about me." Gu promised, and then told his mother.

She laughed and said, "What a strange girl! She rejects my son's proposal of marriage but then conducts a secret affair with him." She happily followed the girl's plan to see what would happen.

After more than a month passed, the girl suddenly didn't show up for several days. Gu's mother became concerned, and went to her gate to find out why. Dreary and lonely, the house was locked up and still. She knocked for a very long time, till the girl finally came out, her hair disheveled and her face dirty. She opened the door to Gu's mother, then shut it after her.

Once inside the girl's room, she discovered a crying infant lying on the bed. Shocked, Gu's mother asked, "How long has it been since you gave birth?"

"Three days," replied the girl.

Gu's mother picked up the baby and examined it, determining it to be a boy; furthermore, he had plump cheeks and a broad forehead. Delighted, she exclaimed, "You've given birth to a grandson for me, but now you'll be left alone, so what will you do for support?"

The girl answered, "I dare not reveal the trivial secrets of my heart to you, mother. Wait until evening, when no one's around, then you can take the child and go." Gu's mother went home and informed her son, both of them finding the girl's response quite odd. That night, they went to pick up the baby, and brought it home.

Several nights later, at about midnight, the girl suddenly appeared at the door and came in, carrying a leather bag in her hand, announcing with a smile, "I've

---

'*My body isn't clearly my own*': This is a line from "The Newlywed's Departure" (*xinhun bie*) by Du Fu (712-770 C.E.); see Zhu (215n23). The reference is to the uncertainty of the girl's identity as Gu's wife.

concluded a great mission, so please allow me to take my leave now." Gu anxiously inquired her reason for leaving, and she replied, "I'll never fail to remember your kindness in helping my mother. When I told you 'this was a one-time affair—it can never happen again,' it was to suggest that I wasn't trying to recompense you in the privacy of bed. Because you're poor and cannot afford to marry, I've helped you to continue your family line. I'd hoped we'd succeed with one attempt, but unexpectedly, my period came as usual, so I had to break my oath and try again. Now that your kindness has been repaid and I have carried out my intentions, I have no more regrets."

"What's in your bag?" Gu asked.

She replied, "It's my enemy's head." Gu examined the bag and then peered inside it, turning the head over to find its facial hair matted with blood, its face unrecognizable. Horrified by it, he returned to his questions for an accounting.

"All along, I didn't tell you everything," she explained, "since I couldn't reveal the details to you, for fear that you might divulge them. Now that the business has been successfully concluded, there's no harm in telling you: I'm from Zhejiang. My father was a Sima, falsely condemned to death by an enemy who also confiscated our family's holdings. I carried my mother away on my back, concealed our family name, covered my face, and disappeared for the last three years.

"Hence I didn't pursue my revenge immediately, because I still had my mother to think about; once mother was gone, there was that lump of flesh in my belly, and for those reasons I had to delay for so long. On the nights when I wasn't in my house, I'd gone out to find my enemy's home, since I was unfamiliar with the roads, and feared that I might miss him."

A Sima: One of the most prominent family names in Chinese literary history, from the author of the *Records of the Grand Historian*, Sima Qian, to Sima Yi, the military strategist from the historical epic, *Romance of the Three Kingdoms*, who founded the Jin Dynasty.

Once she finished speaking, she went out the door. As she did, she admonished him, "Be kind, and watch out for the child I bore. Your good fortune is slight, and you won't live long, but this child will achieve glory for your family. It's late at night, so don't awaken mother— I've got to go!" Before he could sadly inquire about her destination, she vanished in a flash like lightning, so that in the time it took to glance at her, she was no longer to be seen. Gu could do nothing but sigh and stand there numbly, as though he'd lost his very soul.

The next day he told his mother everything, considering with her the strangeness of it all, and that was an end of the matter. After three years, Gu really did die. His son, at eighteen, qualified as a *jinshi,* and they say that he respectfully cared for his grandmother until she died.

The collector of these strange tales remarks, "A man has to have a wife like the swordswoman if he wants to keep a boyfriend as livestock. Otherwise while you're loving your handsome boar, he'll be loving your breeder pig!"

Jinshi: A successful candidate in the highest level of the imperial civil service examination.

68. The Drinking Buddy

Scholar Che's family was not well fixed for money, but he was addicted to drinking. When night fell, unless he helped himself to three cups of wine, he couldn't get to sleep, and for that reason he never allowed the wine bottle by his bedside to become empty.

One night he woke up, and as he turned over, he sensed that there was someone lying in the bed with him, so he figured that the bedclothes he'd used to cover himself must have slid off into a pile. He felt around till he found something soft and fluffy, like a cat, but larger; he brought a candle over—and there was a fox, dead drunk, and sleeping it off. He looked over at his wine bottle and found it empty.

Hence he laughed, and said, "This'll be my drinking buddy." Not wishing to rouse the fox, he tucked it in and laid his arm over it, so they could sleep next to each other. He kept the light burning, so he could observe the fox if it changed into something else.

At midnight, the fox yawned and stretched itself. Che chuckled, and declared, "You've had such a nice nap!" When he lifted up the bedclothes and looked beneath them, there wearing a Confucian scholar's cap was a handsome young man.

He got up from the bed and did obeisance to Che, thanking him for his kindness in not killing him. Che replied, "I'm always into the liquor, so people take me for a fool; pal, you'll be a Bao Shu to me. If you have no misgivings about the proposition, I'd like for you to be my drinking buddy." He pulled the fox back down onto the bed, and again lay down to sleep, adding, "If you can visit often, don't hesitate for any reason." The fox agreed to return. When Che next woke up, the fox had already gone. He then acquired a good quantity of excellent wine and waited for the fox.

When night came, the fox did return and they happily drank together in private. The fox was a prodigious drinker, and its words were so humorous that Che was sorry they hadn't met sooner. The fox said, "I've enjoyed your fine wine repeatedly, so what can I do to repay your kindness?"

Che replied, "That piddling amount of wine is hardly worth mentioning!"

"Be that as it may," persisted the fox, "you're a poor scholar, and it's not easy for you to get money for drinks. Therefore I'd like to devise a modest plan for you to come up with drinking money."

The next night, the fox showed up and announced, "If you go seven *li* southeast of here, by the side of the road there's some gold that's been left behind, and you can go there to collect it."

Che went there as he was told, found two pieces of gold, then bought some delicacies at the market to go with their wine that night. The fox responded by informing him, "Behind your courtyard, stored in a cellar there, is something you should check out."

Che did as it said, and so discovered more than a hundred strings of cash. Delighted, he declared, "With this in the bag, I have no more worries about buying wine."

"Not so," replied the fox. "When water fills the rut left by a passing wheel, can it last for long? We need to plan for even more."

Bao Shu: A minister to Huan Kong of Chi (c. 685-6 B.C.E.), Bao used his resources to serve as the patron of his devoted friend, Guan Zhong, who in turn later became Prime Minister of Chi (Mayers 97-8, 180-1).
Li: A distance equal to 1/3 mile.

Another day, the fox called on Che, and told him, "The market price for buckwheat is very low now, and this business opportunity will set you up." Che followed this advice, buying up over forty *dan* of buckwheat. Everyone laughed at him for doing so.

It wasn't long before a great drought dried up and withered all the grain and vegetables, until only buckwheat could still grow; Che sold his buckwheat for a tenfold profit. Thanks to the transaction, he became a rich man, and acquired two hundred *mu* of irrigated farmland.

He still asked the fox for advice, and when it told him to sow lots of wheat, he did, and reaped accordingly, and when it advised sowing lots of millet, he did, and reaped in kind—the appropriate species and planting times were always as selected by the fox.

Over time they grew even closer, the fox calling Che's wife his sister-in-law and treating Che's son like his own. But after Che died, t,he fox never came back.

Forty dan: One *dan* equals about fifty kilograms.
Two hundred mu: A *mu* is equal to about .0667 hectares, so Che's 13.34 hectares equals about 33 acres.

69. *Lian Xiang*

Sang Xiao, whose courtesy name was Ziming, lived in Yizhou. Orphaned when he was young, he lived in a house near the Honghua [Saffron] Market. It was Sang's nature to live quietly and contentedly by himself, usually going out for a walk twice a day, and resolving to sit at home all by himself the rest of the time after taking his meals with his neighbor to the east.

This neighbor happened to visit him once, and teased him, "Since you live all alone, aren't you afraid of ghosts and foxes?"

Sang laughed, and answered, "What's there for a man to fear about ghosts and foxes? If they show up as men, I'll meet them with my sword, and if as women, I'll just open my door and invite them in."

The neighbor went home and contrived with a friend to use a ladder to send a prostitute over Sang's wall, who knocked at his door softly with her fingers. Sang peeked out to ask who was there, and the woman replied she was a ghost. Sang was so terrified that his teeth chattered noisily. The prostitute backed away and left.

In the morning, the neighbor came over to Sang's study, so he described what he'd seen, and announced his intention of returning to his hometown. The neighbor clapped his hands and said, "Why didn't you open your door and invite her in?" Sang paused and realized that he'd been tricked, so he returned to living placidly as he had before.

Half a year went by, then a girl came one evening

and knocked at his study's door. Sang figured his friend was fooling with him again, so he opened the door and invited her to enter, discovering her to be a devastatingly gorgeous girl. Amazed, he asked her where she'd come from, and she answered, "I'm Lian Xiang, a prostitute from a brothel just west of here."

Since he knew there were several brothels in that vicinity, he believed her. They extinguished the lights, climbed into bed, and wove themselves together like exquisite silk. From then on, she dropped by regularly every few nights.

One evening, Sang was sitting alone with his thoughts, when a girl entered quietly. He figured it was Lian and got up to greet her. When he saw her face, he realized his mistake: she was only about fifteen or sixteen years old, wore expansive sleeves and an unmarried girl's hairstyle which hung down her foreheard, yet she looked sophisticated and beautiful, walking into the room with steps that seemed to be both coming and going. Greatly startled, Sang suspected that she was a fox.

The girl declared, "I'm from a good family, by the name of Li. Admiring your refinement, it's my good luck to be able to make your acquaintance." Sang was quite flattered.

He took her by the hand, which was cold as ice, and asked, "Why are your hands so chilly?"

"All my life, my body's been too weak to be very warm," Li replied, "besides, being out in the evening's frost and dew, how can my hands be warm!" Then she loosened her silk robe, and Sang believed she truly was a virgin. She told him, "Because I love you, I want to offer myself to you this evening. If you don't think it too low of me, I hope to take care of your needs often while next to you on your pillow and mat. Do you have anyone else seeing you?"

"No one except a nearby prostitute," Sang replied, "but she doesn't attend to me very often."

Li said, "I'll be careful to avoid her. I'm not one of those kinds of people, so you mustn't reveal our secret to her. When she comes, I'll go, and when she goes, I'll come whenever I can." Just as the rooster was about to crow, she offered Sang an embroidered slipper as a present, declaring, "I've worn this on my foot, so just touch it whenever you yearn for me. However, if anyone's around, you must be careful not to bring it out!"

He took the slipper, examining it carefully, noting it was so tiny that it came to a point at the end, like an awl. He loved her for it. The following evening, when no one was around, he took out the slipper and began playing with it. Li gracefully appeared all of a sudden, and the two joined together intimately. Henceforth, every time he took out the slipper, the girl would inevitably show up, as if she could sense his thoughts.

It seemed pretty odd, so he asked her about it. She laughed, "It's just a coincidence."

One night, Lian arrived, and became terribly shocked, asking Sang, "Why do you look so washed out?"

"I can't feel anything wrong," he replied. Lian then bid him farewell, making a date that they would meet again in ten days.

After she left, Li came to him without missing an evening. "Why's it been so long since your lover's shown up here?" she asked him. When he told her about the appointment she'd made with him, Li laughed and inquired, "Who do you find the more beautiful, Lian Xiang or me?"

Sang replied, "The two of you are matchless. But Lian's flesh is warmer."

Li's facial expression changed, and she declared, "You claim our beauty is equal, but you're only saying that in my presence. She must be another goddess of the Moon Palace, so I'm clearly no match for her." Hence she was no longer cheerful. Then she counted on her

---

Lian's flesh is warmer: Pu's double pun here implies that both Lian's "skin and muscle" *and* her "intimate relationship" (*jifu*) with Sang are both "more moderate" and literally "warmer" (*wenhe*) than his *jifu* with Li.

Goddess of the Moon Palace: A reference to Chang'e, the Chinese goddess of the moon.

fingers that ten days had just elapsed, so warning Sang not to give her away, she planned to spy on Lian.

The next night, after Lian Xiang arrived, they laughed and chatted together in perfect harmony. When they made ready to go to bed, Lian, quite startled, cried, "How awful! I haven't seen you in ten days, so what could have done you so much harm? Can you swear you haven't been meeting with someone else?" Sang asked her why she was wondering. "I can see it in your expression," she explained, "and your pulse is whispy, like unraveled silk—you have the ghost disease."

The following night, when Li appeared, Sang asked, "Did you get a peek at Lian Xiang?"

"She's a beauty, alright," she replied. "I'm sure there's no one else so lovely in the whole world—she must be a fox. When she left, I followed her to her den in the southern hills." Sang suspected this was just a matter of jealousy, and casually dismissed it.

The next evening, he teased Lian Xiang, "While I put no credence in it, there are some who say you're a fox."

"Who's been saying this to you?" Lian anxiously asked.

Sang smiled and said, "It's just my own notion, darling."

Lian then asked, "What is the difference between a fox and a human?"

"Foxes seduce people and make them sick, and the sickness can grow serious enough to make people die, which is why they're feared," he explained.

Lian Xiang exclaimed, "That's not true. For someone as young as you, the vitality can return in just three days, so how can sex with a fox prove harmful to you? Doing it daily, however, would curtail your vitality, so in that way the person choosing to do so would be doing more harm than the fox. Are you saying that foxes are to blame for everyone who dies of consumption? That's why I believe someone's been saying things about me."

Though Sang vigorously asserted that nothing had been said against her, Lian kept questioning him earnestly. He couldn't stand to keep it from her, so he told her everything.

Lian replied, "No wonder I could tell you'd become fatigued recently. But what could've caused this to happen so quickly? Is it because she's not human? You must say nothing about it, and tomorrow night I'll do as she did and spy on her."

When night came, Li appeared, and hadn't spoken three words when she heard the sound of a cough outside the window, then swiftly ran off. Lian entered and cried, "You're doomed! She's truly a ghost! If you continue to fall prey to her beauty and don't break with her immediately, you're heading straight for the underworld!"

Sang thought she was simply jealous, and refused to comment.

Lian remarked, "It's clear that you're not going to give up your feelings for her, but I just can't bear to see you die. Tomorrow, I'll bring some medicine for you to dispel your fatal disease. With any luck, the disease has taken only shallow root in you, and in ten days you should be cured. Please stay in bed with me and I'll watch over you, so we can make you well."

The next night, she took out a measure of medicine, and Sang swallowed it down. Instantly, it circulated throughout his innards, till his guts felt clear and calm, and his spirit immediately brightened. Although he was grateful to Lian Xiang, in the end he still wouldn't believe that Li was a ghost.

Night after night, Lian Xiang stayed under the quilt, and snuggled close to Sang; but if he started to get amorous, she'd always turn away. After several days, his flesh filled out again. Before she left, Lian sincerely urged him to stop seeing Li. Sang disingenuously agreed he would do so.

But as soon as he'd closed the door, he turned up the wick of his lamp, took out Li's slipper, laid down and began lusting for her. Li suddenly appeared.

Because quite a number of days had gone by since they'd seen each other, she gave him a very resentful look. Sang explained, "She stayed with me these nights to work some medical magic, so please don't be angry—I

have genuine feelings for you." Li was somewhat pla-
cated by this.

Sang laid down with her, and in a bedroom con-
fidence told her, "I care for you very much, but there are
some who say you're a ghost."

Li was at a loss for words for quite some time, then
shrieked, "You must have been listening to the lies of that
fucking fox! If you don't stop seeing her, I'm not coming
back!" Then she began sobbing and weeping. Sang tried
everything he could think of to console her, till she finally calmed down.

A night later, Lian Xiang arrived and could tell that
Li had been back, angrily declaring, "You certainly want
to die!"

Sang laughed, "Why are you so deeply jealous of
her?"

Lian became even more furious: "You were cultivating your own death till I stopped you, and if I hadn't
been jealous, what would've become of you?"

Sang made excuses, then jokingly said, "She told me
yesterday that my sickness was the work of a fox spirit."

Lian sighed, then responded, "It's clear from your
words that you don't realize how mistaken you are, which
I hadn't expected, but even with a hundred mouths, how
could I justify myself to you? Now I must ask to part with
you. One hundred days from now, I will see you lying in
your bed." He couldn't convince her to stay, so with a
look of disappointment, she went away directly. From
this time forward, Li was together with him every night.

About two months went by, and he began to feel
exhausted. At first he just tried to console himself; but as
the days passed, he gradually became exceedingly thin,
and couldn't take in more than a single bowl of congee.
He wanted to return to his hometown, where he could
be supported and cared for while recovering, yet he was
so passionately attached to Li that he just couldn't bear

One hundred days: Pu's original reads *bairi*, a ritual held on the
100th day after a birth or death.

to rush off.

Since he decided to stay, in a few days the effects became so severe that he was unable to get out of bed. His neighbor noticed how his illness had devastated him, and sent a boy each day to take him food and drink.

Sang finally came around to entertaining suspicions about Li, so he said to her, "I'm sorry I didn't listen to Lian Xiang's advice before it all came to this!" When he finished speaking, he shut his eyes and lost consciousness. He revived a moment later, opened his eyes and looked around, but Li had vanished—and that was the end of their affair.

Sang lay wasting away in his lonely studio, wishing with the intensity of someone who's starving for Lian Xiang to come. One day, just as he was concentrating his thoughts on her, someone suddenly pulled aside the curtain and entered: Lian Xiang. She approached his bed, smiling, and said, "This village boy, how can I forget you!"

Choked with sobbing for a long time, and knowing that he was to blame, Sang begged her to save him. "Your disease has entered the vital organs," Lian explained, "so it's truly no longer possible for me to treat and cure you. I came because we're about to be parted by your death, and I want to make it clear that I wasn't jealous before."

Extremely distraught, Sang cried, "There's a thing under my pillow that I must trouble you to destroy." Lian searched and retrieved the slipper, then held it near the lamp, turning it over and over. Li suddenly entered, halting when she saw Lian Xiang, and turning to flee.

When Lian moved to block the doorway, Li found herself in such a difficult position that she didn't know where to go. Sang reproached her repeatedly, and Li found herself unable to reply. Lian smiled and said, "Finally we have met face to face. Earlier you told this gentleman that his lingering illness could only have been caused by me, but now what do you have to say?" Li bowed her head to acknowledge her wrongdoing. "A girl as beautiful as you," Lian exclaimed, "how can you twist love into hatred?"

Li flung herself to the ground, begging Lian to have pity and save Sang. Lian then helped her up, and asked her about her life before she died. Li replied, "I was the daughter of assistant magistrate Li, but died young and was buried next to the wall outside. Like a spring silkworm who dies too soon, I died too young to have fallen in love with anyone. To be together in love with Sang was my sole desire; but that I never meant to cause his death, I swear with all my heart."

Lian observed, "I've heard that a ghost can bring about a person's death so that after the person's dead, they can always be together—isn't that so?"

"Not at all," answered Li. "When two ghosts come together, neither is the happier for their union; if that kind of happiness were possible, the underworld would've provided me plenty of young men!"

Lian cried, "Ah, you're crazy! Every night you've been doing it, even though Sang can't take it, and yet you're a ghost!"

"Since foxes can kill people," Li demanded, "what magic makes you exempt?"

Lian replied, "There are those foxes who make themselves strong by stealing the energy of mortal men, but I'm not one of them. There are foxes who do no harm to people, but there are absolutely no ghosts who do not kill, because the yin energy is too powerful in them."

Sang heard her words and finally realized that the two actually were a fox and a ghost. Fortunately, since he'd grown accustomed to seeing them so often, he really wasn't frightened of them at all. Nevertheless, he felt his breathing dwindle to a thread, and couldn't suppress a loud cry of pain.

Lian, turning to look his direction, asked, "How shall we relieve him?" Li, shamefaced, humbly backed away. Lian laughed, and said, "I'm afraid that when his health recovers, your jealousy will devour him again."

Li gestured respectfully, and answered, "If there's a doctor sufficiently talented to undo what I've done, I'll gladly bury my head in the ground, for I could never dare to face the world again!"

Lian opened her bag and withdrew some medicine, declaring, "I knew today would come, so after I left, I went to pick herbs from three mountains over the course of three months, and now the ingredients are all prepared, so any man dying of consumption could be cured by this fool-proof medicine. However, there's one condition—that it's only effective if the one who caused the disease donates something to its cure."

"What do you need me to do?" asked Li.

Lian replied, "You must give him a drop of your saliva. I'll put the pill in his mouth, then you must drip saliva into it." Li, embarrassed all the more, lowered her head, turned aside, and glanced at her slipper. Lian made fun of her, crying, "Sister, you're still only interested in your slipper!"

Li's shame increased while she raised and lowered her head, unable to contain her embarrassment. "This is one of your usual practices," Lian remarked, "so why withhold it now?" Then she slipped a pill through Sang's lips, and turned to compel Li to act. She responded with a drop of her saliva.

"Again!" Lian demanded. Li offered her spit once more. In all, she spat three or four times, so Sang could swallow the pill. After a little while, his stomach began to make a great noise like cracks of thunder. Lian placed yet another pill in his mouth, then put her lips to his and breathed into him. Sang felt a burning heat in his lower abdomen sending the glow of energy throughout him. Lian cried, "He's recovered!"

Li heard the rooster crowing, looked around anxiously, then disappeared. Lian stayed with the newly-revived Sang, to build up his health again, since he couldn't yet feed himself; hence she kept the outside door bolted shut, to pretend that Sang had returned to his hometown, thus breaking off contact with others, and watched over him day and night.

Li also came without fail every night, offering her own earnest care to him, and treating Lian like her elder sister. Lian reciprocated with sincere sympathy and fondness. Three months later, Sang was as good as new.

Then, for several nights, Li didn't come around, and even when she did come, she just took a quick look at them and left right away. Whenever the three faced each other, Li seemed quite unhappy, so Lian often asked her to stay with them and rest, but she never agreed to do so.

Once Sang chased after her, and carried her back home in his arms, her body as light as one of the paper effigies burned to mourn the dead. She made no attempt to resist, laid down with her clothes on, and curled herself up tightly into a length less than two *chi*.

Lian, filled with pity for her, discreetly asked Sang to make love to her, but though he nudged her, Li wouldn't wake up. Finally Sang also fell asleep; when he awoke, she was gone from sight.

After more than ten days, she still hadn't returned. Sang was feeling particularly unsettled, constantly taking out her slipper and caressing it. Lian remarked, "Even I've taken a fancy to her—let alone how you, a man, must feel."

"In the past," Sang replied, "when I toyed with this slipper, she'd come, and though I suspected it quite often, I still didn't expect that she'd really be a ghost. Now, thinking about her as I hold her slipper, I feel terribly sad." Then he commenced to weep.

Prior to this, in the wealthy Zhang family, there had been a fifteen-year-old daughter named Yan'er, who suddenly died without any warning signs. In the course of the night, she returned to life, got up, looked around, and wanted to rush off. The Zhangs bolted the door so she couldn't get out.

Yan'er told them, "I am the spirit of an assistant magistrate's daughter; feeling obliged to a gentleman named Sang, who thinks of me tenderly, I have left my slipper at his house. I'm really a ghost, so what's the point of holding me here?"

Since her words seemed reasonable enough, they

Two chi: Li shrinks herself to less than 2/3 of a meter.

asked her why she had come there. The girl lowered her head, pacing nervously and glancing about, unable to explain herself. When someone mentioned that Sang had been sick and had returned to his hometown, the girl insisted it couldn't be. This quite puzzled her family members.

Sang's neighbor to the east heard about all this, and when he climbed over the wall to sneak a peek, he saw Sang and a lovely woman speaking together; as he quietly entered and pressed onward, Sang's visitor suddenly vanished from where she'd been. The neighbor, astonished, asked Sang what was going on.

Sang laughed, and said, "It's like I told you: if any women come to visit, I'll let them in."

His neighbor then repeated Yan'er's words to him. Sang consequently unbolted his door, and was about to go out and have a look for himself, but had no pretext to do so. Yan'er's mother heard that he truly had not returned to his hometown, and was most amazed. When she sent an old servant woman to retrieve the slipper, Sang took it right out and gave it to her.

Yan'er was delighted. When she tried to put it on, however, the slipper proved too small for her foot by at least an inch, which really shook her up. She grabbed a mirror and looked at her reflection, suddenly realizing that she had come to life in someone else's body, and then she explained the whole thing to the mother. From then on, the mother began to believe her.

The girl faced the mirror and cried, "There was a time when my appearance was nice, and I was quite self-confident, but even so, every time I saw elder sister Lian, I became more and more ashamed. Now my face has changed to this—I'd be better off as a ghost!" She held the slipper and wailed her sorrow inconsolably.

Covering herself with a large quilt, she laid down, absolutely stiff. She ate nothing, so her body's skin became swollen; for seven days she refused food, but still she didn't die, and the swelling gradually receded; she felt so famished she couldn't stand it, so she began to eat again. For several days her body itched all over, then all of her skin peeled off.

When she got up in the morning, she found that her slippers had fallen off in her sleep, and as she tried to put them on, she discovered they were so large that they no longer fit her. Hence she tried on her former slipper and found its size to be a perfect fit, delighting her.

As she looked in the mirror, seeing her own eyebrows, eyes, and cheeks, just as they had always been, her joy increased. She washed and combed her hair before going to see her mother, and those who saw her couldn't help but stare.

When Lian Xiang heard the strange tale, she advised Sang to send a go-between to propose a marriage; but since he was poor while she was wealthy, and there seemed little chance of success, he didn't dare go through with it.

On the birthday of Yan'er's mother, he accompanied the mother's other sons-in-law as they visited her to celebrate her longevity. When the old lady noticed Sang's name among the others, she sent Yan'er to peep through the curtain, to survey the guests. Sang was the last to arrive, and Yan'er suddenly rushed out and caught hold of his sleeve, wanting to go back home with him. Her mother gave her quite a scolding, so she went back inside, ashamed.

Sang, who'd gotten a careful look at her and knew it was truly Li, couldn't keep himself from crying, and subsequently prostrated himself, refusing to get up. The old lady finally raised him up, without thinking any the less of him. Sang went away and invited Yan'er's uncle to serve as matchmaker. The old lady discussed the matter with him, and they selected an auspicious day for the wedding, after which Sang would come to Yan'er's house to live.

Sang went home and told Lian Xiang, then discussed what to do next with her. Lian was upset for quite a long time, then expressed the wish to part with him. Sang, devastated, wept freely. Lian told him, "You'll light the wedding candles with your new family, and if I were to go with you, how would I save face?"

Sang came up with the idea of returning to his home first with Lian, then afterwards welcoming Yan'er, and Lian went along with it. Sang then expressed his intentions to the Zhangs. When the Zhangs learned that he'd already set up a family, they became angry, expressing their resentment and indignation. Yan'er earnestly explained everything to their satisfaction.

When the appointed day arrived, Sang went and brought Yan'er home. Everything in the house had been carefully prepared, though extremely inexpensively; yet when they arrived home, stretching from the gate to the end of the hall, woven carpets had been laid out and countless decorative lanterns hung as brightly-colored as brocade.

Lian Xiang assisted with the bride's entrance to her new abode and removed her veil, to reveal her looking as radiant as she'd ever appeared. Lian joined them in drinking from the wedding cup, then they asked for the details of her strange return to life.

Yan'er replied, "When I was last with you, I was unable to restrain my sorrow. I began to despise my body as an alien thing, and felt unclean. After leaving you, I angrily refused to return to my grave and drifted aimlessly. Every time I saw living persons, I envied them.

"In the daytime, I dwelt among the flora, and by night I wandered where my feet took me. Unexpectedly, I came to the Zhangs' house and saw a young girl lying on her bed, approached and attached myself to her without realizing that I could return to life that way." When Lian heard this she became silent, lost in thought.

Two more months went by, and Lian bore a son. After giving birth, she suddenly fell violently ill, and as the days went by, her condition steadily worsened. She clutched at Yan'er's arm and told her, "I must burden you to take care of this child, your son as much as mine." Yan'er's tears fell as she tried hard to comfort Lian. She wanted to hire some magical healers for Lian Xiang, but Lian refused to allow it.

Her condition deteriorated till she lay dying, her breathing as thin as a strand of silk. Sang stood by with

Yan'er, both of them sobbing. Suddenly Lian opened her eyes and declared, "Don't weep for me! Our child is happy to be alive, so I'm happy to die. If fate will have it so, in ten years we can see each other again." Once she finished speaking the words, she died.

When they opened her clothing as they were about to place her into a coffin, her body changed into that of a fox. Sang, unable to bear seeing Lian as a strange creature, gave her a lavish burial. The son was named Hu'er, and Yan'er loved him like he was her own child. Each Tomb-Sweeping Day, Sang and she hugged the boy at Lian's grave, and wept together there.

After Sang became a successful candidate in the imperial examination at the provincial level, his family gradually began to prosper. Yan'er, however, was deeply sad that she couldn't bear him a child. Hu'er was quite intelligent, though frail and prone to sicknesses. Yan'er frequently wished that Sang would marry a second wife.

One day, a servant suddenly reported, "There's an old woman outside the gate, accompanied by a girl whom she's interested in selling." Yan'er called out for them to enter.

The moment she saw the girl, Yan'er cried out in astonishment, "Sister Lian has come back!"

Sang looked her over and was equally amazed to find her exactly like Lian. He asked, "How old is she?"

"Fourteen," came the reply.

"What's her selling price?"

The old lady answered, "I only have this one child, but still I have to find a place for her, while all I need is simple food and somewhere to live, and to be sure that when I die, these old bones won't be tossed into some ravine. Then I'll be satisfied." Sang offered her a good price, and had her stay.

Yan'er took the girl's hand, and they stepped into a

Hu'er: Literally, the name means "fox-child."
Tomb-Sweeping Day: Part of the Clear Brightness (*qingming*) Festival, where families honor their ancestors at family grave sites.

private room, where Yaner lifted the girl's chin, smiled, and asked, "Do you know me?"

"No, I don't," she answered. When Yan'er inquired about her name, the girl replied, "My surname is Wei. My father sold starch in Xucheng, but died three years ago."

Yan'er counted on her fingers and realized that Lian had died exactly fourteen years earlier. She looked closely at the girl again: in both appearance and manner, she resembled no one so much as Lian. Yan'er then patted the top of her head, and exclaimed, "Sister Lian, sister Lian! The ten-year date you set before hasn't let us down!"

The girl suddenly woke up as though from a dream, and spontaneously cried out in surprise, staring hard at Yan'er. Joining them, Sang laughed and said, "This is 'like an old, familiar swallow that has come back home.'"

The girl, tears streaming from her eyes, declared, "It's true. My mother once said that at the time I was born, I was able to speak, and thinking this inauspicious, I was given dog's blood to drink, so I'd lose memory of my previous incarnation. But now it's like I'm just awakening from a dream. Aren't you little sister Li, who was ashamed to be a ghost?" They talked about their previous existence together, by turns saddened and jubilant.

One particular Qingming, Yan'er explained, "Every year, this is the day when the master and I go to weep for elder sister." So they went to Lian's grave, which was covered with weeds, while the tree growing over her coffin had grown so it took two arms to reach around it. The girl sighed deeply at the sight.

Yan'er said to Sang, "Sister Lian and I have cared for each other in two different worlds, and we can't stand being separated, so it's only right that our bones be buried in the same site." Sang went along with their request, opened Li's grave to retrieve her bones, and

---

'*Like an old familiar swallow*': A line from the classical poem, "*huan xi sha*" ("Washing in a sandy stream"); see Zhu (228n80).

carried them back to be buried with Lian's. Relatives and friends who had heard the strange story dressed auspiciously and gathered about the grave, not expecting the several hundred people who were there.

A number of years into the reign of Kangxi, I was traveling south in Shandong when, hindered by rain, I stopped at an inn. A scholar there named Liu Zijing, Sang's cousin, took out the biography of Sang, written by his colleague, Wang Zizhang—over ten thousand words long—for me to read. This story only covers its main points.

The collector of these strange tales remarks: "It makes me sigh! One of them, dying, wishes to live, while another one, alive, wishes to die—everywhere under heaven, is there anything as hard as finding a human body? Those who possess such a body often don't care for it as they should, so they're equally uncomfortable as a living creature like the fox, or a dying spirit like the ghost."

Reign of Kangxi: 1662-1723.

70. A-Bao

In the western part of Guangxi, there lived a famous scholar named Sun Zichu. He was born with an extra finger. Sun had a slow, deliberative way of speaking, and people always tried to cheat him, for he always believed whatever he was told. If there were singing girls sitting anywhere in his vicinity, even when he was spotting them from a distance, he'd try to run away from them shyly. Those who knew he responded this way would lure him into coming where prostitutes could be hired to act indecently familiar with him, whereupon he'd blush the entire length of his neck, while sweat rolled down his face in pearly drops.

For these reasons, everyone laughed at him. This made him look like such a dumbbell that people circulated malicious tales about him until he was nicknamed "Goofy Sun."

In his town, there was a certain old man who was an influential merchant and was as wealthy as a prince. His relatives were all of noble descent. He had a daughter, called A-Bao, who was extremely beautiful. At that time, he wanted to choose a good mate for her, and the sons of all the great families sent their intentions with gifts, expressing their wishes to marry her, but none of them were suitable, in the old man's opinion.

Since Sun then had lost his wife, someone played a trick on him, advising him to contact a marriage broker about A-Bao. Sun naively had little notion that he was out of his depth, and hence proceeded to follow the advice.

The old man had known for some time that Sun was a talented scholar, but disapproved of him for his poverty. Just as the marriage broker was leaving, she happened to run into A-Bao, who asked why she'd come and was told.

The girl jokingly said, "If he lops off his extra finger, he can take me home with him." The marriage broker then informed Sun.

Sun replied, "That's not tough at all." Once the broker left, Sun used an axe to cut off his extra finger, the severe pain of it penetrating to the heart of him, and so much blood poured out that he was on the verge of dying. It took several days before he was able to get up again, then went out to see the broker and showed her the finger.

Horrified, the old lady broker ran off to inform A-Bao. The girl also found this startling, but in jest invited him this time to quit being goofy.

When Sun heard this, he became upset, asserting that he was no fool; however, he had no way to see her and demonstrate that himself. He began to reconsider that maybe A-Bao wasn't necessarily a celestial beauty after all, for what gave her the right to act so superior? Because of this, his former infatuation with her suddenly cooled.

Then Qingming arrived, with its custom of women going out to walk through the streets; frivolous young men would join together and follow after them, unrestrainedly rating each of them. There were several young men of Sun's acquaintance who strongly urged him to join them.

In mocking derision, one of them demanded, "Don't you want a glance at your sweetie?" Sun knew they were making fun of him; but he'd already endured the girl's ridicule, so he thought he'd get a look at her, and hence was delighted to follow along with the group and search her out.

From a distance, they spotted a young woman resting beneath a tree, with a mob of insufferable young men surrounding her like a restraining wall. The group members agreed, "This has to be A-Bao."

They hurried over and verified her identity. Attentive to every detail, they found her to be an unparalleled beauty. In a short while, the crowd became even more dense. A-Bao stood up and hastily left. The crowd was thrown into chaotic discussion about her appearance, the lot of them as disoriented as if they were crazy. Sun alone remained silent. The group went on ahead, and when they turned back to look at him, seeing Sun standing like an idiot in the same spot, they called to him, but he didn't answer.

The group pulled him over to where they were, taunting him, "Did your spirit abandon you to follow A-Bao?" He still didn't reply. The group knew him to be a fellow of few words, so no one thought this strange, and either by pushing or by pulling, they finally got him back home.

Once at home, he went straight to bed, laying there all day without getting up, unconscious as though he was passed out drunk, and though they shouted to him, he couldn't be roused.

His family was afraid that his spirit had indeed abandoned him, and searched the countryside outside the household, calling out to it, but this proved to have no effect. They slapped Sun and questioned him, but his only response was the drowsy remark, "I'm at A-Bao's house." But when they asked for more information, he went silent again. His family members, anxious and perplexed, didn't understand what was happening.

Originally, when Sun saw A-Bao leave, he couldn't allow himself to be parted from her, so he felt his body following along behind her as she walked, till gradually he was right up next to her, and no one criticized him about it.

Thus he followed A-Bao home, where he sat and laid down next to her, and every night he made love to her, which they both found exceedingly pleasant; afterwards, however, Sun would feel extremely hungry, and though he longed to return home, he felt disoriented and didn't know how to get there.

A-Bao continually dreamt about having sex with a particular man, and when she'd ask him his name, he'd say, "I'm Sun Zichu." She felt this to be very strange, but was unable to bring herself to tell anyone about it.

Sun lay in bed for three days, his breath dwindling as if it was just about to stop altogether. His family grew extremely worried, and went to break the matter gently to the old man, in hopes that he might invite them to search for Sun's spirit in his household.

The old man laughed and said, "In the past, we never made a practice of visiting each other, so why would his spirit have become lost in my house?" Sun's family remained resolute in their pleading, so the old man finally agreed to permit the search.

A master of magic arrived, carrying some of Sun's old clothing and a straw mat. A-Bao, upon asking him the reason for his visit, was astonished that Sun's spirit was in her family's house, and guided the master directly to her bedroom, where she let him summon the spirit and then take his leave.

By the time the magic master had reached the Sun family's gate, Sun was already moaning from his bed. Upon awakening, he was able to describe what toiletries and possessions A-Bao kept in her room, what they looked like, what they were called, and all without a mistake.

When A-Bao heard about this, her amazement increased, and she secretly felt moved by the profound degree of his love.

Once Sun was able to leave his bed, he became totally engrossed in his thoughts, completely absent-minded. He was always trying to catch a glimpse of A-Bao, hoping for the good fortune of encountering her once again. During the Buddha Bathing Festival, he heard that she was going to offer incense at the Shuiyue Monastery, so at

---

Buddha Bathing Festival: In celebration of the Buddha's birthday, on the eighth day of the fourth month of the lunar calendar, celebrants bathe the Buddha's image with fragrant water.

daybreak he went to wait for her by the side of the road, his eyes dazzled from straining so hard to watch for her.

The sun had already passed noon when A-Bao appeared, spotting Sun when she peered out from her carriage, and subsequently pulled aside the curtain with her delicate hands while staring at him without turning away. Sun moved forward, trailing along after her.

A-Bao suddenly ordered a maid servant to go ask the gentleman his name. Sun eagerly answered the question, his spirit feeling even more agitated than before. When the carriage left the monastery, he headed home.

At home, he became sick once more, fell into a trance, and stopped eating, in his dreams always calling out A-Bao's name. He berated his spirit for not being able to follow her once again.

When the old parrot which belonged to his family suddenly died, a child held its body and played with it on a bed. Sun thought to himself that if only he had the parrot's body, with just a flap of the wings he could be in A-Bao's room. As his mind fixated on the parrot, he felt his body become the parrot's, and he hastily flew off, straight to A-Bao's place.

The girl, delighted, caught the bird, tied it to a perch, and fed it hempseeds. With a loud squawk, it cried, "Elder sister, don't tie me up! It's me, Sun Zichu!"

A-Bao, utterly shocked, untied the string, but the bird didn't fly away. The girl blessed it, saying, "Your sincerity has engraved itself on my heart. But now we're of different species, human and bird, so how can we be joined in love together?"

The parrot replied, "Just to be near the fragrance of you is everything I desire." If other people tried to feed it, the parrot wouldn't eat; when A-Bao herself fed it, it ate, and when she sat down, it would perch on her knee; and when she laid down, it would sit next to her bed.

So it went for three days. A-Bao felt great pity for the bird, and privately sent someone to check on Sun's condition. The scholar had lain stiff, without breathing, for three days, yet the area over his heart had not turned cold.

Once again, A-Bao gave the parrot her blessings: "If you can become human again, I swear I'll be yours till I die."

"You're lying to me!" squawked the parrot. A-Bao swore she wasn't. The parrot cocked its head to the side, as though thinking it over.

A little later, when A-Bao decided to bind her feet a bit tighter, and hence took off her shoes, putting them under her bed, the parrot suddenly swooped down, snatched the shoes in its beak, and flew off, with A-Bao calling out to it as it disappeared into the distance.

A-Bao sent an old woman to go and discern Sun's condition, and the old woman found the scholar already awake. His family members had seen the parrot arrive with the shoes in its beak, then fall to the ground dead, and everyone had agreed it was incredibly strange. As soon as he had revived, Sun called for the shoes. No one there could figure out what had happened to him.

When the old woman arrived and walked in to see Sun, she demanded the whereabouts of the shoes. "A-Bao gave them to me as a betrothal gift," replied Sun. "Tell her for me that I have not forgotten her precious promise." The old woman did as she was directed.

A-Bao thought this all the more strange. Hence she sent a maid servant to describe everything to her mother. Her mother carefully verified the report's accuracy, then said, "This young man's reputation for talent isn't bad, but he's as poor as Xiangru. If after several years of searching we choose a son-in-law like this, I'm afraid the prominent families will laugh at us." However, because of the shoes incident, A-Bao swore that she would have no one else but him. Her mother and father went along with her decision.

They sent the news quickly to Sun, who was overjoyed, and suddenly recovered from his illness.

Xiangru: Sima Xiangru (179-113 B.C.E.), a famous poet who was impoverished, but successfully wooed the wealthy widow, Zhuo Wenjun, with his lyrics while playing his zither-like *qin*.

A-Bao's father discussed having Sun move in with them. "A son-in-law can't live for long in the household of his wife's parents," A-Bao responded. "Besides, Sun's already poor, so that would simply give people more reason to think him worthless. I've given him my word, so I'll live in his thatched hut and enjoy his humble food without regret." Sun then married A-Bao and took her home with him, and they seemed together like beloveds who'd been separated in a previous life, now rejoined.

Of course, A-Bao's family gave her a dowry, a small fortune that significantly improved their circumstances. But "Goofy" Sun, who was too obsessed with studying, didn't know how to manage the family's business interests; fortunately, A-Bao was adept at handling their assets, so she didn't burden Sun with business matters. After managing things thus for three years, they became quite rich.

Sun suddenly fell ill with diabetes, then died of it. A-Bao wept piteously, crying her eyes out, then just stopped sleeping or eating. When others tried to encourage her, she wouldn't listen, hence she took advantage of nightfall to hang herself. A maid servant discovered her attempt and quickly rescued her, so A-Bao revived, yet she still refused to eat.

Three days later, Sun's relatives had gathered and were just about to inter his body. They heard a groan and gasp of breath from inside his coffin, then opened it, verifying that he'd come back to life. He told them, "I appeared before the Hell King, and because I've been a just and honest person, he ordered that I be given an official appointment. Suddenly a man announced, 'Minister Sun's wife is about to arrive.'

"The King checked his registry of ghosts and declared, 'It's not yet her time to die.'

"The man replied, 'She didn't eat for three days.'

"The King turned to look at me and said, 'Being moved by your wife's devotion, for the time being I will allow you to return to life.' Hence he sent a servant to harness horses and bring me home." From this time forward, Sun's health steadily improved.

It happened then that the date arrived for the pro-vincial civil service examination, and as it approached, some young men decided to play a joke on Sun by secret-ly drawing up seven odd, phony examination topics, then luring him to a secluded place to tell him, "Thanks to somebody's bribes, we're able to show you the examiners' topics."

Sun believed them, working day and night on these seven topics, till he'd successfully completed the seven essays. The group hid their laughter from him.

At that time, the civil service examiners, concerned that overly-familiar themes might promote the copying of previous work, did everything they could to turn the usual topics into unusual ones. When the examination papers were distributed, all seven matched up with Sun's essays. Accordingly, he was selected as the best of the examinees. The following year, Sun qualified as a *jinshi* and was granted a place in the Hanlin Academy.

When the emperor heard of these curious events, he summoned Sun to appear for questioning. Sun delivered his report to the emperor and awaited his reactions. The delighted ruler praised him effusively. Afterwards, the empress also summoned A-Bao, and lavished expensive gifts on her.

The collector of these strange tales remarks, "The quality of foolishness may assist an individual in de-veloping determination, for it's the case that someone who's crazy for books will certainly prove to be a skilled writer, while someone who's nuts for art will have what it takes to develop fine artistic ability; those who fail to develop themselves, and never accomplish anything, would all say that there's nothing goofy about *them*. It's the same with those who squander money on painted

---

Jinshi . . . Hanlin Academy: Jinshi is the title awarded a successful candidate in the highest imperial examination. The Hanlin Academy, founded in the 8th century C.E., was a scholarly institute that provided a variety of scribal and archival services for the imperial court.

ladies, or who ruin their families through gambling—
such people, on examination, are the ones who're really
foolish! Therefore, if one is clever and artful, even to
excess, then one can be said to be truly goofy, and what
goofiness Master Sun has in that sense!"

Here's a collection of ten sayings that really exhibit
foolishness: "Save your money—but if you do, you'll eat
poorly. Boast of your son's intelligence in front of your
guests. You can love a child, but never teach him to
read. Be afraid of telling people about the disease you
have. Invest your earnings in prostitutes. Steal so you
can spend your gains on drinking and gambling. Fool
the debt collector by signing your IOUs with the names
of your father and brothers. A father and son's accounts
are always perfectly balanced. The family should be used
the way one uses a machine. Always like your students
who are good at gambling."

71. *King of the Nine Mountains*

A man named Li, who lived in Caozhou, was a successful candidate there in the first level civil service examination. While his family had traditionally been well off, their home wasn't very extensive; behind it was a garden, several *mu* in size, that had not been used for a long time. One day, an old man arrived to rent a room from Li, and straightaway took out a hundred taels.

Li explained that they didn't have any rooms to let, so he'd have to decline. The old man replied, "Please accept it, don't trouble yourself about it." Li didn't understand what he meant, so he accepted the money, figuring that he'd wait and see what would happen.

The next day, the villagers saw swarms of horses and carriages filled with people entering the Li family's gate, one after another, seriously doubting that Li could find room for them all, and asked him what was going on. Li had no idea, either; he hurried home to look into it, and found no traces of them whatsoever.

After several days had gone by, the old man suddenly showed up to pay a visit. He declared, "We've come to you for shelter for several days and nights. Everything's already been put together, a stove's been set up for cooking—we haven't had time to arrange an invitation to show you our gratitude until now. I've sent my daughters to prepare some food, so I hope you'll come and honor us with your presence." Li followed him.

Several mu in size: One *mu* is equal to .0667 hectare (1/6 acre).

As they entered the garden, Li suddenly saw a splendid house that looked brand new. When he walked inside, he discovered the furnishings to be quite beautiful. A cauldron of wine was heating on the verandah, and the delicate scent of steaming tea issued from the kitchen. Instantly, wine and food were brought out that included fabulous delicacies.

Soon Li saw young men appear in the courtyard, going and coming in large numbers. He also heard children whispering, making the sounds of laughter, and words from behind a screen. With all the servants, it seemed like there were nearly a hundred people working for the old man's family. Li realized that they had to be foxes. When the banquet was finished, he went back to his house, darkly entertaining thoughts of killing them.

Each time he went to the market he bought some saltpeter and sulfur, till he'd accumulated several hundred *jin* worth, and hid it, buried in the garden, until he was ready to use it. When he suddenly ignited the saltpeter and sulfur, the blaze stretched up into the sky like a black fungus, so the burnt stench of the ashes made Li squint, unable to go near the fire; he heard the cry of animals howling and fleeing, a horrible clamor of noise. As soon as the fire was put out, he went into the garden to take a look, and found the ground covered with dead foxes, their heads horribly charred, so he was unable to count them exactly.

While he surveyed the grounds, he encountered the old man entering the garden from outside, wearing a deeply grieved expression, and reproaching Li bitterly: "We had no permanent enmity; your garden was leased for one hundred taels, which was no small amount of money; so how could you mastermind the extermination of my clan? This extraordinarily cruel act of malice must be recompensed!" He left in a fit of anger. Li feared that the old man would begin heaving stones at his household, but for more than a year, nothing at all strange occurred.

Several hundred jin worth: One *jin* is equal to ½ kilogram.

In the early years of Shunzhi's reign in the Qing dynasty, a gang of thieves came into being in the mountains, with vast numbers of men banding together, and the officials were unable to arrest them. With so many members having sprung up, Li was constantly concerned about being attacked by the bandits. A man who could predict the future appeared in Li's village, calling himself "The Old Man of the Southern Mountains," telling people tales of good fortune and bad which were so close to real events that they made him quite famous in the village.

Li had him summoned to his home, and asked him to tell him his fortune, according to his birthdate. The old man, stunned, kowtowed to Li and exclaimed, "The man with this birthday is really an emperor!" When Li heard this, he was quite astonished, considering the comment absurd. The old man's face and voice became solemn, to confirm that his words were serious.

Li, suspicious that the old fellow wasn't all there, asked him, "How can that be, since a person can't just become emperor from being empty-handed."

"That's not true," the old man answered. "Since ancient times, haven't many emperors grown up as ordinary people, proving that not every emperor became one through birthright?" Li was puzzled by this, and moved his seat closer to the old man. The old man determinedly regarded himself as a "sleeping dragon." He asked for Li to equip himself with the very finest armor and helmet, and the very best bow and crossbow.

Li pondered this, and felt it unlikely that anybody would support him in such a claim. The old man declared, "I'd like to ask that you issue the order for me to go and communicate with the bandit leaders on the several mountains, and draw up an alliance with them. I can

Shunzhi's reign: The third Qing emperor, but the first to govern all China, ruled from 1644-1661.
A "sleeping dragon": A reference to the nickname of Zhuge Liang (181-234 C.E.), renowned for his almost preternatural foresight while minister and strategist for the Shu-Han leader, Liu Bei, during the Three Kingdoms period.

send someone to spread the rumor that you are the real emperor, and then the soldiers in the mountains would certainly agree to support you." Li was flattered, and sent the old man on his way. He drew upon his cash reserves in order to have armor made.

After several days, the old man returned to make the trip with him, and advised, "Take advantage of your fortune and blessings, plus my skills as an orator, and all of the bandit leaders on the mountains will agree to listen to you and to fight for you." Over the space of the next ten days, over a thousand men joined Li's army.

He paid respect appropriately to the old man, and regarded him as his military strategist; he had an enormous banner made, and set up a forest of colored flags; as Li's army grew stronger and more people began to hear about it, the cities sent out troops to take punitive action against the bandits, and with the old man commanding Li's forces, the city troops were soundly defeated. Badly demoralized, the county officials requested reinforcements from the official in the provincial prefecture. The prefecture's soldiers would have to make a long, arduous journey to arrive there, so the old man again advanced the bandit forces to attack, completely routing the city soldiers, his officers and men inflicting widespread casualties.

Their reputation continued to expand as the gang members reached to over ten thousand, and for that reason Li gave himself the name, "King of the Nine Mountains." The old man, worried about the scant number of their horses, heard from the capital that some horses were being sent to this province, so he dispatched a brigade to seize and hold the horses that were on the way. After this, the reputation of the "King of the Nine Mountains" became all the greater. The old man also declared him "Guardian of the State and Supreme Commander of the Army." Living in seclusion in their mountain lair, Li openly boasted about himself, and declared that in just a limited number of days, he would soon be wearing the imperial yellow robe.

Meanwhile, because of the incident involving

seizure of the horses, the provincial governor sent out troops to oppose Li, and received support from higher officials, who sent out their most excellent troops in further aid; they surrounded the bandits from six directions, and then closed in. The government troops' banners filled the entire mountain valley.

The "King of the Nine Mountains" was terrified, and summoned the old man to work out a plan, but no one knew where he'd gone. Hard-pressed and with no tactics of his own, the "King of the Nine Mountains" climbed to the top of the mountain and exasperatedly cried out, "Now I know how great is the power of this dynasty!"

The mountain stronghold was captured, its inhabitants taken prisoner, their wives and children killed. Li suddenly understood that the old man was really the old fox, who'd avenged the extermination of his clan by wiping out Li's own.

The collector of these strange tales remarks, "If husbands would just live with their wives and children happily, with the doors of their households closed, how could they ever kill anyone? And even if they could kill, why would they ever destroy an entire clan? The fox's plan was quite ingenious. However, if there had been no evil thoughts in Li's own mind, the plot wouldn't have germinated, even with the old man trying to cultivate it; the man who killed the foxes was savage, and that shows that his heart already possessed evil roots, so the fox encouraged those roots to sprout and then conducted his plan of revenge. Now we can directly test passersby by saying to them, 'You're really an emperor!' Henceforth, everybody will be shaken up, and run away.

"Obviously, Li was guided towards the sacrifice of his entire family, but he was still happy to listen to the advice. Hence he can't blame anyone else for his family being destroyed, can he? A man listens to insane comments and initially is angered by them, but if he becomes intrigued, he'll continue to give credence to those suspicions until his life and reputation are both destroyed, and then he realizes that his own faults have led to the disaster; this is the general rule of this kind of thing."

72. The Foxes in the Zunhua Office

Master Qiu, of Zhucheng, governed the Zunhua district. Many foxes had gotten into the office there. Finally, the last building was taken by them to use as their home. Occasionally they went out and did bad things to people, but trying to dispel them just made them behave even worse. The officials who had once lived there had made sacrifices, and had prayed, but no one dared to oppose the foxes.

When Master Qiu arrived at his post, and heard about all this, he became furious. The foxes feared him as upright and unyielding, so one changed into an old woman and told his servants, "I'd like to make this petition to His Excellency: there's no point in mutual enmity. If he can give me three days, I'll take the others with me and we'll slink away." Master Qiu overheard this, but said nothing.

The next day, when he finished reviewing the troops, he ordered them not to disperse, sent them to their camp to bring over all of their large cannons, and then surrounded the Zunhua office's last building with them; over a thousand cannons fired on the last building—which collapsed at once despite being several stories tall—while skin, flesh, fur, and blood began to rain down from the sky.

They also saw that in the midst of the resulting dark, dense, poisonous fog, a wisp of white vapor was belched out, and then vanished. The crowd of soldiers looked into the distance and cried, "There's a fox running off." Afterwards, everything was once again safe and sound in

333

the Zunhua office.

After two years, Master Qiu, angling for a transfer and promotion, sent a loyal and canny servant to carry a certain amount of silver to the capital. When the business didn't work out, he stored it temporarily in a pit at the house of one of the office's employees.

Suddenly, an old man appeared, claiming he'd been wronged, saying his wife and children had been violently murdered. He accused Master Qiu of cutting back on the army's provisions, in order to use the money to ingratiate himself with powerful people, as would be immediately apparent at a certain household if they would investigate and verify it. Someone accepted the petition and pledged to look into it.

Arriving at the employee's house, they searched everywhere but found nothing. The old man kept pacing the same plot of ground. Realizing what it meant, they pointed out the spot, and soon they discovered the silver; engraved on it were characters spelling out, "Transported and guarded by this county." They stopped to look for the old man, but he'd vanished from the premises.

When they searched for him, according to the name and address he left them, this, too, turned up nothing. As a consequence, Master Qiu got into some hot water and was sentenced for his deed. That's when he realized that the old man was the fox that had fled.

The collector of these strange tales remarks, "Foxes that plague people deserve to be severely punished. However, if they obey and abandon their wickedness, we should also treat them humanely. It can be said of Master Qiu that 'he hated the fox too aggressively.' But if his actions had been carried out by Guan Xi, even a hundred foxes couldn't have achieved revenge on him!"

Guan Xi: Guan, whose courtesy name was Yangzheng (and who was also known as Guan Xi Kongzi, or "Guan Xi Confucius," because of his broad knowledge), was once the target of some lavish bribes that he resolutely refused. By citing Guan Xi, Pu indicates that if Qiu had been as honest and clear of blame as Guan Xi, the foxes' efforts would have been in vain (Zhu 242n21).

73. Zhang Cheng

There was a Henan man named Zhang, who had lived in Shandong before that. At the end of the Ming dynasty, when Shandong fell into general chaos, his wife was carried off by northern soldiers. Zhang had often been a trader to Henan, so he fled there with his family. He married a Henan woman who bore him a son named Ne. Before long, she died, and he remarried, that wife giving birth to a son named Cheng.

Zhang's new wife, named Niu, was overbearing and constantly hateful towards Ne, treating him like a beast of burden, and feeding him only marginally edible fodder. He was sent to collect firewood, and each day it was his responsibility to bring back a shoulder's load; whenever he failed to do so, he was soundly whipped and abusively cursed, till it was almost more than Ne could stand. Meanwhile, Niu secretly set aside tasty cakes for Cheng, and sent him to a private tutor for reading instruction.

As Cheng grew up over time, he proved by nature to be full of filial piety and brotherly love, and since he couldn't stand to see his elder brother, Ne, exhausted all the time, he confidentially tried to dissuade his mother from her treatment of him. But she wouldn't listen to him.

One day, Ne went into the mountains to collect firewood, but before he'd gathered enough, a huge storm blew up and he took refuge beneath a rock outcropping,

---

Northern soldiers: That is, by Manchus.

and by the time the rain stopped and it cleared off, it was already late. He was utterly famished, so he slung the firewood over his back and headed home.

Niu checked and found him short of the expected load, so in anger she refused him anything to eat; his hunger burning inside him, he went to his room and laid down, stiff and motionless. When Cheng came home from studying with his tutor, and saw Ne looking so dejected, he asked, "Are you feeling sick?"

Ne replied, "I'm just hungry." Cheng asked him to explain, and when Ne told him what had happened, Cheng's expression became grave, and he rushed out.

A moment later, he returned with some cakes stuck inside his robe for his brother. Ne asked him where he'd gotten them. Cheng replied, "I took some flour and asked the neighbor lady to make them, so don't talk—just eat." Ne gobbled them down.

Then he advised his younger brother, "After this, don't do it again. If word gets out, you'll be blamed. I get one meal a day, so the hunger isn't going to kill me."

"Brother, you've been weakened," Cheng insisted, "so you don't have the strength to collect firewood!"

The following day, after eating, Cheng stole off to the mountains to the place where Ne was collecting his firewood. His older brother spotted him, and asked in surprise, "What are you doing here?"

Cheng replied, "I'm here to help gather firewood."

"Who sent you?" asked Ne.

He replied, "I came by myself."

Ne told him, "There's no point talking about it, since you can't cut firewood—but even if you could, you mustn't." Consequently, he urged him to go home. Cheng wouldn't listen, using his hands and feet to break up limbs to help his brother.

Then he told Ne, "Tomorrow I should bring an axe when I come."

Ne came over to dissuade him. He saw that his brother's fingers had been scratched up, and that he'd worn holes in his shoes, so he felt bad about it, and cried out, "If you don't go home quickly, I'll take this axe to my throat and kill myself!'"

Cheng then headed home. Ne accompanied him halfway there, then turned back around. Once he'd gathered his firewood, he, too, went home, stopping by the tutor's school to pay a visit, where he advised the master, "My brother is still young, so you should keep him inside here. There are many tigers and wolves out there in the mountains."

The master said, "I didn't know where he'd been going before noon, but I've already beaten him for it." Ne went home and told Cheng, "You didn't listen to my words, so now you've suffered a beating for it."

Cheng smiled, and said, "No big deal."

The next day, Cheng hefted the axe, and again headed out.

Ne, astonished at his arrival, said, "I specifically told you not to come back, so why have you returned?" Cheng didn't reply, but simply chopped up firewood for a long while, eager to help, the sweat pouring down his cheeks as he worked without ceasing. When he'd collected enough to make up a bundle, he turned back without a word of farewell.

The master scolded him again, so Cheng revealed the truth to him. Expressing admiration for his virtue, the master lifted the prohibition on his leaving.

One day, the brothers were out in the mountains with several other men, when suddenly a tiger appeared. The frightened group spread themselves flat on the ground. The tiger eventually lifted Cheng up in its mouth and carried him off. Lugging Cheng, the tiger made very little progress, so Ne was able to chase it and catch up with it. He swung his axe at it, and caught the tiger in the thigh. The beast roared in agony and ran off so swiftly that Ne was unable to keep up with it, and had to turn back, bitterly weeping.

The others tried to console him, but he sobbed all the more miserably, crying out, "My younger brother was one of a kind; besides, he died for me, so how can I go on living!" Then he raised his axe up to cut his own throat. The group rushed to stop him, but the axe had already entered his flesh about a *cun,* and blood was gushing out. He became dizzy and fainted. The men, aghast, ripped up some of his clothing and used it to stop the bleeding, then helped him get home.

His mother, weeping and cursing, cried, "You killed my son, now you want a nick in the neck to take you off the hook!"

Ne groaned, "Mother, don't vex yourself. Younger brother is dead, and I have no reason to go on living!" He was placed on his bed, but with the pain from his wound he couldn't sleep, so day and night he huddled against the wall, sobbing.

His father was afraid that Ne, too, might die, so he frequently came to his bedside to feed him, with Niu reproaching him for it each time. Ne then stopped eating, and three days later, he died.

In their village lived a mage, who acted as a courier to the underworld, and Ne ran into him en route there, subsequently recounting to him the suffering of the past several days. When he inquired about Cheng's whereabouts, the mage told him that he hadn't heard anything. Then he turned, and led Ne along with him.

They came to a large city, where they saw a man in black coming their way. The mage stepped in front of him, and asked him some questions. The man took out a document from a bag he wore at his waist, and looked it over carefully, examining the hundred-odd names of men and women there, but didn't find a Zhang among them.

The mage suspected that it was listed in someone else's documents. But the man told them, "This is my jurisdiction, so there's no reason for Zhang Cheng to be taken by the others." Ne refused to accept this, and strongly insisted that the mage accompany him inside the city.

Once they were inside the city walls, they saw recent ghosts as well as ones who'd been there awhile, gliding

---

About a cun: The Chinese "inch" is equal to 1/3 decimeter.

here and there, and when they recognized some of them, they went to make inquiries, but found that no one yet knew anything about Cheng.

Suddenly they all raised their voices to exclaim, "The Bodhisattva has come!"

When Ne looked up into the clouds, there was an enormous figure, with dazzling rays of light emanating from her, till suddenly everything around them was brightly lit. The mage congratulated Ne: "Young sir, you're in luck! The Bodhisattva only comes to the underworld once every so many decades, to attend to things regarding the disposition of spirits, so now's the perfect time to be here." Then he pulled Ne down onto his knees.

The multitude of ghosts also noisily knelt, putting their palms together and chanting for the merciful one to rescue them from their suffering, till the sound of their entreaties shook the ground. The Bodhisattva waved her willow branch, sprinkling sweet dew over everyone, its spray as fine as mist. Suddenly the mist ceased, the light faded, and the Bodhisattva vanished.

Ne felt some of the dew on his neck, and the place where the axe had wounded him no longer caused him any pain. The mage, as before, led Ne away with him and they returned home. Not until they could see the village gates in the distance did the mage take his leave and depart.

Ne had been dead for two days, when all of a sudden he revived, related everything that had transpired in the underworld, and then reported that Cheng wasn't dead. Niu figured he was making it all up and accused him of falsifying, heaping more verbal abuse on him. Though Ne was being wronged, he had no way to defend himself, yet when he touched his wound, he felt a scar there and knew he truly had been healed.

Bodhisattva . . . willow branch: Refers to Guanyin ("She Who Hears All Cries"), the Buddhist goddess of mercy, "considered the embodiment of compassion, wisdom, and love" (Perkins 196). Her willow branch, a Buddhist symbol of humility, is revered for its cleansing and healing properties.

He marshaled his strength to get up, and pledged to his father, "I'm going to enter the clouds and scour the seas to search for my brother, and if I can't find him, don't look for me to return as long as this body has life in it. I want you to think of me, father, as if I were still dead." The old man led him over to a private space, and there he wept with him, not daring to ask him to stay.

Ne then departed. At every thoroughfare, he invested his resources to search for his brother, and once he'd exhausted his traveling money en route, he became a beggar and continued on. A year passed, till he reached Jinling, his clothing in tatters, having become hunchbacked along the way.

He spotted a group of ten or so riders passing through, and had to step aside to get out of their way. Ne noticed one man who looked like a senior official, about forty years old, accompanied by robust men on sturdy, powerful mounts, galloping and capering before and behind him. A young man, riding a smaller horse, kept staring over at Ne. Ne figured that the young man must be the son of a high official, so he didn't dare return his glance.

The young man reined in and halted his modest steed, then suddenly dismounted and cried out, "If it isn't my elder brother!" Ne raised his head to take a careful look, and sure enough, it was Cheng. As he grasped Cheng's hands, Ne felt a great pang of sorrow and broke down in tears.

Weeping along with him, Cheng asked, "Elder brother, what has happened to bring you to this state?" As Ne described his experiences to him, Cheng's sympathy increased all the more. The other riders dismounted to ask what was going on, then explained it to the senior official.

The official ordered them to provide a horse for Ne to ride, then the brothers joined their reins and rode together back to the official's home, with Ne asking

---

Jinling: Modern Nanjing.

Cheng to tell him his story from the beginning.

Originally, after the tiger carried Cheng off, he'd been unconscious when it dropped him along the road, and he lay there all night long. It happened that the official, Zhang Biejia, had just come from the capital, and as he passed, noticing Cheng's cultured appearance, he took pity on him and cared for him, till he gradually regained consciousness.

Cheng told the official his address, which was a long distance away. Hence the official took him home with him. There he applied medicine to Cheng's wounds, and several days later, he'd begun to recover. Biejia had no heir, so he adopted Cheng. They had just been out for a ride when he caught sight of Ne.

While he was explaining everything to his brother, Biejia entered, and Ne respectfully thanked him over and over. Cheng went inside and carried out some silk clothing for his elder brother, then he put on a feast for him, so they could chat while enjoying the food.

Biejia asked him, "Since your family is in Henan, how many able-bodied men are there in your hometown?"

"There aren't any," Ne replied. "Father grew up in Shandong, only later relocating to Henan."

Biejia commented, "I'm also from Shandong. What county is your village part of?"

"In the past," Ne replied, "father said that it was part of Dongchang's administrative territory."

Amazed, Biejia exclaimed, "I'm from the same hometown! Why did you move to Henan?"

Ne explained, "At the close of the Ming, soldiers poured in, abducted my father's first wife, and then left. My father had to endure soldiers burning everything down, and carrying off his wife. Earlier he'd conducted business in the west, going and coming, so he was quite familiar with the area, and for that reason he settled there."

Even more amazed, Biejia asked, "What is your father's name?" Ne told him. Biejia stared at him with his eyes wide, lowered his head as if pondering something, then quickly rushed inside.

Before long, Biejia's mother came out. Together the brothers kowtowed to her, and once they'd finished, she asked Ne, "Are you Zhang Bingzhi's grandson?"

"That's correct," he answered.

Biejia's mother began to weep, saying to Biejia, "These are your younger brothers." The brothers found themselves tongue-tied. Biejia's mother explained, "I was married to your father for three years, then carried off to the north by a commander named Hei, and half a year afterwards, I gave birth to your elder brother. Another six months later, the commander died, and your elder brother in time filled a vacancy under his banner, moving up gradually to take the commander's place. Now he's been released from that appointment.

"Each and every moment, I think about my real home, so I separated myself from the northerners and resumed my previous identity. Time and again, when I sent people to Shandong, no one could learn anything, but how was anyone to know that your father had moved west!" Then she added to Biejia, "But making your younger brother your son—you destroy your own blessings and posterity!"

Biejia answered, "In the past, when I asked Cheng about himself, he never said anything about being from Shandong, so he must have been too young to recall it."

Then they organized themselves by age: Biejia, forty-one years old, was the elder Zhang son; Cheng, at sixteen, was the youngest; Ne was twenty-two, previously the elder of Zhang's sons, but now the middle brother of all three. Having two younger brothers made Biejia very happy, and they all slept together in the same room so he could learn the causes behind their having become separated, while he made plans for them to return home.

His mother was afraid that Niu wouldn't accept them. Biejia told her, "If she can accept us, we'll live together, and if not, we'll split up. Who in the world wouldn't want to return to his father's home?" Thereupon, he sold his house and packed up everything, having set the day when they would head westward.

As soon as they arrived at their village, Ne joined

Strange Tales from Liaozhai

Cheng to ride ahead and announce the news to their father. After Ne left home, Niu died; their father had become a solitary old widower, perpetually in mourning. When he suddenly saw Ne enter, he was so happy that he felt faint from the strain; upon seeing Cheng, he was absolutely ecstatic, unable even to speak a word, his tears falling freely.

Then they told him that Biejia and his mother would arrive soon, so the old man stopped his weeping, stunned, torn between joy and sorrow, and just stood there like a simpleton. It wasn't long until Biejia entered and paid his respects to his father; his mother clasped the old man in her arms, and they wept together.

Since all the female and male servants had come down to meet them, and were all over the place, inside and outside, the old man didn't know what to do, whether to sit or to stand. When Cheng didn't see his own mother, and asked after her, he learned that she had died; wailing until he was hoarse, he then fainted, but shortly afterward began to revive.

Biejia financed the building of a new house, and engaged a tutor to instruct his two younger brothers; horses were soon capering in the stables, the rooms of the house were filled with boisterous chatter, and, surprisingly, they became a rich and influential family.

The collector of these strange tales remarks, "Hearing this business all the way to its conclusion provokes my tears to fall: a boy ten years or so old, chopping wood to help his brother; I admire him, and cry out, 'This is another Wang Lan in the world!' And then my tears fall

Tears to fall: A refrain in this particular commentary is *duo*, a character signifying "to fall down" or "to sink," used metaphorically here (it appears five times) to communicate the depth of Pu's emotion.

Wang Lan: Wang Lan was the stepbrother of Wang Xiang, who was abused by his stepmother during childhood yet remained filial to her. Wang Lan felt so badly for the beatings given to his elder stepbrother that he tried to intercede, helping Wang Xiang finish the hard work assigned by the mother and saving the first time. When I hear that the tiger has carried off Cheng, I can't help wailing and sobbing, "Why must heaven be so unfair!" So I cry for the second time. Elder and younger brothers unexpectedly meet again, which causes me to weep anew, for the young brothers suddenly have an elder brother, and I feel sorry for Biejia for having lost so many years of brotherhood—hence I shed tears once again. A family is reunited out of both sad and happy circumstances, and though I shouldn't cry, I cry also for the old man. I wonder whether in later generations there will be people like me who shed tears so easily."

---

his stepbrother's life several times when his mother tried to poison Wang Xiang (see Zhu 248n44).

74. The Fenzhou Fox

Master Zhu was a Fenzhou magistrate, whose government office was overrun by foxes. As he sat there at night, a woman was going and coming beneath his lantern light. At first he thought she was his wife's servant, so he didn't look up at her; and when he did raise his eyes, he realized that he didn't recognize her, though she looked quite beautiful. He knew in his heart that she was a fox, but he lusted for her nonetheless, and hastily called for her to come.

She stopped with a smile, and said, "That stern sound's meant for me, but who are you calling your maidservant?"

Zhu laughed and stood up, dragging her over to sit with him, where he could apologize for his mistake. Then he made love to her, and for a long while they lived together happily as husband and wife.

Suddenly one day, she said to him, "You're going to have to give up your appointment—there isn't much time."

"When must I do it?" he asked.

"Right away," she smiled. "There may be congratulations at your gates now, but there will be mourning in your village soon, so you can't remain an official."

Three days later, he received an announcement that he should relinquish his appointment. The next day, he was given news of his mother's death. Zhu resigned his post, desiring that the fox accompany him to his hometown. But his fox wife couldn't agree to do so.

346

She accompanied him to the river's edge. There he tried to force her aboard the ferry with him. The girl told him, "You wouldn't know this, but foxes can't cross rivers." Zhu couldn't bear to be apart from her, and expressed his love for her there at the river bank. The girl suddenly rushed off, saying she had to visit an old friend. After a bit she returned, and now she had a man with her, returning the visit she'd just made. The girl uttered something to her guest. Once he'd left, the fox came back to Zhu, saying, "Please climb aboard the ferry at your convenience—I'll be joining you for the crossing."

Zhu replied, "According to your own words, you can't make the crossing, so why are you saying this now?"

"The one who just paid us a visit is the river god," explained the fox wife. "I used you as the rationale for making a special request of him. He gave me permission to cross the river within the next ten days, so I can accompany you and stay with you for that long." Then they crossed the river together. On the tenth day, consequently, she said farewell and left.

75. *Qiaoniang*

In Guandong, there was a government official named Fu, who was over sixty when he had a son, named Lian. Lian was extremely bright, but he'd been endowed with rather inadequate reproductive equipment, so even at the age of seventeen his private parts were still as small as a silkworm. Everyone far and near learned of this by rumor, so no one would offer him their daughters to marry. Facing the possibility of being denied descendents, Fu fretted about it day and night, but didn't know what he could do.

Lian meanwhile was studying with a teacher. When the teacher unexpectedly had to step out one day, it happened that a monkey show was playing just beyond their gate, and Lian went outside to watch, abandoning his studies. Upon reflecting that the teacher must be about to return, he became afraid of being punished, and ran off.

Once he was several *li* from home, he saw a girl dressed in white, walking ahead of him, with a maidservant. The girl turned her head towards him, revealing that she was bewitchingly beautiful, beyond compare. She was walking slowly with her tiny feet, so Lian hurriedly walked past her.

The girl turned to look at her maidservant, and said, "Why don't you try to ask the gentleman whether he'll be traveling to Hainan?" The maid servant then called out

---

Li: A distance equal to 1/3 mile.

348

the question. Lian asked why she was wondering.

"If you're going to Hainan," the girl replied, "there's a letter I'd like to send home with you. My mother would be a grateful hostess." When Lian originally ran off, he did so without a particular direction in mind, so he decided that crossing the sea might be the thing to do, and gave the girl his consent. She took out the letter and gave it to her maidservant, who in turn gave it to Lian.

When he asked the girl for her name and home town, she replied, "My family name is Hua, and we live outside Qinnü village, three or four *li* from the northern part of Qiongzhou." Lian then went aboard a boat and departed.

The sun was already setting as he arrived in northern Qiongzhou. He asked about Qinnü village, but no one seemed to know of the place. Heading to the north, he walked four or five *li*, and though the moon and stars were shining brilliantly, the road was so overgrown with grass, and the place was so wild, that he couldn't find an inn where he might rest. He felt completely bewildered.

He noticed a tomb by the side of the road, so he thought he'd stop there to rest a bit, even though he was afraid that there might be tigers and wolves about. Consequently, he clambered up into a tree as nimbly as a monkey and settled onto a branch. He listened to the sounds of rustling in the tall pine trees, and to the chirping of insects in the night, which made him feel uneasy, so he regretted having impetuously agreed to come.

Suddenly hearing the sounds of people below him, he looked down and saw what seemed to be a courtyard; a beauty was sitting on a stone, flanked by a pair of maid-servants carrying painted lanterns, standing on each side to wait on her. The beauty turned to the maid on her left and said, "Tonight the moon is bright, outshining the stars, so we can take out the tea Auntie Hua gave me and make a cup of it to drink, while appreciating this lovely evening." Lian assumed them to be ghosts or evil spirits, which made his hair stand on end, and he hardly dared take a breath.

One of the maidservants looked up at him all of a

sudden and cried, "There's someone in the tree!"

The frightened girl stood up and said, "What a brave fellow, to spy on people in the dark!"

Lian was horrified, but with no place to run and hide, he climbed down, prostrated himself on the ground, and begged her to pardon him. When the beauty came over to take a casual look at him, her anger turned to pleasure—she pulled him up and sat him down next to her. With a sidelong glance, Lian could make out that she was seventeen or eighteen years old, and stunningly gorgeous. When he listened to her speak, he could tell she had a local accent.

She asked him, "What are you doing here?"

"I've been sent to take a letter to someone," he replied.

She informed him, "There are many bandits in the countryside, so sleeping out in the open can be risky. If you don't mind the clutter, I'd like you to rest here." Then she invited Lian inside.

There was a room with only one bed in it, so she directed a maidservant to spread out two quilts on it for them. Since Lian was ashamed of his physical inadequacy, he offered to sleep on the floor. The girl laughed and said, "Having received our honored guest, how dare I neglect tending to you?" Lian couldn't get out of it, so he laid down together with her on the bed, though he was so mortified that he didn't have the nerve to relax and stretch out.

Soon afterwards, the girl secretly slipped her hand in under Lian's quilt to explore, lightly stroking his thigh. Lian pretended to be asleep, like he hadn't felt anything. Then, a little while later, she lifted his quilt and slid under it, nudging him, though he still showed no reaction. The girl slid her hand down to his private parts. Then,

---

How dare I neglect tending to you: The "*yuanlong*" portion of this colloquialism is derived ironically from the name Chen Yuanlong, a figure from the Three Kingdoms period, noted for taking a large bed for himself and giving a small bed to his guest (Zhu 256n25).

disappointed, she stopped stroking, quietly slid out from under the quilt, and left. Presently, Lian heard the sound of weeping. Feeling nervous and humiliated, uncertain what to do, he cursed heaven for his deficiency.

The beauty called for her maidservant to bring a light. The maid saw signs of tears on the beauty's face, and asked in surprise what was making her unhappy. The girl shook her head and replied, "I'm just sighing over my destiny." The maid stood before the bed and looked searchingly into the girl's face. The beauty said, "If you can wake him up, send him on his way." Lian heard all this, which doubled his feelings of shame; in addition, he worried about finding a place to stay in the middle of the night.

While he was thinking things over, the maid declared, "Auntie Hua's come."

Lian took a quick peek, and saw that she was in her fifties, though still very stylish. When Auntie Hua saw that the girl wasn't asleep, she asked why. The beauty refused to reply. Then the woman noticed there was someone lying on the bed, and demanded, "Who's that sharing your bed?"

"This evening a young gentleman asked for lodging," the maid answered for the girl.

Auntie Hua laughed and said, "I didn't realize Qiaoniang was celebrating her wedding." When she noticed that Qiaoniang's tears hadn't yet dried, she was startled, and said, "Tears have no place on one's wedding night; has the gentleman been rough with you?"

Qiaoniang said nothing, sobbing all the more. Auntie Hua wanted to have a grope to examine the young man, but as she lifted his clothing, the letter fell onto the bed. She picked it up and looked at it, then cried in amazement, "This is my daughter's handwriting!" She opened it up and read it, both sighing and exclaiming.

Qiaoniang asked her what it was. "It's from Sanniang," Auntie Hua explained, "who says that her husband Wu has died, leaving her alone with no place to go—so what's she going to do?"

The girl replied, "This fellow said he had a letter to

deliver, so it's fortunate we hadn't sent him away yet."
Auntie Hua told him to get up, then inquired as to how
he came by the letter. Lian carefully explained. Auntie
Hua replied, "You've gone to a lot of trouble to bring this
letter, so how can we recompense you?" She gave him a
searching look, and asked with a laugh, "How have you
managed to upset Qiaoniang?"

Lian answered, "I don't know what I've done." Then
she asked Qiaoniang her question.

The girl sighed and explained, "I'm upset at myself
for having married a eunuch when I was alive, and for not
running away from the fate of having another eunuch,
that's why."

Auntie Hua turned to Lian and declared, "Clever
boy—unaware that you're really a woman, I thought you
were a man, eh? You're my guest, so for a bit let's not
bother the others."

Then she conducted him into one of the rooms
on the east corridor, and slid her hand into his pants to
examine him. Laughing, she said, "It's no surprise that
Qiaoniang's all in tears. However, you're lucky that
there's a physical foundation, so it can still be fortified."
She held up a lamp and scavenged through her chests
and baskets, till she came across a black pill that she told
Lian to swallow down at once, mysteriously ordering him
not to move, and then went out. Lian lay there musing
by himself, not knowing what disease the medicine was
supposed to remedy.

Just as the fifth watch was beginning, he became
conscious of feeling a moist warmth just below his navel,
directly going into his private parts, suffusing the area
until there was something hanging down between his
thighs; when he touched himself, he found an impressive
male organ. He was shocked and ecstatic, like he'd been
awarded the highest distinction imaginable from the
emperor.

The fifth watch: The final of the five two-hour divisions of the
night, from approximately 3:00-5:00 a.m.

As daylight spilled over the windowsills, Auntie Hua entered, carrying steamed cakes into the room for him, warning him to sit still, and upon leaving, shut the door behind her. She went and told Qiaoniang, "Since the young man performed a worthy deed by delivering the letter, we need to detain him until Sanniang arrives, so they can get to know each other, like elder and younger sisters. For the time being, keep him shut up in there so we can avoid upsetting or annoying anyone." Then she walked out the door and departed.

Lian was pacing in boredom, every so often opening the door a crack, like a bird peeking out of its cage. He spotted Qiaoniang, and felt the urge to summon her so he could display himself to her, but was too bashful and stopped himself. He was involved thus till about midnight, when Auntie Hua brought her daughter home.

She opened his door and remarked, "The gentleman must be very bored! Sanniang, come here and formally thank him." The girl from his road encounter shyly entered, then turned to face Lian, and greeted him respectfully. Auntie Hua directed them to call each other elder brother and younger sister.

Qiaoniang giggled and said, "They can also call each other elder sister and younger sister." They all went together into the main room, where the group sat together while wine was served.

As they were drinking, Qiaoniang teasingly asked Lian, "Are eunuchs also aroused by beautiful women?"

"The lame never forget what it's like to have walked," Lian replied, "and the blind never forget what it's like to have seen." They all smiled broadly at his words.

Qiaoniang noticed that Sanniang was fatigued from traveling, so she forced her to go to bed. Auntie Hua then gave Sanniang a glance to indicate that she should go and sleep with Lian. Sanniang, embarrassed and nervous, wouldn't move. Auntie Hua encouraged her, "This so-called man is actually a woman, so what's there to be afraid of?" She urged the two to leave together.

Privately she advised Lian, "In secret, you're my son-in-law; publicly, you're my son—that's the deal."

Delighted, Lian took Sanniang's arm, and led her onto his bed, where it was like he was using a grindstone to test a new blade, and his pleasure was obvious. Once they were finished and resting on pillows, he asked her, "What kind of person is Qiaoniang?"

"She's a ghost," Sanniang answered. "Her talent and looks are unequalled, but it's her fate to suffer misfortune. She married a young gentleman of the Mao family, but he was impotent, and by the age of eighteen he still couldn't function, so she became depressed and moribund, till the regret she harbored sent her to her grave."

Lian was shocked and began to suspect that Sanniang, too, was a ghost. "To tell you the truth," she said, "I'm not a ghost, but a fox. Qiaoniang was living alone without a mate, while I and my mother had no home, so we took advantage of the situation to settle here." Lian was quite stunned. Sanniang told him, "Don't worry, we may be ghosts and foxes, but we won't cause you any misfortune."

Henceforth, they chatted and ate together every day. Though Lian knew Qiaoniang wasn't human, yet he loved her for her beauty and goodness, and his sole regret was that he hadn't had an opportunity to expose himself to her. Lian was cultured and restrained, yet good at pleasing people by telling them jokes, so Qiaoniang began to feel affection for him.

One day, as Auntie Hua and Sanniang were about to go out, they shut Lian up again in his room. Lian sulked, pacing the room in circles, and calling through the door to Qiaoniang. Qiaoniang ordered a maidservant to try out several keys, then finally got the door open. Lian leaned close to her ear and asked her to come in with him. Qiaoniang sent the maidservant away.

Lian then pulled her close to him on the bed, snuggling face to face with her. Qiaoniang mockingly reached down below his navel with both hands, and said, "It's a pity that this part of my boyfriend is lost." She hadn't even finished these words before she found her hands absolutely full.

Astonished, she exclaimed, "What was so tiny last

time, is suddenly huge!"

Lian laughed as he told her, "Last time it was too shy to come out for a visitor, so it remained shrunken; now with all the embarrassing ridicule and slander, it grew bigger, just like a frog when it gets angry." Then they made love together.

When they were finished, Qiaoniang angrily exclaimed, "Now I know why they've kept your door shut. Before, when mother and daughter were drifting without a place to stay, they availed themselves of my home. Sanniang learned to embroider from me, and I never kept even the smallest secret from her. For her to act like this now out of jealousy—!"

Lian calmed her down, and explained what had happened. Qiaoniang finally relented. "It's a secret," Lian said, "and Auntie Hua urged me to keep it that way." He'd just finished speaking, when Auntie Hua suddenly entered. The two, surprised, leapt out of bed.

The woman cast an angry eye, and demanded, "Who opened his door?" With a smile, Qiaoniang admitted she was responsible. This made Auntie Hua even more furious, prompting a stream of curses from her.

Qiaoniang just laughed, and exclaimed, "Granny, what a big laugh! This is a man who's really a woman, so what use can he possibly be?" Sanniang, upset from observing the acerbic exchange between her mother and Qiaoniang, tried to intervene between the two, and finally managed to turn their stubborn anger into amity. While Qiaoniang's words still seemed resentful and resistant, subsequently she recognized Sanniang's intention and cooperated with her. But Auntie Hua remained vigilant day and night, so the two lovers had no chance to act on their desires for each other, and could only express their emotions through significant glances.

One day, Auntie Hua told Lian, "My two daughters—the elder sister and the younger sister—are now both devoted to you. I've been thinking that your staying here may be improper, so you should return home and explain things to your father and mother, towards concluding a marriage agreement." She immediately made preparations for him, and hurried him to leave.

Together, the two girls faced him with sorrowful expressions; but Qiaoniang looked especially distraught, her tears spilling like the pearls from a broken necklace, and this went on for quite some time. Auntie Hua tried to stop them from crying, and at her earliest opportunity pulled Lian outside. Once they stepped outside the gate, the house and grounds ceased to exist, and in their place Lian saw an untended grave.

Auntie Hua accompanied him till he was aboard a boat, and told him, "Once you've gone, I'll take my two daughters away and rent a house in your village. If you won't forget your beloveds, go to the abandoned garden of the Li family, and there you can claim them for marrying." Lian then returned home.

After Lian's father had searched for his son unsuccessfully, he was naturally apprehensive, so when he saw his son return home, he was overjoyed. Lian outlined the whole story, and described Auntie Hua's plan. "How can you trust that fiend's words?" demanded his father. "The only reason you're still alive is your male deficiency; otherwise, you'd be dead!"

"Even though they're supernatural beings," Lian countered, "they have feelings just like people do; besides, the girls are both intelligent and lovely, and if I marry them, I won't receive any more teasing from our relatives." His father had nothing to say, and simply sneered at him. Lian then left, but he found himself itching to show off his new ability again, so he began making love often to the maidservants; eventually, he even began doing it publicly in the daytime, just because he wanted to scandalize his parents.

One day, a young maidservant happened to spy him doing it, and ran off to tell his mother. Since she didn't believe her, she went to have a peek for herself and was astonished. She summoned the maids to get to the bottom of the matter, and hence she learned the whole story.

Ecstatically happy, she exuberantly announced to

everyone she met that her son wasn't sexually incapable, and that they would soon choose a daughter from among the influential families for her son to marry. Lian told his mother confidentially, "I'll marry into the Hua family, or I won't marry at all."

His mother remarked, ""There's no shortage of beautiful women in the world, so why settle on some spirit?"

"If not for Auntie Hua," he answered, "I'd never have been able to perform sexually. It would be inauspicious to turn my back on them." His father was persuaded, so he sent a servant and an old woman to go and look at Auntie Hua and her daughters discreetly.

The two traveled four or five *li* east of the city wall, looking for the Li family garden. Among some collapsed walls, bamboo, and trees, they saw the wispy signs of kitchen fire smoke. The old woman climbed down from the carriage, and walked right up to the door, where Auntie Hua and Sanniang were wiping the table and washing up, as though they were waiting for someone.

The old woman paid her respects, and then revealed her master's orders. Upon looking at Sanniang, she declared in surprise, "Is this the lady our young master would bring into the family? When I see her, I can understand why young master's spirit yearns for her, and why his dreams revolve around her." Then she asked about Qiaoniang.

Auntie Hua sighed, and said, "She's my adopted daughter. Three days ago, she suddenly passed away." Then she entertained the old woman and the servant with wine and food.

When the old woman returned home, she gave an account of Sanniang's demeanor that pleased both father and mother. When she got around to news of Qiaoniang's death, Lian was so grief-sticken that he sobbed and sobbed.

The night of the wedding ceremony, Lian met with Auntie Hua to ask her about Qiaoniang. She told him,

"She's already been reborn in the northern lands." Lian cried for a long while.

He took Sanniang home with him, but in the end he couldn't forget his love for Qiaoniang, and whenever anyone arrived from Hainan, he was certain to ask them in, to interview them about her. Someone said that at the Qinnü graveyard by night, one could hear a ghost weeping. Lian was surprised at this, and ran in to tell Sanniang.

Sanniang sat deep in thought for a good long time, then, bursting into tears, exclaimed, "I've abandoned my elder sister!" Lian asked her what she meant, and she explained, "When my mother and I came here, we didn't let her know the plan. This suffering spirit, couldn't it be her? I've wanted to tell you, but was afraid of being scolded by my mother."

Lian listened, saddened, but then became hopeful. He ordered a carriage and traveled at double speed day and night, hurrying to the site of Qiaoniang's grave. He kowtowed at her grave tablet, and cried out, "Qiaoniang! Qiaoniang! I'm here."

Instantly, he saw Qiaoniang, carrying a baby in her arms as she emerged from the grave, raise her head and piteously sob, staring unstintingly at him with anguished regret. Lian also wept. When he inquired whose child it was, Qiaoniang replied, "This is your son, born three months ago."

Lian sighed, and said, "Because I believed Auntie Hua's lies, the suffering of mother and son has been been hidden away in a grave—what a wrong I have to rectify!" Then he took them away in his carriage, crossed the sea, and returned home.

He held the baby in his arms as he told his mother everything. When she saw the child with its sturdy appearance, not like a ghost at all, she was exceedingly

---

In the northern lands: This might be seen as dually painful for Lian, given both his loss and the post-Ming dynasty animosity of the Han Chinese toward the northern invaders, to which Pu makes occasional allusions.

pleased. Qiaoniang and Sanniang lived harmoniously, and were filial daughters to Lian's mother and father.

Afterwards, Lian's father fell ill, so they sent for a doctor to come. But Qiaoniang told them, "His sickness can't be cured, because his spirit has already left him." She supervised as they prepared for his funeral, and as soon as they were finished, he died.

The child grew up to resemble his father quite remarkably; he proved particularly adept, and at fourteen, he passed the examination for *xiucai*.

Old Zi Xia, from Gaoyou (though he moved to Guangdong), heard all this. He's lost track of what the place was called, and he also doesn't know how everything turned out in the end.

Xiucai: A successful candidate in the imperial civil service examination at the county level.

76. The Wu Official

There was a certain official in Wu, whose name I've forgotten. He had a reputation for being firm and honorable. Wu's customs treasured the city god so greatly, that the people carved a wooden effigy of it, and dressed it in brocade, which made it look alive.

For the god's birthday, the local residents would all collect money and throw a festival party, during which an imperial carriage drawn by men would parade through their thoroughfare; they constructed a series of banners, then organized all kinds of officials into rows and lines to parade together, accompanied by musicians and the sound of drums.

The event was treated as a custom, so for years no one had dared not to participate.

The official, who had just come to take up his new post, came across the celebration, and stopped to ask what was going on. Some of the Wu residents explained it to him. He asked further questions, and learned how much they were spending on the lavish displays.

Outraged, the official pointed to their deity and scolded them, "The city god is supposed to serve the city. If it is too ignorant to cast its magic, or if it's just some disgusting ghost, then it doesn't deserve to be worshipped; even if it's a useful spirit, it should make economical use of resources and manpower—isn't it counter-productive to spend money on it, raised from collecting the residents' possessions?" When he'd finished speaking, he set the effigy on the ground and gave it twenty lashes.

Following this, the elaborate custom was abandoned. The upright and just official was never secretive about his public practices, but he'd also enjoyed such celebrations when he was a young man.

Once he'd occupied his office for some years, he was outside his office building, climbing a ladder to look into a bird nest, when he unexpectedly missed his footing and fell down, breaking his hip and subsequently dying. The people heard the official's loud voice angrily arguing with the city god from inside the city god's temple, and he carried on thus for several days without stopping.

Wu's people hadn't forgotten the official's virtuousness, so a crowd gathered to discuss a solution to this conflict, then they built another temple for the official, and the sounds of the argument finally ceased. This temple was also dedicated to the city god, with sacrifices offered there year round, and consequently the god's influence seemed particularly manifest there. Wu since then has had two city god temples, they say.

77. Ventriloquism

A woman came to our village who was twenty-four or twenty-five. She was carrying a medicine bag, and peddling her curative abilities. A person came to her for a diagnosis, but the woman explained she couldn't offer a prescription herself—she had to wait until sunset, when she could ask for the advice of various spirits.

That evening, she thoroughly cleaned her small room, then shut herself up inside. A crowd gathered outside her door and window, quietly pressing their ears close to listen in, but they couldn't catch any words, though no one dared even cough. Inside and out, everything came to a dead stop.

About halfway through the evening watches, suddenly they heard the sound of a curtain being pulled open. From inside, the woman asked, "Have you come, Ninth Aunt?"

"I have come," replied a woman's voice.

The woman again asked, "Has Lamei come with Ninth Aunt?"

What seemed to be the voice of a maidservant replied, "I'm here." The voices of the three became intermingled in incessant chatter, on and on without a lull.

Presently, they heard the sound of curtain hooks being pulled again, and the woman announced, "Sixth Aunt has come." The other woman's voice asked, "Has Chunmei also come, cradling the young master in her arms?"

Another female voice declared, "The stubborn little rascal! Wailing and refusing to go to sleep, yet he insisted on coming with his mama. He must weigh a hundred *jun*; I'm so tired of carrying him on my back, the little goblin!" Before long, they heard the sounds of Chunmei's courteous greetings, of Ninth Aunt asking about others, of Sixth Aunt exchanging greetings, of the two maidservants expressing their appreciation, of the little boy's merry laughter, and of a cat, blending into a noisy clamor.

Then they heard the woman say, "The little gentleman really loves to play, since he came from so far away, holding that kitty all the while."

Later on, the sounds gradually hushed, and at the sound of the curtains being drawn again, the room erupted with voices inquiring, "Fourth Aunt, why have you come so late?"

A small, delicate voice answered, "The road here is longer than a thousand *li*, and it took a while for mother-in-law and I to walk it. Besides, she walks rather slowly." Then each of them, in their own ways, greeted Fourth Aunt and her mother-in-law warmly, combining the sound of seats being moved and calls for additional seating, the noise filling the room for the length of time it would take to have a meal.

Then they heard the woman ask about someone's ailment. Ninth Aunt believed that ginseng should be given, Sixth Aunt felt that it would be best to prescribe milk vetch, while Fourth Aunt suggested applying some atractylodes. The voices consulted for a while, then they

---

Lamei . . . Chunmei: These names mean "Plum Flower" and "Spring Plum," respectively.

Hundred jun: One *jin* weighs a catty, or ½ kilogram; one *jun* equals thirty *jin*; hence the young master supposedly feels like he weighs 1,500 kg.

Li: A distance equal to 1/3 mile.

Milk vetch . . . atractylodes: The roots/rhizomes of the Milk vetch (*astragalus adsurgens*) and the Atractylodes (*atractylodes macrocephalia koidz*) are employed to make decoctions for treating the stomach and spleen.

heard Ninth Aunt call for a brush and inkstone.

Before long, there came the shuffling of paper being folded, the clatter of the writing brush's cap being pulled off and tossed down, and the scraping of the inkstone to make ink; then when the brush was dropped onto the table, it made a rattling sound, and they heard the rustling of medicinal herbs being combined and wrapped up.

An instant later, the woman emerged, calling for the sick person, so she could explain the use of the remedy and the prescription. Then when she turned and went back inside, they heard the three Aunts taking their leave, the three maidservants saying their farewells, the child's incoherent mumbling, and the cat's meows, all at the same time. Ninth Aunt's voice was clear and penetrating, Sixth Aunt's slow and elderly, Fourth Aunt's delicate and pleasing, and along with the voices of the three maids, each had a unique tone that could easily be identified and distinguished by anyone listening.

The astounded crowd took them to be authentic spirit voices. But when they tested her prescriptions later, they proved not to be very effective. Thus they were party to what is known as ventriloquism, an unusual skill used there to sell medicine. Still and all, pretty rare!

Wang Xinyi once reported that when he was in the capital, passing through the market district, he heard the sound of a stringed instrument accompanying a singer, and people watching, blocking the way like a wall.

As he got close enough to catch a peek, he saw a young man with a lovely voice singing a song. But there was no instrument accompanying him—only his finger pressed against his cheek while he sang, sometimes pressing it in, sometimes pulling it out; it sounded no different than the vibrations of a bow string. He was also a descendant of practitioners of ventriloquism.

78. The Fox Duo

Scholar Jiao was the third younger brother of Jiao Shihong of Zhangqiu. On one occasion, he was reading a book in his garden. At midnight, two beauties appeared, and they were extraordinarily pretty. One was about seventeen or eighteen, the other fourteen or fifteen, and they began caressing his study table, while smiling suggestively at him. Jiao knew they were foxes, so he adopted a stern countenance and resisted them.

The older of the two remarked, "You're as long and stiff as a halberd, so why don't you exercise your manhood?"

"I won't engage in intimacy with any woman except for my wife," Jiao replied.

The girl laughed as she cried, "What a stubborn pedant! Are you still holding onto your old-fashioned morals? The fifteenth day of the tenth month celebrates the spirits, allowing everyone to turn values on their heads—and besides, climbing into bed for a little while is a trivial matter, right?" Jiao again fended them off.

Jiao Shihong: Jiao Yurui, whose courtesy names were Jiwu and Shihong, became a *jinshi* in the fourth year (1647) of the emperor Shunzhi's reign, and served as an assistant minister in the Ministry of Revenue (Zhu 264n1).
The fifteenth day of the tenth month: Following the lunar calendar, this is when the birthday of the Three August Ones, legendary demigods who taught the essentials of civilization to humanity (Palmer 15, 211), is celebrated.

The girl, realizing they couldn't arouse him, then declared, "You're a famous scholar, so we'll challenge you to a poetry contest, and if you can respond, we'll leave: '*wu* and *xu* have similarly shaped characters, with the only difference being a point between them.'" Jiao thought it over, but refused to participate.

Laughing, the girl said, "An official as resolute as this—? Oh well, I can do it for you: '*ji* and *si* have been linked, so just jump in with both feet.'" One more laugh and they were gone.

A poetry contest: The *zhudui* is a call/response kind of verse challenge; one opponent recites something in a particular form, and the other recites a response to it in the same form (here, one line four characters long, followed by one line six characters long). But the girl's challenge to Jiao operates on two levels: both to echo her poetic structure, and to give in to her seduction.

'Wu and xu . . . a point between them: The character *wu* (戊) is drawn with one fewer stroke than the character *xu* (戌); the fox-girl's suggestive subtext is "the time is right to bring our bodies together, if you'll just come a little closer."

'Ji and si . . . with both feet: The characters *ji* (己) and *si* (巳) also differ from each other by only a single stroke; the fox-girl is implying that they'll end up in bed together, so "eventually our feet will meet where yours have walked, then you won't be able to help but touch us."

79. The Wei County Fox

The Li family owned a second home in Wei county. Unexpectedly, an old man came to them to lease the residence, guaranteeing faithfully to pay them fifty taels a year for it. Li agreed to rent it to him. After he'd left, however, there was no more news of him, so Mr. Li advised his servants to rent the place to someone else.

The next day after they did so, the old man showed up and said to him, "You agreed to lease the residence to me, so why are you about to switch and rent it to someone else?" Li then explained his doubts. The old man replied, "I intend to be in the house for a long time; I was delayed, then, because I had to choose an auspicious time to move in, which will arrive after ten more days." Proceeding to pay a year's rent up front, he remarked, "Even if in the end it seems unoccupied for the year, don't become concerned." Li accompanied him out, inquiring about the date, and the old man told it to him.

Several days past that date, there was still no sign of him moving in. Li then went to take a look for himself, but found the pair of gates bolted from the inside, smoke emerging from the kitchen chimney, and miscellaneous sounds of people inside. Surprised, he sent in his visiting card, offering to pay his respects.

The old man hurried out and ushered him inside, laughing and chatting with him like he was family.

Wei County: The title of the story actually refers to Weishui, a river in Shandong's Wei county.

Once Li returned home, he sent some people back to present gifts from his family; the old man graciously and generously rewarded them with food, drink, and other nice things.

After another several days, Li set up a banquet, invited the old man, and they merrily continued their happy conversations. When Li asked him about his birthplace, he identified it as Qinzhong. Li expressed surprise that he was so far from home. The old man explained, "Your county here is a most fortunate place. Qinzhong can no longer be home to me, for a great catastrophe is about to befall it." At that time, peace prevailed everywhere, so Li didn't question him any further.

The following day, the old man sent him an invitation, announcing that he was ready to repay his landlord's courtesy, providing décor, drinks, and food that were lavish and elegant. Li, amazed by it all, began to wonder whether his tenant was actually an influential official. The old man was on such close terms with him that he informed Li he was a fox. Li was so astonished at this that he mentioned it to everyone he came across.

County officials who heard about the strange affair came in their carriages daily to the old man's gate, hoping for a chance to meet and to make friends with him, and without exception he kindly agreed to see them. It was just a matter of time before higher officials also began showing up there. Only one particular county magistrate was repeatedly refused and forced to take his leave. The magistrate solicited Li's help in gaining him admission, but still the old man refused to see him.

Li asked him what was up. The old man left his seat and came near Li, whispering, "You wouldn't know this, but in a previous life he was an ass, though he's now the magistrate passing judgment on the people, and is so greedy that even helping himself to somebody's rice soup makes him drunk with power. I may not be human, but I'd feel ashamed to have him for a friend."

Qinzhong: another name for Shaanxi province.

Li then made up an excuse to tell the magistrate that the fox feared his godlike nature, and hence simply didn't dare see him. The magistrate believed him and stopped coming. This was in the eleventh year of Kangxi's reign. Not long after, Shaanxi was afflicted by the fires of rebellion. This gives credence to the belief that foxes can foretell the future.

The collector of these strange tales remarks, "The ass is a large creature. When angered, it kicks out its legs and brays itself hoarse, its eyes larger than wine jars, till it's snorting like an ox; not only is its noise unpleasant, but so is its appearance. If you hold up a bundle of hay, however, you can persuade it to lower its head in docile compliance, happy to accept a harness. If someone is a magistrate of the people with a character like this, he will become intoxicated with his authority even by taking someone's rice soup. I hope that those who govern the people will caution themselves not to be like the ass, but instead to seek the counsel of the fox, thereby growing in virtue daily."

Eleventh year of Kangxi's reign: That is, in 1672.

80. Hongyu

In Guangping, old man Feng had a son named Xiangru. Father and son had both been successful in the initial level of the civil service examination. The old man was nearly sixty, upright and honest, yet his family was so poor that the cupboards were often bare.

Over the course of a number of years, old Feng's wife and Xiangru's wife both died, one after the other, so all of the housework, from fetching water from the well, to cooking their rice, fell upon the two men.

One night as Xiangru was sitting under the moon, he suddenly caught a glimpse of his neighbor woman from the east side, peeking over the wall, so he went up to the wall to look at her. When he got a better glimpse, he discovered that she was beautiful. He came closer, uttering a small chuckle. He beckoned to her with his hand to come nearer, but she wouldn't move. He insistently invited her, and then, when he put a ladder up, she climbed over and afterwards they went to bed together.

When he asked what her name was, she replied, "I'm your neighbor, Hongyu." Xiangru was lovestruck, and swore he would love her forever. Hongyu promised the same. Night after night she came and went, with the assignations continuing for about six months.

On one occasion, old Feng got up during the night, heard his son exchanging witty comments with someone, and then when he stole a peek, he saw the girl there. Furious, he loudly swore, "You animal, how dare you behave this way! Though we're so poor, you're learning to be a playboy rather than studying as hard as you can? If people find out about this, you'll lose your reputation; even if they don't know about it, it'll ruin your life!" Xiangru fell to his knees, tearfully expressing how sorry he was.

His father then rebuked Hongyu, "You haven't o-beyed the rules for female morality. Since you didn't guard your own reputation, you've already disgraced yourself, but now you're disgracing other people. In this case, your lack of restraint has brought shame on my house!" When he finished his tirade, he angrily went back to bed.

Hongyu's tears fell as she cried, "Your father blamed you so heartily that I feel terribly ashamed! We two must be destined to end like this!"

"Since my father is still alive," Xiangru replied, "I cannot freely make my own decision about this. But we're so deeply in love with each other, we should just keep it as our secret."

As Hongyu took her leave to part from him, Xiangru began to weep. She stopped and told him, "Since our relationship didn't result from a matchmaker, or from our parents' decision, and was just a matter of me coming over the wall to get together with you, how can we expect it to last until we die? There'll be a nice marriage waiting for you somewhere here, so you can go and make a proposal." Xiangru informed her that he was penniless. She replied, "I'll come tomorrow night and help you find a solution."

Later, the next night, Hongyu appeared as she promised, took out forty silver taels, and presented them to Xiangru. She explained, "If you travel sixty *li*, you'll come to Wu village and Mr. Wei, who values his eighteen-year-old daughter so highly that he hasn't married her off. But if you offer him enough money, he'll certainly agree to it." As soon as she finished speaking, she left.

Sixty li: Since one *li* equals 1/3 mile, this will be a 20-mile trip.

Xiangru seized the opportunity to tell his father that he wished to go look for a prospective wife. But he hid the silver and didn't venture to tell him about it. The old man was concerned that since they were penniless, there was no use in pursuing the matter, so he would have stopped him. Xiangru then gently remarked, "I'd like to try it first, before giving up." The old man nodded his assent.

Borrowing someone's horse and a servant, Xiangru went to pay his respects to Mr. Wei. Wei turned out to be the head of a farming family. Xiangru called out his name, then was led to speak with him. Wei knew that Xiangru belonged to a distinguished family, and seeing that his bearing and expression were open and clear, found him to be admirable, but worried that Xiangru didn't have enough money to get married.

Sensing this in Wei's hemming and hawing, Xiangru poured all the taels in his bag out on the table. Wei, then quite pleased, called upon a neighbor to serve as witness, and in a book with red pages, recorded the marriage agreement.

Xiangru went inside to pay his respects to Wei's wife. In a narrow room, the daughter shyly held a welcome banner for her mother. He took a cursory glance at her, and although she was simply dressed, she seemed so radiantly beautiful that he was secretly delighted.

Wei then welcomed Xiangru as his son-in-law, and said, "There's really no need for a formal ceremony, son. Wait a little, while the wedding clothes are made, then when that's done, I'll send my daughter to your house." Xiangru set up a time with him and then left for home.

He fibbed to old Feng, telling him that Wei cherished their family's reputation, and wasn't demanding any money from them. The old man was quite pleased. When the appointed day arrived, Wei sent his daughter as promised. The girl, hardworking and thrifty, made a virtue of docility, and very earnestly worked for marital harmony.

After two years, they had a boy, named Fu'er. On the occasion of Tomb-Sweeping Day, they were carrying the infant up to a grave site, when they met a gentleman named Song. Official Song, an imperial censor who had been dismissed from his office for taking bribes, lived brashly in the community.

On that day, after also visiting a grave, Song returned home after having seen the beautiful lady. He asked a villager about her and learned that she was Xiangru's wife. Counting on the fact that the Fengs were impoverished scholars, he hoped to seduce them with a large bribe into wavering and sending the wife over to him, to use as he wished.

When Xiangru happened to hear about this, he became livid with anger; but since he thought he couldn't oppose Song's power, he covered his anger with a laugh, and returned home to tell his father.

Infuriated, old Feng rushed out to inform Song's servants, gesturing wildly, berating Song with a wide variety of curses. Song's servants scattered like rats.

Song was also angry, seething like a boiling cauldron, so he ended up sending several people to Xiangru's house, to beat up old Feng and his son. When Xiangru's wife heard them, she abandoned Fu'er in bed, her hair all disheveled, and wailed for help. The mob grabbed the woman, boisterously dragged her off, and then left.

Father and son lay wounded and disabled, groaning on the ground, while Fu'er was choking and crying from in his room. The neighbors took pity on the Fengs, and helped them onto their beds. As the days went by, Xiangru was able to get out of bed with a cane. But his father was so angry that he couldn't eat, vomited blood, and soon died.

Xiangru howled in sorrow, and with Fu'er in his arms, he went to the governor to file a complaint—and though the lawsuit went all the way to the highest provincial officer, in the end he received no justice. Afterward, he heard that his wife had refused to give in to Song and had consequently died, exacerbating his sorrow.

His many wrongs choked his chest and throat, but he saw no way out. Every time he thought of his desire to find a way to kill Song, he recalled that Song was surrounded by servants, making it hard to get to him, and besides, his infant son would have no one to care for him. He grieved day and night, unable even to close his eyes.

Suddenly, an impressively virile fellow with curly beard and broad jaw, whom Xiangru had never met before, appeared in his room to console him. He invited the man to have a seat and asked him about his family background. The man hastily demanded, "Don't you want revenge on the enemy who killed your father and viciously forced your wife?"

Xiangru suspected him to be one of Song's people come to spy on him, so he knowingly falsified his answer. The stranger's eyes angrily bulged in their sockets as he exclaimed, "I thought you were a true gentleman before, but now it's clear that one doesn't have to be lowborn to be contemptible!"

Xiangru sensed that he wasn't a spy after all, fell to his knees, and drew near the stranger, declaring, "I was honestly afraid that you were one of Song's people. Now I'll let you know my thoughts: I've been concealing my hatred, waiting on a chance for revenge for quite some time. However, I've got to protect my infant son, or I fear our family line will die out. You're a righteous person, so can you take my place as his guardian?"

"That's women's business," the stranger replied, "not something I can do. You know how to raise an infant, so please take care of that yourself, and I will work faithfully on your behalf." When Xiangru heard this, he threw himself down and touched his forehead to the ground in gratitude. The stranger left without turning around to look at him.

Xiangru chased after him to inquire his name, and he answered, "I won't tell you my name, and thus if I'm unsuccessful, you won't have my name to blame; if successful, you won't have to worry about thanking me." Then he left. Xiangru was afraid of being involved in the pending violence, so he took Fu'er in his arms and fled.

That night, as the entire Song household was sleeping, someone climbed over several house walls and entered, killed the imperial censor, his father, son, daughter-in-law, and a maidservant. The Song family put charges against Xiangru in writing, and then informed the local officials. The officials were utterly astonished. The local official sent his people to capture Xiangru, but found no trace of him, which effectively implicated him as the apparent murderer.

Meanwhile, Song's servants and the official's followers hunted everywhere for Xiangru and his son. When night fell on the southern mountains, they heard an infant's crying and tracked Xiangru's footprints, seized the two of them, and dragged them back. As Fu'er began to cry more and more, the captors grew so angry that they grabbed the child away and cast him aside. Xiangru, maddened by this injustice, wanted to die.

When the city commander saw him, he demanded, "Why'd you murder them?"

Xiangru cried, "I've been framed! He died during the night, but I left the village during the daytime—and besides, I was holding a crying baby in my arms, so how could I have climbed over the walls to kill people?"

The commander insisted, "If you didn't kill anyone, why'd you run away?" Xiangru was unable to argue successfully in his own defense. Then the officials put him in jail.

Xiangru, sobbing, cried, "It doesn't matter if I die, but what was my baby's crime?"

"You murdered others' children; your child was killed," the commander replied, "so what's your complaint?" Xiangru, who had already been stripped in the commander's office, and had been repeatedly subjected to cruel punishment, refused to confess any guilt on his part.

That evening, the commander had just laid down when he heard something strike his bed, followed by a shaking, which frightened him greatly as he felt it. He shouted out, and the whole household was awakened into springing up and gathering lights, revealing thereby a short sword, as keenly sharp as frost, which had penetrated the wood of his bed more than a *cun* and couldn't be pulled free. When the commander saw it, he lost all spirit.

People with weapons searched all over in the vicinity of the house, but could find no traces of anyone. The commander was frightened out of his mind. He considered that Song was already dead, and hence he had nothing to fear from him; he described everything in detail, reporting to a higher official, and pleading for Xiangru until he was cleared of blame and finally released from jail.

Xiangru returned home, where there was no rice in the clay pot, alone among the shadows of his four walls. Fortunately, his neighbors took pity on him and brought him food and drink, since he was neglecting his own needs. Thinking about how his great enemy had been repaid, he would suddenly burst into loud laughter; then considering the cruel misfortunes that had virtually exterminated his family, his tears would fall without cease; thinking about it the least bit reminded Xiangru that he was poor to the bone, and that his family line would not continue, so he found a place where no one was around and wept loudly, unable to stop himself from crying. He was like this for half a year, trapped and increasingly disengaged.

Then he begged the city commander for pity, and asked to have the body of his wife returned to him. After burying her and returning home, sad and grieving, wanting to die, he tossed and turned in his empty bed, but there was just no relief for him.

Suddenly there was a knock on the door, and as he concentrated his attention on being very still and on listening, he heard someone outside the door murmuring words to a child. Xiangru anxiously got up and covertly peered out at what seemed to be a woman. As soon as he opened the door, she exclaimed, "With so much injustice to be redressed, it's fortunate that you're not sick!" The voice had a familiar sound, but on the spur of the moment, he couldn't place it.

When he brought a candle near, he saw it was Hongyu. She picked up a child, who'd been playing and laughing as she stood over him. Xiangru didn't take the time to ask anything, he just embraced Hongyu and wept openly. The woman also shared his grief. Then she prodded the little boy and said, "Have you forgotten your father?" The child clung to Hongyu's clothes, his bright eyes looking at Xiangru.

He carefully examined the boy till he recognized the blessing that it was his own Fu'er. Quite shocked, weeping, he asked, "How did my son come to be here?"

Hongyu replied, "I'll tell you the truth: the former references to me as a neighbor woman were lies. I'm really a fox. Just as I was going out one night, I saw your son crying at the mouth of a valley, so I adopted him in Shaanxi province. When I heard the news that your great troubles had been settled, I brought him here so you could be reunited." Xiangru wiped away his tears as he thanked her formally. Fu'er was nestled at Hongyu's breast like she was his mother, but he couldn't yet remember his father.

Just before dawn, Hongyu hastily got up. When Xiangru asked what she was doing, she told him, "I was about to leave." Xiangru abjectly knelt at the bedside, weeping, unable to look up at her. Hongyu smiled and said, "I tricked you before. Now that your family's newly restored, we should get up earlier and work hard." Hongyu began clearing away the wild grass that had grown up, working like a man.

Xiangru lamented that since he was so poor, he had no way to support them. "Please just concentrate on studying hard," Hongyu replied. "I don't know how much we'll earn, but at least we won't starve to death." Then she took out money for him to purchase sewing supplies; she leased a field containing several plots of ten *mu* each and hired servants to cultivate them. She worked very hard at the farming, and mended clothes in the house, as the normal routine for her days. The village folk heard of Hongyu's kindness and generously offered their own assistance.

In about six months, things had begun to flourish,

Ten mu: Or about 1.66 acres.

and Xiangru's family was becoming wealthy. He told Hongyu, "From heaps of ashes, you have delivered into my empty hands a new lease on life. However, in one matter I'm still not secure, so how can I settle it?" She asked him to explain, and he replied, "The time for the civil service examination is already near, but I'm not registered to take it."

Hongyu laughed and said, "I'm sending four taels to the official in charge, and your name is already on the examination record—if I'd waited until you'd said something, it would've been too late to make arrangements." Xiangru put the money inside his sleeve.

He was a successful candidate in the imperial examination at the provincial level. By the time he was thirty-six years old, he owned fertile fields joined by footpaths, and a summer house that was large and spacious. Hongyu was so svelte that she seemed she might just blow away, yet she made an exceptional farm family wife, although the severe winters were harsh and the skin of her hands was smooth and soft like cream. It's said that she was thirty-eight, but when people saw Hongru, they often took her for a woman of about twenty.

The collector of these strange tales remarks, "His son was sturdy, his father virtuous, and hence he's rewarded with a good ending. Not only was this man knightly in behavior; the fox was, too. It was also a pretty strange situation! The commander inaccurately judged things, inciting a frightening anger; and the shock of the blade as it entered the wood—couldn't it have easily gone half a *chi* higher into the bed? If Su Zimei had read this story, he would've declared something like, 'What a shame it couldn't just hit him!'"

Half a chi: A *chi* is equal to about 1/3 of a meter.
Su Zimei: Best known as Su Shunqin (1008-48), a Song dynasty writer.

81. Dragons

Near the border of Beizhi, a dragon fell from the sky into a village. It moved ponderously and awkwardly, as it entered the home of a certain notable family. Their house couldn't hold its enormous body, so it squeezed itself small and went inside. The family members all fled. It made its way clamorously to the upper floor, while the family fired a cannon to scare it away. Then the dragon went back outside.

Just outside the door, there was a shallow puddle of dirty, stagnant water. The dragon jumped into it, rolling about and covering itself with mud, then leaped up into the air more than a *chi* before falling back down. It lay coiled in the mud there for three days, with flies gathering all over its scaly hide. Suddenly there came a heavy rain, and when a thunderbolt flashed across the sky, the dragon disappeared.

A scholar climbed Mt. Niu with some friends to enter the monastery there for a visit, and to look around. They noticed that in its rafters, on a yellow tile, there was a little snake coiled up, as thin and insignificant as an earthworm. All of a sudden, it began to wrap around the tile like a finger; then it looped around another circuit, like a belt. Everyone became frightened, realizing it must be a dragon, so the group hurried and began climbing down.

Beizhi: Modern Hebei province.

Just as they got halfway down the mountain, they heard the sound of a thunderbolt, from inside the monastery, that shook the entire the mountain valley. Black clouds covered the sky like a shell, and a massive dragon emerged from inside them for a moment, then plunged back inside and vanished.

In the little village of Zhangqiu, there was a peasant woman who was out in the fields working when a fierce wind blew dust in her face. Some of it got into one of her eyes, and made it feel like there were grains of wheat in it, so she rubbed and puffed at it, but it still didn't feel comfortable.

When she opened her eyes and carefully looked around, her eye wasn't hurt, but there was an expanse of red flesh that appeared between her eyeball and the flesh around it. Someone said, "This must be a hiberating dragon." The woman was worried that she was going to die.

After more than three months, while a torrential rain was falling from the sky, suddenly there came the sound of a huge thunderbolt, a flash, and the dragon was gone. The woman wasn't harmed in the least.

Yuan Xuansi reports, "At Suzhou, a thunderbolt exploded out of the darkness. The people saw a dragon swoop down from the clouds, its scaly hide stretching as it moved, clutching in its talons a human head, the beard and eyebrows of which were clearly visible; a moment later, it went into a cloud and disappeared. In addition, they never heard that anyone had lost his head."

Yuan Xuansi: Also known as Yuan Songfa, a writer during the reign of Qing emperor Kangxi, from modern Shandong's Zibo City.

82. Fourth Lady Lin

In Qingzhou administrative district, there was an official named Chen Baoyue, from Fujian. One night, he was sitting by himself, when a woman pulled aside the curtain and entered. He looked at her, but didn't recognize her; yet she was stunningly beautiful, and her long sleeves were in the style of the serving ladies of the imperial palace. She smiled and said, "Isn't it lonely to sit here by yourself in the still of the night?"

Startled, Chen demanded, "Who are you?"

"My home's not far from here," she replied, "as close as your neighbor to the west." Chen figured her for a ghost, but he felt attracted to her. He clutched at her sleeve and pulled her down next to him, where her refined conversation delighted him greatly. When he embraced her, she did little to resist.

She turned to look around her, and asked, "There isn't anyone else here, is there?"

Chen anxiously closed the door and answered, "No one." When he encouraged her to take off her skirt, she turned out to be very shy. Chen eagerly offered his assistance.

"I'm twenty years old, though still a virgin," she said. "If you're too violent with me, I won't be able to bear it." When they finished making love, they noticed she'd bled a little, which made the mattress wet.

Then, as they lay on the bed exchanging bed talk, she told him she was "Fourth Lady Lin." Chen pressed her for details. She explained, "Though all my life I've

383

been chaste, now because of your wanton act, I've lost my virginity. If you truly love me, just wish that we can love each other forever—why bother asking so many questions?" Before long, the cock crowed, so she rose and left.

From that time forward, she came every night. Each time, they conversed and drank together behind closed doors. Whenever their chats came to the topic of music, Lin could always dissect a song note-by-note. Chen hinted that she must be a professional musician. She explained, "When I was a child, I practiced music regularly."

Chen implored her to perform a song. Lin replied, "I haven't practiced my music for such a long time, I've forgotten the rhythm of most of the songs, and I'm afraid that those who know better will laugh at me." After he tried again to persuade her, she bowed her head and began then to beat time, singing tunes from Yizhou and Liangzhou in tones that were sad and moving. When the songs were finished, she burst into tears.

Chen, touched as well by the sorrow of the music, held her in his arms and comforted her, saying, "Darling, no more songs of fallen kingdoms—they make people unhappy."

"Tunes like these reflect one's feelings," Lin replied, "and someone who is sad cannot sing a joyful song, any more than a happy person can sing a sorrowful one." And so the two took great pleasure in their relationship, living in extraordinary harmony.

Over time, family members began eavesdropping on them, and when they heard Lin's singing, they couldn't restrain their tears. Chen's wife caught a glimpse of Lin's beauty, and doubting that any human being could be so hauntingly lovely, she decided that if Lin wasn't a ghost, she must certainly be a fox; fearing that Chen had taken up with some dreadful monster, she tried to convince him to cut off the relationship.

Chen couldn't stand listening to this, yet he adamantly demanded the truth of Lin. She paled as she answered, "I was once a maid in the palace of Prince Heng. I met with disaster and died, seventeen years ago.

Because you are so very honorable, I've given myself to you in pleasure, but in all honesty, I couldn't bear to bring trouble down on you. If you see me now with suspicion or fear, then I should go."

Chen insisted, "I don't doubt you; but since it's the case that we're as close as a married couple, I must know the truth about you." Then he asked her about things inside the palace. She described her past with full detail and artistry. When her narration came to the decay of Prince Heng's fortunes, she became choked by sobs and couldn't continue speaking.

Since Lin didn't really need to sleep, every night she got up and chanted the sutras for protection, praying to the Buddha with scriptures and recitations. Chen asked her, "Can someone in the underworld still reflect upon personal sins?"

"One may," she replied. "When I consider how my last life sank into ruin, I hope to do a measure of good to improve my next one."

She frequently evaluated poetry and lyrics with Chen, and when there were some defects, she would critique them; as for the best phrases, she gracefully recited them with her lovely voice. Her frame of mind was so literary and unconstrained, Chen would simply forget he was tired. "Do you write poetry?" he asked her.

"When I was alive," Lin replied, "I did occasionally." Chen begged her for some of it. Lin smiled and told him, "They were a child's words, hardly adequate to show a learned person like you."

Lin lived with Chen for three years. One evening, she suddenly appeared, grief-stricken, to bid him farewell. Terribly shaken, Chen asked her to explain. She told him, "The Hell King has decided that since I wasn't guilty of any crimes in my previous life, and I've never neglected since then to read and chant the scriptures, he will allow me to be reborn into the Wang household. I must leave tonight, and we can never hope to see each other again." She concluded her words in wrenching sorrow. Chen, too, was weeping.

Then Chen set out some wine for them to drink

away their pain. Lin began to sing with mournful passion, taking the music of each word in a hundred directions with her grief; each time she came to a particularly sad point in the song, she would break into sobs. She had to stop and begin again several times before she could finish the song, and they took no joy from their drinking.

Lin rose then, wavering on the point of leaving. Chen pulled her to him firmly, and they sat together for a few moments more. At the sound of the cock suddenly crowing, Lin told him, "You mustn't detain me any longer. Yet you have often chided me for not agreeing to show you my homely writing; now that I'm about to part from you forever, I'll try quickly to write something for you, though the rhythm won't be very good."

She asked for a brush, and once she'd composed the poem, declared, "With a saddened heart and confused mind, I can't give you a polished piece, and since its cadences may be divided wrongly, please don't take it out and show it to anyone." Then she covered her face with her sleeve and departed. Chen accompanied her just outside his gate, where she simply disappeared.

Chen, devastated, stood there a good long time. When he looked at Lin's poem, he noticed that her characters were beautifully shaped, a treasure that he would always cherish. The poem read:

> Still and calm, I lay buried near the palace for
>   seventeen years,
> And wondered—who will think of the vanished
>   empire?
> I think upon the vacant palace, its arbors sealed
>   up,
> And weep, hoping that you, my Prince, have been
>   reborn a cuckoo.
> As the sea's billowy waves wash over the land at
>   sunset,
> The Han dynasty's pipes and drums have been
>   silenced, its beacon fires extinguished.
> This weak, beautiful woman cannot become an
>   evil spirit after death,

> For with a pure heart, grieving, I think only of
>   the Buddhist truth.
> I've chanted the bodhi's phrases many, many
>   times a day,
> And when not busy, I've read two or three sutras.
> I have sung for you the spirited songs of Liyuan
>   instead of weeping;
> Now, in your solitude, you may also shed your
>   tears.

In being repeated many times, this poem may no longer be completely intact, and I suspect it may contain some errors.

This poem: This twelve-line poem, consisting of seven characters per line, is structurally reminiscent of the *"jiang shang yin"* ("River Poem") of Li Bo (699-762 C.E.), China's most famous poet. However, its subject and tone are almost precisely the opposite of those in the Li poem, treating Buddhism and nostalgic sadness rather than Daoism and exuberant joy.

83. In the River

Wang Shengyu, who had been sailing south, anchored his boat in the middle of the river for the night. He was already lying on his bed when the moon began shining as bright as white silk, and being unable to fall asleep, he'd had his servant boy give him a massage.

Later, he suddenly heard something on the roof of the boat, like a child walking over a reed mat, starting at the far end of the boat and coming closer, gradually approaching his part of the cabin. Concerned that someone might be trying to rob him, he anxiously got up and asked his servant about it. The boy had also heard it.

While Wang was questioning the boy, he saw someone lean over the top of the boat and support himself, so he could lower his head upside down and spy into the cabin. Quite shaken, Wang grabbed his sword and cried out for all of his servants, awakening everyone on board.

Wang reported to them what he had seen. Some of them wondered if perhaps he'd made a mistake. All at once, something made the sound again. The group began looking around, but there was no sign of an intruder, only a few stars and the bright moon, along with the endless lapping of the river's waves.

The group took their seats in the boat, and before long, they saw a blue fire in the shape of a lantern suddenly emerging from the water and floating; little by little, it drew closer to the boat, till the blue fire suddenly dissipated. At once a dark figure stood up there, towering above the water, and using its hands to cling to the boat, began walking alongside it.

Everyone made a clamor and cried, "Surely this is the thing!" They wanted to shoot it. Just as they were drawing their bows, it hastily dove into the water, and they could no longer see it. They asked the boatman about it. He told them, "In ancient times, this was the site of a battlefield, so if ghosts occasionally appear and then disappear, one shouldn't think it strange."

Works Cited

Primary Source

Zhu, Qikai, ed. *Liaozhai zhi yi.* 3 vols. Beijing: People's Literary Press, 1995. Volume 1 (*shang*).

Secondary and Contextual Sources

Allan, Sarah. *The Shape of the Turtle: Myth, Art, and Cosmos in Early China.* Albany: State University of New York Press, 1991.

Barr, Allan. "Pu Songling and the Qing Examination System." *Late Imperial China* 7.1 (1986): 87-111.

---. "Disarming Intruders: Alien Women in *Liaozhai zhiyi.*" *Harvard Journal of Asiatic Studies* 49.2 (1989): 501-17.

Blakeley, Barry B. "Chu Society and State: Image versus Reality." *Defining Chu: Image and Reality in Ancient China.* Ed. Constance A. Cook and John S. Major. Honolulu: University of Hawai'i Press, 1999. 51-66.

Blunden, Caroline and Mark Elvin. *Cultural Atlas of China.* New York: Facts on File, 1983.

Bonnefoy, Yves. *Asian Mythologies.* Trans. Wendy Doniger *et al.* Chicago: Chicago University Press, 1991.

Cahill, Suzanne. *Transcendence and Divine Passion: The Queen Mother of the West in Medieval China.* Stanford: Stanford University Press, 1993.

Campany, Robert Ford. *Strange Writing: Anomaly Accounts in Early Medieval China.* Albany: State University of

New York Press, 1996.

Chan, Leo Tak-hung. *The Discourse of Foxes and Ghosts: Ji Yun and Eighteenth-Century Literati Storytelling*. Hong Kong: The Chinese University Press, 1998.

Clunas, Craig. *Superfluous Things: Material Culture and Social Status in Early Modern China*. Urbana: University of Illinois Press, 1991.

Eberhard, Wolfram. *Chinese Festivals*. New York: Henry Schuman, 1952.

---. *A Dictionary of Chinese Symbols: Hidden Symbols in Chinese Life and Thought*. New York: Routledge, 1986.

Far East Chinese-English Dictionary [*yuandong hanying da cidian*]. New York: U.S. International Publishing, Inc., 2000.

Gan, Bao. *sou shen ji* [*Anecdotes about Spirits and Immortals*]. Trans. Ding Wangdao. Beijing: Foreign Languages Press, 2004.

Hammond, Charles. "Factual Framing in *Liao Zhai Zhi Yi*." *Acta Orientalia Academiae Scientiarum Hungarica* 59.2 (2006): 205-30.

Hucker, Charles O. *A Dictionary of Official Titles in Imperial China*. Taipei: SMC Publishing, Inc., 1985.

Huntington, Rania. "Tigers, Foxes, and the Margins of Humanity in Tang *Chuanqi* Fiction." *Papers on Chinese Literature* 1 (1993): 40-64.

---. "Foxes and Sex in Late Imperial Chinese Narrative." *Nan nü: Men, Women and Gender in Early and Imperial China* 2.1 (2000): 78-128.

Idema, Wilt and Lloyd Haft. *A Guide to Chinese Literature*. Ann Arbor: Center for Chinese Studies, University of Michigan, 1997.

Kang, Xiaofei. "The Fox and the Barbarian: Unraveling Representations of the Other in Late Tang Tales." *Journal of Chinese Religions* 27 (1999): 35-67.

Lanciotti, Lionello. "An Introduction to the Work of Pu Songling." *Ming Qing yanjiu* n.v. (1993): 67-80.

Lao, An, trans. *The Book of Rites: Selections*. Jinan: Shandong Friendship Press, 2000.

Mathews, R.H. *Mathews' Chinese-English Dictionary*.

1931; Rev. American Edition. Cambridge, MA: Harvard University Press, 1943.

Mayers, William Frederick. *The Chinese Reader's Manual.* 1874; rpt. Shanghai: American Presbyterian Mission Press, 1910.

Mercatante, Anthony S. *The Facts on File Encyclopedia of World Mythology and Legend.* New York: Facts on File, 1988.

Miyazaki, Ichisada. *China's Examination Hell: The Civil Service Examinations of Imperial China.* Trans. Conrad Schirokauer. New York: John Weatherhill, Inc., 1976.

Naquin, Susan. "Connections Between Rebellions: Sect Family Networks in Qing China." *Modern China* 8.3 (1982): 337-60.

The New Grove Dictionary of Music and Musicians. 2nd ed. 27 vols. Vol. 27: Wagon to Żywny. Ed. Stanley Sadie. New York: Grove, 2001.

Paludan, Ann. *Chronicle of the Chinese Emperors: The Reign-by-Reign Record of the Rulers of Imperial China.* London: Thames & Hudson, 1998.

Palmer, Martin *et al.*, eds. and trans. *T'ung Shu: The Ancient Chinese Almanac.* London: Rider & Company, 1986.

Perkins, Dorothy. *Encyclopedia of China: The Essential Reference to China, Its History and Culture.* New York: Facts on File, Inc., 1999.

Pines, Yuri. *Foundations of Confucian Thought: Intellectual Life in the Chunqiu Period, 722-453 B.C.E.* Honolulu: University of Hawai'i Press, 2002.

Prusek, Jaroslav. "Liao-chai chi-I by P'u Sung-ling: An Inquiry into the Circumstances under which the Collection Arose." *Studia Serica Bernhard Karlgren Dedicata.* Ed. Søren Egerod and Else Glahn. Copenhagen: Ejnar Munksgaard, 1959. 128-46.

Schafer, Edward H. *The Vermilion Bird: T'ang Images of the South.* Los Angeles: University of California Press, 1967.

Sivin, Nathan. "Chinese Alchemy." *Hidden Truths: Magic, Alchemy, and the Occult.* Ed. Lawrence E. Sullivan.

New York: Macmillan Publishing Company, 1987. 253-60.

Sondergard, Sidney L., and Will G. Collins. "Young and Dangerous(ly Traditional): Reading Guangong and the Act of Obeisance in Hong Kong Films Since 1986." *Studies in the Humanities* 32.1 (2005): 50-73.

Sterckx, Roel. *The Animal and the Daemon in Early China.* Albany: SUNY Press, 2002.

von Falkenhausen, Lothar. "The Waning of the Bronze Age: Material Cultue and Social Developments, 770-481 B.C." *The Cambridge History of Ancient China: From the Origins of Civilization to 221 B.C.* Ed. Michael Loewe and Edward L. Shaughnessy. New York: Cambridge University Press, 1999. 450-544.

von Glahn, Richard. *The Sinister Way: The Divine and the Demonic in Chinese Religious Culture.* Los Angeles: University of California Press, 2004.

Wang, Aihe. "Creators of an Emperor: The Political Group behind the Founding of the Han Empire." *Asia Major* 14.1 (2001): 19-50.

Wang, Panling. *Pu songling yu minjian wenxue [Pu Songling and Folk Literature].* Shanghai: Wenyi chubanshe, 1985.

Willoughby-Meade, G. *Chinese Ghouls and Goblins.* New York: Frederick A. Stokes Company, 1926.

Wu, Fatima. "Foxes in Chinese Supernatural Tales (Part II)." *Tamkang Review* 17.3 (1987): 263-94.

The Yellow Emperor's Classic of Medicine. Trans. Ni Maoshing. Boston: Shambhala, 1995.

Zeitlin, Judith T. *Historian of the Strange: Pu Songling and the Chinese Classical Tale.* Stanford: Stanford University Press, 1993.